The Gamble

They were lying in the darkness on a
blanket. Madame Mai snuggled up to him, and
said, "Do you think you could learn
to love me?"

Ruxton told her what she wanted to hear.

She said softly, "When you first spoke to me—
remember that first day? I was thrilled
inside. My husband is such a forbidding personality
that no other man had ever shown awareness
of me as a woman. . . ."

Ruxton showed appropriate surprise and gratitude.

"If I hadn't written that note," she asked,
"you wouldn't have called on me during
the trial—isn't that true?"

Ruxton said truthfully that it was true.
He guessed that she was trying to
bind him to her. So much the better—
all part of his plan.

Books by A. E. van Vogt

The Best of A. E. van Vogt
The Mind Cage
The Violent Man

Published by POCKET BOOKS

A.E. van Vogt
THE VIOLENT MAN

A KANGAROO BOOK
PUBLISHED BY POCKET BOOKS NEW YORK

Distributed in Canada by PaperJacks Ltd., a Licensee
of the trademarks of Simon & Schuster, a division of
Gulf+Western Corporation.

POCKET BOOKS, a Simon & Schuster division of
GULF & WESTERN CORPORATION
1230 Avenue of the Americas, New York, N.Y. 10020
In Canada distributed by PaperJacks Ltd.,
330 Steelcase Road, Markham, Ontario.

Published by arrangement with Farrar, Straus and Giroux
Library of Congress Catalog Card Number: 62-16951

ISBN: 0-671-82004-4

First Pocket Books printing April, 1978

Trademarks registered in the United States and other countries.

PRINTED IN CANADA

PART ONE

I

The prison sprawled on the flat Chinese plain. Even at a distance it seemed large, a spread-out mass of gray buildings. As the truck carried him with eight other white men and four Chinese "landlords" along the deep ruts that made up the road, Seal Ruxton kept glancing at the massive penitentiary ahead.

The first shock of being sentenced to death was over. He had been unlucky, he realized, to have fallen into the hands of these angry orientals at a time when they were planning another experiment. It was too soon to decide what he should do.

He held onto the side of the small truck, balanced himself against the steady, uneven jolting, and studied the terrain. It depressed him. One might have to walk a whole day to reach a sizable hill. Far south, he could see rising land, uncertainly visible. Though perhaps that was an illusion of the hot, hazy morning.

He had been on a train three days and two nights. So this remote prison was at least 1,000 miles from the ocean. The dialect of the truck driver and the two guards in the cab had a far north harshness. That fitted.

It hurt him to realize it was so far. He was a tall, strong man, with bitter, knowing lines around his mouth. It was a worldly knowingness, a conscious awareness that men were not any better than they were. The knowledge had long ago given him a feeling of self-sufficiency, for he expected nothing of other people except, perhaps, betrayal, or brutality, or weakness. Expecting so little, he could not be surprised. And he was not surprised now that he, and these others, were being taken such an immense distance from that ocean which, he felt, could be a jumping off place for escape. Being realistic, he knew that a white man could not hope to cross a thousand yellow miles. Therefore, this was easily the most threatening situation he had been in in his thirty-eight years.

He had just estimated that they were about three miles from the prison when the man beside him spoke haltingly, in English.

"You—American?"

Ruxton did not turn, or show that he had heard.

The man persisted, "We be friends, hey?"

Ruxton had no real friends. He looked around the truck, hoping to exchange position with someone. It was impossible.

"By jeez," said his tormentor in a low, angry voice, "you have speak to no one since you join us. And, by jeez, when Jarnoz speak to you, you speak to me."

Now, when it was too late, Ruxton recognized that the other was in a rage. The next moment the man's fist struck the top of his head. The fury that motivated the blow left him no recourse but to retaliate.

His hands were down at hip level as he swung about. Ruxton had a glimpse of a big man, bigger than himself, with a sensitive look to him even at this moment of extreme anger—a Turk, he had guessed casually on the train, and he thought it now. He grabbed at the man. In a single, sustained effort, he lifted him and flung him out of the truck.

The sun glared down from the late morning sky. The truck throbbed throatily, and careened along at a steady twenty miles an hour. It was a '48 Dodge, probably one small item of the vast total of American equipment captured by the Chinese Reds from Chiang Kai-shek when they drove him and the remnant of his army to the coast and off the mainland to Formosa in 1949.

Ruxton regained his balancing hold on the side of the truck, and glanced back along the primitive road. Jarnoz was getting to his feet. He stood for a moment, apparently uncertain as to his course of action. Incredibly, no one seemed to notice. No one yelled, or pointed. Ruxton had time to feel regret that he had been so quick to react. There would probably be severe repercussions from these ferocious Chinese captors.

In the distance, Jarnoz started after the truck, gesticulating. Ruxton was relieved. An unplanned escape had no chance of success.

He turned, reached past two men toward the rear window of the cab, and banged on the glass. A scowling Chinese face appeared at the window. Ruxton pointed back along the road. The face disappeared. A moment later, the brake jammed on. The truck squealed to a stop. And the two guards jumped out.

Evidently, they did not see Jarnoz, for they brandished their guns at the prisoners, and seemed uncertain as to what was wrong. Ruxton pointed again.

10

This time, they glanced back along the road, and backed off, guns at the ready. Their conversation indicated that they thought it an attempt to escape.

Ruxton felt irritably sorry for Jarnoz. The Turk was about to experience the peculiar literal stupidity of these people. Ruxton thought, "Jarnoz may accuse me." He decided to admit nothing, not even that he understood Chinese.

A few moments later, the man came running up, red-faced and breathless. One of the guards said something which Ruxton couldn't hear. And then he stepped forward, and clubbed the big man over the head with his rifle. Jarnoz staggered, and fell. An ugly, bloody welt began to show across the top of his head as he lay twitching on the road.

The guard motioned at the prisoners with his gun, and yelled threateningly, in Chinese, "Pick him up!"

Ruxton was one of the three men who swung down and lifted the victim up to where several other prisoners pulled him over onto the floor of the truck. When they were once more under way, Ruxton asked himself, guiltily, "Why did I really refuse to communicate when he spoke to me?" He decided finally that the man's imperfect English had aroused in him an unsuspected sentiment—a subconscious judgment against a person who had not been born into the English language. It was an amazing realization for one who spoke several languages fluently and had always had a facility for other tongues.

He pushed the unpleasant awareness from the forefront of his thought.

As they drew nearer the penitentiary, Ruxton made out smaller structures standing in the shadow of the bigger buildings. The developing size of the place took some of the power out of a grim joke he had had with himself the past few days. "I've been in a better jail," he had told himself, "than anything these so-and-so's have to offer."

It was a foolish humor, for it was more than six years since he had been in prison. He had returned from the South Pacific after World War II feeling perfectly normal and glad to have it over with. His intention was to re-enter his family business and start enjoying life again, which he did.

And then one day he almost killed a man in an argument over what—so he was told later—he reportedly conceived to be the other's pro-Soviet views.

As he explained it to his attorneys later, "The fact is I have no strong feelings on the subject. But I had had a couple of drinks. I don't remember the fight at all."

11

It was assumed that he had drunk more than he admitted. He was heavily fined and given a warning.

Ruxton, who knew that he had actually had only two drinks, was puzzled—but he drank more sparingly after that.

On an evening in mid-1947 he beat up a complete stranger unmercifully. In court, the victim claimed he had merely said, "Heil Hitler!" jokingly, whereupon he received the first of many vicious blows.

Ruxton did not remember the remark or his attack. In defense, he told the court, "So far as I know I expect those in charge of this country to look after the enemies of this country, and I have never given either Hitler or Stalin much thought. I had nothing to drink."

A few weeks after he was released from jail, acquaintances pulled him off of one of their number before he could do any damage. This third assault was hushed up, but Ruxton was now an intensely worried man, and he had the sensible thought that he had had no such violent impulses overseas, and that something about the American civilization and himself didn't mix any more. He promptly departed from the United States.

The British at Hong Kong accepted his credentials. From the beginning he considered the city a fabulous place and felt at home.

During the years since, he had not once lost control of himself.

There were incidents of anger, but these were outgrowths of his normal irritability, and fitted in with his ordinary behavior.

His two trips into China were made because of Anna Chen, that intense young woman who managed his businesses with an expert's astuteness and a Chinese intuition. But Anna's family was still on the mainland, and Anna— as she admitted one day when he found her crying—grieved often because she had not heard from her parents and two sisters for years.

Ruxton, being wise in many ways, suspected that his finding her openly tearful was no accident. But he had the somewhat unique idea for a white man in the far east, that the Chinese had feelings also, and so he felt instant sympathy. Yet he couldn't help remembering his father's practical advice: "Women, Seal, are the damnedest people. Once a female starts to work on you for something, you have two alternatives: Either tell her never to bring up the matter again, or do something about it."

Ruxton suspected there was nothing he could do. However, he inquired among his British business acquaintances if they might find a way for him to visit Red China. He received no encouragement. Finally, after it seemed as if his request had been forgotten, it was proposed to him that he act as agent for a British syndicate to buy spices. Ruxton hesitated, since America was still not doing business with Red China. Yet in the end he agreed on condition that he receive no pay and no share of the profits.

He bought the spices, and then made a detour to follow out one of Anna's clues. He stayed as long as he dared, searching, and then, having found no sign of the Chen family, he returned to Hong Kong.

He had crossed to the mainland this second time as unobtrusively as the first. And he had no illusions. It would be some time before inquiries were made about him. And when those inquiries were ignored, his business "associates" would not pursue the matter. It was understood by all parties that humanitarian principles of behavior were not followed by the Red Chinese.

Ruxton stopped the recollection with an irritated shake of his head. For days, ever since his arrest and sentence his mind had been like a broken record, going over and over the same thoughts. Since there was no true Cause and Effect here, he had nothing to learn from the experience except that it was a hard world even for a man as capable as he was.

He grew aware that Jarnoz was regaining consciousness and, simultaneously, that a long line of limousines was coming up behind the truck.

A horn honked. Some of the prisoners had already seen the fancy-looking machines, and were staring. Now, the others also turned to look at the motorcade. Ruxton was curious, but after one glance he restrained himself. He had something more urgent to attend to. He knelt beside the Turk.

The big man blinked at him, uneasily. Ruxton said, accentuating every word, "If it's necessary, I will say you fell out. I will say I tried to catch you but could not help you."

Jarnoz nodded. "Good." He added, "I have no business hit you. My nerves bad. We be friends, hey?"

Ruxton shook his head. "Not yet. It's too dangerous."

He did not wait for a reply, but stood up hastily. He had

13

actually no wish to be seen in an act of mercy. The Chinese Reds did not understand the parable of the Good Samaritan.

During the next half minute he had all he could do to hold himself erect. The truck was pulling off the road, and the ride grew bumpier. Ruxton hung on, as the first of the limousines drew up alongside of them. He expected the car to pass, but instead a man in army uniform beside the driver leaned out, and yelled in Chinese, "Who are these people?"

The truck driver yelled back, "Special prisoners!"

The officer shouted, "The ones who have been sentenced to death under Plan 'Future Victory'?"

The driver answered, "Yes, these are the ones."

"Then stop your truck," said the officer. "We want to meet our soon-to-be-friends."

He began to wave at the cars behind his own. The truck edged off the road and came to a halt. As the two guards climbed out, the cars in the motorcade pulled up all around the truck, some of them slanting almost at right angles off the road.

As nearly two dozen men and women emerged from the interiors, Ruxton counted all together seven cars: three Cadillacs, two Chryslers, a Mercedes-Benz, and a Rolls-Royce. It must be a group of high-powered people indeed to have such cars at their disposal. In face and manner, they looked above average in alertness and intelligence. Their dress was dutifully lacking in ornamentation. The eight women were dressed simply, in cotton dresses. The men all wore that peculiar, bulky, army blue affected by Mao Tse-tung and other top Reds. Even for these people, drab clothing was evidently still the surest way to prove that they were having humble thoughts, Ruxton observed cynically.

The officer who had been giving all the orders paused in front of the truck, and looked up at the prisoners. He was as fine a looking Chinese as Ruxton had seen. Taller than average, with only a hint of Mongol features, in his manner was both command and deference. His bright eyes moved visibly as he glanced from face to face. His gaze came to Ruxton, and there was no doubt in the latter's mind that he was being sized up, carefully and intently. The eyes moved on, then came back to Ruxton. He spoke in perfect, almost colloquial American English, looking straight at Ruxton.

"My name is Mai Lin Yin, and I am in charge of Plan 'Future Victory.' These people that you see here—" he politely indicated the men and women who were approaching from the various cars—"will be associated in our program, which, I can assure you, will be conducted with a minimum of discipline and a maximum of courtesy. But now, will you all step down? It will give you an opportunity to stretch yourselves before proceeding on this wearisome journey."

It was only about two miles farther to the prison, but Ruxton climbed over the side, and welcomed the feel of the ground. The other prisoners did not speak English, but they recognized what was meant, and also climbed down.

Introductions began, and Ruxton gave his own name.

". . . And this is my wife, Phenix—" Mai Lin Yin said to Ruxton.

The woman who came forward was lean, young, good-looking, with a confident manner. As she shook his hand, she said, "We are all excited about this experiment. If it works, then millions of lives will be saved when the free peoples of the world finally liberate America. We have a great obligation, you and we—all of us."

Until this moment, he hadn't thought there would be women involved. The prospect of two years without a woman had been one of the stunning realities of his terrible sentence. He had always had a certain attraction for women, and now, with a sidelong glance at Mai Lin Yin, he looked straight in Mrs. Mai's eyes as he said, "You are a beautiful and desirable woman. I sincerely hope that we shall be very good friends."

She met his direct gaze for an instant. "I'm sorry, Mr. Ruxton, if we already have a misunderstanding. I am everybody's friend."

"Then I am fortunate," said Ruxton smoothly, "for I cannot help but be included."

"I might make an exception in your case," she said coldly. "But—" she unfroze, "not yet. Misunderstandings can be forgiven and forgotten provided—"

There was an interruption. Ruxton had been keeping a tiny portion of his awareness on Mai Lin Yin. He was conscious that the man was affably shaking hands and introducing his colleagues to others of the prisoners. Now, abruptly, his voice ceased, and it was as if a machine had turned off. For everyone fell silent.

Ruxton and the woman turned. It took a moment to grasp what was happening. And then he saw that Mai Lin Yin had discovered Jarnoz lying at the bottom of the truck.

A soft, hot breeze was blowing, a portent of the greater heat yet to come to this far plain of interior China. Except for the almost desert-like bleakness, and that there were so

15

many Chinese involved, it might have been a scene on a back country road in Kansas.

Mai glanced at the two guards, and said in Chinese, "What has happened to this man?"

The guard who had hit Jarnoz said, "He tried to escape."

Mai stood somber, seeming to consider that. Then he turned to Ruxton. "Is that what happened?" he asked.

Ruxton, who had not yet admitted to any one that he understood several Chinese dialects, stared at him blankly, and then said, "What did he say?"

Mai translated, and Ruxton shook his head. "He fell out," he said. He explained briefly.

The officer turned toward the guard. "Give me your gun," he said. The guard handed it over. He looked unhappy. Mai toyed with the rifle for a moment, and then he spun it rapidly in his hands, and struck the man over the temple. The guard fell to the ground, and lay still.

Handing the rifle to the truck driver, Mai said in Chinese, "That will teach him that special prisoners are not to be mishandled."

He faced Ruxton and the others, companionably. "And so," he said in English, "I have punished the soldier who struck your associate." He smiled, as he added, "I hope you will accept my punishment of him as a friendly act, and that it is a happy augury for the success of Plan 'Future Victory'."

Ruxton, who had his own hardness, wondered, "Does he really believe that what he just did is a recommendation?"

Mai was turning away. He gave curt commands. The unconscious guard was lifted into the cab of the truck. Mai now suggested that the prisoners climb back into the truck. As they started to do so, he laid a restraining hand on Ruxton's arm. "Not you," he said. "I would be most honored if you would ride the remainder of the journey with my wife and myself."

Ruxton nodded his acceptance.

"Thank you," said Mai. And turned away.

Ruxton looked significantly at Mrs. Mai. Her angry eyes met his, and he did her the courtesy of glancing away.

"You have a very unusual name," he said. "Phenix—beautiful."

"It is an old Chinese name," she said. "But come, please enter the car."

She walked beside him, and she seemed curious suddenly,

rather than annoyed. "Have you any idea why my husband wants you to ride with us?"

Ruxton shook his head.

Minutes later the line of cars was once more moving toward the prison.

2

"This is Tosti, assigned to cook and work for us," Mrs. Mai said.

Ruxton faced forward. He had noticed the second young woman as he climbed into the car. Now, he inclined his head, an acknowledgment of the introduction. Mrs. Mai spoke in Chinese to the maid—for that was what she was, however they worded it. The young woman bowed her head, and then looked momentarily into Ruxton's eyes, a quick, searching glance. He had an impression of being appraised, for what purpose he could not imagine.

Tosti's eyes were a rich, wide-eyed, chocolate brown, her face delicately oval, her lips very red, and her body slender. She was twenty-eight or nine, he thought, and very subdued.

Although she evidently understood Chinese, Ruxton saw that Tosti had Japanese features. He said so to Mrs. Mai.

"Yes," was the answer. "Tosti is Japanese."

Ruxton considered the emotional value to a Chinese woman of having a Japanese maid. It seemed like a very simple way of being socially superior in a country where the opportunity must be fading fast.

Far more important, after Phenix' cold rejection of his advances, Tosti offered him a second chance for the days ahead. It seemed a particularly good opportunity because Japanese was one of the several languages he knew well.

Alerted by the possibility, he settled back into the seat. And awaited events.

The Cadillac, one of the long '54 Fleetwoods, glided over the country road with a minimum of swaying. Its speed was not great, about thirty-five miles an hour at the fastest, with frequent slowdowns as the chauffeur, a plump Chinese soldier, adjusted his beautiful machine to road conditions.

Ruxton sat directly behind the driver. Tosti was next to him, and beyond her, Mrs. Mai. Her husband, in the seat directly in front of her, stared straight ahead. The introductions over, no one said anything for at least a minute.

17

Finally, Mai Lin Yin stirred, and turned. "You may be wondering," he said, "why I invited you to ride with us."

Ruxton nodded, and waited.

Mai continued, "First of all, I thought I might find out from you, what is your opinion of the chances of the success of Plan 'Future Victory'?" He spread his hands amicably. "—Find it out in an atmosphere more congenial than the back of a truck or the inside of a prison interrogation office."

Ruxton said now, slowly, trying to recall the details as he vaguely remembered hearing them at the time of his sentencing, "You people are supposed to know how to change thinking—you Chinese even coined the word for it. Brainwash. I assume you will give me the brainwash treatment."

"Not exactly," said Mrs. Mai, leaning towards him, intent and actually quite emotional. "This is different. You must change yourself. You may come to us for help, and in the end you must convince special interrogators of the Party that you have truly changed. You see—you must wash your own brain. This is the new plan, different from anything we have attempted before."

Mai Lin Yin nodded in agreement with his wife's somewhat excited words. "Yes," he said, "this is different. We say to you, in effect: Mr. Ruxton, here is a problem. You solve it for us."

"How many of us are there with this problem?"

"Twenty-three. Nationals of the principal Western nations," said Mai.

"Are we all here now?"

"Yes. When this truckload arrives that will complete the experimental group. In addition, of course, there are more than two thousand political prisoners representing the various reactionary groups of the old regime. Millions of these have not yet been liquidated."

"You can see," said Mrs. Mai earnestly, "how much depends on the success of the experiment."

Ruxton abruptly felt sorry for her. "Would you really like my true thought?" he asked.

"Of course—" Mai seemed surprised—"that is the perfection of the new plan. Nothing need be held back, on a thought level. Of course, we cannot permit violence. Speak."

"Yes," encouraged the woman from his right, her voice gentle, "say what you think."

"What I'm thinking," said Ruxton, "is that I come from the most advanced civilization on earth, and these poor, ignorant people want me, a product of that great civiliza-

18

tion, to start thinking in their simple fashion. I think it can never happen."

He gazed first at the woman and then the man, challengingly. "That's the problem as it really is," he said. And settled back firmly in his seat.

Ruxton was astonished after a moment to hear soft laughter. He twisted his head. It was Mrs. Mai. She seemed genuinely amused. She caught his glance, and sobered.

"After all," she said, "Chinese civilization is 6,000 years old."

Ruxton thought. "Yes, but over all this vast land you still use human excretion for fertilizer. You have cholera plagues, and uncontrolled floods. You have poverty the drabness of which is equalled only by what exists in other old, faded civilizations. You have for centuries had a disregard of human life that in the West we only have in periods of aberration, such as when the Nazis ravaged Europe and the Soviets murdered the Kulaks."

Long ago the ancient Chinese culture, lost in the apathy of the centuries, had come into contact with Western machine civilization. Foolishly it had resisted it, and fought it, and slowly yielded, becoming the halting type of democracy it was capable of being. And then the communist idea, with outside military aid and its "ant" philosophy, overwhelmed the plodding democracy. In the same way, more than a generation before, a gang of nihilistic bandits in Russia had murdered the first tiny democracy in that country and had terrorized masses of illiterate peasants into accepting a new set of chains. That was Ruxton's picture of communism.

"And now," he thought, "they want me to believe that these half-starved human beings have enough light of reason in their eyes to see what is good for all men.

They actually expect me to think that way before I'm through."

For an instant, then, the awareness of what the future held for him was a sharp, painful sensation in his throat. The feeling of shock faded. He smiled, suddenly amused by Mrs. Mai's amusement. "She will never understand," he realized. "She and I are an entire ocean apart, and perhaps millennia in time."

He felt a need to explain, perhaps even to re-educate—for obviously they didn't know the truth of things.

He said aloud, tolerantly, "That's right. China is a very venerable civilization. But those who gave it what life it had

19

have nearly all been shot. The victors do not believe in the values of the old civilization. Therefore China is no longer old, but extremely new. It must be judged for what it is, not for what it was."

"And what do you think it is?" That was Mai Lin Yin. There was an edge of emotion in his voice, an antagonism, disappointment. Ruxton thought, "He naively expected a cooperative friend. Now he thinks I'm just another reactionary enemy."

Aloud, Ruxton said, "A beehive, an ant hill—mindless fear conforming to brutality." He glanced at the two people, and had a moment of compassion. "You asked for my opinion," he said. "I gave it. This is where I start."

Mrs. Mai was staring straight ahead. Her husband seemed lost in thought. It was he who spoke, slowly. "It's not our problem," he said. "We are like parents who stand by to give a helping hand and a word of advice to their growing children, in this case, only if they ask for it."

He became pensive. "You whites will not be living in the main prison. You will be free to come and go within the confines of the village."

Mrs. Mai turned to Ruxton. "You have three months," she said earnestly, "to show your first evidence of intent. We must report then, have you, have you not, shown any willingness to change. Please do not put us in the position of having to report that you have not."

Ruxton said, startled, "I thought my death sentence was automatically suspended for two years to give me time to make the change."

She murmured hastily, "There's a review at three months, six months, one year, two years. It's awfully simple. You must show some sincere sign that—" She broke off. "But here—we are at the end of our journey."

It took a long moment for Ruxton to come back from his shock, to realize that they were entering a street, and to an awareness that he had other, more immediate things to do than worry about what progress he might have made three months hence.

3

He looked around with intense interest. For there was a village, and it was outside of the prison with its high concrete wall. He saw that it was actually quite a small village, and that it had looked spread out from a distance because its principal street ran parallel to, and right beside the wall.

His car, coming in from the east at right angles to this main street, passed a straggle of shacks, and then turned left, and there was the long, dirt avenue stretching in front of him, and behind him—he saw fleetingly—well beyond the farthest reach of the prison itself.

All the buildings were on the east side of the street, across from the wall. Mostly, they were shacks, or small stores. But there was a long, low hut with many windows that looked like a soldiers' barracks. And a three-story wooden building that could have been a grimy unpainted skid row hotel in an American city. Several other larger buildings seemed to be for warehouse or storage purposes.

Soldiers were on guard everywhere—so it appeared to his skimming gaze.

The chauffeur evidently knew his duty, for he made a U-turn and came back so that Mai Lin Yin could step directly onto the wooden sidewalk in front of the hotel-like structure. He opened Mrs. Mai's door, and she got out. The driver began to climb out also.

It was the moment Ruxton had been waiting for. He parted his lips to speak. Before he could utter a word, Tosti said in English, "You be—" she touched her bosom —"lover me?"

Ruxton was so taken aback by her saying what he had intended to say that he sat momentarily speechless. Then he said hurriedly in Japanese, "I shall find a place where we can meet. Go now."

Her answer was in Japanese, breathless, "Such a situation as this—no time for feminine wiles. You are very attractive man. I shall love you with my whole heart."

As she got out onto the sidewalk, Ruxton opened the door on his side of the car, stepped down to the dirt road, and walked around the car.

All the tension seemed gone out of him. The threat of death was somehow far away. The feeling he had had about the impossibility of training himself to be a communist was temporarily unimportant.

For the nine years he had lived in Hong Kong, he had been concerned with small things: the wholesale price of spices, storage of goods, details of transportation, ship charges, actual methods of making and selling goods. He had bought considerable property, not on the beautiful, steep slopes of Victoria Peak, but down where the press of

21

population was nearly two thousand to the acre, an incredible mass of humanity. The details of such ownership made hard work, and some of it was better left to shrewd Anna Chen. But, still, he did not delegate too much, ever. He believed in doing his own haggling, and he set his own terms.

With that same acute interest in details, he stood now in the dirt street of the prison village, and he saw that it was like other villages in communist China. There were several shops that had the appearance of being privately owned. Ruxton had already heard of the way the Reds diluted the ownership, but that didn't matter to the customer. He walked over to the nearest, and purchased a boiled duck egg, two small oranges, and a cooked rice cake. The cake was surprisingly tasty, and he said to the shopkeeper, in English, "Good cook—my compliments."

The man, a small, scrawny, elderly individual, shrugged his lack of understanding. From behind Ruxton, Mrs. Mai's voice translated the compliment into Chinese. The man bowed and smiled, and said, "I will tell my wife."

Ruxton faced around to Mrs. Mai, as she translated the old man's reply. She added, "You make yourself at home quickly."

"I saw the food," he replied. "I was hungry. I still have my money, so I was able to buy."

"Wouldn't you like to see your room?"

"Sooner or later, why not now?"

She led the way into the hotel, for that was exactly what it was. It was a rickety old place, but it had the foyer, the desk with its little cubbyhole postal boxes, and to the right of the desk a wide staircase. The ornamentation of the ceiling told of better times. Ruxton wondered aloud how such a basically good structure had found its way to so remote and barren a part of otherwise teeming China.

"It was moved here," Mrs. Mai said. "It was put on skids, and five thousand men and several tractors hauled it thirty miles from Wanchan."

Ruxton made a mental note of the distance to Wanchan, but made no comment on her explanation.

In entering the hotel, he had noticed that several white men sat in wooden chairs near the windows to the left of the door. For the first few moments after his entrance, they were only a group, not yet identified. But now he saw that one was a Catholic priest, and one was an officer of the United States Air Force.

22

Ruxton stared at the officer in amazement and then, unmindful of Mrs. Mai, walked over to the man. "My God," he said, "what are you doing here?"

The intensity of his words was so great that the man evidently misunderstood.

"Do we know each other?" he asked.

"No. I meant—your uniform. U.S. Air Force."

"Oh!" the officer acknowledged. "I'll tell you later when there are none of these Chinese s.o.b.'s around."

Ruxton said, "My name is Seal Ruxton."

"Mine is Captain Edward Gregory."

Ruxton turned, paused as he became aware of the priest again and then, his resistance to communication re-asserted itself and he walked on to rejoin Mrs. Mai.

She was busy writing something on a small piece of paper. As he came up, she glanced at his face, started to speak, and then seemed to think better of it. Instead, she faced the soldier on duty behind the desk, and said in Chinese, "What rooms do you have left for the prisoners?" He answered, "Two doubles and three singles." She said, "My husband wishes Mr. Ruxton to have the best of the singles." He said, "That would be number 39, for it faces north and thus avoids the summer sun, and the heat from the furnace reaches it first in winter." She said, "Good. Take him to room 39."

She turned back to Ruxton. "The soldier will take you to your room. Lunch is at one in the dining room through that door." She pointed at some portieres. "When you get to your room, read these further instructions."

She handed him the slip of paper on which she had been writing, and walked past him out of the hotel. The soldier clerk came out from behind the desk, and beckoned Ruxton with a nod of the head. They went up the stairway to the second floor. There were three desks set up near the stairs.

A hard-faced Mongol officer sat at one of them. Two warrant officers were busy with many papers at the other two desks.

Ruxton and his guide continued on up to the third floor. Here, two soldiers, impassive of face, each carrying a shouldered rifle, walked side by side along the corridor of the third floor. The desk man said to them, in Chinese, "This one's room is 39."

They nodded and marched on. The guide opened the door, motioned Ruxton inside. Ruxton crossed the threshold, and stopped. The room in which he found himself was not large, but it had a bed with an ancient wooden headboard in faded ivory. There was a hard-seat chair, and an escritoire, both painted in ivory color. An attempt had also been made to use the ivory paint on the old rocking chair by the window, but the dark red of the cherry-wood showed through streakily.

Ruxton heard a click. Turning, he saw that the door had closed, and that he was alone.

4

With a sigh, Ruxton sank down on the bed. It uttered a hideous, protesting creak, almost as if it were a living creature. The sound was so unexpected that he half stood up. Then, realizing, he settled down again. But already he was resigned to his squeaking vessel of sleep. Ignoring its noisy response, he unfolded the note Mrs. Mai had given him, and read:

> Success of Plan "Future Victory" is very important to my husband, and I feel sure that if he thinks you might not change, he will see to it that you suffer an accident, and are replaced by someone in whose conversion he has more confidence. Since he already has one incorrigible American in the Air Force man, I feel he will scarcely desire to have another. So be on your guard, for he has tens of thousands of executions to his credit. Destroy this letter.

Ruxton re-read the note with a faint feeling of triumph. The fact that it had been written suggested that Mrs. Mai was not the one-hundred-percent communist that her verbal enthusiasms had implied, and also that it had been wise of him to speak to her as a woman, and not as an enemy agent.

He climbed to his feet and, note in hand, walked over to the east window, drawn by the sound of a motor. It was a glass window, except that a part of the lower pane was broken, and the broken part had been replaced by rice paper. As he glanced out, he was in time to see the truck with the other prisoners, entering the village. It bounced over a bump, and at this distance the way the men in the back grabbed for balance made them look ridiculous. A few moments later, the automobile disappeared from his sight.

But he could hear it as it shifted gears, turned into the main street, and came toward the hotel. The engine coughed, and died. And he knew his fellow passengers had arrived.

He thought: "This is all real."

Merely thinking that was somehow unconvincing. He said it aloud, softly, trying to make it have meaning. But he was tired now, and certainty was hard to come by. He surmised, from the contents of the note, that Mai Lin Yin would have to present an overwhelming success to the party. "They won't accept failure," he analyzed. "They've gone too far. This is for keeps."

His anxious thought was interrupted. Footsteps sounded outside his door. The thin panel reverberated with the knock that came a moment later.

Ruxton started forward, and then became aware of Mrs. Mai's note clutched in his palm. Since he did not intend to destroy it, he hastily slipped it into his pocket. That done, he opened the door.

Captain Gregory, the Catholic priest, and a slim, dandified white man stood there. The Captain said, "May we come in?"

Ruxton sighed inwardly. His feeling that he should avoid quick friendships till he could size up this situation was being overwhelmed by weight of numbers. Without a word he stepped back and motioned the men to enter.

They came in, one following the other, first the priest, then the strange young man, and then Gregory. They all seemed tense, each in his own way. These were threatened men, and they showed it in the way they held themselves, and in the way they walked. Captain Gregory closed the door. It was he who spoke in a low, firm voice. "This is Father de Melanier," he introduced the priest. He explained, "The good father can just barely make himself understood in English, so he has brought along his compatriot, Jean Lemoine, who speaks a much more recognizable English."

"I speak better," said Lemoine. He added cheerfully, "We are all in the box, eh?"

Gregory said, "I guess he means the same boat . . . you know." He shrugged.

Ruxton had decided to be sociable. "It's a trap all right," he said.

"No trap for me," said Lemoine. "In France, I have been communist three times. No problem to become one again."

Such an attempted airy dismissal of the problem hardened

25

Ruxton against the man. "Maybe they won't like backsliders," he said.

Lemoine was abruptly less cheerful. He sat down on the bed, jumped at the enormous creaking sound that welcomed him, and then said unhappily, "You say unfortunate things."

Father de Melanier said in French, "Ask him if he is going to become a communist."

He was an intellectual-looking man in his middle forties, soft of face, manner and voice. Ruxton looked at him, hesitated, and then answered him in French: "How does one become a communist?"

"You speak French?" The priest was delighted. "Then we can converse."

Ruxton had come suddenly to the decision to reveal that he understood the language. It was not a well-thought-out decision. But it seemed to him that concealing his knowledge of Japanese, Russian, and two Chinese languages would be difficult enough.

Lemoine recovered from his gloom. "I shall translate for Captain Gregory," he said.

Father de Melanier said, "I have decided as a preliminary step to read their literature. I have advised Captain Gregory to do the same."

Ruxton said, "You feel that they will construe the reading of Communist literature as evidence of intent?"

"Yes," said the priest. Then he spread his hands in a gesture of frustration. "I admit it is only a method of gaining time. I have already read most Communist literature published in China. It is aimed at a very low class of mind."

Ruxton said slowly, "Maybe reading the stuff will do for the first three months. But after that there is the next quarter. Can you make another, further compromise?"

Father de Melanier shook his head sadly. "As a missionary," he said, "I shall never abandon my faith, never miss a prayer, never lose a chance of winning another soul for Christ. But I have been in this part of the world for eighteen years, and I am prepared to live and let live under any government or economic system, provided I can continue the work of the church. If this is not sufficient, then—" he spread his hands, helplessly, this time—"the commandant will have to report that I am incorrigible."

Ruxton was silent. He stared at the priest with unhappy compassion. "It won't work," he thought. He had as devious a mind as any Chinese, and he sensed that this experiment was different. These others couldn't see it, except perhaps Captain Gregory.

He looked directly at the officer. "You refuse?" he asked.

The other nodded. "After the Korean war, the President issued a directive on Communist indoctrination. I intend to carry that directive out to the letter."

"Does the American government know you are a prisoner?" Ruxton asked.

"No."

"How come?"

"My plane was forced down over the Pacific in a storm. We put our rafts out. I never saw my crew again, but I was rescued by a Red China fishing boat. I have since been told none of the other bodies was recovered, and that it is presumed we were all lost."

"I see." Ruxton nodded. It was a typical violation of international law by the Chinese Reds. But it had given them an American Air Force officer for their experiment, without any questions asked, so they were evidently satisfied.

Captain Gregory interrupted his thought: "Have you ever served in the U.S. armed forces?"

"Three years during World War II."

"What rank did you attain?"

Ruxton had an idea of what was coming, and he stiffened. But he was icily amused. "Idiot, first class," he said. "By that I mean, I obeyed all orders given me regardless of their stupidity." He added apologetically, "I was too young to know any better."

A faintly clouded look had come into Captain Gregory's face. He seemed uncertain. "I gather you didn't like your officers," he said finally, tolerantly.

Ruxton said, "I thought ninety per cent of them were unfit to clean diapers. God only knows whose idea it was to put them in charge of human beings."

He saw that the other was not unfamiliar with the attitude of lower ranks in service. For the captain's expression became obviously tolerant, and somewhat patronizing. Also he must have decided he was talking to a former private, for there was a touch of command in his voice, as he said, "I expect you as an American to make the same stand that I'm making. Refuse even to read their literature!"

Ruxton laughed; he couldn't help himself. "Captain," he said when he recovered control, "remind me to consult you about all my other activities. I never was able to make up my mind about anything and it's good to know there's someone around who can make it up for me."

The Captain flushed. "I beg your pardon," he said. "I didn't mean to sound undemocratic. But surely you see the value of a united front and of not giving in to these s.o.b.'s."

Ruxton remembered Mrs. Mai's grim reference in her note to Captain Gregory's recalcitrance. He said roughly, "What I see is that you're going to get yourself shot in short order. Personally, I plan to read their junk. Do you know," he went on in a wondering tone, "I couldn't tell you what communism is. It always seemed such a dull subject, but—" he smiled savagely—"it's got more exciting suddenly." He frowned at the captain. "Are you seriously saying that you are not curious as to what the alternative is to your death sentence?"

Gregory's lips tightened. He seemed to come to a decision. He said in a formal tone, "You know, sir, that the American people expect us to sacrifice our lives if necessary."

Ruxton stiffened, then said coolly, "Captain, I have an idea that if Mr. Gallup were to poll popular opinion as to what each American would do in this situation he wouldn't get the same answer from everybody, and I doubt if more than one per cent would adopt your extreme solution. Wait—" He spoke sharply, and held up his hand with a sudden gesture. "Now, take my personal situation. I served a prison term in the United States and do not feel all Americans are to be regarded with equal respect—"

In the background Lemoine, who had been translating in a low tone to Father de Melanier, suddenly raised his voice in excitement.

Ruxton went on, "I'd like to wring the neck of the judge who sentenced me for the phony moral lesson he read me. And there was one guard in that prison—if I ever get my hands on him, I'll strangle him. Also, a certain psychiatrist would get a black eye at least."

Gregory was pale. "Surely you cannot hold the treatment you received in prison against the American people?"

It was such a complete misunderstanding of what he was trying to say that Ruxton shrugged, and said pityingly, "I'm sorry I've hurt your feelings, Captain. But I believe you ought to change your views, not I mine."

Captain Gregory walked rigidly to the door. He opened it, and turned. "I'll thank you," he said coldly, "never to speak to me for any reason while we are together in this prison."

"Goodbye," said Ruxton impatiently.

The American officer went out, and closed the door.

Lemoine caught Ruxton's eye and nodded his head, admiringly. "You are a man who speak the mind," he said. "Perhaps, you and I, yes, very definitely you and I have similar philosophies. We are both citizens of the world, hey? Only there is no such status, hey? And so we must constantly—what is it you Americans say?—'suck up' to madmen in order to live."

Ruxton, who had already decided he did not like Lemoine, did not think there was any similarity between himself and a man who admitted that he had been a Communist three times. He made no reply, merely stared at the young man.

The priest said to Lemoine, "We had better go."

Father de Melanier paused at the door, and said with a friendly smile, "I sense that you and Captain Gregory are closer together than he realizes."

Ruxton said quietly, "I differ, sir. Being in the military, he cannot really grasp that there is a civilian point of view. In essence all I said was that I'm finally going to find out what these Communists are up to. For that he cut me off from further communication."

"I feel that you will be friends," said the priest.

Ruxton was not prepared to argue the matter. He said, "You have my good wishes, Father. I have no idea whether or not I have a soul, but I give you permission to pray for it if it exists."

"I shall most certainly do so," said the priest.

"Lunch is at one," said Lemoine. He looked at his watch. "And it is now twenty of. The dining room—"

"I know where it is," Ruxton said.

"It's through a door to the left of the desk, main floor. Entrance of dining room, lunch room, breakfast room." Lemoine was at the door now. He turned owlishly. "Bathroom on every floor," he said. "American style, it says."

"With running water?" Ruxton was incredulous.

"In a way." Lemoine spoke cautiously. "There's a stream on far side of prison—that's where life begins again on this desert. They pump water from the stream to tanks on the roof. One day, no water. Forget to pump, maybe. But every other day there's been water."

"How many days have you been here?"

"Two days." Lemoine laughed.

"You seem to know your way around."

"What is there to learn in a little Chinese village?" He

shuddered. His eyes lost their glow. "If I am so bored in two days, what will it be like in two years?"

He went out, shaking his head gloomily.

Ruxton started to follow, then paused and examined the door. He could find no way to lock it. He shrugged, thought, "Oh, well, who has secrets?" He wondered if twenty-three condemned men would develop habits of thieving on each other. It was a strangely unpleasant thought.

He left the room, pulling the door shut after him. The two sentinels were coming towards him as he walked along the hallway. They paused alertly to let him pass, then marched on. Ruxton found the bathroom.

As he entered he saw that someone was already there. The rushing water must have drowned out the sound of the door opening for the boy at one of the washbowls jumped as Ruxton stepped up to the second bowl.

His was a thin, clean-shaven boyish face. Ruxton remembered having seen him, silent and morose, sitting near Gregory in the lobby, body twisted and awkward. What was visible now, at close quarters, was the pallor of fear, the bloodshot eyes, the lax, frightened mouth. Ruxton had not intended to speak, but the boy's terror broke through his own barriers. He said gently, "Do you understand English?"

The boy looked at him, blank, glazed-eyed.

Ruxton asked in French, "Do you speak French?" Still there was no recognition, nothing but the terror, naked, uncontrolled. Ruxton turned away, shrugging; then decided on one more effort, and he faced the boy again. He pointed at himself. "Seal Ruxton," he said.

He was watching the boy's face closely, but there was no sign of any reaction. If his words went in—there was no one home to receive the message.

He bent to wash himself, and he was reveling in the fresh feel of it when the door opened. The newcomer was a lean, angry man in his early forties. He glanced at Ruxton, then immediately focussed his attention on the boy. He spoke sharply in a tongue strange to Ruxton. The boy stood blank. Without another word, the man struck him in the face with the back of his fingertips. Then struck again. Then again.

Ruxton straightened, and watched the tense scene, curious. He did not consider what was happening as brutal, nor did he think of interfering. There was a race-similarity of appearance between the two. He guessed they knew each other, and that the older man was trying to help the younger one control his fear.

Abruptly, the boy broke into a frustrated, angry crying. Tears mixed with rage. He struck back weakly at his tormentor. The action brought a satirical comment from the older man. Again, the boy tried to strike him. He missed, but his face was contorted with a new, stronger emotion; hate. He lunged at the older man, missed him as the man stepped aside, and lunged again. It was an awkward movement. The man caught his arm, neatly opened the door with his free hand, and with a twist of his body, propelled the boy out into the hall.

He closed the door, regarded Ruxton quizzically, and then, pointing at himself, spoke a word that sounded like "Diogo." Ruxton reciprocated with his own name. Diogo hesitated, then smiled helplessly, and began to wash himself.

5

Luncheon.

Cooked green vegetables, rice in abundance, pork and chicken in various forms, and hot tea—that was the meal.

Ruxton enjoyed every bite. Finally content, he thought: "Evidently they don't intend to starve us the first day." He had a feeling that things might become strained later on in the experiment, and he divined that food scarcity might be used as a lever on recalcitrants.

From where he sat, he counted twenty-two whites (besides himself) and fifteen Chinese, all men. Mai Lin Yin was not among them but, except for him and the women, the Chinese were those he had seen in the chauffeur-driven cars. The whites sat at the tables that extended down either side of the room, and the Chinese in a long row at the head table. Windows were open. Everybody, captor and captive alike, suffered equally from the atmospheric conditions. Ruxton wondered suddenly, "What am I waiting for? Orders?" He climbed to his feet, and started for the door.

"Mr. Ruxton!"

Ruxton turned toward the head table where a plump Chinese officer had risen to his feet. The man spoke again. "For this one occasion, please remain at your seat. We wish to issue general instructions to newcomers."

Ruxton returned to his chair without comment. There was a stir at the portieres. Mai Lin Yin entered the room. He paused and said, "Please turn your chairs, and face this way."

The command was repeated by his aides in various languages. There was a creaking and scraping, but soon silence. Mai Lin Yin glanced at his watch, and spoke again. "By July 12, 1957, midnight, by the power and authority vested in me by the Chinese Communist Party, I shall be in a position to inform all of those here present who have survived interrogations and intermediate trials by people's courts, whether or not they have successfully achieved the goals set. You will find an adequate library of Communist literature in all languages needed for this group in the front room of my home. Reading must be done in that room between ten in the morning and ten at night. It is forbidden to remove any books. Call on me or my staff for whatever assistance you may desire."

He paused, and the interpreters spoke, each in turn. They were still interpreting when, across the room from Ruxton, Captain Gregory climbed to his feet. He was flushed. In a voice thick with anger he said: "By what authority does the gang of murderers and bandits up in Peking hold prisoner an officer of the armed forces of a country with which China is not at war?"

Mai Lin Yin stared at him steadily. A proud look came into his face. "By the authority," he said, "of the people of China."

"That's a lie!" said Captain Gregory.

"This is strong language," said Mai Lin Yin, and it seemed to Ruxton that his voice was deceptively mild. "Why not use the language of reason, Captain?"

Captain Gregory raged: "Don't give me any of that double talk. The people of China have been terrorized by wholesale massacres of their relatives and friends. Now you pretend that these frightened individuals were, and are being consulted. But you are not consulting a man when you hold a knife at his throat, tell him what to think, and then ask him if he thinks it. That, my terrified little man, is the kind of reasoning the scum up in Peking are doing with the people of China."

Mai Lin Yin said in the same mild tone: "You do not seem to be showing a spirit of cooperation with the people, Captain. Have you seriously considered the consequences to you, personally, of such an attitude?"

"God damn your cooperation!" roared Captain Gregory.

"You'll get none of it from me. And as for consequences, I expect to be murdered."

The silence was longer this time. Finally, Mai Lin Yin said quietly: "You have three months, Captain, to alter your views on these matters. But I must warn you, no violence please, during that period." He looked around. "Now, are there any questions?"

The interpreters made no attempt to translate the interchange between Mai and the air force officer, but they now, each in turn, translated the question. When they had finished, only one man raised a hand. He spoke in a language which, Ruxton guessed from his appearance, was one of the Scandinavian tongues. The words were translated into Chinese by an interpreter who said, "He wants to know if there is any value in subjecting citizens of such neutrals as Sweden, his own country, to such experiments as this, when the fact is that Sweden would probably remain neutral in the event of war between Russia and China on the one hand, and America and the West on the other?"

Mai Lin Yin said earnestly, in Chinese, "Tell him that the free peoples of the world have a duty to the enslaved masses of all the capitalistic countries, and that the greatest service he can render to the people of his country, which after all is a capitalistic nation, is to co-operate with us, so that at the proper time knowledge gained now can be effectively used to save the lives of many who would otherwise have to be destroyed because they will themselves be centers of capitalistic infection."

As the interpreters were completing their translations a few minutes later, Ruxton saw that Gregory was again climbing to his feet. Gregory said loudly, "One more thing I want to say. There is present in this room a character born in America who, I am presuming, you regard as representative of the people of the United States. I want to tell you that this man is an ex-convict, that winning him over will probably be a pushover, but that it will prove nothing. He represents nobody. He—"

Almost as Gregory began speaking, Ruxton felt his first flash of rage. Before the man had said more than a few words, Ruxton realized what was coming, and he was on his feet. At the word "ex-convict," Ruxton was already rounding the table, and racing across the room. He saw that Gregory was aware of him, but some kind of verbal momentum was involved, an emotion from which there was no turning back, for it was not until Ruxton snatched his arm

33

and swung him around that he stopped, and said with a sneer: "It's the truth, isn't it?"

Ruxton struck him, a single smashing blow on the chest. Gregory went down with an amazed look on his face. And came up again, his jaw set, his eyes narrowed. As he gathered himself for what was unmistakably going to be a counter-attack, the voice of Mai Lin Yin, no longer mild, but high pitched and commanding, yelled, "The first man to strike another blow gets shot."

That ended the fight. Gregory straightened slowly, and Ruxton glanced toward Mai. The Chinese leader had a pistol in his hand. He seemed to realize there would be no more squabbling, because he slipped the weapon into a pocket, and walked to the portieres, and yelled in Chinese at some-one on the other side, "Send a guard of three in here."

He returned into the room, and stood gazing at Ruxton with an expression that was presently alarming. Ruxton said uneasily, "This man came to my room, and we had already had a quarrel, so his mention of me was a provocation which I could not let go by."

As he finished speaking, three soldiers entered through the portieres, rifles at the ready, and at a curt command from Mai Lin Yin, took up positions beside him. Mai said, "Mr. Ruxton, you do not for a moment believe that I was fooled by this little drama between you and your country-man. It has been reported to me that you recognized him as you entered the hotel this morning, and I have no doubt that the two of you are now making elaborate efforts to ensure that no significance is attached to your reaction when you first saw him."

Ruxton was suddenly frightened. For such a misreading as this could never be proved or disproved. "I was surprised to see an officer of the American armed forces in such a situation as this."

Mai was calm again. He stroked his jaw, speculatively. "I ask myself, what could you two be desirous of concealing, and the answer which comes most readily to mind is that you are an American intelligence officer. What a pity!"

It was such a fantastic idea that Ruxton recovered. "Holy smoke!" he said. "You people must see spies in every bush."

Mai said in an icy voice, "Your jesting manner under-rates the seriousness of your situation."

Ruxton was temporarily beyond the reach of fear. He said, "Until this instant, Mr. Mai, I thought you were an intelligent man." He stopped, because there was a stubborn

34

expression on Mai's face, a suspicion that mere words could not erase. The threat was increasing, but he braced himself and said, "All right, all right, just skip the whole thing. I can see that no argument is going to reach you. So do what you damn well please, and let's get it over with."

Mai Lin Yin shook his head. "It is not what I please, Mr. Ruxton. The people shall judge you. We have law and order in this country, based upon democratic principles." He turned to the head table, and said in Chinese, "Bring the furniture for a people's court. A trial is about to commence. Tell these prisoners to remain, since they shall be the court, and render the decision."

As the interpreters began talking, several aides rushed out of the room, and others jabbered excitedly among themselves. At Mai's command, two of the three guards took up positions beside Ruxton.

The third man stationed himself at the door.

6

As he waited, Ruxton felt the anger fading out of him. He watched unhappily as a desk was eased past the portieres, and set down near the door. He realized he was fighting a developing anxiety. Abruptly, he lost the fight. An alarm reaction surged through his body, and a fearful conviction came that he would be shot this very afternoon.

How many seconds passed while he stood there gripped by pure fright, he could only estimate afterwards; not too many. But presently, some automatic defensive mechanism was triggered, and the ability to resist the internal disaster began to return. As he stood there, trembling in spite of his effort at self-control, someone placed a chair behind the desk. Mai Lin Yin sat down in it. Another chair was brought, and put down beside the desk. Indicating the second chair, Mai ordered in his Mandarin Chinese, "Bring the prisoner here." The two guards motioned Ruxton, and he allowed himself to be guided into the chair.

As soon as Ruxton was seated, Mai Lin Yin asked in English, "What is your name?"

Ruxton did not reply. The flashing image of himself standing in front of a firing squad was fading a little . . . replaced by a quiet, seething resentment that held him taut, like a tube inflated by air pressure. Against that pressure, speech was impossible.

Mai Lin Yin spoke again, his voice edged. "Am I to understand, Mr. Ruxton, that you do not plan to reply?"

From somewhere in the room, the voice of Captain Gregory said, "Don't you realize you've got a frightened man on your hands? He can't answer."

Mai said sharply, "Captain, we understand your eagerness to aid this spy of your country, but it is he who is being questioned, not you."

"You're an idiot!" Gregory retorted in a disgusted tone.

"One more insult from you," Mai replied, "and I shall have you escorted from this room. This will mean that your compatriot will lose your vote when the time comes for the people's judgment."

The interchange between the two men had given Ruxton a few of the precious seconds he needed. The tight band of his resentment seemed to let go a little. His anger changed. Suddenly, he felt the need for cunning. With that need, the ability to speak returned. He said aloud, "My name is Seal Ruxton."

As he spoke, his glance met Mai's. The man's eyes lighted up with satisfaction. "I congratulate you, Mr. Ruxton, on your decision to cooperate with the people."

Ruxton felt a flush of shame creep into his cheeks. It was momentary only. He told himself that he was not so much cooperating as gaining time to recover from the fear that had suddenly shattered him. He had to get back to the point where he could face all this madness again.

Mai Lin Yin said, "Is Seal Ruxton your true name?"

Ruxton hesitated.

Mai said loudly, "Come, come, it is or it isn't!"

Ruxton said, "Yes, it is my true name."

"Why did you hesitate?" Mai demanded.

"It's a long story."

"We have all afternoon."

Ruxton sighed. He had entered Hong Kong on a false passport, and had then gone through a period of legally recovering the use of his own name. What was astonishing was that he could not recall the false name he had used. He was explaining the situation to Mai when he realized that his voice was reasonably under his control.

He sat up in his chair. His shoulders straightened. He sighed again, with relief this time. He felt himself a man again.

But the trial continued.

"What is your home address?"

Ruxton gave it, absently. He was re-discovering his immediate environment. He realized that his fear had put him out of touch. For the first time, now, since the trial had been ordered, he saw the "people" as Mai had called them, who were his judges and his jury in this incredible drama. And what he saw brought a memory of things he had heard about trials like this.

In such situations, the Chinese had proved that people who were confronted by the fear that a negative judgment would be held against them, invariably voted whatever sentence was suggested to them. This group of twenty-two whites were under the same kind of pressure. To be a juror in such a trial was also to be on trial. Not three months hence, but this very first day, these men were being forced to make some kind of a decision as to whether or not they were going to be communists.

As he observed these things, Ruxton answered that he had been born in up-state New York; that he was no longer an American citizen, but a permanent resident of Hong Kong; and that he was engaged in the import-export business. At that point, he braced himself and, drawing a deep breath, made the first conscious effort to save his life. "Mr. Mai," he said, "I have heard of these People's Courts. Those present who have been terrified by the continuous threat of the actions taken against law-abiding people, will vote against me now—right now, before the evidence is in." He looked straight into the man's narrowed, dark eyes. "Why don't you ask them for a judgment, boy?"

"Don't call me boy," said Mai Lin Yin harshly.

"What is your rank?" Ruxton asked.

"Major."

Ruxton shrugged. "I recognize your military status, Major."

Mai seemed mollified. He pursed his lips; and he spoke as if he were analyzing a condition that could be observed. "You have the hardness of a trained intelligence officer, Mr. Ruxton."

"I learned to be tough when I was in prison, Major."

"Are you an ex-convict, as your compatriot stated?"

"I served two years for attempted manslaughter."

Mai was scowling. "How did you manage to leave the United States, and enter Hong Kong, with a criminal record?"

Ruxton smiled wanly, and said, "The key to entering Hong Kong for an American is that he have enough money to support himself. After I got there I realized that that in

37

itself would have been sufficient. But when I was in prison I learned where I could obtain any kind of a forged document. I entered Hong Kong with a forged passport. Later, when I was granted the status of permanent resident, I petitioned to have my name changed—back to what was actually my true name."

Mai Lin Yin said earnestly, "Mr. Ruxton, you will have to admit that this is the kind of background an intelligence agent would seek to build up."

"First of all," said Ruxton irritably, "I'm not an agent, and I don't think you're being logical to believe that an intelligence agent would spend two years in prison and seven years in Hong Kong for any such purpose. Americans don't think like that. Life is too short."

"We have only your word for it that you were in prison. It seems an unusual confession to make so quickly."

"I was told that brainwashing gets the truth out of you sooner or later, and so I decided to withhold nothing."

"Mr. Ruxton, what is your opinion of communism?"

It was such an abrupt switchover to a new level of questioning that Ruxton parted his lips to answer before he realized that this was different territory indeed. By now, he had concluded that he knew nothing of communism, and that any lengthy opinion would only make him sound ignorant. So he said, "A new religion." It was the most evasive good answer he could think of.

"And what is your opinion of capitalism?"

Ruxton leaned back and closed his eyes, and finally he opened them and shook his head. "I don't know."

"Surely, you have some opinion."

But Ruxton had decided not to commit himself. "Some people do well under capitalism," he temporized, "and others do not."

"What you are saying is that capitalists are despoilers of the laboring and farmer classes."

It was such a far-fetched interpretation of what he had said that Ruxton was transfixed by the thought, "Is he offering me a way out?"

It was not a possibility that he could leave to chance, or so it seemed to him. He said in a low tone directly at Mai, "If you agree to end the trial right now, I'll agree that I said that."

As he finished speaking, he glanced into Mai's eyes. And he saw that he had made a mistake.

Ruxton turned away from Mai, and wiped the perspiration from his face. He was trembling again, for he had put more hope into his bargaining offer than he intended. He decided uneasily, "Mai *believes* all this junk."

He grew aware that Mai was denouncing him to the "jury" for having attempted to bribe the interrogator. But Ruxton's interest was not in dramatics. He was remembering more of what he had heard about trials like this. In the days when the Reds first took over cities, five hundred to a thousand "landlords" would be tried simultaneously, in some large, open space, before the entire populace.

The trial would begin with a single "landlord" being placed where the crowd could see him. Then one of a large group of accusers would shout loudly what the man was being tried for. This usually consisted of the information that he owned a few acres of land. As soon as the charge was made, the accusers, in chorus, demanded the death penalty for the reactionary "beast."

Reluctantly, the crowd picked up this chant. Communist agitators, circulating among the people, singled out and yelled at individuals who were not participating. These persons, taking alarm, immediately joined the yelling until finally the "people" were unanimously demanding the death sentence.

The bewildered victim, who had not been allowed to offer one word in defense of himself, was now shot to death. In this way the servants of the people—the Reds—carried out the judgment of the people.

A few more of the accused were then dealt with individually. Next, several persons at a time were "tried," found guilty by the crowd, and shot. Finally, the 800 or so prisoners who were left were accused *en masse,* again the stereotyped chanting and finally the mass execution, with machine guns mowing down the victims.

There was no doubt at all but that the onlookers got the idea. However, it was more than that. So many impacts, so much violence, so much bloodshed, did emotional things to the mind of each person. Some of those who watched were actually brought to such a frenzy that their personalities changed. While in a state of shock, every member of the crowd heard the communist slogans. Heard them, learned what the party line was, and what happened to the enemies of the "people."

Sitting there, Ruxton realized that Mai also was uttering slogans: *Capitalist . . . despoilers of the laboring and farmer Class . . .* These white men, too, were in a state of shock, and they were being given the word. The recollection of such trials, tens of thousands of them over the vast region of China, drew him into a profound introspection, from which he emerged with a start to realize that Mai had twice asked him the question: "What was the reason for your visit to China?"

It seemed to Ruxton that, rather than meekly answer questions, he must make an attempt to gain control of this interrogation.

"Major Mai," said Ruxton in a low voice that only Mai could hear, "I protest this mockery of a trial."

"Mr. Ruxton," said Mai loudly, "you will receive justice. No man can expect more."

There came to Ruxton the anguished feeling that it had indeed been foolish of him to speak his true thoughts in the car to a man who somehow naively expected that foreigners, given the opportunity, would eagerly welcome the hand of "friendship" when it was "sincerely" offered. Mrs. Mai had correctly realized her husband's disappointment.

Ruxton slipped his hand into his pocket, located there the note she had written and then, as the interpreters finished their translations he said, "I would like to introduce some evidence of my own."

Mai seemed surprised, "What evidence could you possibly have?"

"I'm going to prove that the interrogator entered this trial prejudiced against the accused."

Mai looked at him in frank disbelief. "And how," he asked in a dangerous tone, "do you propose to establish this?"

"I wish to call your wife as my witness."

Mai looked around the room, uncertainly. The Chinese who were present showed a marked degree of interest. Ruxton could imagine that Mai's handling of this situation might be the subject of future group criticism meetings in which every detail of his decision would be subjected to scrutiny. Whatever the motive, Mai said abruptly, "Bring my lover, and tell her it is urgent."

He settled back, scowling. Ruxton, who had observed himself after his more impatient moments, realized that the man needed outside thoughts that would justify a change of mind, and so he said quietly: "There is nothing wrong in a man defending himself. You have me trapped here in this prison village. I promise to bear no ill will if, as an outcome of your wife's evidence, you see fit to release me. I realize you are only doing your duty. But according to my court sentence, your duty is not to kill me but to change me."

He was watching Mai's face closely as he spoke. With almost every word, some of the stubborn expression disappeared. When it had completely gone, Ruxton allowed his voice to trail off, and he sat silent.

The portieres stirred, and Mrs. Mai came in. She glanced at her husband questioningly, and Mai said, "We are trying this man as an American intelligence agent, and he claims that you can give evidence on his behalf."

Mrs. Mai seemed puzzled, then she gave Ruxton an astounded look, and then for a moment she seemed anxious. Slowly, she stiffened, and gazed at him questioningly. Ruxton said, "I don't know what he's saying to you, but he made this fantastic accusation against me right after lunch. I'm fighting for my life."

The woman continued to stare at him. She was pale but composed, finally, as she turned to her husband and said to him, "Does it matter if he is an intelligence agent? Do we care? Would not our purpose remain the same?"

Mai seemed nettled by the question. "Then you *are* on his side?"

Mrs. Mai said, "I am on *our* side, but I was present when you received your directive. In having a trial you are still using old-style methods. Remember, we are to test new methods. That was the directive."

Mai said angrily, "I am surprised to hear you make such a public statement." But there was a querulous quality in the anger.

His wife was calm, some of the color returning to her cheeks, as she said, "We must all learn the new methods."

Mai seemed unnerved. And at that point he made a *non sequitur* statement. "But my dear, he insulted the Chinese people—calling us low class and ignorant, when in fact as you pointed out we are the oldest—"

He stopped. He seemed to realize that his words had nothing to do with the issue. He climbed to his feet, stood very still for a moment, then said in English, his voice hoarse, "The prisoner is released, and rejoins his group."

He turned abruptly and walked out of the room.

7

Breakfast was over.

It was the second day, and Ruxton walked along the street toward the Mai residence. He saw that a guard stood outside the gate of the bamboo stockade, a small, sturdy Chinese with a huge shock of black hair. The hair gave him a superficial resemblance to the formidable Mao Tse-tung, the Chinese Red leader. But there the resemblance ended. Instead of radiating power and cruelty, this guard merely looked stupid.

He made no move as Ruxton opened the gate, stepped through, and closed it behind him. Inside, Ruxton found himself on a curving walk that led toward the house.

He came to a door, which had lettered on it the words "READING ROOM" in several languages. Ruxton hesitated, then glanced back the way he had come. What attracted his attention instantly was that he could see a guard in a watch-tower on top of the wall of the great prison. The man didn't look at him, but Ruxton entered the reading room silently furious at the bad luck that had placed a sentinel at such a vantage point. The fury passed as he realized that he could not afford to be concerned by the man's presence.

He entered the book room and saw that another guard stood inside the entrance. The soldier glanced indifferently at him, then looked away. Ruxton moved over to a shelf, and began examining books. One of the white men in the room stood up and fumbled at a nearby shelf, took a book, and returned to his seat.

Ruxton picked up a propaganda pamphlet in English, and also found himself a chair.

The pamphlet was as foolish and deadly an item as he had ever seen—foolish in that it was aimed at simple minds, and deadly in that it combined anti-Americanism with a larger than life view of a communist, depicting him as a father figure—superior, commanding, privileged.

As he continued to glance through the pamphlet, Ruxton was remembering that he had last seen Major and Madame Mai sitting at separate desks on the second floor of the hotel, processing piles of documents. He must assume that they were still there.

He climbed to his feet, walked past a closed door which

evidently connected with the rest of the house—locked, he presumed, although that wasn't certain—and placed the pamphlet on a table on which a printed placard stated, in several languages: DO NOT REPLACE BOOKS ON SHELF. PUT THEM HERE. He paused at the table, as if to look at some of the books already there. But he was actually recalling the geography of the house as he had observed it on coming through the gate.

Satisfied that his memory was correct, he went outside and walked toward the rear of the house, along a stone walk that followed the terracing of the land down hill and behind a huge, flowering shrub. He had a strong impulse to look back, to see if the guard on the wall was observing him. But he restrained himself. A fear came that one of the prisoners might follow him out of the book room. But if someone did, Ruxton failed to hear him, and took the chance that it was not so. Nevertheless, he breathed easier as he rounded the shrub and was no longer in view of either the wall or of the door from which he had emerged.

Still in a hurry, still conscious that he must risk whatever lay in store, he reached the rear of the house. He came to an entrance, a teakwood door. He opened it without a moment's hesitation and stepped inside. He found himself in a room with carved, coal-black furniture, paneled walls, and a deep-piled rug.

Several doors led from the room. He walked to one and glanced through it, and there was Tosti. She was dressed coolie style but neat, and her black hair had a sheen and was nicely coiled. He saw instantly that she was not as tall as Mrs. Mai by several inches, but there was a dainty beauty to her that had its own quality. She must have heard a sound, for she turned and looked straight at him.

Her limpid brown eyes grew very wide as she recognized Ruxton. Then she put her hand over her mouth in a silencing gesture, and beckoned him to come with her. She took him back through the room with the black furniture, across the threshold of one of the other doors into a hallway, and so into a small bedroom at the far back of the house. Hastily, she lowered the bamboo strip curtains over the rice-paper window. She had a small, soft body that she offered him without a word being spoken.

Later, she said, in Japanese, "She is gone all morning, and besides she has never come to my room."

"How long have you been with her?" Ruxton asked.

"Ever since I come out of prison—long time now."

43

"You were in prison?"

"Three years—until I became a communist. No other way out. So I became one." Her delicate, oval face was very earnest.

"What about you and me?"

"That's different. We only make love."

Ruxton pictured this little creature in a Chinese prison for three long years, being brainwashed. Although she had been present every second of the time, she would probably never be able to tell how she had come to change her mind. He recalled a young American woman who had been passed through to Hong Kong by the Chinese authorities. She had not been released till she agreed that her imprisonment was just. She had held to this story, so the treatment must have been effective. He assumed that Tosti had made the same agreement.

She said now, "I have a private entrance." She led the way for him from her room and along the hallway to a door, which she opened. She pointed to the left. "Tomorrow again, maybe?" she asked.

"Yes," said Ruxton.

He strode toward the hotel with a lighthearted feeling. It was the feeling of victory. Incredibly, here in the heart of a Chinese prison system, with sentinels pacing the streets, or posted a few yards from his rendezvous, he had found himself an eager young mistress.

As he entered the hotel lobby, he saw that Captain Gregory and Jarnoz were talking to each other near one of the windows. The Swede who had asked about citizens of a neutral country at yesterday's luncheon, sat near them.

As Ruxton came in, Jarnoz turned, waved and then came over to intercept him. He fingered his head and said ruefully, "I must have hard nut—seems all well. No pain."

He had stopped in Ruxton's direct path to the stairs, and so Ruxton paused and stared at the man, coolly. He did not acknowledge the words.

Some of the smile faded from the other's face, but he tried again. "I professor of history. This my year to study. Come to China to study." He grinned. "You ask: 'What does Turkish professor study in China?' Remember, many old caravan trails to China cross Turkey. Ancient connections with this land."

Ruxton stared at him, and said nothing. Jarnoz returned his gaze, and his face was completely unsmiling now. He said, "One piece of information. That boy, Gongoe—youngest—

very frightened—missing, is rumored. What will happen when recaptured can only speculate."

Ruxton surmised instantly from the description that Gongoe was the boy who had been so terrified in the washroom the previous day. He felt disappointment. It would have been more fitting if a very capable man had made the break—someone who might have a chance of carrying the story of this criminal Chinese Red conspiracy to the outside world. Gongoe would never make it. He shrugged. "Too bad," he said, and his tone carried as much of a dismissal as had his earlier silence.

Jarnoz turned, and walked off, shaking his head. As he approached Gregory he said, "I not understand that man."

Gregory was contemptuous. Ruxton caught the words: "Criminal—what do you expect?" Ruxton was immune. The other prisoners did not seem to realize yet that easy camaraderie among the prisoners might not be acceptable. Back in his room, he remembered his feeling of glee over Tosti. "I'm like a small boy," he decided, "who has put something over on the old man." He wondered if that was in fact the explanation. His father was a man who had tolerated no nonsense from adults or children. What motivated such a man was not clear even at this vast distance of more than a decade in time and seven thousand miles of space.

Thought of his father carried him back, mentally and emotionally.

8

On Seal's sixteenth birthday, his father took him to one of his mistresses and told her, "Take care of him, and be sure you don't make a sissy out of him." The woman, a well-built brunette in her late thirties, showed by her reaction that this injunction put her in as great a state of shock as it did Seal. She looked at the older man, her lover, and kept shaking her head in a dazed way and mumbled something about not understanding. He stepped close to her, and said, "You do this for me, dear. You know I've talked to you often about the importance of boys having early experience."

"But you should have warned me," she said in a stricken voice.

"I'll see you later," he said, and hastily departed.

When he was gone, she invited Seal to sit down, and talked nervously about how she had always admired what his father

45

had said about him, and that she agreed with his father's ideas about "such things." She must have been almost out of her mind, for she also made the indiscreet statement that his father was her sole support. Having made her timid overture, Doris—her name was Doris Matson—waited for him to take the initiative. When he showed no sign (he was numb), she abruptly started to cry. That put him into confusion and he headed for the door intending to leave, if a fear-driven impulse to flight could be called an intention. She barred his way. It was as he was trying to break past her that their bodies began to touch.

And so he stayed with her.

During the next few days, he ate very little and could not settle down to his studies. His mother, a sad-eyed woman, was roused to wonder and anxiety. But he resisted all her questions.

He did not visit Doris again till one day he found her waiting for him at the school gate. When they reached her apartment, she gave him his first intellectual lesson in the man-woman relationship. "You mustn't ever expect a woman to ask a man, because if she's a lady she won't do it." As a result of this and other hints from her, he soon took the initiative.

He startled her one day by arriving during his lunch hour, and he departed with the words, "See you after school."

He was a virile youth with the immense potency of a six-teen-year-old. And there was a day, then, when he came in the morning before school . . . at lunch-time . . . after school . . . and about ten o'clock that night. It was nearly midnight when he left a dismayed woman, who was finally confronted by the need to make a decision.

All her adult life, her problem had been to gain security by having a man move in her direction. Not just any man, but exactly and only one who provided for her. Her solitary marriage, earlier, had failed to give her a home, or even enough to eat.

When she was thirty-two, and still pretty in a faded way, she met Seal's father, at that time a red-faced young business man. He insisted on exclusive possession and moved her into a small apartment. For the first time in her life, then, she was secure. It was only on a month to month basis, but it made possible the realization of a lifetime dream. She went back to school.

She told Seal a great deal about her training during their friendship. It was her only defense against the total degrada-

46

tion that had been visited on her. By letting him know that she did have the means to leave, she was able to gain confidence in her pretense that she was doing all this for the love of his father. Like an alcoholic, she was still not admitting that she had lost control. Seal was not fooled. Gradually, he pieced together the woman's story.

She lay awake most of the night of Seal's four visits, in a state of profound shock. Shortly after dawn, or so it seemed to her, the doorbell rang. She shuddered, but did not answer. At noon he was back. This time he rang so long she knew she would have to talk to him if he came again.

When she heard his ring shortly after four o'clock, she called through the door panel, "Go away! I'm through with the Ruxtons." When he did not come back that night, or the next day, or the next, she grew resigned, and began to think sadly about looking for a job.

Seal, on his part, was baffled. For a time he did nothing. Finally he bought a book, titled *Marriage Technique*. And so he discovered that according to the experts average American women were not capable of a great deal of sex until they reached the age of 58 or 60. Armed with this knowledge, Seal went up to Doris' apartment. It was Saturday, the eighth day since she had sent him off. She had not looked for a job, and she was relieved to see him.

By the time Seal left her it was with the understanding that his visits would now be curtailed to three times a week. Since he had been over-awed by the book, and so prepared to accept less, her offer was a surprise and gave him his first wonder about books on that particular subject. The agreement took the madness out of their relationship.

A year to the day after Ruxton, Senior, had taken his son to the woman, he stopped Seal at the garage door, and said to him with his usual finality, "You're through over there with Doris. I'm taking her back. From now on find girls of your own age. And if you don't find a few," he concluded threateningly, "you'll do without your allowance."

To feel resentment against so powerful a being, yet not dare show it—for a week that was the conflict that built up inside Seal. Resentment—and a scheme—won. He called on Doris early one morning. She let him enter the apartment, but expressed herself as helpless before his father's command.

After swearing her to secrecy, he told her the one hidden fact about his father: "He had a heart attack two years ago. He could go any time."

47

His father had threatened him with disinheritance if he ever mentioned his shame. The older man felt humiliated by anything in himself that was less than perfection.

When he had told her, Seal was as pale as the woman. He was revolted at himself for having used such an argument. And afraid that she might tell the elder Ruxton.

But he didn't back down.

After a long pause, Doris began to talk herself into accepting. "Seal, I'm ashamed of myself. You'll have to forgive me for being weak. I didn't want to give you up. I feel just awful, and, yes, you may come to see me. We'll just have to be careful."

It was after that victory, as he walked away from her apartment, that Seal felt the glee. For the first time in his life, or so it seemed, he had put something over on the old man.

9

Lying on his creaky bed in the Chinese prison hotel, Ruxton realized that his triumph at getting Tosti was the same feeling he had had about Doris. For a moment, that was merely interesting, and then . . . "Careful," he thought, "or I'll begin acting as if my captors are the same as father." He had to admit there were many similarities. As he grew older, he had come to realize that his father was not so rare a bird in America—or anywhere for that matter—as he had believed at sixteen and younger. The combination of extreme subjectiveness and the feeling that he and he alone was right seemed to come as naturally to a driving, successful man as it did to the communists. Emotionally, it would appear, all these angry people were brothers.

Ruxton thought, "I wonder what the Mais would think of my old man and that situation with Doris?" He slipped off the bed, put on his shoes, buttoned his shirt, and walked down to the second floor. As he had hoped, Mai Lin Yin and his wife were still at work. They looked up at his approach. He paused at the man's desk, and said, "I was just thinking of an aspect of my past life, and I wondered what the Communist interpretation of it might be."

Mai was at ease, momentarily like a typical old-style Chinese who dealt with foreigners on a friendly basis, ingratiating, smiling. "Ask my wife," he said. "She has a special skill in such interpretations."

"It's personal—early sex training," Ruxton said.

Mai's expression grew pained. "Mr. Ruxton, that is typical bourgeois thinking. My wife is an adult. She is aware that there are two sexes, and is no more shocked by what might have befallen some child or teen-ager than you or I."

Ruxton hesitated, but only to savor the unexpected opportunity. Then somewhat jauntily he walked over to the woman. She looked up, glanced over at her husband, and then gave Ruxton a puzzled stare. Ruxton said, "Your husband referred me to you—" She made no comment, simply looked at him steadily, so he repeated what he had already said to the man. Then, with a quick glance over his shoulder to make certain Mai was not paying attention—he wasn't —he said, "I'm somewhat reluctant to tell you of my past, in view of what I said to you yesterday. I still mean that, you know."

She did not chide him. She said quietly, "Tell me your story."

Ruxton described his experience, beginning at age sixteen, with Doris, his father's kept woman. Half way through the story he was aware of Mai coming up behind him, but he gave no sign. He finished finally: "What I want to know is, what would the Communist interpretation of that whole affair be?"

He showed his awareness of Mai's presence by glancing around. "I'd like your opinion also, Major."

Mrs. Mai spoke coldly. "We do not give personal opinions, Mr. Ruxton. We are trained Marxists—" She paused, then, "—and we give organization interpretations." She continued, "Your father was evidently a member of the vicious landlord reactionary class of America, who possessed a number of concubines. In handing one of his concubines over to you, his intention was to debauch you for the purpose of miseducating you into his own feudalistic ideas of enslavement of the property-less class. By thus instilling in you the feeling that you could buy or sell a property-less woman, he laid part of the groundwork for your future as a Reactionary-thinking person who thinks nothing of buying and selling human beings and human labor for personal gain."

"I see," said Ruxton.

He rejected the analysis instantly, for it was already notorious that Red Chinese leaders were using their power to get women, and the women were willing. It was obvious that many Marxists, like all the other single-track philosophers, were trying to explain the most basic biologic impulses in terms of their doctrine. He suspected that the desire of people—men as well as women—to be taken care of, might be better explained by Freud than Marx. Because of the marriage situation, and the need for protection during pregnancy, women were more easily frightened into believing they should be taken care of, and thus they surrendered their freedom.

Mrs. Mai's answer also by-passed the fact that what his father had done had always been illegal in America.

The thought ran its course, and he said, "What about when I continued to pursue the woman?"

Mai cleared his throat, and his wife, who had been about to speak, waited respectfully. Mai said, "A hopeful sign for you. Your role as a rebellious son in a landlord's family augurs well for you personally."

"How long did you stay with this woman?" asked Mrs. Mai. It was an irrelevant question, and she must have realized it. She bit her lip; and then, in control again, said quietly, "Never mind that. That's unimportant." But she was flushing as she said, "Perhaps your mis-education about sex explains why you were sent to prison." There was an unhappy note in her voice, and it dawned on Ruxton that his jail background bothered her.

Quickly he explained what had happened, but in general terms. He avoided any reference to the fact that one of his victims had been a vociferous pro-Soviet.

She seemed relieved, but she said nothing.

This was a good point, Ruxton decided, to leave the subject of his prison record. He said quickly, "How should young people be educated, sex-wise?"

"There are two aspects to my view," she answered in a severe tone. "One is the official practice at Yenan where we Communists had our headquarters for so many years. Each person was required to discipline himself. If he could not do so by his own will power, then the State came to his assistance. The State wisely limited sex to once a week."

Ruxton glanced around to see how Mai was taking her words. The man was glum. He muttered that he had things to do and returned to his desk. Ruxton said to Mrs. Mai, "What is your second view?"

"It's personal," she said. "I have observed that men pursue women much as they would untamed animals, using every cunning device to trap them. It is generally assumed that animals have no rights, and there is a type of male who stops at nothing in order to possess a woman, obviously believing that she does not deserve to be treated honestly."

"I tried honesty once," said Ruxton ruefully. "I told a woman I didn't love her, but that I wanted her."

"What happened?"

"I had the anguish of watching her go off with another man who, to my knowledge, had other mistresses. She preferred his lies to my truth."

"But why were you concerned at all—if you didn't love her?"

"Because," said Ruxton patiently, "she was a desirable woman."

"My point exactly!" Mrs. Mai flashed. "Why couldn't you simply find a woman whom you could love, marry her and be faithful to her?"

"Eh!" said Ruxton.

He parted his lips to speak again, then closed them, annoyed at how staggered he felt. The remark had penetrated to the hidden guilt inside him. A kaleidoscope of memories of his relations with women swept through his mind. Like a person who has momentarily lost his identity, he felt panic.

With a tremendous effort, he began to recover from the flood of awareness that had breached half a lifetime of subjective feelings. To his surprise, his voice showed none of that shattering, as he explained, "When a woman is suddenly available, a man has to act fast. You can't take time to decide whether or not you really love her."

"Are you serious?" Mrs. Mai sounded breathless. "You consider the timing of the pursuit to be that important? In a similar circumstance it would take me a year or more to make up my mind." She broke off, and said sharply, "Would you rob a bank merely because the opportunity offered?"

"No—of course not."

"But there are people who would?"

"Yes."

"Then according to your reasoning, you should steal the money because someone is going to get it, and it might as well be you."

Watching her, Ruxton had the feeling that he had made too many admissions. She was dangerously close to turning against him. He gave a swift glance at Mai, and then bent down and said in a low voice, "I promise that I shall never tell you a lie."

Phenix stood up. Her color was high. "I believe," she said, "that it's nearly lunch time for you."

Ruxton was reluctant to end the interview on a personal

defeat. He said, "After all, a woman has a very simple solution. She can hold out for marriage."

"Many men promise marriage."

Ruxton urged, "Still, if she insists on the actual marriage before making any concessions—no problem."

Madame Mai avoided his eyes as she said stiffly, "Nature made woman vulnerable in her need to hold a man who has won her heart." Her lips tightened, and now she looked at him angrily, as she continued, "And there is a difference between the calculating male who lies and the gentle-hearted woman who believes his lies."

Ruxton said softly, "I see that the male-female problem is fundamentally the same in China as elsewhere."

Her voice was harsh as she answered, "Laws will have to be enacted to make men more honest."

It was not actually a good moment to end the discussion. But Ruxton was suddenly aware that he was still trembling. He excused himself and walked to the third floor. There he paused.

"What is the matter?" he asked himself. "Why don't I have any more desire for a family or home?" But there was nothing like that in him. He wanted women, not a woman—yet he was guilty.

He thought, "She really blasted me wide open with those questions of hers, and here I stand exposed."

What was most disturbing, he sensed a feeling of superiority underlay his attitude, and that feeling was not directed only toward women. The feeling was an emotional sense of being right, needing nothing and no one else.

He felt more noble, more idealistic, more aware, more humble, and on occasion more capable of kindness—so many more good things were in him than in other men.

So he could judge, and punish others.

It was an amazing self-discovery, with more implications than he felt immediately prepared to investigate.

Still very disturbed, he headed for the bathroom.

As he was washing his hands, he remembered he had intended to ask Mai about Gongoe. A few minutes later, on his way down to lunch, he paused at the commandant's desk. "What's the latest on the escape of that boy?" he said.

The moment the question was out, he knew he had made a mistake in asking it. Major Mai stiffened. Slowly, he turned, his brown eyes narrowed and bleak. "Mr. Ruxton," he said in a steely voice, "you may safely leave the capture and punishment of the escaped prisoner to us."

The ferocity of the reply was startling. But far more up-setting to Ruxton was the fact that he had not even vaguely realized how serious the matter was. He had asked about Gongoe casually, without really thinking about it.

For a long moment, he gazed into the other's unrelenting eyes. Then, shaken, he turned away.

10

As the twenty-two white men and fifteen Chinese finished eating lunch, Mai Lin Yin came in. He was smiling again, and when he spoke his voice was cheerful: "I won't detain you long, gentlemen. But we are engaged on an important proj-ect. Does anyone have any questions?"

He waited patiently while his words were translated, and then glanced from face to face, questioningly. He paused as he came to Ruxton, and waited until Ruxton shook his head. His gaze moved on, but then came back. "You visited the reading room today, Mr. Ruxton?"

"Yes." Ruxton spoke warily. It seemed to him that this man had from the first meeting selected him as a special target.

"Do you recall what you read?" Mai asked.

"A pamphlet."

The faintest frown clouded the friendly face. "Did you find it interesting?"

"Very much so." That was true. Interesting, clever, un-scrupulous, full of lies, childish.

"But it had no effect on you?"

Ruxton had been thinking hard as the question and an-swer game continued. He must decide whether to tell the truth, or to lie as to what he had thought. He was not ready to do either. He said, and there was impatience in his tone that he could not suppress, "Mr. Mai, we should understand each other. My problem will not be resolved by you and me having intellectual arguments. What I want to know is, where are all those methods that work on a person below the level of his intellect? In the outside world, we have heard of these techniques. Since I am a condemned man, I'd like to find out if these special methods will affect me. If not, I'd like to know it and we can go on from there."

As he finished, he saw that the words, simple and straight-forward though they had seemed to him, were too strong for the other man.

Mai's brows were knit into an unsmiling stubbornness. Ruxton said quickly, "I'm an intelligent man. The pamphlet I read was for children eight to ten."

The stubborn look on Mai's face was partly replaced by a kind of tolerant contempt. He said, "We are all children, Mr. Ruxton, on the level of basic beliefs. Perhaps, some day you will realize that no great change is required of you. A dozen insane tenets, perhaps, need to be erased from your subconscious, and replaced by a dozen sane concepts. Nothing more. It's that simple."

"I'm willing to be shown," Ruxton retorted. "So if you will make up a list of what I should get rid of, and what I must replace it with, I'll be glad to look it over."

When the interpreters translated these words, there was an immediate clamor from some of the other white men which, when translated, meant: "Yes, what are the dozen points of change?"

Across the room, Captain Gregory climbed to his feet, and said deliberately, "Point one, Give up your soul. Point two, Start sucking up to a gang of murderers. Point three, Start spouting their jargon—"

That was as far as he got. Mai let out a yell of rage. It was such a screech that Gregory faltered, stared at him, and then abruptly sat down. Mai stood trembling, his face working—but when he spoke he seemed to be fully recovered. He said quietly, "We would prefer that you read further. Then when you finally seek to belong to a discussion group of your own free will, develop the theme as rapidly as you can understand it."

It was an evasion, so far as Ruxton was concerned. He stood up and said firmly, "Just a moment, Mr. Mai. There are enough of us here who are interested in finding out what the twelve points might be—so interested that we are not influenced by the comments of Captain Gregory. Suppose that we stay right here with some of your people and work out *at least*—" he emphasized the words—"twelve points. There are probably more, but if we know what twelve of them are, we can have an initial over-all picture."

Mai had gone to the door, and there he paused. As Ruxton spoke, he turned slowly, until he faced the group again. He seemed uncertain. Ruxton read in the man's face the moment by moment emotional changes, from an adamant state through a kind of angry resistance to change, and then, actually an expression of frustration. This was followed, penultimately, by a grudging recognition that Ruxton's words were sensible, and the facial muscles relaxed into outright acceptance. Mai turned to his interpreters and said in Chinese, "Translate what he said for those who wish to stay for such a meeting."

After Mai departed, what seemed to Ruxton a surprising number of men got up and left. They included, besides Gregory, Lemoine, Father de Melanier, Jarnoz, the two Scandinavian types, Diogo, and several of the men who had been in the library that morning.

On his way to the door, the priest paused and leaned over Ruxton. He spoke in a low voice, in French, "I could probably tell you the twelve points myself. It will be interesting to compare notes with you later, but my cooperation during the first three months is limited to reading their abominable literature. No group meetings."

He walked on. Ruxton was left with a faint feeling of surprise, and a considerable feeling of respect. He had somehow expected that almost everyone would be interested to find out what the twelve points were. There were more brave men in this little world than he had thought.

He grew aware that Lemoine had stopped at the door. Their gazes met, and that seemed to decide the man. He hurried over. Bending close to Ruxton, he said, "A group of us is planning to escape this week on the assumption that the Chinese won't expect such a quick attempt following Gongoe's disappearance. I'm sure Jarnoz, Gregory, and Diogo would like to have you come along."

Ruxton was instantly furious. The naming of names, the open invitation to join, was so indiscreet that he had an impulse to jump up and strike the man.

"Get away from me!" he said in a low, threatening voice. "I'm not interested in any half-baked schemes."

Lemoine gave him a startled look, and backed away. He hesitated, then turned and hurried off. His walk was disoriented as he stumbled through the portieres. Ruxton realized furiously, "Now he'll tell the others what he's done, and they'll think I'm going to betray them."

After a moment, the implications of Lemoine's indiscretion seemed so serious that he half-rose to his feet to run after the man. Slowly, seething with frustration and anger, he settled back in his seat. He had a sickening feeling that he had not heard the last of that affair.

With so much turmoil in him, it was hard to concentrate on the discussion. Only bits and pieces of the words spoken came in to him. He realized presently, however, that the first point had an ancient tradition indeed in the history of conquered and conqueror:

". . . Respect for Chairman Mao . . ."

Kneel to the emperor, praise the king, obey the high priest. It was an irony of the twentieth century that mild designations were replacing words that had become intolerable. And so, Mao Tse-tung, the new absolute lord of five hundred million people, was called "Chairman." After enough human beings were slaughtered, that mild word might have such evil connotations that a future dictator would call himself "chief clerk." They were, of course, all servants of the people. Of course—that thought passed by as some new words came in:

". . . We must lean toward the Soviet Union, who is our big brother."

That reminded Ruxton of something. He straightened, and looked toward the line of Chinese sitting at the head table. He said, "How does the People's Government explain the action of the Russians in stealing all Japanese industrial equipment from Manchuria, instead of turning it over to the Chinese people?"

His interpreter, a moon-faced Chinese who spoke English with a British accent said, "That would be an incorrect question, Mr. Ruxton, and brings up what would actually be another of the twelve points."

"What's that?" said Ruxton.

"You must ask only correct questions. The correct way to word your question would be, Was it not wise of our big brother, the Soviet Union, to seize Japanese equipment in Manchuria, and so prevent it from falling into the hands of the Kuomintang gang?"

"That," Ruxton asked in surprise, "is a correct question?"

"That," said the interpreter firmly, "is a correct way to ask a question that, when incorrectly asked, might lead to the holding of incorrect ideas about our big brother, the Soviet Union."

The wording was so peculiar that Ruxton gave the man a long, questioning look. But the moon face was bland and unrevealing, and the brown eyes calm and fathomless. "I can see," said Ruxton slowly, "the importance of wording questions correctly."

"I feel that you are learning rapidly," said the man. Again, the words seemed to have a double meaning. Ruxton came to a decision. "What is your name?" he asked.

"Ho Sin Go."

"Thank you."

By the time Ruxton had mentally noted that Ho Sin Go might be useful to him in an emergency—if he were carefully cultivated—another of the twelve requirements was being listed:

". . . Hold correct concepts . . ."

That turned out to be not just a re-statement of asking only correct questions. A correct concept covered literally anything that was good for the revolution. One of the prisoners seemed to be stubbornly arguing this point with the interpreter who understood his language. The prisoner was a small, stocky man, swarthy of face, with a way of tightening his lips that seemed also to be a tightening of his mind. The argument grew long, so the interpreter finally turned to his colleagues, and said in Chinese, "He says he has been a good man all his life, holding correct moral principles. I asked him, 'Have you been a Communist all your life?' 'No,' he answered. So I said, 'Then you have not been a good man, for only a Communist can be a good man, and hold correct moral principles.' "

As he waited for the English translation of that to come to him, Ruxton toyed fleetingly with the idea that, if he were to admire the Reds for their methods, he might thus find his road to Communism. He shook his head again, gloomily. That wouldn't work. He had never admired enemy generals, no matter how skillful they were, and in World War II, he had developed a chronic fury against skillful Zero pilots. He hated them all because they threatened him.

As he watched the stocky little man tenaciously defend his moral principles, Ruxton almost forgot his own anxiety over what Lemoine had said. The Chinese mentors were exceedingly polite at first. But finally they became impatient, and then sharp. At the end, an older Chinese said curtly, "Tell that Greek we can spend no more time while he tells us how he helped his brother through college and his sister to find a suitable husband. These are tails that he will have to cut when he becomes a Communist."

And that was the next point on the list:

". . . Cut all your tails . . ."

Break with your past. The fact that you were born of a particular mother, in a particular country and district is unimportant. Is your brother a Communist? No. Then he is your enemy. Is your sister soft and dependent? She must learn to look after herself. Give the other members of your family no more thought than you would a stranger. If they are in need, they will be looked after by the street government. Does your wife come from a landlord's family? Divorce her, for she will attempt to use your affection for her to turn you against Communism. You must marry only another Communist. Cut the tail of identification with any other group. Cut the tail of identification with any local geographic area. It is better to live in the worst part of any Communist country than in the best part of an imperialistic reactionary state.

For Ruxton, who had already cut more "tails" than most men, the Red requirement seemed like a big order. How could a man break with his entire past, short of total forgetfulness? But the requirement was that big: *All* old society concepts, such as filial love, must be cut.

In his exile, Ruxton had occasionally thought it would be pleasant to see his mother. Tearful, ineffectual woman she had been, but she loved him. Yet he seldom even wrote a letter—why not, he could never quite decide.

He realized that around him, they were verbally cutting tails: ". . . For loyalty to friends, substitute duty to and love of the State, and of the Marxist-Leninist ideal—"

Ruxton had many acquaintances, but his friends were primarily the women who were his mistresses.

". . . Dispense with conscience . . ."

Ruxton had either very little, or a lot—he could never quite decide which.

". . . Eliminate all bourgeois emotions such as pity and sympathy. A good Communist must steel himself to be able to participate in struggle meetings wherein it might be necessary to denounce someone for execution . . ."

Ruxton was willing to denounce for any purpose whatsoever 80 percent of the officers of the U.S. armed forces of World War II.

More tail cutting: "Old style" national loyalties had to go, for only a Communist could be a patriot. The others were all "running dogs of the Capitalist reactionary beasts—" Tail cutting was indeed a tremendous subject.

After tail cutting came a puzzler: "Make sacrifices."

Ruxton asked, "Sacrifice what?"

"You'll have to figure that out yourself," said his interpreter, with a faint smile.

"Look," said Ruxton, "we have nothing. The Chinese people have nothing. What can anybody except a Communist with privileges sacrifice?"

"You eat well," said his mentor, significantly.

Ruxton sighed. "I suppose," he said with resignation, "we ought to be grateful. But you can cut down on our food supply whenever you want to."

"That," said Ho Sin Go, "is entirely up to you. Your food supply will not be cut by us."

And then Ruxton got it. He was outraged. "You mean to tell me," he said, "you expect us to go on some kind of a starvation diet of our own free will to prove some obscure point—" He became silent, inwardly fuming.

"That brings us to the next point," said the interpreter. "You must prove that what has been good enough for peasants and farmers for centuries is good enough for you."

Ruxton was silent and, when the translations had been made, none of the other white men spoke. Ruxton thought grimly, "If they're having the same kind of thought as I am, I'm not surprised that they have no comment." He sensed a kind of mindless anger in the reference to the peasants and farmers. Implicit was an attempt to make somebody pay for millennia of scarcity and suffering. Who? They could never catch the culprit, if there was one. And so the agony of a thousand years or more was to be alleviated by having everyone do a kind of physical penance. Since only a few hundred people would ever see the person serving out his "guilt," it couldn't possibly have any real meaning. But the Red leaders presumably gained some certainty about individuals who voluntarily undertook to redress the economic imbalances of the ages by a method of self-flagellation.

Impatient with such rationalization—as he analyzed it— Ruxton glanced at his watch. He was astounded to see that it was a few minutes of six o'clock, and that he would barely have time to clean up before dinner. He noticed wryly that his notebook showed only eight points, not ten, of a dozen. But he had had enough. He stood up. The others followed suit. It seemed to Ruxton, as he made his way out of the dining room, that his seven companions each in his own way visibly reflected his personal conviction that the whole project was impossible.

He spent the evening in his room, angry and baffled. The very extent of his emotion finally made him wonder. He asked himself, "Am I thinking of giving in, and was I hoping they would make it easy?" He shook his head, finally. No, that wasn't it. He felt insulted that, in addition to the enormous invalidation of a sentence of death, he must agree to accept nonsense and personal degradation. There was, Ruxton realized, one other explanation for his towering anger. "I'm going to stay alive," he thought. "And if I finally decide I can't make it, I'll try to take as many of these miserable Reds with me as I can."

It was pleasure of a sort to have such a thought. He slept on that feeling of savage satisfaction.

But in the morning, his problem remained.

II

At the "library" on that third day, Ruxton read a remarkable work. Undoubtedly, along with Machiavelli's *The Prince,* and a handful of similar treatises on practical government politics, one of the most remarkable books of all time. It was titled, *The State and Revolution,* and it was by Vladimir Ilyich, who in his later days called himself Nicolai Lenin and led the Russian Bolsheviks to their total victory in 1917.

It was a thin little volume, and it basically had nothing to do with communism as such. But it described what a revolutionary group must do to take over a country. It was a handbook for revolutionary governments by a Marxian theorist who had temporarily put aside his communism and devoted himself exclusively to revolutionary methods. What he prescribed was universally sound, and could be used as easily by any unscrupulous politicians.

The book rehabilitated almost forgotten ideas, originally propounded by Marx and Engels, some of which at the time of Lenin's writing had been obscured for half a hundred years. In dusting them off on the eve of the Russian revolution, Lenin certainly showed what could be done by a man with enough venom in him to kill half the population of the planet.

The elements of a revolutionary take-over, as Marx and Engels—and then Lenin—accurately foresaw, consisted of a policy of terrorism and agitation by a precise method. The tactic was to enter a village, a town, or any community—select 50% of the poorest men, and some women. Arm them. Tell them that they now owned the country, but make it clear that the Communist Party would give the orders. Then shoot the police and all other former officials. Disband the local army post, and kill the officers. Announce that in future the armed workers would police themselves and unite in the formation of a "people's" army. Lay down a policy of hard labor for everyone except, peculiarly, members of the Communist Party.

Incredibly, it worked. The armed laborers were immediately put back to work. In addition they had the job of seeing to it that everyone, including themselves, worked the same period of time. This simple equalitarianism for everyone but members of the CP seemed to satisfy their simple minds, for in over thirty years in Russia—and now six years in China—no one or group had been able to break out of the trap thus created.

Ruxton read with absorption, and it was purely accidental that he suddenly noticed it was ten minutes after eleven. He had set a quarter to as the time he would leave·to keep his rendezvous with Tosti, and so he was already dangerously late. But he felt reckless, and unconcerned with the risk. He put the book aside, went out boldly, and made his way to the side entrance which led to Tosti's room.

She heard him enter, and came running. "We have forty minutes," she said breathlessly, "before madame returns."

She was already disrobing as she entered her room. Her passion matched her urgency. Later, when he was dressed again and on his way out, he paused and squeezed her slim little body to him. She clung with a sudden surprising desperation, despite the shortage of time. "You be good now," she whispered. "No more chances like today. Don't you get shot!"

"All right," he said, but inwardly he shrugged aside her concern.

Once outside, however, he realized that he was actually quite tense, and it struck him that, with two years to go, it was thoroughly irrational of him to risk cutting off his source of sex. Presumably Tosti might find another lover, but it was obvious that if he were ever caught, he would not be allowed another opportunity.

The realization was highly disturbing, and that disturbance remained with him after lunch, so much so that he couldn't read, couldn't sit, couldn't stay in one place. On impulse, he returned to the hotel, found Mai at his desk on the second floor, and asked him, "Would you have any objection if I followed the prison wall to the village on the far side?"

Mai looked up momentarily from his desk work and said, "Not at all, Mr. Ruxton. But be back before bed-time." He laughed, as at a joke.

Ruxton hesitated, thought better of answering, and went down the stairs and outside. He walked across this tiny portion of the vast land of China, following the north wall where there was shade, and he had a thought that transcended the centuries and the nations of the era in which he lived. These were primitive times. Man was at the bare beginning of his emergence from superstition, and there was no real sign of change. The problem, as he was now realizing, was internal, not external.

He came to the end of the wall, and to a creek. The stream was at its low ebb, for it flowed through a ten foot wide channel in a much wider stream bed. There were indications that at spring flood it overflowed its far banks. Ruxton knelt beside the water. It was clear and unpolluted, perhaps because it had crossed many miles of desert, and flowed into the village at this point, not out of it. He cupped his hands, filled them with water, and drank. The water was almost too warm, but it satisfied his thirst. After drinking, he washed his face, and that felt even better. On impulse, he removed his shoes and bathed his feet. As he did so, Chinese children of varying ages appeared on the far side of the stream, and stood watching him.

Ruxton waded the stream, dried his feet as well as he could on a patch of grass, and put on his socks and shoes.

At this point one of the older children, a boy of sixteen or so, yelled that this was a foreign dog, whereupon they all started to run, squealing with fear. Ruxton watched them in their mad panic to scramble out of sight.

He walked on into the village along a typical narrow street, noticing the fields beyond and certain large buildings. From his recent travelling in China, he recognized them for what they were. This was a collective farm, Chinese style. Probably a feeding farm for the prison. Somewhere in the near distance, behind some brush, he heard the grunting of pigs. A moment later, a cow made a mooing sound from a hidden pasture.

When he came to the end of the village, he walked over to a small rise to the right of the road. From it, he viewed the country-side. There were some cattle in a field far to his left. He could see men working among rows of green vegetables, and these extended for a good mile ahead and to the left. Where the farm ended was brush and open land, and then a developing sparseness. Ruxton assumed that the encroaching desert reached that close to the garden land which paralleled the precious flowing creek. Far down stream, almost lost in the distance, were the rooftops of another village.

Ruxton wasn't sure what he had expected. But he was disappointed. "Did I hope to find a way of escape?" he asked himself gloomily. If so, this was not it.

He walked to the road. As he started back through the village, he saw that a group of men were gathering in the village street. There was a loud sound of voices, high-pitched, nervous, unfriendly. Ruxton fought off a rising tension, but he did not slow down. He walked to within half a dozen feet of the nearest of the group, and was amazed to hear that they were discussing an attack he had made on their children. He thought: "Those little stinkers made up a tale of a boogie-man chasing them." He had an instant intuitive awareness that there was no way of disproving the lie.

He had already selected from among the men the one with the cleanest looking cotton coat—that would be the local Communist Agent. Now he pointed at himself and said to the man in Chinese, "American imperialist."

What passed through the minds of these villagers as they heard those words, Ruxton couldn't decide. But he did know that for six years the drumbeat of hate against the reactionary American beasts had been part of the thought education of all Chinese.

A man stepped forward. "I'm from Shanghai," he said in excellent English. "What happened between you and the children?"

"They threw stones at me," said Ruxton coolly.

He listened as his words were translated into Chinese. When the man had finished there were nods of understanding. "Oh, so that's it." They seemed to accept the statement as truth. It would have been an astonishing reaction except that Ruxton had noticed among adults in other parts of Red China a certain distrust of their Communist-trained children.

Ruxton started to push through the crowd, when he saw the boy who had frightened the other children standing at the rear of the group of men. The boy raised his voice plaintively in protest. "We didn't throw any stones."

The crowd as a whole paid no attention. The Red leader said to him, sharply, "Get back to your house, and hereafter behave well toward people who enter the village peacefully."

The boy backed away, then turned and ran.

Ruxton walked on, the crowd making way for him. He was almost at the stream when he heard quick footsteps behind him. He faced about. It was the man from Shanghai and the Red leader of the village. Ruxton waited for them to come up. Though short in stature, they were both rugged looking men, sun-and-wind-burned farmers, quite a different breed from the restaurant waiters and store keepers of America, and the street masses of Hong Kong.

The man from Shanghai said, "My name is Johnny Liu. My friend here is Lo Hin Yo. He's the local Representative of the People's Patriotic Land Workers Group, and also he doubles in as the local representative of the People's Democratic Dictatorship, and he's a former soldier of the People's Liberation Army."

Ruxton surmised that Lo Hin Yo was one of the armed laborers, a hard worker indoctrinated to see to it that others worked hard also.

Johnny Liu continued, "He wants to know, what do the American people think of what is going on in China?"

Ruxton hesitated. Could he tell the truth? These men probably did not realize the continuing strong feeling in the U.S. over the blackguard role played by China in the invasion by Red Korea of Southern Korea. He finally said, "Many Americans supported the Yenan group led by Mao Tse-tung, when they were pretending to be agrarian reformers. During this period, top American leaders tried to bring the Yenan group and the Kuomintang together. Then the Chinese people grew weary of freedom, preferring to be enslaved, and the Nationalist armies surrendered to the People's Liberation Army. Suddenly, the Yenan group whipped off its mask. Its members stood starkly revealed as Communists trained in Russia. This, therefore, is the opinion of the American people: That China is now ruled by running dogs of the Soviets."

Johnny Liu looked disturbed. "I don't think I can tell him that. That's not a correct concept."

Ruxton felt frustrated. He wondered helplessly, "Can truth and falsehood ever talk to each other?" He considered what a correct concept would be, and said, though it was hard going: "The Imperialist reactionary Americans, defeated in their attempts to prevent the People's Army from liberating China from the Kuomintang beasts, were again defeated in their try to reimpose Imperialist rule over liberated North Korea but, through cunning, temporarily prevented the liberation of South Korea. Now, they have retreated to their own shores, and are waiting to use as a pretext for another attack on liberated China the legitimate desire of the Chinese people to liberate neighboring countries from the yoke of Imperialism."

When he had finished, Johnny Liu looked at him for a long moment. Then he stepped in front of Lo Hin Yo, and winked. "You really know the lingo, don't you?" he said cheerfully.

"That's a correct concept, isn't it?" Ruxton said, unsmiling.

The man nodded. "That's a correct concept all right, but would you really want me to translate that?"

Ruxton shrugged. "Why not?"

"It might give the wrong impression."

Ruxton felt indifferent. "You don't think," he said, "that what you and I say to your friend is going to change the history of the world."

"No, I suppose not." Johnny Liu seemed doubtful. "Still, I kind of hate to be so damned cynical. Suppose I give him a mixture of your two statements?"

"That should be interesting," said Ruxton soberly.

Johnny Liu turned to Lo Hin Yo, "He says the Americans are licking their wounds over their failure to prevent China from being liberated, but they're happy that they were able to prevent the liberation of South Korea. They are still very strong, and will try to prevent the liberation of other areas of the world."

Lo Hin Yo nodded. He said earnestly, "Ask him, is there any chance that the workers and farmers in America will soon free themselves from the yoke of Wall Street?"

Ruxton waited for the translation, and then said, "The workers and farmers have been very cunning in the past twenty years. They've been buying shares in American companies, until now millions of workers and farmers own parts of Wall Street."

Johnny Liu stared at Ruxton unhappily. "Are you kidding?" he said. "I can't tell him that." He turned to Lo Hin Yo and said, "He doesn't know anything about Wall Street."

This unimportant Chinese Red in this remote Chinese village answered that: "He and other Americans need to be awakened to the danger. Perhaps we can contribute to his knowledge."

Johnny Liu said to Ruxton, "He says, if you wish, we will educate you about Wall Street."

Ruxton said wearily, "He is obviously the logical person for the job."

Liu glanced at his boss, and said, "The American says

thank you, but he's got to go back to his prison now."

He held out his hand to Ruxton. "Good-bye. Come and see us again."

"Maybe sooner than you think," said Ruxton. "Tomorrow afternoon I'll come and help with the work."

It seemed to him, as he crossed a rickety wooden bridge further downstream, and headed back the way he had come, that this collective farm might be the place for him to make his first attempt to find out if he could actually change.

12

As Ruxton walked onto the field the following afternoon, a worker called out in Chinese to Lo Hin Yo, "They are having trouble with the machine." When Ruxton came up, it seemed to him that trouble was a mild term for what was happening. The tractor engine neither coughed nor stuttered, when the mechanic spun the starting crank. Ruxton stood beside Lo and Johnny Liu, and stared at the machine curiously. It was Soviet-built, but it looked suspiciously like an Allis-Chalmers 20-30 of the late 1920's. Ruxton, who had had aircraft mechanics ground into him during World War II, said to Johnny, "Perhaps, I can fix it."

Johnny Liu translated that for Lo. Lo said to the mechanic, "The American, like all Americans, though a reactionary is an expert with machines. He will fix it."

The Chinese mechanic stepped back respectfully. He also evidently believed that all Americans were skilled mechanics. Ruxton checked the carburetor and the wiring, cleaned the sparkplugs, blew dirt out of the gas line, poured in some ethyl, stepped back, and nodded to the mechanic. The man spun the motor. It sputtered, and then took hold with a roar.

It was a good moment. Men who knew mechanics had a peculiar standing in a world where machines were needed but were not well understood. His skill would not be forgotten. At his request, he was assigned to a harvest sled, and he worked with the men, silent, hard, and without complaint. They dug turnips until dark, and then trooped back into the village. He ate dinner at the communal table for unmarried laborers. And then, in pitch darkness—for there was no moon, bathed in the stream, dressed, and started along the stone wall back toward the hotel. The night sky was clouded, and it was difficult to see. But he felt at peace with the universe.

The torments of man struggling with his soul, and with the mad ideas that seized him, seemed far away. The desires of his flesh, though already reviving, were still dimmed for he had possessed Tosti again that morning. And this time there had been no need for haste. Ruxton came to the village street, bought a sweet rice cake from one of the shops—which was still open—and then under the strung-up lights walked to the hotel entrance. He entered the lobby—and stopped.

All the prisoners, so it seemed to Ruxton's first glance, were there. Men turned as he entered, and the conversation died away. Ruxton hesitated. Then he realized that his basic purpose was still to remain aloof and uncommunicative. Deliberately, he strode toward the stairway. From the corner of his eye, he saw Jarnoz and Lemoine detach themselves from the group. They intercepted him at the foot of the stairs. Lemoine said in French, "Mai says Gongoe will be shot when recaptured."

Jarnoz said, "For a little—when you not come for dinner—we think maybe you make the jump, too."

Ruxton did not explain where he had been. His decision to work afternoons might be misunderstood by his fellow prisoners. Actually, it seemed to him a healthy thing to do. Work was neutral. These stupid Communists had already twisted its meaning. But the act of physical labor took away from the tension and the anxieties of his situation, and from the broken record of his own repetitious thoughts.

"Where is Mai?" he asked.

"Upstairs," Lemoine answered.

Ruxton took the stairs three at a time, and reached the desk of Mai Lin Yin breathing hard. "Look, Major," he said, "that boy can't have got very far. Let us look for him, and if we find him that's the end of the matter. No penalties."

Mai Lin Yin's bleak eyes stared up at him without softening. There were stubborn lines in his face that did not change, as he said in a taut, uncompromising voice, "Mr. Ruxton, if you or the other prisoners venture out of this village for any reason, without permission, it will be treated as an attempt to escape and punished accordingly. Take care."

"But look—" Ruxton began. "This boy is mentally ill. If we could find him—"

He stopped. The merciless eyes seemed like opaque ice.

"Mr. Ruxton," said Mai, "if you don't leave my presence immediately, I will have soldiers escort you."

Ruxton backed away slowly. "Okey, boy," he said deliberately. "Have it your own way—boy."

He turned without waiting to see the effect of his words, and went up to his room. He slept fitfully that night and woke up several times cursing Gongoe. Didn't the idiot realize the kind of people they were up against? Each time the curse and the thought ended with a sigh. Of course the boy didn't realize.

Morning brought the ever more surprising information that Gongoe had not yet been found.

On the collective farm—actually, it was not yet collective, said Johnny Liu, just mutual aid—it was another day of digging turnips. But part of the time as he labored, Ruxton wondered, "Where can that so-and-so have gone?" Late in the afternoon, he came to a remarkable explanation. He thought: "He's still in the village somewhere." The moment that realization struck him, he knew with a deep conviction that he had solved the mystery.

He began to tremble. It was a sick feeling of excitement that stayed with him every moment thereafter as he worked, and all the way back to the hotel.

He saw Lemoine as he entered, hesitated, then walked over to him. "Have they found the kid yet?" he asked. Lemoine shook his head. Ruxton said, "Thanks," and hurried up to the second floor. From the top of the stairway, he saw Mai at his desk. He called, "Major Mai, may I speak with you?"

Mai had glanced up at the sound of the footsteps. His eyes met Ruxton's with an obvious deliberateness. Then he looked down, and began to write. Silently, Ruxton cursed at the impulse that had made him use the epithet, boy, the day before. He said, "Major, surely it is to your advantage to recapture Gongoe without delay. Surely that is more important than punishment."

No answer. As if he were alone, Mai transferred some papers to the side of the desk and started writing again.

Ruxton tried once more. He said, "Give us till sundown tomorrow to find him. Send soldiers with us. Everyone should have at least one chance to be foolish. Surely somewhere in your life you yourself must have got a second chance."

Even as he spoke the appeal, he knew it was in vain. The ears it fell on were not so much deaf as controlled by a strange and terrible distortion. From his own experience with such distortion, he could guess now how completely immune Mai was to his words. Not once, but many times, he himself had been in that state. Standing there, he remembered a girl.

Foolish girl! After he had rejected her, she began coming to his apartment in the early morning hours. She had a key that she refused to surrender, and she let herself in with it, and crawled into bed with him. Sometimes, he would casually make love to her. Sometimes, he ignored her. In either event, she would leave by 8:30, for she had a job as secretary to a bank executive. For a year she degraded herself in this fashion. During that time he never talked to her, hung up when she phoned him, and ignored any pleas she made to him when she was with him.

Her visits became less frequent. Three times a week, twice a week, and then once a week. For about three months she came every two weeks, and, while he made love to her, she would say wistfully, "Did you miss me?" Always, he gave no answer. Finally, she stopped coming. He saw her twice after that. Once at a theater with a portly man whom he recognized as her boss, and once in newspaper rotogravure sections, which stated that she had married a lieutenant in the marines. The lieutenant's family was important in Philadelphia; and so there was the beautiful, haunted face of his rejected mistress in the society pages of the *Times*.

Seeing the picture gave him a peculiar satisfaction, which now—staring at Mai—he wondered about for the first time. "What did I gain by that?" The remembered emotion included stubbornness, yes. But above everything was a feeling that she had been wrong to be critical of him. At no time had he asked himself, "Should I have had other women while I had her?" That was a forbidden subject. And so, for a year and a half he had sustained a timeless hostility toward her. And in all the years since he had never reviewed the experience. No wonder Stalin and Hitler and Mao Tsetung could murder a hundred and fifty million people among them and not once have a qualm, or a feeling of guilt, or give even a passing thought to their countless victims. What they felt must be simply a more intensely sustained anger than anything he was capable of. How right could a human being feel? As right, apparently, as Seal Ruxton in his relations with women.

He forgot about that for the question right now was, what should he do about Mai?

As he stood there at the head of the stairs on the second floor of that ancient hotel, Ruxton remembered: "In the American army, all the little Hitlers jumped when the Big Hitlers yelped. That means Mai will do what his superiors want."

He thought instantly of who the only possible superior within reach might be. Down the stairs he ran, slowed to a relatively sedate walk as he crossed the foyer, and then hurried to the Mai residence. A wide-eyed Tosti let him into the room with the magnificent black furniture. Then she hurried off to get her mistress.

A few moments later, Madame Mai came in. She wore a slit skirt that showed one leg inches above the knee. A faint, pleasing perfume emanated from her.

She listened to his appeal, then shook her head firmly. "In these matters," she said with finality, "where no previous directive exists, I do not try to influence my husband. He has been assigned the task of determining a plan for the rehabilitation after liberation of the entire population of a highly civilized capitalist state, and Mr. Gongoe has chosen an unfortunate time to attempt to escape."

Ruxton saw reluctantly that she meant it, and that it would be useless to try to dissuade her. He turned away, then faced her again, curious. "How long have you been married to him?"

Mrs. Mai said without hesitation, "The party married me to him when I was nineteen."

"The Party—married—you—to—him?" echoed Ruxton.

"I was attending Peking University," she said, and sighed. For a moment, she seemed far away. Then she continued, "I was unhappy over my country, and full of ideals. So at the end of my senior year, I made my way to the North, and crossed the lines into Communist territory. There was a perennial shortage of lovers—they called all married women 'lovers'—and so I was told that one of my duties would be to marry a long-time communist. After crying about it for two weeks, I agreed. And really I was very lucky, for they produced Mai Lin Yin. Most of the girls in the same position as I—and there were many of us—were married to vulgar old peasants. My husband isn't young, but he at least has good manners and good breeding. Like any girl, I used to weave romantic thoughts around him. But he couldn't make the grade. So now we follow the old Party dictum on sex, and live a placid married existence."

"No children?" asked Ruxton.

She shrugged. "I have managed to avoid it."

Ruxton looked at her with a steady gaze. He was being given a very candid account—the kind of statement a woman might give to her lover, but surely to no one else. He said as much, and suggested that her placing so much confidence in him had implications.

The woman shook her head. "I thought about your proposal," she said frankly. "The idea attracted me. But I can't do it. Discovery would mean that you would undoubtedly be executed."

"Why should there be discovery?" Ruxton asked. His tone did not urge her. He had a feeling for these things. And this was not the moment when this woman would surrender.

"An affair in a military prison, surrounded by sentries and soldiers!" she said incredulously. "You must be quite mad, Mr. Ruxton."

"It would be more difficult in a crowded city in today's China than right here," said Ruxton.

"I think you had better go," said Mrs. Mai. "What you suggest is out of the question. Good night."

She turned, and left the room. Ruxton heard her call Tosti, and say, "Show Mr. Ruxton the way out."

Tosti came in timidly. Ruxton whispered to her in Japanese, "Is there a flashlight in the house? I will return it in the morning."

She nodded, and whispered, "You go now, and I will throw the flashlight out in a minute."

She opened the door for him. Ruxton turned on the threshold. "If someone were hiding in your basement, where would he hide?"

Her eyes widened. He could see the instant understanding leap through them. Then, "In the front, among the boxes, there is a pile of American mattresses." She sounded anxious.

He whispered, "Don't worry. If he's there, I'll get him out."

Her lips formed the words, "Be careful." Then she closed the door on him.

Ruxton waited in the darkness. Abruptly, the door opened a crack, and a flashlight was poked through. It landed on the ground beside him.

He picked it up, and straightened slowly. He stood there then, not moving, and listened to the noises of the night. They were numerous. Night birds. The ubiquitous cricket. And from beyond the walls of the great prison, the strange music of Chinese stringed instruments. Guards entertaining each other? Or prisoners? It didn't matter. He could move around, and the uneven medley out there would give him some protection from being overheard.

In his daytime visits to Tosti, he had noticed a basement door. Trusting his memory, he made his way to it in the darkness and, after a little fumbling, opened it. Not knowing what kind of steps there would be he stayed hard against the door as he pulled it shut. It was pitch dark inside. He probed cautiously with one foot, and found a step.

After he had edged his way down the stairway to a concrete floor, he turned the flashlight on for an instant—just long enough to see that there was an open, though low-ceilinged passageway between piled furniture on the left and boxes on the right. Stooping, he made his way forward a measured number of steps, and stopped. He estimated he had come about as far as he had seen open space.

He decided, "If Gongoe is here, he's already heard me, because I haven't been that silent. Therefore—" he switched on the flashlight and directed it to where, visible behind some boxes, a pile of mattresses showed. Ruxton walked over to them, and flashed his light into the face of a sleeping Gongoe.

He shut off the light hastily, and waited. There was no sound but the sound of shallow breathing, and no reaction. Ruxton tried to feel that the boy's exhaustion was lucky for both of them.

He visualized the position of Gongoe's body, as he had fleetingly observed it.

He braced himself.

He reached down, put his right hand firmly over Gongoe's mouth. With his other hand, he caught the back of the neck.

He lifted smoothly but with all his strength, and pulled the thin body out, up and beside him.

He kept his right hand over Gongoe's mouth. With his left arm and hand, he took a boa-constrictor's hold around both arms and body. And he started back the way he had come.

Under his constricting hold, Gongoe's body gave a convulsive jerk. But Ruxton held him. The language barrier allowed no room for argument. Against the other's spasmodic movements, Ruxton tightened his cruelly strong grasp. On the way to the door, Gongoe kicked at his shins. Ruxton squeezed his face, hard. Gongoe groaned, and he ceased to struggle.

Physical strength, thus applied, spoke a language that bypassed speech. The communication method proved adequate for his purpose. He got outside safely, carried Gongoe to the back fence, and threw him over.

As swiftly and silently as possible, Ruxton vaulted the fence and sought in the darkness to recapture the boy.

His grasping, swinging hands found nothing. Appalled, Ruxton thought, "Good God—the damn fool got away!" After a minute he felt resigned. His plan had been to carry Gongoe into the hotel, up to the second floor, and deposit him at Mai's desk. Whatever hope existed for the boy would surely lie in his being returned without having to be re-captured—so Ruxton reasoned.

Perhaps the boy would have sense enough to sneak up to his room. But there had been no way of conveying to him that such a course might be best.

Uneasy, Ruxton climbed back over the fence and returned to the Mai house. He laid the flashlight inside the basement door and softly closed it. Then he walked to the front of the house and out of the gate.

Back in his room, Ruxton's uneasiness grew. He shouldn't have interfered. He had forced an impossible situation to a crisis, and so had created for himself a potential nightmare of self-recrimination. He told himself finally, "I've got to decide that I will feel no regrets."

He slept on that. And awakened in confusion, his heart pounding. He saw that it was daylight, but it took a moment to realize what had brought him out of his deep sleep. The door was partly open, and the head of Ho Sin Go, the Chinese-English interpreter, poked through the opening.

"Mr. Ruxton," said Ho, "the individual who escaped has been recaptured, and Major Mai orders all prisoners to dress immediately and come down for the execution."

"For the what?" yelled Ruxton.

But the man had already pulled back his head. The door closed.

13

As Ruxton emerged from the hotel entrance, the soldier standing outside the door yelled incomprehensible sounds at him, but he pointed south along the street. And so Ruxton got the idea.

As he walked in the indicated direction, he saw that a number of white men were gathered about two hundred feet away. Ruxton joined them, and waited unhappily as others of the white prisoners came over from the hotel. He avoided looking directly at any of the men with whom he was acquainted. In spite of this, he noticed presently that Father de Melanier seemed about to address him. Ruxton turned his back on the group.

From where he stood, he could see the sun. It was barely above the horizon. The earliness of the hour gave the scene a reality which at some more ordinary time of the day it might not have had. He realized with a sense of shock that he believed that a genuine execution was about to take place.

As he stood there with the others, there was a movement further along the street, looking south. Ruxton watched, curious now, too resigned to be angry as four soldiers came out of a yard, pulling Gongoe. The boy was half-carried, half-dragged to the prison wall directly in front of the group of white men. For the first time then, Ruxton saw that two metal rings, about three feet apart, hung from the wall somewhat above the height of a man's head. The soldiers tied the boy's wrists to the rings, so that his arms were spread-eagled, his back to the wall. When they stepped away, he sagged. His head hung down, and his body was loose, and at first sight he seemed to be unconscious. But—Ruxton observed—there was movement. The boy shifted his feet, and twisted his body slightly, and opened his eyes.

He stared dully at his fellow prisoners. He seemed mortally tired, and even at twenty-five feet, his eyes had a visibly sick look. Ruxton was inwardly bracing himself for the murder he expected to witness, when a man spoke beside him.

"Ah, Mr. Ruxton, I see that you are regretfully surveying the result of your foolishness."

Ruxton turned slowly. He saw that it was Major Mai who had come up to him, and who had spoken the meaningless words. His own expression must have been blank and questioning, for Mai spoke again, sharply this time. "Come now, Mr. Ruxton. Don't pretend that you are not a member of the escape group, of which Mr. Gongoe's effort was a facet."

Ruxton looked at the Chinese commander with a disbelief that abruptly changed to a towering rage. He said in a dangerous voice, "Mr. Mai, will you stop being a bigger fool than you have to be. I know nothing of this child's action."

"You deny that you are intimately involved in an escape plan?"

Ruxton clenched his fist, and drew back to strike the other's stubborn face. Mai took a hasty step backward. He

74

looked startled. He said quickly, "I warn you—don't hit me."

Ruxton said through clenched teeth, "If you don't stop assigning blame to me for every goddam thing that happens around here, I won't even read your goddam literature—and do what you please about it."

Mai smiled obstinately, "Your rage undoubtedly reflects your disappointment, Mr. Ruxton. If you did not know of an escape plan, then explain your attempts to intervene for Gongoe, beginning with your first inquiry asking if he had been recaptured."

Ruxton stood very still, seeing the step-by-step logic by which this paranoid character had reasoned the situation.

"Yes, yes, Mr. Ruxton," Mai said slyly, "your interest in Mr. Gongoe's welfare was not as touching to me as you hoped it would be. You evidently knew where he was, and wanted permission from me to produce him. I saw through that little scheme, and all of you conspirators will now learn a lesson." He added, "I was not at first inclined to take this extreme step, but your inquiries and transparent machinations left me no alternative."

Ruxton stared into those cunning eyes, and knew that denials would be useless. The "plot" as Mai had pictured it had a certain plausibility. It was never easy to know what people were up to. What was fantastic in this situation was that Mai felt that his unverified conclusions were correct enough to justify killing someone.

Ruxton said contemptuously, "It's typical of the idiotic way you're handling this project that you would assume that I know everything that's going on here."

Mai's lips tightened. "Mr. Ruxton, your remarks are too personal for your future welfare."

"Stop bothering me," said Ruxton, "and get on with murdering that child."

Mai stood quite still for a moment. His face showed an uncertain rage. Abruptly, he smiled grimly with understanding, and said, "You hope to dissuade me by taunts and innuendoes from performing my duty."

It seemed to Ruxton suddenly that a conversation with this distorted personality was futile. He sighed resignedly, "Look, Major, I wouldn't even be talking to you if you hadn't spoken to me first."

Mai went on as if he had not heard, "The use of the word 'child' in referring to a grown-up male of one of the more hateful colonial powers is a technique for relieving him of responsibility for his own acts and for the acts of his government. The term 'murder' is a propaganda word which suggests that fitting punishment for a crime is in itself a heinous offense."

Ruxton was silent. He was being verbally out-maneuvered now. But he actually felt far away from the problem, and unconcerned with the reasoning of this psychotic Chinese. He had a mental picture of millions of the more able Chinese of the China of the past confronted by these madmen. They must have realized their doom in such crafty faces as he now saw in front of him.

Mai was continuing, "Fully aware of the danger to himself, Mr. Gongoe last night left his hiding place and attempted to seize a truck. He was evidently familiar with automobiles, for he broke into the dashboard, and connected the wires of the ignition. Had not sentry Yu Hin Gan been alert, Gongoe may well have succeeded in his escape."

The description of the pitiful plan pulled Ruxton's attention back to the scene. Where Gongoe had thought he would drive, or how far he would be able to go, was a puzzle. The escape chances of even an astute white man in the interior of this primitive country, every area of which was patrolled, were close to zero. Gongoe had no chance at all.

"You have nothing further to say, Mr. Ruxton?" Mai asked.

"Get it over with," said Ruxton roughly. "I want to go back to bed."

He was immune now, and he turned his back on Mai, and walked off a few feet. He heard Mai say, "Tell these people that Mr. Gongoe is to be shot for his attempt to escape, and that this will be the fate of all persons who make a similar attempt."

As the translations began, Ruxton grew aware that Mai had again come up beside him. "You cannot turn your back, Mr. Ruxton. We absolutely require that everyone here witness the punishment."

Ruxton faced forward without comment.

Father de Melanier edged over to him. "M'sieu Ruxton," he said plaintively in French, "perhaps I could have permission to pray for this poor fellow. Is he Catholic, by any chance? You seem to have some influence with Mr. Mai—"

"Influence!" Ruxton echoed. He caught himself, and thought in amazement, "Is that what all this looks like to these people?" It was such an unexpected evaluation that it was only after several moments that he said in a low voice,

"I'm the last man you should ask for such a purpose. Why not ask Lemoine?"

"Frankly," whispered the priest, "I do not trust my compatriot."

Ruxton was silent, but he agreed. He had thought several times that Lemoine inviting him to escape, and then naming names, was an action of a type engaged in by *agents provocateurs*. Still, this was an emergency. "Ask Lemoine, nonetheless," he urged. "He just might have influence."

A few moments later, he watched Father de Melanier cross the road trailed by Diogo and two Chinese interpreters. Mai must have realized it would be a difficult communication for he called after the group in Chinese, "See that they don't waste any time."

Ruxton assumed that the priest was administering Extreme Unction. If so, there was no response from the doomed man.

Abruptly, Major Mai yelled a command. "End this farce. Let us get on with our duty."

One of the Chinese translators tugged at the kneeling priest, who slowly rose to his feet, backed a few steps, then turned and walked, head down, across the road. His fingers were interlaced, and he was saying something that was not audible. A prayer? What else? Diogo walked beside the priest. He was shaking his head, scowling. Suddenly, Diogo turned, and shouted something at the boy.

"What is he saying?" Mai asked the interpreter, who answered, "He says, 'Die like a man, you coward.' " Once more Diogo shouted. The translator said to Mai, "He says, 'Do not disgrace your country.' "

The boy stirred, and seemed to become conscious of surroundings. He spoke in a puzzled tone, and the interpreter translated, "What is this? Where am I?" Mai said, "Tell him he is to be shot for attempting to escape." The statement was communicated, and there was a long silence, and then Gongoe started to cry. It was a wailing cry, not that of an adult at all, but a child's crying.

Ruxton walked over to Mai. "You're shooting a baby," he said. "This boy never developed beyond mother's knee."

Mai studied him with a sarcastic smile. "Mr. Ruxton," he said, "if you are asking me not to do what I must do, you are talking to the wrong man. Many bitter duties must be performed by those who genuinely wish a bright new future for man."

Ruxton said, "The epitaph on your gravestone will be,

'This man by himself created a cemetery five miles square, in every grave of which lies an honest man.' " He broke off, "Why don't you hold one of your People's trials?"

"This is an administrative judgment, requiring no trial," said Mai calmly.

He turned abruptly away from Ruxton, and walked over to the soldiers. "Firing squad, ready," he commanded. The soldiers sprang forward to line up. "Aim rifles," yelled Mai. Up came the captured American rifles. "Fire!" yelled Mai.

There was an uneven crackling of gunfire. Ruxton saw the boy jerk wildly, then go limp. With that, he turned and walked off toward the hotel. There was an outraged shout from Mai, "Mr. Ruxton, come back here!"

Ruxton turned. "I've watched the execution. Is there more?"

"I want your opinion of the execution. You agree that it was necessary, do you not?"

It took a long moment to realize that Mai was asking a serious question. Ruxton thought hard, and then said in a steady voice, "I'm glad he's dead, Major. There's no place for weaklings in such a project as this."

If Mai detected any irony in the remark, he did not show it. "Thank you, Mr. Ruxton. You may go." He turned to the interpreters, and said, "Tell your friends that they must all remain until they have given their opinion of how right I was to carry out this execution."

Ruxton heard no more. He was walking rapidly toward the hotel.

PART TWO

14

Two months and twenty-five days went by.

The harvest was completed . . .

Winter came to north-west China, and that was a phenomenon in itself. There was neither snow nor rain, but the icy winds brought great clouds of dust from the desert. The dust settled like a pall over man and his works. Each day, groups of prisoners were brought out of the big prison to sweep off the street.

Ruxton read one hundred and eleven of the peculiar cartoon books that were among the principal mass propaganda weapons of the Reds. Each had its own anti-American bias and its pro-Communist moral. He read also a number of books, including several that gave the correct concepts about China's military history since the early 1920's.

He had visited Tosti seventy-nine times, twice a day for three days while the Mais were away.

The ninetieth day of his imprisonment was clear and bright and cold. Ruxton emerged from the hotel, and shuddered as the chill hit him. However, it required only a few moments to adjust to the temperature. He wore the padded cotton clothes which were virtually the national Chinese dress in winter time, and which all the prisoners had been issued early in the autumn. The padding did provide some warmth.

As Ruxton started along toward the Mai residence, Father de Melanier rounded the corner of the hotel, and hailed him. Ruxton stopped, but he was puzzled. Because of his association with Tosti, he had avoided communication with the other men. Even with the priest his tactic had been to answer questions politely but never to initiate a conversation, or offer a thought of his own. It had proved adequately discouraging until this moment. This sounded different, more determined. Ruxton waited, resigned.

Father de Melanier came up, and said in French, "Ah, Mr. Ruxton, bear with me on a delicate subject matter. Your compatriot, Captain Gregory—he has today and tomorrow to make some concession to our captors."

So that was it. Ruxton sighed inwardly. He had no solution. He said, "Don't you think he's made that his business?"

The priest replied firmly, "I think it is the business of us all."

Ruxton stared at the man, curious and suddenly sardonic. "Father," he said, "during the second three months of our imprisonment, you will be expected to make some concession—other than just reading. Suppose *your* compatriot, Lemoine, comes to me two days before the end of the six months, and says, 'Mr. Ruxton, what are we going to do about Father de Melanier?' What shall I answer him?"

An expression of grief momentarily came into the man's face. Then he shook his head, grew calm, and said, "Let us take a logical step away from the individual to the general. Mai is trying to learn from Plan 'Future Victory' a formula which Chinese occupation forces can later apply to conquered western Nations. Is that not so?"

"True," Ruxton agreed.

"It seems to me," the priest went on, "that if we could reason out what plan Mai is formulating, we might even persuade an American air force officer to make a countermove as in a game, and so apparently compromise."

Ruxton conjured up an image of Gregory's stubborn countenance, and strongly doubted it. But he listened quietly, as Father de Melanier continued. "We must remember," the man said, "that the Communists can bide their time as few other conspiratorial groups have ever been able to do. In their early days, instead of killing them, they patiently indoctrinated captured Nationalist soldiers and members of the *Mintuan*, the counter-revolutionary force, and turned them loose, knowing the story would gradually spread that the Reds were merciful. Chiang Kai-shek repeatedly asked them to abandon the Marx-Leninist idea of mass extermination of the upper classes, but the Communists would never agree. As we know now, they subsequently carried out the extermination plan to the letter. But at the time it looked to the gullible that the Reds were kind-hearted idealists, and only the government was cruel."

It was such a clear-cut picture that Ruxton decided the priest's argument about Gregory had merit. Mai undoubtedly made his moves according to some preconceived idea. That would mean even Gongoe had died within the frame of a plan. "We might ask ourselves," Ruxton conjectured out loud, "what effect did Gongoe's execution, for example, have on the populace—meaning the twenty-two of us who remained alive?"

"No further attempts to escape have been made," interjected the priest.

"Yes," Ruxton acknowledged, "but I feel as if it had no particular after-effect on me that way, since I had already decided that escape would be virtually impossible. Perhaps, you should inquire of the others how they reacted. Did it make them feel that they had better give in? Or did they become two-faced, determined never to give in but pretending that they would?" He was interested now. "You might ask them," he concluded.

The priest hesitated, and then nodded decisively. "I'll do it," he said. "If we can reason out Mai's plan, we might persuade your compatriot—"

It was certainly the best possibility, and so Ruxton said, "I don't know what I can do to help, but call on me for anything that's within my power."

As he turned, and started off along the street, he saw that Madame Mai was just emerging from the gate of the Mai residence.

He couldn't help but notice as they approached each other, and not for the first time, that even in her padded cotton winter clothing, she looked neat and attractive. She was alone, and seemed to be in a bemused state, for she started to walk past him, unseeing. Abruptly, she paused, and said, "Mr. Ruxton, wait!"

Ruxton stopped, and turned.

The woman went on in a distressed tone, "I feel I should tell you. We have been going over the files of all the prisoners, and only your fellow American is being reported as recalcitrant."

Ruxton couldn't help wondering if she weren't taking a risk in giving him such information in advance. It reminded him. He said, "In that note which you wrote me, and which I have not yet destroyed, in case you may wonder—" He paused, and looked at her questioningly.

"I wondered," she said, and her voice was little more than a whisper.

Ruxton continued, "In that note you said that the American officer had been forced on your husband. Does that mean he will receive special consideration?"

She shook her head fiercely. "My husband has complete autonomy. His plan includes the possibility of execution under all circumstances."

Her explanation matched so exactly what Father de Melanier had analyzed that Ruxton hesitated, and then told her his idea that Gongoe's execution fitted in with her husband's formula. When he had finished, the woman said quietly, "I'm sorry, I'm not at liberty to tell you his plan." She broke off. "Please, Mr. Ruxton, destroy the note I gave you. Surely you would rather have me as your friend than as your enemy."

Ruxton asked, "Why did you give me such a note?"

She ignored the question. "Now that the name of Gongoe has been brought up," she said, "do you recall the night you came to see me?"

"Yes?" Ruxton was suddenly wary.

"After I left you that night," she went on, "I waited for you to pass my bedroom window."

Ruxton said, "Oh!" But that was a mild word compared to the shock that went through him.

Mrs. Mai continued, "When you didn't come, I got curious at a sound I heard, and I went across the house—and I saw you through the shutters carrying a man's body from the basement. Was that Mr. Gongoe?"

Ruxton was thinking, in anguish, "Trust a woman who is beginning to get interested in a man to start listening for his footsteps." His mind leaped past her question. "Did you tell your husband?" he asked.

"You answer my question," she said curtly, "then I'll answer yours."

Ruxton decided that denial was useless. "It was Gongoe," he admitted. "I guessed where he had hidden himself, so I captured him and threw him out." He shrugged. "I hoped if he showed up at the hotel it would restrain your husband's blood lust."

"You had nothing to do with his escape?" She sounded incredulous.

"Not a thing."

"Aren't you disturbed that you forced him out into the open, where he was caught and executed?"

Ruxton admitted that it had disturbed him very much.

"If you had left him alone to follow through on his own plan, he might have made good his escape."

Ruxton shook his head. "That I don't believe, but I felt guilty."

"You are certainly responsible for his death," she said positively.

Ruxton frowned. She was pressing the point beyond good sense. He said, "Not really. After all, Major Mai actually murdered the boy, not me."

To his astonishment, she grew angry. "He had a job to do. You had no reason to interfere and so force him to act."

Ruxton was taken aback by her logic. He was realizing that he should have known better than to talk to a woman about anything other than personal feelings. From her anger, he drew the conclusion that she had tried to argue her husband out of the execution, and in the privacy of the bedroom Major Mai had pointed out to her the inexorable requirements of his position.

He said aloud, softly, "Thank you."

She seemed amazed. "For what?"

"For trying to save Gongoe."

She stared at him, briefly silent. "There was really nothing I could do," she said at last, "because I had seen you with Gongoe, so I knew that my husband was correct in his analysis of your part in the escape."

"He was incorrect," said Ruxton. "I reasoned out where Gongoe was, and I carried him from the basement because it was *your* home."

The lie had a profound effect on the woman, as he had hoped it would. Her face softened. She said, "Oh!"

Her expression changed even more. It was as if an excitement possessed her, an inner joy. It was obvious that the entire reality of the situation had altered in her mind. She said slowly, "I didn't tell my husband."

It was a moment for dramatic gestures. Ruxton said, "Wait!" He knelt on the hard road, rolled up his trouser leg, ripped open a carefully sewn pocket, took out her note, stood up, and handed it to her. "Are we even?" he asked.

"A woman and a man are never even," she said. She laughed lightheartedly, and flushed as she brushed past him. Ruxton whirled after her. She heard his footsteps, and turned. She was still breathless. Gazing into her face, Ruxton knew that it was time for him to make a stronger play for this woman. He said in a low voice, "Are you going to let me go on much longer without the companionship of a woman?"

Some of the color drained from her face. She said uneasily, "Mr. Ruxton, I am a married woman. You shouldn't expect this of me."

It was a perfectly true statement. But all Ruxton said was, "I'm at your mercy, and I hope you will be merciful."

She was a beautiful Chinese woman who had been holding back from men since she was nineteen. So, not knowing her own passion, obviously only vaguely stirred as yet—but stirred—she could temporize enough to say unhappily, "With this three month period ending, I feel in a state of distraction. Let me think about it for two days, and I'll give you a final answer then."

She seemed so close to the edge of strong emotion that Ruxton realized he had pushed her far enough. He said, "The mattresses where I found Gongoe . . . would be a good place for us to meet."

". . . But it's dusty down there."

"Clean it up," Ruxton urged.

She closed her eyes. She stood like that for a long moment, then she opened them again, and asked simply, "Do you love me?"

The question clearly came so directly from her heart that Ruxton felt sorry for her. "She is like all the others," he thought, "wanting exclusive love from a man whose affection seemed to embrace all women." He said, pitying her, "Not yet. But from the first moment that we met I had a feeling for you."

She nodded, half to herself. He saw that his words held a truth for her beyond what he meant. She said, "Give me . . . two days."

Ruxton said, "Thank you—Phenix."

She sent him a quick, almost grief-stricken look. Then she turned, and walked on again toward the hotel. This time Ruxton let her go. He moved slowly toward the reading room, moment by moment pushing away the sympathy that had gripped him.

He was remembering what his father had once said: "Seal, if a man ever starts feeling sorry for a woman because of the trouble she gets herself into, then he's in the biggest trap in this universe. He'll be completely stunned at the game she will then play with him. Nobody knows why a woman treats such a man so badly, but whatever the reason it's one hundred percent destructive of the man's right to have any identity of his own. Let me tell you what happened to me.

"Like most young philanderers I didn't want to marry any girl who had had premarital relations. And so, I proposed to your mother because she let me know in no uncertain terms that she was pure, and would stay that way until the minister said, 'I pronounce you man and wife.'

"I still don't know why I wanted to marry a virgin, but I did.

86

"After the wedding when I started to join her in bed, she said, 'John, I want you to sleep on the couch tonight.'

"I said, 'For heaven's sake, why?'

"She said, 'I'm sure that in your mind the wedding ceremony meant that now you have an exclusive license to have carnal knowledge of my body. Marriage means more than that to me, John. Human beings don't have to be like animals. Sex is important, of course. But it should always be secondary. I want us to enjoy our honeymoon. Good night, John. I love you.'

"And she rolled over on her side, turned out the bed light, and presumably went to sleep.

"When we finally had sex, I could sense that she was the kind of woman who could really enjoy it. But she rose above her animal instincts and let me know that we would sleep together every two weeks.

"After this had gone on for some months, I called some old girl friends and resumed relations with them. And so, no longer under pressure, I let your mother play her little game, with interest and curiosity as to how it would develop.

"I got the idea that having a child would change her attitude about sex. But when, after giving birth to you, she started the two week routine again, that's when I'd had enough. I told her that since the purpose of sex was actually to have children, and since I didn't want any more children immediately, it was wrong of us to engage in sex for idle pleasure. And therefore I set up a plan whereby she and I would co-habit three or four times a year. The purpose of this was to ease any tensions that might build up, I said.

"Having played out that game as far as I cared to, I busied myself with the office, while, presumably, she spent her time with you."

It would be unwise, it seemed to Ruxton, to accept his father's philosophy on women without question. And yet he knew it to be superficially true. What it really added up to was that he could not afford to become too involved emotionally with either Tosti or Phenix.

He had come to the reading room by the time he had this thought. Dutifully, he wiped his feet on the mat inside the door, and silently procured for himself the latest of the military books he was studying.

Presently, he was able to settle down to reading.

15

As Ruxton rose to his feet shortly before eleven, he was dismayed to see Lemoine also get up. Lemoine paused beside him, and whispered, "When you are ready to leave, I wish to speak with you."

"Speak to me after lunch!" said Ruxton curtly.

The Frenchman hesitated. "It is important," he said.

"To whom?" Ruxton's tone was brusque.

Lemoine agreed unhappily, "Very well, after lunch." He returned to his chair, and sat down again gloomily.

Ruxton's feeling of disturbance continued. The interruption had broken the even pattern of his life, and he had a hunch he should take no chances. He had been phenomenally lucky up to now in being able to keep his numerous rendezvoux with Tosti. It seemed to him that he must remember that everything would be difficult these last two days, and that he should be cautious. With that thought, he strode over to Lemoine.

"All right," he said. "C'mon outside."

Lemoine came hastily to his feet. As they walked along the frozen road, Lemoine said, "I notice you reading the military books. Very interesting, yes?"

"Yes," said Ruxton warily.

Probably, Lemoine was merely trying to make some friendly remarks, and had not drawn him outside to discuss China's military history. Nevertheless, this man could be working for Mai, and it would be unwise to give his true thoughts even about something as far from present time as a past war.

Lemoine continued, "One thing seem to stand out. Chiang Kai-shek tried to avoid fighting with the Japanese, but the Communists never cease pushing for full scale war against the invaders."

In the course of his seven years in Hong Kong, Ruxton had picked up considerable information about China's wars. And so, though it was true that the Yenan group had wanted to involve China in total war with Japan, it was equally true that every Nationalist soldier engaged in such a war was one less opponent for the Communists in their conspiracy against the central Chinese government. In this case the arithmetic had worked out exactly according to calculation. The Japanese, ostensibly in Asia to keep the Communist menace from their doors, succeeded only in knocking down the walls of China's house. Through the openings swarmed the destroyers.

A kaleidoscope memory of these mighty events flitted through Ruxton's mind. He nodded, and said quietly, "Yes, the Reds certainly wanted China to fight the Japanese." He broke off. "But you didn't call me out here to talk about the dead past."

Lemoine said, "Are you not anxious? Within two days, the judgment will be rendered on us, and the sheep will be separated from the goats."

Ruxton did not reply immediately. The information he had from Madame Mai had been given to him alone. He said finally, "Why should you be anxious? You've been a good little collaborator."

Lemoine shuddered. "Don't use that word. It have bad meaning for Frenchman—from Nazi days."

Ruxton could believe that it had. But the fact was, this was different. The Germans had made no effort to subvert the majority of their prisoners, had simply treated them with brutality. They required the person to be inferior, but he was accepted as himself. If they murdered him, he died in his own identity. To the bitter end he knew who he was.

Hitler had aligned himself not with an ideal, but with a philosophy of realism. Its thesis: force brought the world to its present condition, and equally force would make the future. Any other idea he labeled as so much propaganda to lull the timid masses.

The Frenchmen who had collaborated with the Nazis had had no excuse. Nothing was offered them except the right to be scoundrels along with the master race. But if Lemoine survived *this* collaboration, he might as well change his name.

Brainwashing, as Ruxton saw it, resulted in loss of identity.

Lemoine was speaking again, soberly, "All right. Let us say you and I are safe. What about your fellow American?" He broke off. "This is the fact. He is who I wish to speak about. He will be shot tomorrow night unless we do something."

In spite of himself, Ruxton felt a chill. He would have imagined—without reason, actually—that any executions would take place two mornings hence. But the naming of the evening hour had an authoritative ring to it. It seemed to him that Lemoine had unwittingly revealed that he also had advance information.

Ruxton said deliberately, "Personally, I don't see what I can do. He hates my guts."

Lemoine said emotionally, "He have no way to help himself. We must lift him over the hurdle, somehow."

Surprisingly, that sounded sincere. Whatever other game Lemoine was playing, his manner made it acceptable to Ruxton that he wanted to aid Captain Gregory.

Ruxton stopped short in the street, and thought, "How do you change the mind of a dedicated officer, so that he will cooperate with a gang of Communists enough to get him over the first three months?" There was no easy answer. Gregory undoubtedly had an idea that if he gave in to any degree it would be a complete defeat and an acceptance of collaboration.

The problem began to interest Ruxton in a purely technical way. "Let's see," he thought. "We've got national allegiance" —but that was the bugbear. That was what Gregory would have to slide over. To tackle that one head-on was to ask for failure.

He glanced at Lemoine, "Have you any suggestions?"

The Frenchman said gloomily, "I have argue with him. He have tole me to shut up. I go down on my knees. He give me a kick. He say I am not his friend if I try to save him from being shot. I am only his friend if I let him be shot. He have gone entirely mad."

"We're all mad," said Ruxton absently. "C'mon." He started to walk again. Lemoine fell into step beside him, and thus they headed on past the hotel. It occurred to Ruxton that he would have to act as if his companion was one of Mai's counter-agents but also that he genuinely wanted to save Gregory. It was sort of a transition for Lemoine. He was still capable of human feelings. Presently, being human would be too dangerous, and he would feel safe only if he were expressing correct concepts. It would make a very involved conflict at some future time. Thank God, he didn't have to think about it now. After a minute, he still didn't have a plan, and so, temporizing, he repeated, "Any suggestions?"

"If you speak to him, perhaps."

Ruxton visualized that, scowled, and parted his lips. Before he could answer, Lemoine said quickly, "Do not say it! I sense hostility. Leave it unsaid, please."

Ruxton stopped walking, and stared at the man, with narrowed eyes. He wasn't hostile. But he was irritated with Lemoine. "Look," he said roughly, "If you've called me out

90

here to offer me some stupid illogicality, get away from me. Don't bother me with a bunch of chatter and a half-baked scheme."

Lemoine backed away slowly, shaking his head. "What a man you are. But you see why everyone wants you either dead or on his side. Even Mai."

"Stop talking nonsense!" said Ruxton impatiently.

Lemoine urged, "But you will not give up thinking about him?"

Ruxton said without hesitation, "If I can think of anything sensible, I'll do it."

With that, he turned and walked back toward the Mai residence.

Lemoine called after him, "There's no time to waste on thinking."

16

Ruxton did not look back. He felt that he had been swindled into a useless conversation, and that he had unnecessarily allowed Lemoine to weaken him. He was suddenly determined to have Tosti.

It was twenty to twelve as he let himself into the hallway near Tosti's room. She came hurrying, and slipped quickly into his arms. She was more relaxed in their relationship, even though he was late; more acceptant of her rights with him. In many ways she showed that she felt secure. And the fact was, except for her increasing tendency to chatter—and that exercised his Japanese—he had no reason to find fault with her. She was wonderfully available to him.

She said now, in her teasing tone, "The end of the three month period has come. You think maybe you be shot?"

"No," said Ruxton, "I don't think I may be shot, not this time."

She must have known that was true, for she cuddled up to him, and said in a happy voice, "We shall be lovers for a long, long time."

Tosti had told him many things about herself in the course of their three months' intimacy. Caught in the maelstrom of the war's end, she had witnessed scenes of revenge against Japanese nationals in the city where she had been stationed as a clerk in a government storehouse. Her memories of the experience were on the horrifying side. She seemed almost wholly unaware that the Japanese had been vicious almost beyond belief in their role of occupying power.

She believed that she had been converted to Communism. Yet he had already discovered a core of race superiority in her. She could accept an American "as a lover" because the Americans and the Japanese fought each other like equals, "face to face." Since the war had been settled by an outside force—the atomic bomb—it had taken nothing away from the equal bravery of Japanese and Americans. So it was all right for members of the opposite sex of each of these powerful but equal nations to hold each other, face to face, as lovers.

Tosti's attitude towards the Chinese was that they had been dirty and worthless until the Soviets put some sense into them. She gave no credit to the Chinese Communists for any benefits that had resulted from the "liberation." She did accept that the Russians had brought order at the end of the Japanese occupation to a country that was of itself not able to achieve it. Given time and peace, the Japanese would have done it better, but it was certainly time that someone was taking care of all these dirty people. Her opinion of the Mais was that they were not truly Red. Proof: Mrs. Mai bathed every day, and that certainly was not a Communist custom. It was quite an involved line of reasoning, but it satisfied Tosti.

As usual, it took him a little longer to dress than it did her. When he was ready, she opened the door, started out into the hallway—and stopped.

From beyond her, and out of Ruxton's line of vision, came the voice of Madame Mai, speaking in Chinese: "I was coming to get you—"

What happened then could not be avoided. Even as she was speaking, she came into view. As she saw Ruxton, she stopped. Her eyes widened. She glanced quickly from Tosti to Ruxton again, and there was instant total understanding in her face. What was surprising then was her speed of recovery. She said to Tosti, in Chinese, "The prisoners are not allowed in this part of the building."

Ruxton, after that first moment of shock, had become irrationally calm. He had an inner understanding with women, and he accepted this situation differently than other men might have. Before he could say anything, Madame Mai said, "What was it you said earlier, Mr. Ruxton, about having been denied the companionship of a woman for three months?"

It was a moment for reaction, not thought. And his reaction was strictly rage. "Don't be so damned quick to jump to conclusions," he said roughly.

"Then what are you doing in the girl's room?" Her voice was high-pitched, unnatural.

"None of your damned business!" Ruxton snapped. "If you want to have me killed, you can tell your husband I was here. Otherwise, I'll explain it to you some time. Goodbye."

What he implied was all lies. But it was the best he could do. As he passed Tosti at the door, he whispered, in Japanese, "Deny everything." And then he was outside, leaving the two women to confront each other.

As he walked toward the hotel a few minutes later, his rage, instead of diminishing, was mounting. The feeling that Madame Mai was wrong grew upon him. By lunch time he was seething with anger at her. He had the full, furious conviction that he was the injured party and, by god, she had better watch out. He had a strong impulse to do her physical damage.

He ate lunch, a black scowl twisting his face. He thought, "If she turns against me, I'll pay her back if it's the last thing I ever do." He had the choleric thought that she had no right to regard what she had seen as having any bearing on her potential relationship with him.

As lunch ended, he walked over to Jarnoz and held out his hand. He said, "It is time we became friends."

The Turk looked surprised. He glanced at Ruxton's face, and then stared down at the outstretched hand, blinked, and then slowly extended his own hand. Ruxton grabbed the man's rather limp palm, and pumped away. He heard himself say cheerfully, "We have a problem confronting all of us, and I have finally come to believe it will be solved only by a joint effort and not by each person by himself."

He believed nothing of the kind. Yet it was as if his tongue, in speaking the words, was seized by an inner compulsion.

Jarnoz said in a low tone, "We have problem for sure. What we do with Captain Gregory?"

Ruxton said, "Introduce me to some of these other people."

And that was the first time he actually talked to some of his fellow prisoners—if a conversation through one or more interpreters could actually be said to be "talking." First of all, Jarnoz called Lemoine, who introduced Ruxton to Señor de la Santa. De la Santa, though Spanish, could speak French and Italian. He said, "Ah, the angry American is going to join the human race." Ruxton asked him, "What brought you to China?" The Spaniard explained that he had a brother married to a Portuguese woman on the island of Macao, a Portuguese possession off the coast of China. One day, he decided to cross over to the Chinese mainland, and he was picked up by the police. The Reds accused him of espionage, and he was tried and sentenced within a week. "So here I am."

Tittoni spoke German. It was through him that Lemoine introduced Spie and Holsenamer. The former was a tall, fair-haired German; the latter, dark-haired, somewhat over-weight, was also German. Spie was forty, a mature, determined man. Holsenamer seemed in his early thirties. It was Spie, speaking through the two interpreters, who said, "We Germans realized right away that we had better collaborate. They talk as if Imperialist America is the big enemy, but somehow we get the feeling that there will be less patience with Germans. We are not allowed to take a moral attitude, because the implication is Hitler forfeited any moral rights we ever had."

Holsenamer added, "So we plan to become good little Communists as fast as we can."

How had they come to China? Holsenamer's answer: German industry was hoping to penetrate the Chinese market. So he had conceived the idea of coming on his own to get orders for goods, even though he represented no firm. He had expected that he could get the orders filled in Germany. "If I came as an agent," he said, "I would get a commission —small change. If I came on my own, then I had a good chance of being a genuine middle man, and of making a million."

Rudolph Spie had left his country as soon as possible after World War II, and he had been on the move ever since. He had come to China, hoping that his experience as a major in the German artillery would win him a worthwhile post in the Communist army.

Both men were arrested shortly after their arrival in China, and sentenced without explanation to Project "Future Victory." The total disregard of their rights seemed to bear out their feeling that West Germans were given a lower status in China than other European nationals, since no specific charge was preferred in either case.

De la Santa commented, "If an accusation of espionage

can be considered a granting of status, then I was treated with respect."

Through various nationals, Ruxton now met several more of his fellow prisoners.

Tittoni, one of the Italians, who had already acted as interpreter, now spoke for himself. He said, "I would rather not say why I came to China. It was a big mistake."

The other Italian, Pescara—a small, dark man—said excitedly, "I am a seaman. I came ashore at Foochow, and I meet my Chinese girl friend there. We make love with an Italian ardor intermingled with strong Chinese emotion. The police pick us up and say there are no more prostitutes in China. I never said she was a prostitute. They said it. I say she has been my girl since I first came to China fourteen years ago—well, first her mother was my girl, then her. After all, she was only eight when I met her mother. But when she got to be sixteen—what a woman! So they sentence me for what?"

Ruxton said drily, "Contributing to the delinquency of a minor."

"But she's no minor. She's twenty-two now."

There was an argument between Pescara and de la Santa who was translating. The latter turned to Ruxton, and said in French, "The Italian says he admitted that he had first had the girl when she was sixteen, so he agrees maybe they did have the right to take him on a morals charge."

It seemed to Ruxton that the crime of statutory rape hardly justified a sentence of death. But he did not say it. He was now introduced to one of the Swedes, named Sugurd Lund; a Dane, Niels Madsen; and the Greek who had maintained his moral rights for so many hours months before. The Greek's name was Dmitri Mapoulis. Somewhere in there he began to feel like a person at a party who is introduced to too many people. In this case, all the faces were familiar, but the information about each person, and from them, grew confusing. There were too many interpreters. Waiting for translations became incredibly boring.

He became weary, and he sat down beside Jarnoz, and they discussed the theories of the terrorists of the 19th century. The Turkish professor had previous knowledge of the movement, and Ruxton had read about it in the Mai library. He was particularly fascinated by that sub-group of the Populist society which called itself the *People's Will*. This was the group that had maintained the highest "ideals" of the terrorist organization. After assassinating Czar Alexander

95

II, the executive committee of the group had written the new czar stating that terrorist activity would cease when full democratic freedom was granted. Ruxton could find no flaw in the reasoning of the terrorist philosophers, Stepniak and Burtsev. They were confronted by a despotic regime in Russia, headed by an absolute monarchy, and so a group, the total membership of which was never more than five hundred persons declared war on a government with 1,200,000 soldiers under arms at all times.

The techniques of terrorism, since those days, had become widely understood. In many countries, groups seeking to overthrow or influence the existing regime did so through terror. Some terrorist organizations were so powerful and numerous that they imposed orderly taxation on the populations of the cities and towns around them.

Ruxton was objectively discussing this increasing use of murder as a political weapon—when he had a thought. It was a simple idea, and not for a moment (when it first struck him) did it appear to have any special implication.

He said, "Fortunately, not everyone is terrorist material."

Jarnoz laughed. "What a world, hey, if everyone were terrorist!"

Ruxton, still not suspecting what lay ahead, said, "There must be a special type of person who can be a terrorist."

Jarnoz was attracted by the possibility, and suggested they analyze known terrorists of the *People's Will* to see if there was a common denominator. It quickly developed—insofar as Ruxton could recall—that the author of the brief biographies in the Mai library had not thought in such terms. He was interested in the theories of the men, and in their acts of terror, not in their characters. With one exception. The terrorist, Tkachev, was described as believing himself to be the only true Messiah, and his theory of combining terror with seizure of government as the only true scriptures. Tkachev died in an insane asylum.

These facts seemed to provide no common factor, except, as Ruxton put it, "In order to be a terrorist, you really have to believe that you're right in what you're doing. We could assume that Tkachev's Messiah feelings were an exaggerated version of every terrorist's attitudes."

Jarnoz pointed out that the membership of the *People's Will* rejected Tkachev's ideas and cast him out of the society. "So he too extreme for them."

"That's true," Ruxton acknowledged. "Still, we know that Tkachev's theories were later picked up by none other than

Nicolai Lenin, the man who led the Communists to victory in Russia, in 1917."

But he spoke absently. His interest was not in the rightness of this or that terrorist's ideas, but in the terrorist type, as such.

Jarnoz was frowning. He seemed to be thinking hard.

Ruxton continued, "A psychiatrist in the prison I was in in the United States said that the rages that had got me jailed showed an unconscious impulse to violence. He said when a person who had such impulses was finally able to rationalize them, and so felt justified in using them consciously, he would then be able to do physical damage to the extent of the rationalization. Now, if we were to suppose that all terrorists had this unconscious impulse, and had rationalized it—"

Ruxton stopped.

He had a sudden blank feeling of disbelief.

Then he thought wonderingly, "Good God, I also am a terrorist type."

The colossal insight ran through all its changes in his mind, became an accepted part of his awareness as something that *could* happen to him if the buried rage ever broke through to consciousness. And he was about to make a dissembling remark to Jarnoz, when the second wave of the idea hit him.

He thought, "In my relationship with women, the rage has already broken through. I've already justified it."

He had suggested that the key to the terrorist had to be the feeling that he was right in what he did.

With women Seal Ruxton felt himself right. So right that for several hours now he had been in a sweat of fury at Madame Mai. During those hours, he had been absolutely determined that she had better not resist him, or he would do something violent.

Sitting there, he recalled women whom he had actually struck, consciously, and with a feeling of justification.

Ruxton was shaken now. He stood up abruptly, mumbled an excuse, and went up to his room. He felt strangely exhausted.

He slept for an hour. When he awakened, he lay for a while realizing that he was relieved. At last he knew. For years he had had the uneasy conviction that unknown and uncontrollable forces might at any moment impel him to dangerous actions.

The additional data, which had so suddenly burst into view, would surely help him.

He realized presently that his intense anger against Mrs. Mai was gone. He thought half-heartedly, "Actually, she is right to be angry. And I really couldn't blame her if she turned against me one hundred per cent."

Yet he also knew that women didn't turn easily against men. "But she'll do something," he thought. And shivered with a vague memory of what women had done in other similar situations. He allowed no clear picture to come through, just the feeling of uneasiness. "Something," he thought.

Disturbed, Ruxton got off the noisy bed, walked to the east window, and looked out over the cold, snow-less plain. The scene reminded him of a train trip he had once made across northern Kansas during a dry winter. True, there had been a great deal of grain stubble, and here was only sandy, level ground. But the mood of wintry desolation was the same. Sight of it brought him back to Gregory's dilemma.

He thought somberly, "It's too late for him to escape, and it's six months to warm weather."

For the Captain, any solution he achieved tonight or tomorrow must also include a solution for three months hence, since winter would not release its frigid grip on this remote land till April or May. It seemed impossible that anything could be done for Gregory, with little more than twenty-four hours left to do it in.

He was still feeling baffled when the time came to go down for the evening meal.

17

Dinner that night consisted of porterhouse steak, and a baked potato, with a side plate of green vegetables. The meat was cooked medium well, and Ruxton liked his steak very rare; but it was steak, and he ate his portion with relish and a feeling of nostalgia for American restaurants. As he glanced around the room, he saw that he was not the only one who had done justice to the Occidental meal.

Captain Gregory said in a loud, sarcastic voice, "I suppose this is a reward for the good Commie collaborators, and a last meal for the condemned."

Fa 'tze, the chief interpreter, said to his aides, "Tell them they must remain. Major Mai will be here in a few minutes to speak to them."

When that was translated, Gregory said cheerfully, "Ah, another slapstick performance by our junior comedian." He raised his voice, "Hey, Ruxton, you know what?" Ruxton straightened, and looked across at him questioningly, but said nothing. Gregory continued, "I have an idea that bastard was going to execute somebody as a lesson for us all and, looking back, I think you were his first choice. That poor kid was an after-thought."

It was a possibility that had several times occurred to Ruxton. Gregory went on, "Reason I mention it, there must be some good left in a fellow that Mai would want to kill."

Ruxton was startled by the friendly tone, but he rejected the overture. "Captain," he said ironically, "my problem is, how does a man change himself into a Communist? I can't seem to figure that out. Maybe you can help me."

Gregory stared at him, the cheerfulness fading from his lean face. Yet he hesitated. He seemed disappointed. But when he spoke finally, it was with a sneer: "Just keep sucking, boy. You'll get there."

Gazing at the man, Ruxton had an awful insight: "He's going to do something desperate tonight, and he has in mind involving me." Nothing but madness could be expected from Gregory at this late hour of his life. The smile, the apparent friendliness, the casualness, concealed a tension that must be approaching the point where his entire being was consumed by emotion. Ruxton smiled grimly to himself, and thought, "Oh, no, you don't. I'm not getting into anything right now." It was Gregory who would have to make the change.

As he had that thought, the portieres parted, and Mai Lin Yin entered the room. There was something about the way he walked that alerted Ruxton instantly. Suddenly, he realized that this was the hour of judgment. Not tomorrow night, but right now.

Mai strode to the center of the room in that purposeful way, waited for the silence that came quickly, and said, "It has come to my attention that there has at this late date been criticism of my action in having Mr. Gongoe shot. Since my action was of course completely justified, I believe that this execution is an excellent point on which we can have a self-criticism meeting."

Ruxton's first thought was: "Criticism of Gongoe's death? Who? . . ." And then he remembered. Was it possible that a distorted version of his suggestion to the priest about the boy's execution had been reported to Mai? He saw that Captain Gregory was rising to his feet.

The air force officer said in a deliberate tone, "Am I to understand that you are going to criticise yourself, or that we are going to criticise you?"

Mai said quickly to the translators, "Do not translate that." Having spoken, he stared at Gregory in a baleful manner, but finally said in a mild voice, "Captain, I had my period of self-criticism long ago, and no longer require it. I shall adjudicate this particular self-criticism meeting, holding it to correct concepts and correct questions, so that each individual may learn from my wide experience in these matters."

"Since this self-criticism is not going to be of you," replied Gregory, "I think I'll beg off, and go take a nap."

"No one leaves this room, Captain." Mai's voice went up at least half an octave.

Gregory sat down. "Sleeping in a sitting-up position is a little harder," he said cheerfully. "But I've done it before. I guess I can again."

Mai glared at him. Then he smiled, his mouth twisting wryly. He said in a surprisingly relaxed voice, "Captain, if you fail to take advantage of the opportunities given you, that is your funeral—to use an American colloquialism. Please notice that it is you who make the choice."

"I understand you're going to murder me tomorrow," said Gregory. "But don't try to pretend it isn't murder."

Mai walked over to the table near Ruxton, drew out a chair, and carried it back to the center of the room. He sat down in it. There was a grimness in his manner, and Ruxton realized that here and now might be the last opportunity to save Gregory's life.

"Major Mai!" he said sharply.

"Yes?" The commandant gave him a questioning glance.

"We have a shadowy personality in Captain Gregory," Ruxton continued. "Perhaps he might be willing to fill out some details about himself." He hesitated, and then finished his thought, "If he were by some chance to, uh, leave us now, we would have almost nothing on which to base a memory."

Mai looked over at Gregory. "Well, Captain?" he said.

A stubborn expression came into Gregory's face. "My name is Edward Gregory," he said. "My rank is Captain, and I am in the United States Air Force. That is the information I am authorized to give by my commander-in-chief, the President of the United States."

Ruxton saw the man's dilemma only too clearly. He was doomed, caught between two relentless forces, neither of which permitted him any latitude. Communists everywhere rejected *in toto* the kind of morality on which it was based. They had already proved that they could massacre any number of dissenters. The passing years had established that the survivors forgot the dead, and in record time started mouthing the *clichés* fed them by the massive propaganda machine of the winners. There was no solution for Gregory except collaboration—or death.

"Captain," said Ruxton, "I think you should recognize a special situation exists here. This is not a military prisoners' camp. It's an experimental prison, and you and I have had the incredible bad luck of being forcibly made a part of the experiment. Now, I want to ask you a question—"

Gregory said harshly, "I don't want to hear any treason from a traitor."

"Look," said Ruxton in a reasonable tone, "as individuals we are confronted by a whole group of men who are caught up in that special madness which is associated with support of an economic system. These men operate under a government directive, and are made to answer with their lives if they fail. So they feel as helpless as you are."

Gregory was shaking his head angrily. "I cannot accept that they are not responsible for their actions," he said. With deliberation, he turned, and faced the Chinese at the head table. He said slowly, emphasizing each word, "I warn you, men. You are all, each, individually, responsible for your participation in any murder that takes place here. No government has any right to ask you to commit murder, and don't think that there is any protection for you on the grounds that you are following orders."

Mai said to his aides, "Do not translate that." To the Captain, he said, "You are appealing to a bourgeois morality, which does not exist in this country. In establishing a new society, we require from each individual that if necessary he sacrifice himself—"

Captain Gregory sneered, "Big talk now. Watch them squeal in a court of justice."

Mai said, "To the notion that at some future time an Imperialistic judgment will be rendered on myself and my colleagues, I say very simply, *Ta ma ti*—"

Gregory snapped, "Speak for yourself. Every man in a

court stands alone, and he stands alone on the gallows."

Mai continued, "We know what such cunning courts of so-called justice will do, and so we can say, captain, let the Wall Street beasts do what they can—"

"You poor little peasant," said Captain Gregory, pityingly.

Mai flushed, but he went on, "—Their days are numbered, captain, and even now I suspect they tremble as they hear the marching feet of the peasants and workers whom they have deluded for so many centuries."

"What childish talk," said Gregory with contempt. He hesitated, then continued in an earnest tone, "Major, no one in America has so far wanted to kill Chinese people. In Korea, our small army captured 180,000 of them and treated them with respect and consideration. You captured 7,000 Americans, of whom 3,000 are missing and probably murdered. But the so-called Wall Street beasts are still not angry enough to hit back hard. So you've all got off without really having to face American firepower. Better keep it that way, or you'll get your pants wet, and have to have your diapers changed."

He seemed unaware that Ruxton had made an attempt to save his life, for he twisted in his chair, and said, "As for you—in Korea, we had our first look at your kind. All I can say is, I don't know how you can hold up your head in the presence of a man."

Ruxton said, gently, "Captain, I could dispense with your conversation from now on. But some of these other people seem to like you. So, since it's still early, why don't you go over to the book room and start reading Communist literature? That's the simplest way to make sure that you and I can continue this debate during the dull winter months."

Gregory said grimly, "I wouldn't read their junk if they paid me."

Ruxton shrugged, and gave up. In saying what he had, he had merely exposed himself to additional abuse. Clearly, the man had no solution for himself; and he rejected help. Ruxton leaned back in his chair—as Mai stood up and walked over to him.

"Mr. Ruxton," he said, "I have happy news for you. You are being recommended for continued training during the next three months. Congratulations."

He held out his hand and Ruxton's spirits sagged instantly, for he had no intention of shaking hands. The crisis was upon him so quickly that for a moment he sat dazed. Then, deliberately, as if he did not see what Mai was doing, he looked up at the man, and said slowly, "Major, the journey of a hundred miles begins with one step—is that not an old Chinese proverb?"

Mai lowered his extended hand, and stroked his jaw. He was visibly offended; his face showed the beginning of anger, but he also seemed uncertain.

Ruxton said desperately, "Project 'Future Victory' is being operated on another old proverb, as I see it."

Mai temporized, "What is that?"

"Get the coffin ready, and watch the man mend. . . . Major, it is not easy for the man who is being asked to mend to feel sincere, friendly feelings for the person who is getting the coffin ready."

The Chinese leader laughed curtly. "You are a very clever man, Mr. Ruxton," he said, but he was relaxing now. "And you and Captain Gregory have just demonstrated how close to the edge of the grave it is necessary to force people before they will give up their anti-people bias. Now you can see the problem of those who work for the future well-being of mankind."

The words gave Ruxton an opportunity to make a final point. He said, "Major, this is my decision. I am going to find out if you and other Communists are actually working for the future well-being of mankind."

The commandant smiled tolerantly. "That remark shows an incorrect understanding, Mr. Ruxton. In time to come you will be amused at how naive your thinking is. For the moment, however, I accept your answer."

He turned, walked a few steps to one side, and pulled out a sheet of paper. He said, "The following persons are also recommended." He thereupon read aloud from the paper every name except that of Captain Gregory, explaining when he had done so: "The persons I have named have complied with the minimum requirements for the first three month period of Project 'Future Victory.' This means that the individuals named automatically go forward into the next three month period."

Involuntarily, Ruxton glanced at Gregory. The officer was sitting, staring straight ahead. His jaws were clamped, his face white, his eyes narrowed.

"As for Captain Gregory, who is not recommended," Mai Lin Yin continued, "I expect to receive instructions about him tomorrow from Peking."

Gregory stirred himself, and laughed shortly. He said,

"They're even bigger bastards than you. So we won't have to guess what those gangsters will do."

Mai walked over to him. He seemed calm as he paused beside Gregory. There was no suggestion of threat in the way he held himself. Without warning, he slapped him across the face. "Respect for Chairman Mao, please!" he said harshly.

And then he grunted, as Gregory came up from his chair, and like a football player drove forward head first into Mai's belly. Mai was swept half across the room by that charge. There he managed to sidle to the left and get his hand into his pocket. When it came out, it held a gun. He struck a single, slashing blow at Gregory's head.

The American officer fell, twitched, and lay still.

Mai yelled in high falsetto to the prisoners, "Carry this imperialist dog to his room."

Lemoine, Jarnoz, the Swede and the two Germans came forward, gingerly lifted Gregory and silently bore him through the portieres and out of sight.

"Come back when you're through!" Mai shrilled after them.

Instantly calm again, he faced about. "Let us resume our discussion," he said.

Each man was now put to struggling with his conscience. And soon there was no doubt. This was a self-criticism meeting in earnest.

The emphasis was on criticism in relation to, not merely criticism of. Each person was requested to give reasons why he approved of the execution of Gongoe. Or, if he did not approve, what was the nature of the "old style" thinking that prevented his giving approval. "New style concepts" and "correct principles" were opposed to "old style concepts" and "tails."

It seemed to Ruxton that part of the weariness that descended on the roomful of men derived from the interminable time taken up by translations. By midnight, the tired participants had among them offered every correct and incorrect concept about killing that they could think of. Mai patiently prodded them on, apparently content with repetition if nothing new was offered.

About half past one, de la Santa stood up, and spoke to his Chinese-Spanish interpreter. Translated, his words proved to be directed at all the prisoners: "I have a feeling that Mai wants a specific answer from us, and I don't think he's going to let us go to bed until we give it."

In the end, it was Mai himself who gave the correct concept: "Your imperialistic parents and teachers, seeking to corrupt and control you, implanted in your minds the false idea that deaths inflicted by the imperialistic reactionary courts were justified, whereas the fact is that the peasants and workers, when awakened from slavery, have the only natural right to execute those who have enslaved them. Gongoe, as a tool of imperialistic beasts, could therefore be killed like the running dog that he was, without mercy."

The translators broke into spontaneous clapping after these words were uttered. Then they began their lengthy task of interpretation, while Ruxton waited, thinking, "Now, surely, he'll let us go." But when the translations were completed, Mai launched into a eulogy of peasants and workers, and of how true democracy could only come in any country if the liberation was led by the workers and the peasants. They were the only true source of creativity. Here in China, workers constantly gave practical solutions to problems that baffled scientists and engineers. Simple peasant farmers, it seemed, were solving age-old problems of agriculture with a facility and brilliance that dazzled agricultural experts.

Listening to the harangue, Ruxton found himself wondering sleepily if the time would come when he, also, would believe such legends and myths. He recognized that the lies had a purpose. So long as the people accepted the flattery, they would hold still for the big shakedown, which was the real purpose of the hugest con game in history. Somehow this generation had to be kept confused while the new generation was educated in correct concepts.

Ruxton was still thinking about that when Mai ended his testimonials, and announced, "As soon as that is translated, we will retire."

Some twenty minutes later, Ruxton slumped into his noisy bed. He expected to fall asleep instantly, but he was disconcerted to find himself tormented by the events of the evening. As he tossed and turned, seeking a restful position, he realized that he was impressed by group criticism. The method made an impact on the mind. In an atmosphere of sustained threat, it forced the individual out of his stereotyped thinking. Its weakness as a tool for finding truth was the pre-conceived communist ideology that was attached to it here in this prison. And after only one session, he could see that other dictators, with *their* ideas, could utilize it to force people into their brand of correct concepts. Accordingly, it was a doctrinal weapon, but it was a weapon of dangerous power.

He kept recalling the tactics employed, and the progressive willingness to agree on the part of those who participated, as they became more and more fatigued with the passing of time.

Relaxed at last, he turned on his side, away from the door. And he was slipping off to sleep when the door behind him opened.

. . . And shut.

There was a flare of bright light from the outer hallway during the moment the door was open. Then pitch darkness.

But he knew with an awful thrill that someone had come into the room.

18

Ruxton remembered: *The bed creaks. Therefore—*

He flung off the thin blanket, and rolled to his feet on the far side of the bed. Twisting, he grabbed the bed and propelled it at the door.

He was not surprised when he felt it strike an object, and a man grunted. Whoever it was, gripped the bed and pushed back. Between the two of them shoving in opposition, it was held rigid. Suddenly, there was a grim laugh from the darkness and the voice of Captain Edward Gregory said, "All right, Ruxton, let's call a truce."

Ruxton felt a hot flash of rage as he realized who it was. He had a violent impulse to leap across the bed. He suppressed that with the silent resolve, "I'll teach that son-of-a-bitch to come in here like this, as soon as I've found out what he's after!" Biding his time, nursing the fury that had leaped so instantly through his body, he said, "What do you want?"

"I'd like to have your guts but, failing that, an understanding."

"I see no point in my having an understanding with a man who has one day to live unless he stops being an idiot."

"That's why I'm here. Ruxton, somebody has got to stay alive, and eventually escape from this prison, to tell the world what's going on here. We owe it to our country."

"He's done it," Ruxton thought. "He's tied in national allegiance with staying alive." Until now, anything that had been said to Gregory urging such a course had been rejected. But tonight, suddenly, the pieces had fallen in place. The pressure had reached exactly the right potency. And loyalty to the United States equalled temporary collaboration with the Communists. He felt ever so slightly ashamed for the officer. And yet, what Gregory said was true. Someone should bide his time, and await an opportunity to escape. Whoever succeeded would not be condemned for pretending to have given in.

"Captain," said Ruxton, "I'm happy you've made up your mind to live. But I can't trust you in this room at night. So let's talk about this after you've made your peace with Major Mai."

Gregory said stubbornly, "Ruxton, we've got to have a purpose. There's no use trying to escape in the winter time."

So he had realized that simple, icy truth.

Gregory continued, "We've got to decide now that we're only going to appear to yield to the mental skulduggery of these monkeys. Ruxton, the United States Armed Forces made a complete study of Chinese Red methods with Americans taken prisoner during the Korean war—"

"Damn you," said Ruxton, "I don't want to hear your story." He had always had an instinct for danger, and that feeling was on him now.

Gregory persisted, urgently, "Ruxton, in all the recent wars of the history of West Europe and of America, a man taken prisoner by the enemy was recognized and treated as a member of the opposite side. In many instances, he was roughly handled, but even that was part and parcel of being one of the enemy. The Chinese in Korea changed all that. Once an American was made prisoner, the Chinese attitude was that he was an exploited tool of the reactionary capitalists, and therefore really on the Chinese side, and not on ours. The average American, valuing his own life, took one look at that kind of treatment, heaved a sigh of relief, and decided, 'Oh boy, how long can I keep them playing this crazy game?' Our men hoped it would be until the end of the war, and until they were free to go home. None of them seemed to realize that he had just made the first step of selling his own country down the river."

Ruxton, intent on the other's story, searching his mind for an argument that would end it, relaxed his hold on the bed. Instantly, it moved against him. He shoved back hard.

Gregory seemed not to notice, for he continued, "In all previous wars, an American prisoner could pick up a buddy or two in the prison camp. In the Korean war, the Chinese wrecked the buddy system. Each prisoner was closely observed by one of the Chinese personnel. Suppose a cabbage falls off a truckload of food coming into camp. You pick it up and eat it. At the first group meeting after that, the Chinese observer reports that you were seen eating the cabbage. Then he says that another American prisoner told on you, and by doing so showed an awakening conscience in terms of the 'people'. There is no punishment. You are simply reprimanded, told to think in future of the welfare of your comrades, and then the meeting continues with a lecture on the evils of Wall Street, or some such stuff. Now, the next time you are involved in something—and you can't help it, with your capitalistic style thinking—it is again stated that a fellow prisoner told on you. This time you might be asked, why hadn't you told on yourself? If more incidents occur, veiled threats are made. After all—the Chinese suggest—what can they do with someone who persists in actions inimical to the interests of the 'people,' except eventually punish him, if he fails to show improvement or remorse.

"After a few weeks of these tactics, Americans began to wonder: Are these other guys telling on me? The time came when an American prisoner, realizing he had done something that might be construed as being against the 'people' made sure that he was the first to report it. If he saw someone else doing something 'wrong,' he reported that, too. Why? Because he didn't dare not to. Because, if the fellow who did the so-called wrong thing, accuses himself, and then adds that you saw him do it—the question is, why didn't you report it? Follow that? You're in as much trouble for trying to shield your fellow American as if you had done the thing yourself. First thing you know, you'll find yourself on trial as an 'enemy' of the 'people,' with not a single friend to stand up for you. That was the end of the buddy system. American prisoners could not trust each other, but it all began because they took the first step of co-operating with these Chinese s.o.b.'s. We mustn't do that. Our goal must be to escape as soon as possible."

Ruxton said harshly, "Captain, let's put a period to this little bed-time story. Go ahead with your plans, but don't try to involve me in them. And don't worry about me. I won't tattle on you."

There was a pause. Then Gregory's voice came grimly, "How can I trust a traitor and an ex-convict?"

The feeling of frustration that came over Ruxton at that moment was as strong as anything he had felt at any time in all his years. In spite of his attempt to stop the man from telling him his plans, Gregory had done so. And now: "How can I trust? . . ." But his anger carried no force, even for himself. He had been out-maneuvered by the other man's aberration. Logically, he must now be killed because he knew too much. Perhaps he might save himself by agreeing to Gregory's plan. But he would have to convince the man that he really meant it. If he were Gregory, he would not trust anyone with any information at all. Ruxton thought desperately, I've either got to get down on my knees and beg for my life, or get him out of my room—right now.

He wouldn't beg, and so . . . in a tone of voice that brooked no opposition, he said, "Captain, get out of this room! If you've brought a weapon in here, and you try to use it, I'll wreck you." He broke off. "Listen, I'm going to pull the bed back, away from you. When I do, you open the door, and leave. Do you agree?"

There was a long pause. Finally, with obvious reluctance, Gregory said, "I agree."

It was Ruxton's turn to hesitate. Was there something in this situation that he was missing? He couldn't imagine what it might be. But the alarm feeling remained. He decided, "The more careful I am, the better." Aloud, he said, "I'll let go when I say 'Now!'—" He paused, took a deep breath, and said, *"Now!"*

He released the bed, and started to retreat.

As he did so, Gregory said, in Russian, "Kill!" It seemed meaningless, a nonsense word coming from an American officer. What saved Ruxton then was not his understanding of Russian, but his silent and swift withdrawal all the way to the wall.

Someone leaped across the bed, and landed on the floor about where Ruxton had been a moment earlier. Ruxton had the impression that the fellow flailed the air and, intensely dark though it was, it seemed to him he caught a glint of metal.

The feeling of immense surprise passed. It was too soon to react to his realization that not one, but two, men were in the room. For this instant all that mattered was that he was being attacked.

Judging entirely by memory, he reached for, and successfully grabbed up, the rickety ivory chair, stepped forward, and swung hard. There was a crash, and a splintering of wood. A man—not Gregory—cried out in pain. In the darkness, something fell to the floor with a metallic sound. Ruxton dived for it, fumbled frantically—and came up triumphantly clutching the fallen knife. The time for reaction had come. Ruxton yelled, "Gregory, you puling hypocrite! I'm coming after you with the knife your pal tried to use on me."

"Ruxton, wait! Promise to escape with us when the time comes, and we'll leave. Otherwise, we'll stay here, and fight it out in the dark."

Even in his fury, Ruxton knew that was the wiser course. This was the crisis. They were committed. He cursed the men under his breath. For somehow he divined the kind of madness that underlay the other's stipulation. He required a balancing action, an alleviation, a sacrifice from someone else. Just how such things worked in the mind was not clear. But some kind of catharsis was achieved if a specific other person was hooked into the circuit.

Actually, it was an easy promise to make. For he had already considered the possibility that an attempted escape might be necessary for a last effort at survival.

He said, "All right, I will."

He broke off, savagely, "And now, if you two aren't out of here in twelve seconds—" He started to count. When he reached eight, the door was opened a crack. Momentarily, a man was outlined against it. Gregory stepped between the silhouetted figure and Ruxton. His arm reached up. He opened the door wider. With a quick movement, he shoved the other man through, followed him, and closed the door behind him. It was fast thinking on Gregory's part. In leaving, he had successfully concealed the identity of his companion.

"Except that he speaks Russian," thought Ruxton. It was his one clue, and it was a clue they didn't know he had. Vital clue. For it identified a fellow prisoner who had been prepared to murder him.

Ruxton turned on the light. He was breathing hard, and was furiously angry. But relieved that an actual struggle had been avoided. The light bulb, an ancient type, cast a yellowish glow over the ivory bed and ivory furniture, and the unevenly stained floor.

Ruxton walked to the door, and opened it. In an angry frustration, he examined the lock, and then stepped into the hallway. He realized that what irked him as much as anything was that the two guards outside had allowed someone to enter his room after midnight. As they paced toward him, he beckoned them to come over.

They had been eyeing him. Now, one unlimbered his rifle with a quick, practiced motion. He backed off, and from his vantage point covered the entire end of the hall. The other came forward. Ruxton pointed at his lock, and went through a pantomime which he hoped would convey that he wanted a key for it. The Chinese who had come over, fingered the lock with one hand. Then, glancing at Ruxton, he made a facial gesture of rejection, and shook his head vigorously. He shrugged, and rejoined his companion, who said, "What does he want?" "He wants a key for his lock." "What— with two sentinels walking up and down outside his room." "Perhaps, he didn't like the visitors who entered his room," the other replied. "I'll bet he wouldn't have objected if they had been women."

Both men laughed. Then one said, "Perhaps we shouldn't allow anyone into another person's room after they go to bed." The second man shook his head. "Our orders are to permit free communication among the prisoners." The first man nodded, "You are right." Neither seemed to realize the inconsistency of their attitude. That, under the circumstances, their presence was no help.

Fuming, Ruxton re-entered his room. He pulled the bed over until it was braced against the door, sideways. Then he climbed into bed, and turned out the light. Whoever tried to open the door would have to push the bed with it. What was unsatisfactory about the method was that his sleep could be deep enough that he might not awaken. A bold intruder would take that chance.

Nevertheless, he slept.

19

When breakfast was over, no one stood up. Ruxton glanced surreptitiously around the room. There was a visible expectancy on the faces of the prisoners. He thought, "The word has been passed. They're waiting for Gregory to act." Did the Chinese know? His gaze shifted to the head of the table. Three of Mai's aides, including the senior interpreter, were leaning toward each other, whispering. But their manner reflected an attitude of puzzlement rather than knowledge.

Ruxton swung his gaze to Captain Gregory. The man was very pale. He seemed thinner, as if somehow his whole body had contracted, as if every muscle had tightened a little and drawn him into a smaller space. The overall effect was of gauntness, so that his uniform seemed too small for him.

Gregory raised his head, and his gaze met Ruxton's. His eyes swerved away quickly, but not before they had flashed an unintended message that this man was sick to the bottom of his being with what he was about to do . . . if he could bring himself to do it at all.

Ruxton was alarmed. He jumped up and walked hurriedly over to the Captain. "I want to talk to you," he said. "Outside."

An expression of relief passed across that strained face. It was as if he had needed some life energy other than his own to move him out of his state of shock. He walked with Ruxton to the portieres, and across the lobby, and outside. It was a clear, sunny day, but a strong wind was blowing. The cold impact of the rushing air seemed to brace Gregory. "I'm all right now," he said.

He started to walk along the road, bending a little into the wind. As he did so, Mrs. Mai emerged from the gate of the Mai residence, and stopped as she saw who was coming toward her. Gregory looked straight ahead, as if he did not see her, and walked through the gate and out of Ruxton's line of vision. The woman continued to stand, obviously watching to see where Gregory went.

Finally, she allowed the gate to close, and came along to where Ruxton was standing. Ruxton said, "Did he go into the book room?"

She had paused, before he spoke. Now she stood looking at him thoughtfully. "What did you do?" she asked.

It was not a direct answer to his question, but it said the same thing. Ruxton sighed with relief. Aloud, he said, "I guess I must have persuaded him that he was not truly a prisoner of war—the position he was trying to maintain." He had decided on that explanation, and it seemed the best one even now that he had spoken it aloud. "After all, no one wants to die for no reason."

She nodded, and said, "I'll tell my husband."

She hesitated. Suddenly she looked straight into his eyes. "That matter we discussed yesterday," she said, "It's all right."

The excitement that swept Ruxton made it difficult for him to say anything. But he managed a husky, "Thank you."

"By the way," she added casually, "my housekeeper may be getting married. I was talking about it to her yesterday."

He saw that she was watching him closely. But Ruxton

112

was an old hand at showing false emotion. He said now, with a casualness that matched her own, "A woman should be married. It gives her a sense of security." He paused, then in a puzzled tone, asked, "Who will she marry? I haven't seen any Japanese men around."

Mrs. Mai smiled, and shook her head tolerantly. "Perhaps there will come a time when Japanese women can choose their husbands. But that time has not yet truly come in Japan, so why should she have the privilege here? One of my husband's aides is very attracted to her, so I think that my husband and I will be matchmakers for her."

Ruxton said curiously, "I thought Chinese women were emancipated by Communism, and that hundreds of thousands have been given divorces from husbands they were forced to marry under the old ways."

"Yes, that's true. The Marriage Act of 1950 affirms the equality of the sexes, abolishes child marriages, forbids the adoption of child daughters-in-law, outlaws infanticide, prohibits concubinage, authorizes the remarriage of widows, and accords the right to seek divorce to the woman and the man alike."

"But you're going to force marriage on a Japanese woman."

She was calm. "This may seem bizarre to you. But I understand it fully."

Ruxton understood it also. For the feeling that underlay it explained why she had a Japanese woman as her servant. There had probably been other occasions in history that equalled the degradation visited on Chinese women in cities and towns captured by the Japanese armies from 1937 on. But none, surely, could have surpassed the suffering and outrage. Entire sections of cities were blocked off by top-level command, and all the women in those areas declared prostitutes, and by military law subject to rape by any Japanese soldier.

Nonetheless, it was a bad thought on Phenix' part, to tolerate vicious acts against women of Japan or any country.

Aloud, Ruxton said, "You think it's the women who should be punished for what the armies of their country did?"

She was silent. She gave him a long, thoughtful look, and said finally, "You're a very clever man, Mr. Ruxton." She stepped close to him, and added in a low voice, "But don't, please, think for one moment that you are going to be having two women while you are here."

She moved toward the door. "I plan to be back and

113

forth, today, between the house and the hotel, at irregular intervals, so we may be seeing each other again." She smiled, opened the door, and went inside without a backward glance.

Ruxton followed her inside. He had no intention of going to the library on Gregory's first day there. He was thinking, "Really, the important thing is, no one is going to be killed. And she's promised herself to me. That's enough for one day."

He couldn't even imagine that anything further might still happen.

20

"What can anyone say of a nation that fought for four years in the Pacific, and then stood by while Russia, which fought six days, stole eighty per cent of the rewards of the victor?"

The words were a translation of a comment made by Rudolph Spie.

It was afternoon, and all the prisoners, except Gregory, sat or stood in the lobby. There were no Chinese about, and everybody seemed to be in a profound state of relief. It seemed to Ruxton that during his entire three months in this prison, he had never heard so many people talking at once or speaking so frankly. Perhaps, it was a dangerous situation, perhaps what was now said would later be remembered against the individual. But each man's truth seemed to be spilling out in a slightly exaggerated manner. The voices were high, the laughter lasted too long. Ruxton stayed, first of all because he felt the same need for companionship, and secondly he wanted to discover which prisoners spoke Russian.

After Spie's words were translated by various persons, most of the men present glanced at Ruxton. Lemoine broke the brief silence, and said, "He thinks perhaps you should defend your United States."

Ruxton shook his head. The state of the world reflected on American diplomacy, and not on the American people. He had done his part, risked his life almost every day for three years. When Russia grabbed eastern Europe and Asia, he had felt a sense of helpless frustration. Many times he had pictured himself lying in a grave, along with all those other "poor fools"—for what? So that the world, instead of being taken over by the murderer, Hitler, was handed without a single fight anywhere to the murderer, Stalin. Yet he knew that honest men had tried their best. It was hard to know what should have been done.

De la Santa said, "The Americans acted in good faith. Russia didn't. It was a try to bring those barbarians into the group of nations that lived up to their contracts. It failed. Now we know."

It seemed to Ruxton that what had been most lacking in the United States was guidance. A single statement, repeated often enough, could have steadied men's minds and clarified the confusion of both war-time and war's aftermath. Ruxton mentally wrote the statement as it might have been: "Fellow citizens, a global war is raging, started by an aggressive and dangerous foe. Your government, in fighting so vast a war, is mindful of the possibility that every ally adding its forces to the field of battle will save American lives, and shorten the struggle. Accordingly, it has entered into wartime alliance with various nations which operate under economic and political philosophies which are often alien to the free American way. Be courteous to the nationals of such countries. Treat them with respect, and facilitate their legitimate aims in the pursuit of the war against the common enemy. Do not, however, engage in unseemly discussions about the relative merits of different systems of economics or government, and do not join so-called friendship leagues the existence of which is rendered wholly unnecessary since the legal friendship of the American Government is a sufficient guarantee that the interests of our allies are being faithfully attended to. It may even be that after the war serious and determined actions will be necessary to enforce agreements now being arrived at. Your task should simply be to speed the war effort of the United States and its allies. The watchword is courtesy, respect, and facilitation to our friends, and loyalty to your own country. Nothing more and nothing less is warranted during a period of world-wide danger."

De la Santa was continuing, "In my own country, we speak with caution of political matters, but the fact is that Franco has been very astute. He is the only surviving Fascist in the world today, quite an achievement in view of the total defeat of the fascist powers in World War II. If the Communists anywhere can successfully attach the word, fascist, to an individual or a country, it was a short time ago tantamount to a death sentence, and even today the person will find a thousand doors closing to him. The same crimes as were committed by the fascists, when done by the communists are justified as having been carried out in the name of the 'people,' and for some reason this explanation is not wholly rejected. It would seem to me that those who are taken in by such propaganda are partly to blame for the crimes."

Several men spoke at this time, and there was an argument among them further down the line of interpretation, before they finally seemed to agree. However, the viewpoint that was accepted seemed to be that of the Swede:

"We agreed that fascism as an aggressive force ended with Hitler and Mussolini. If you hear the word fascist applied to someone today, you can be almost certain that you are listening to a communist or communist sympathizer. We agreed that a person who believes in the ballot system where more than one group may contend for the vote is not a fascist. This is the only word that is now used exclusively by Reds, although some of our friends here suggested that if someone uses the words, 'Imperialist' or 'Capitalist,' they must be Communistic. I argued against that, and they quickly agreed that most of the natives of Africa, and the Arabs, and the colored peoples in some other areas are entitled to use the word 'Imperialist' with fervor and indignation, and they don't have to be Reds to feel that way.

"Franco's Spain remains the only fascistic group in the world today, but his regime is not externally aggressive, and he was never anti-Semitic. It is a mistake to consider that a dictatorship is *per se* fascistic, since the Communist regime could then be called fascist. In my opinion this is particularly true of the Chinese, for if ever a country has had one fascist government after another, it's China. We can guess that the Chinese are one of the most hostile and violent people on this planet, fascist to the core, if two thousand years of absolute government is any criterion. Chiang Kai-shek's democratic attempt made only the slightest dent, and those who were influenced toward international good will and democratic feelings were all murdered. However, most of the absolute governments in the world today are developments of primitive rule by one man—a chieftain, witch doctor, or a conqueror. Fascism was an idea and a system."

Ruxton thought, "God only knows what the system was, or if the idea was anything more than one man's egotistic cosmology." But he did not say this thought out loud.

The White Russian, Kuznetoff spoke up at this point, in

French, and gave several illustrations of the disastrous consequences to the West of the destruction by Stalin of the White Russian groups in Europe and Asia. At the end of the war on the German eastern front, the White Russian divisions were compelled to surrender to the Soviets and thus the European White Russian anti-Communist forces were liquidated.

Kuznetoff continued, "The finale of this unhappy story of the White Russians took place here. At the time of the Communist take-over in 1949, there were about 125,000 White Russians in China. These were the original refugees from the revolutionary days, and their descendants. They were offered Soviet citizenship for fifty cents each. Many of them, tired of their long exile, and seeing no alternative, accepted Soviet citizenship, but in great fear. The few who didn't accept were mostly old people. Myself? I had a bitter memory of what I had been told of how my mother was one of the ten thousand officers' wives turned over to the Soviet People's Army to be used as a prostitute. My father and two older brothers, age 8 and 10, were shot. I was visiting an aunt, and she spirited me out of the country. When the Russian offer was made, I was one of the few young people who did not apply for Soviet citizenship. For years, I was left alone. Then, a few months ago, I was arrested, and sent here. So they didn't forget me."

Ruxton thought, "This man can kill. Therefore, since he obviously speaks Russian, he's the one who was most likely with Gregory last night." His own view was that the Russian people, although they had foolishly allowed themselves to be trapped by another crew of despots, were well rid of the old nobility. However, on a purely personal basis, Kuznetoff had ample justification for strong emotion against anyone who was playing the Communist game. But his was surely the one cause in all the world that was as lost as any cause could ever be. With the total capture of the White Russians in Europe and Asia, the Russian Communists had achieved a goal that must have given them many an uneasy hour until it was accomplished.

Ruxton sat down on one step of the stairway, and was lost for a while in contemplating the human tangle. He had his first sense that what had already happened was overwhelming. All by himself, the bear had proved to be a powerful and dangerous opponent. In twenty years, the dragon would be spitting fire beside the bear. Suddenly, Project "Future Victory" seemed a very real experiment. He guessed that its techniques would be applied in due course to hundreds of millions of capitalist "dupes".

He felt a profound inner trembling. Fear? But not for himself. He foresaw the end of democratic freedom on earth. Neither in Russia nor in China had anyone ever experienced what it was like to have individual freedom. So they would never even know what they were destroying. He visualized men and women forever attending group meetings that lasted far into each night, and ended with everyone professing correct principles. Who would dare to have an incorrect thought? For a thousand years there would be respect for Chairman Somebody, correct concepts, correct questions, sacrifice . . . "Oh, God!" thought Ruxton—and forcefully pushed the thought out of his mind.

His glance went to a window across the lobby, and he saw it was becoming dark outside. The bitter winter night was settling down over the vast wilderness of northern China.

Footsteps sounded on the stairway behind him, and drew his attention. He turned. Mrs. Mai was there. She paused several steps above Ruxton, and he came to his feet courteously. She waited, as the men in the lobby grew aware of her, then she smiled, and said in English, "My husband and I have been listening in to this mad conversation. For a time he enjoyed it. But a few moments ago he stood up and walked along the hallway. He seemed unhappy. I suggest you all go to your rooms and get ready for dinner."

She leaned over the banister, and reached behind the lobby desk. When she straightened she had a microphone in her hand. She smiled and came the rest of the way down the steps. At the bottom, she gave Ruxton a fleeting glance, walked across the room, opened the door and went out into the night. A cold wave of air billowed to Ruxton as the door closed behind her.

At that moment, new footsteps sounded. Mai Lin Yin, his face dark with rage, came down the steps, paused at the bottom, and yelled, "No one leave this room!"

His voice held the tone of mad anger, and the sound of it knotted Ruxton's stomach. He looked at that contorted countenance, and there was no question but that the man's wife had understated Mai's unhappiness. Her warning came too late. Her husband was not capable of listening to a spontaneous demonstration of tension release, could not understand or tolerate self-determined memory as distinct from the false facts the Communist indoctrination had tried to force upon them.

Belatedly, Ruxton thought, "We've got to get her back here."

As he had the thought, the outer door started to open. For an instant, Ruxton had the vivid hope that his intense feeling of need had been answered, that she was returning —and then the door swung all the way open and a dozen Chinese soldiers with rifles on the ready poured into the lobby.

Mai motioned them toward his left, and commanded in Chinese, "Over there."

A moment later, the soldiers were lined up, facing the prisoners.

21

Ruxton unfroze. He said, "Major Mai, this was release of tension. We have been under great stress."

Mai gestured at him, cutting him off. "You stay out of this, Mr. Ruxton. Your behavior in this matter was eminently correct."

Ruxton thought, dismayed, "Only because I didn't say aloud what I was thinking." It was fantastic bad judgment on the commandant's part, to judge by words alone.

The glaring eyes were now surveying the men, passing from face to face. Suddenly, Mai's arm went up. He pointed at Sugurd Lund, the Swede. "You," he said harshly, "when did you become a Fascist?"

Somebody translated that. The blond man was pale but composed. He said, "I have never been a Fascist. If anything, I have been a socialist, as are many Swedish people."

Mai yelled, "I heard you say that there are no fascists left in the world now that Hitler and Mussolini are dead. This is a cunning lie. The most Fascist country in the world is America. Admit it."

There was a pause when that command was translated. Lund bit his lip. He obviously realized that he was confronted by a man who was temporarily insane, and should be appeased. In the end, he stiffened, shook his head as if reaching a decision, and spoke in a firm tone. The translation was, "I don't believe that America is Fascist, and I have been surprised at the Communist statements to this effect, and wondered what was behind them."

When the translation was completed, Mai stood stock-still for an instant, and then said, "There is one type of person we will not tolerate in this group, and that is a fascist."

He turned to the soldiers, and commanded the officer in charge, a little wizened Chinese, "Take a squad, take that man out"—he pointed at Sugurd Lund—"and shoot him."

As the soldiers lunged forward and surrounded the Swede, Ruxton said, and his voice was high-pitched, "Major—this is an injustice. This man is not a fascist."

Mai turned to him, his teeth bared, "Mr. Ruxton," he said, "I'm restraining myself from even more punitive action. Another complaint from you and I will take a second person, whose words were very fascistic. Don't try me."

Ruxton kept quiet. He believed with a sick fear that Mai meant exactly what he said.

He stood, then, and watched as the Swede was shoved violently toward the door, a bayonet pushing against his back. And then, as Sugurd Lund realized his fate, he straightened, and head high, walked swiftly through the door without a backward glance.

There was a long pause. The silence was broken by rifle fire. Ruxton closed his eyes, and thought, "It can't be, my God, it can't be!"

But it was.

22

Ruxton opened his eyes, and came rapidly to an awareness of two realities. This was the first morning of the second three month period, and—

He was in a rage.

His body trembled with the force of that anger. He felt huge, as if his insides had swelled up during the night.

He thought of Sugurd Lund's execution, and the rage instantly grew in size. It reminded him . . . What that prison psychiatrist had said . . . If the hidden rage in him ever broke through, and he felt justified—murder!

He thought savagely, "I feel justified right now!"

Yet, as he had that thought, the anger began to subside. He felt it receding, and with it went the sense of being swollen. Even his ideas about the death of the Swede changed.

Sugurd Lund had been unlucky. The glance of a madman had fallen on him. It was like being struck by lightning in a summer storm, a natural phenomenon, in this instance as-

120

sociated with a disordered human mind. Impossible to say of Lund that he was killed because a Communist had found out that he was a former agent of Hitler; he wasn't. Nor could it even be said that he had been murdered because he had used the word, fascist. Several persons had used that word during the course of the discussion.

It was a killing without meaning. Therefore, one could not even be angry about it.

That was Ruxton's explanation for the abrupt subsidence of his rage, though, of course, he also felt helpless.

An hour later, as Ruxton came out of the breakfast room, he heard the sound of automobiles outside. He hesitated as he saw the other men heading for the door. The strong impulse came not to be curious. He was often contrary like that. But the clamor of motors increased. Even more cars must be arriving. Already, it was an event in their routine existence.

As he headed for the door, his need to resist overwhelmed, there came to Ruxton the sound of gay music. It was a familiar strain to him, one of the popular tunes associated with the Yang-ko, a peasant dance which the Communists had modernized and made into China's national dance.

Outside, he found a fantasy-like scene in progress. Buses, trucks, and limousines were parked in long lines next to the prison wall. On a truck opposite the hotel door, a six-piece orchestra was playing. And coming along the street were neatly costumed young men and women who had evidently tumbled out of their vehicles and into their act. They were doing the Yang-ko, and moved as in a parade, in organized groups progressing forward slowly but with the vivacity that was inherent in the dance form itself. Ruxton suppressed a strong impulse to sway with the music, and he thought, "My God, I didn't realize how much I miss the gay spots."

His memory of the theater in Hong Kong was so thoroughly associated with pleasure that the sight of these actors brought intense longing. And the fact was, since he had left America after his jail term, no woman had really ever crossed him, and so life was all pleasure.

As the forefront of the People's dancers reached the prison gate, it opened, and they danced inside. At that point, Ho Sin Go, the Chinese-English interpreter, paused beside Ruxton, and said, "I wonder if I might invite you to my wedding, Mr. Ruxton. It is to take place this afternoon, and we shall have entertainment from the players who will be giving performances here and in the main prison this entire week."

An uneasy premonition swept over Ruxton. "Your wedding?" he said. And swallowed hard.

"Madame Mai suggested that I ask some of the white prisoners to be present, and named you among them."

That was all Ruxton needed. *Madame Mai suggested . . .* This was Tosti's marriage. And Ho Sin Go was the aide who had been attracted by her. He smiled cynically at the tricky way that life sometimes had of confronting people with total irony. Somewhere along the line of his imprisonment, he had hoped to make use of Ho Sin Go . . . And now this.

Physically, then, he stood beside Ho and watched the parade. But mentally and emotionally he was remembering other mistresses of his who had married. He thought, with sudden violence, "To hell with them all!" And then he realized that somehow he believed all these women should hold themselves at his disposal, without regard for their own welfare. The fact that he was dallying elsewhere must make no difference. Each woman must be completely faithful and wait for him with an inhuman serenity.

It was such an incredible expectation that, in the light of his new understanding of himself, standing there, he let Tosti go. His three months of feverishly intense need of her, and the almost daily satisfaction she gave him, seemed to recede in time. "After all," he thought, "Tosti will probably be better off married."

Ruxton said now, in a steady voice, without looking directly at the other man, "I'll come to your wedding, Ho." He stood there, wondering if he could really make love to Madame Mai after what she had done. Then he smiled ruefully. In a few days the pressure of physical desire would become so strong in him that even the wife of the chief interpreter, Fa 'tze Jui-fang, would look good to him. He had always given sex first place. And so he had made love to scores of the best looking women in the world. But also, without a qualm, he had taken some awfully plain females to bed. Under pressure, he drew no lines of color, race, age or appearance. Was she a woman? Was she capable of sexual response? But he preferred beautiful women.

At lunch, he noticed that Ho Sin Go was missing from the head table. Ruxton nibbled at his food absently. He had no sense of having any thoughts. Yet he was disturbed. Once, he visualized his beautiful Tosti in bed with the plump young Chinese. And it wasn't so much that any emotion came as that the picture faded in a flash.

Then he grew aware of a peculiar, burning rage. It brought no thoughts or memories at first. Yet his face grew hot and he realized that he had a strong impulse to commit murder. The impulse was tinged with caution and anxiety. And then out of his subconscious surged the thought: "After all the ways I've opposed Mai, I can't be the person who is openly against this marriage." An instant later, he realized that he was really holding back from action because it might jeopardize his relationship with Madame Mai.

Ruxton grimaced, and put his hands up to his feverish cheeks. He thought, with an attempt to be amused and cynical, "And I believed this didn't matter to me."

He lurched to his feet, walked out of the room, and through the door to the freezing outside. He was standing gulping the icy air into his lungs and feeling the relief of a chill breeze on his cheeks, when the door behind him opened. Father de Melanier stepped out, and closed the door behind him.

"I saw you leave, Mr. Ruxton," the priest said. "You looked ill."

Ruxton turned slowly. He was thinking, "Do I dare?" And realized that he not only dared but had it all figured out. Hurriedly, he explained that he had learned about Tosti, and that the marriage was a forced one, but that he himself could do nothing. He finished, "At first I just shrugged it off. But then it began to bother me. Perhaps something should be done by someone."

When Ruxton concluded, the priest stared off down the street, and there was a look of grief on his face. After a long moment, Father de Melanier nodded. "Leave it to me, Mr. Ruxton," he said quietly. "I shall find an opportunity to talk to this girl. I speak Chinese, and so does she. I shall ask her straightforwardly. If, as you say, she is unwilling, I shall prepare and pass around a petition."

At that moment, when it was already too late, Ruxton had his first conscious misgiving. He had no business bringing so vulnerable a person as a Catholic priest into a problem that Tosti and he had created.

"Since there is no time to waste," Father de Melanier continued firmly, "I shall go right now." He started along the street toward the Mai residence, then paused and turned, "Since you feel you cannot be involved, refuse to sign the petition," he commanded.

Ruxton nodded, not trusting himself to speak. He stood watching the priest walk off with purposeful strides. Then he re-entered the lobby, and went upstairs to his room. A few moments later he was lying down. The bed creaked steadily no matter how quiet he tried to be. And that brought an awareness that he was trembling in every muscle.

How long he lay there he had no idea. But after a time it occurred to him that Father de Melanier must have finished circulating the petition. He got up and went down the flight of steps to the second floor.

Whatever impulse had moved him, his timing was almost too perfect. For as he paused, and glanced toward where the Mais usually sat—there they were. And there was Father de Melanier.

Madame Mai held a sheet of paper in her hand. And her face was as dark as thunder. She said something in Chinese sharply, to her husband. Major Mai stood up quickly, walked over, took the paper and studied it. At that point, Madame Mai saw Ruxton. The dark color drained from her cheeks.

She yelled at him, "Mr. Ruxton, come here!"

Ruxton walked over, unhappy now. He was dismayed at the co-incidence of his appearance at apparently the exact moment the petition was being presented. Yet he knew that he had waited as long as he could. As he came up, Mrs. Mai reached over, tugged the paper from her husband's fingers, and held it out to Ruxton. "Sign this!" she ordered in a voice that was harsh and unnatural.

Ruxton took the paper, saw that the petition itself was in Chinese, and shook his head. "What is it?" he asked.

That seemed to give her pause. She sent him a sharp look, and then said to Father de Melanier, "Did you not ask Mr. Ruxton to sign?"

The priest said, "I could not find him. And since there was not time to waste, I came with what I have here."

Ruxton glanced down to see who had signed. The signatures were, in order, Father de Melanier, Captain Edward Gregory, U.S.A.F., Anton Kuznetoff, Antonio Diogo, and finally, of all people, Lemoine . . . There they were, the brave men of the group of twenty-two.

He had a second thought about Lemoine. If the young Frenchman was an *agent provocateur,* he could gain prestige with the white men by signing, and of course the Mais would understand.

Father de Melanier was speaking again, in Chinese, "I took the liberty of showing Ho Sin Go this petition. I admonished him severely, and told him what I planned to do. He seemed very put out, and—I gathered—was not aware that his attentions were not welcome. Have these two young people not met at all?"

Mai was looking at his wife, with a frown. Abruptly, he spoke to her in the rude, North Country Chinese, a language not understood in most areas of China. But it was Ruxton's second Chinese language, learned from one of his mistresses. Mai said, "Lover, have you gone mad? Are you trying to force a marriage? And why require Mr. Ruxton's signature?"

The woman seemed to come back from some vast distance of the mind. She swallowed, and said in the same North Country tongue, impatiently, "I wish you would leave this matter to me. Tosti should have a husband. Ho Sin Go desires her. After all, I married you without ever talking to you first. And it turned out well. Don't you agree?"

Mai asked, puzzled, "But why have Mr. Ruxton sign the petition?"

Madame Mai hesitated. Ruxton saw that she had regained control of herself. Her problem now was to recover from her indiscreet rage. He surmised that her anger had come from a belief that he was behind the petition. Now, she handed the paper to Mai, and said in an even voice, "Will you translate this to Mr. Ruxton? I should like to have his opinion."

Mai read, "We, the undersigned, out of motives of common humanity, having ascertained that the Japanese woman, known as Tosti, is being forced into a marriage she does not desire, protest such enforcement, and point out that the law of the Chinese People's Government of 1950 specifically forbids enforced marriages." Mai looked up. He still seemed uncertain. "Well, Mr. Ruxton, since my wife desires your opinion, will you give it? Do you support this petition?"

"In principle," Ruxton said, "I support it. But I would not have signed that petition had it been presented to me by Father de Melanier."

"Why not?"

"I am a prisoner who hopes to become a guest. This is a great enough task for one who starts at such a low point as I do."

Mai turned toward his wife. She shook her head ever so slightly, angrily. He hesitated, and then spoke to her again in the North Country language. "Lover, you must give me some reason for this marriage."

Her face was a study, but she was clearly thinking fast. She said, "Tosti, being Japanese, will not herself take the step to marry a Chinese. I realized that recently when I was talking to her, and I determined to break through this barrier for her. Who better for her to marry than a young man who admires her?"

After she had spoken, Mai's face visibly hardened. He turned to Father de Melanier, and said grimly, "The People's Government of China is a democratic-dictatorship. It treats with democratic forbearance only those individuals who support it. It acts with dictatorial harshness toward all its opponents. Since you are one of its opponents, you have no right to circulate petitions against even the smallest action of a government supporter."

The priest protested, "Surely I have the right to point out that the laws of the People's Government were designed and advocated to protect this young woman from the very kind of enforced marriage which Tosti is being compelled to undertake."

Mai said flatly, "As an enemy of the people, you have no rights whatsoever."

"I deny that I am an enemy of the Chinese people," said Father de Melanier boldly. "I call to your attention that the People's Government on coming into power, specifically ordered all its agencies to respect the rights of the Christian and other churches. Therefore, my protest is being made by a legally competent person."

Mai said coldly, "The People's Government recognizes only loyal followers and not spies of foreign groups. As an agent of the Vatican, you are serving a foreign power. My guess is, if we interrogated you closely, we would discover that you have for years reported Chinese affairs to your superiors in Rome. Do not try our benevolence too far."

The stubborn rage of the man, when crossed, was beginning to show. The argument had accordingly become dangerous. Ruxton hesitated, recognizing his responsibility, then said to the priest in French, "Pursue this matter no further. You have done as much as can be done for this girl."

"What is he saying?" Mai asked sharply.

Father de Melanier translated Ruxton's words. Mai turned toward Ruxton. "Why do you give him this advice?"

Ruxton said unhappily, "I can see that you are becoming angry."

Mai scowled, then relaxed with a curt laugh. To Ruxton, he said, "The marriage will take place as arranged."

Madame Mai was calm in her victory. She said to Ruxton, "Thank you for not signing the petition." She glanced at her wrist watch. "It is now twenty minutes to three. Why don't you go down and wait for the—" She smiled sweetly—"the festivities to begin?"

23

The marriage ceremony itself was simple. A book was brought out by Mai Lin Yin. He explained that it was the official record book for all persons at the prison, both prisoners and staff. All records were kept in triplicate, one copy of which was retained at the prison, the remaining two copies being sent, one to the provincial capitol, the other to Peking.

The bridegroom signed first. And then Tosti took the pen and stood with it in her hand. She was dressed in a long silk gown, and she looked as beautiful as a picture postcard. Ruxton, feeling stiff but resigned, presumed that Madame Mai had supervised the bride's preparations. Tosti did not look around, simply stood there for what seemed many seconds. Then, she bent and signed.

The orchestra began to play, and a group of dancers both men and women whirled into the initial steps of a country dance associated with weddings. Ruxton grew aware that Mrs. Mai had come over beside him. He said to her: "You really must have given her a talking to."

Madame Mai nodded. "Would you like to know what I told her?" she asked calmly.

Ruxton hesitated. This woman was disconcertingly direct. "I'm not sure," he said finally.

"I think you should know," was the reply, "just so there is no misunderstanding between us. I told her," said Madame Mai firmly, "that if she didn't sign you would be seriously affected."

Ruxton said, unhappily, "Your ruthlessness dismays me. You're not ashamed of coercing this poor woman?"

He had half turned, and her dark eyes gazed straight into his gray ones. She said, "Now let's not fool each other. You and I know very well that you have been having her.

But I have made my peace with that, and I shall forget the past. One must tolerate the restless emotions of the men of this world, and seek only to guide them, not to stop them." She broke off. "Now, listen carefully. I do not plan to attend the theater tonight, but my husband will be there." She was suddenly a little breathless. "He has one sin. He does not like the Yang-ko theater, but he loves the classical theater with a deep passion. The players will give a classical play in the prison auditorium. Since he knows that I dislike it, he is resigned to going alone, and therefore you come to me in the basement a few minutes after seven."

Ruxton didn't reply.

After a long moment, the woman said uncertainly, "What's the matter?"

That broke the thrall. "Of course, I'll be there," he said.

"Good. I'll see you then." She walked off quickly.

Watching her go, Ruxton breathed easier. Incredibly, his attention had been caught by the possibility of viewing a Chinese classical play in preference to making love.

Along with other expert devotees, Ruxton considered the Chinese classical theater the greatest art form that had ever been created. There was one difficulty. Each individual member of the audience must be educated in appreciation of the form. Such education was prolonged, and in practice was given only to the children of the well-to-do. In the time of the Kuomintang, appreciation had also been taught other groups in the nation. But it remained essentially a mandarin art form. In Hong Kong, his White Russian sweetheart, Antonina, had patiently taught Ruxton to understand the significance of each move, gesture and position, and the meaning of the colorful costumes and masks. Gradually, he had come to realize that he was witnessing art on the highest imaginable level. There came a day when he could tell the difference in performance skills that distinguished a great actor from one who was merely technically perfect. They were all technically perfect, since, as with ballet stars, training began in early childhood, and continued throughout the life of the actor.

Ruxton grew aware that he was perspiring. He remembered how, during the war, he had always been in a sweat before, or during, attacks. The other pilots said it was the heat. But he had always maintained that it was fear. He supposed he was afraid now. And with cause. Tonight, and henceforth, he would be engaged in an affair with the commandant's wife. If Mai ever found out, he, as the offending

lover, would be given one of those slow, Chinese deaths. . . .
An affair that had such a prospect was irrational.

He had been glancing at Tosti at irregular but frequent
intervals, where she stood beside her husband, and now he
did so again. This time he caught her eye. The gloomy expression faded from her face. She gave him a look that said,
"Come over!" and then glanced away. As Ruxton came
near her, one of the women dancers grabbed the sad-faced
Ho Sin Go, and whirled off with him. A male dancer tried
to snatch Tosti. She evaded him, and he danced off, laugh-
ing.

For a minute, they were alone. And the music sheltered
their conversation. Ruxton said in Japanese, quickly, "I sent
the priest. He got up a petition. It didn't work."

Tosti nodded. Her brown eyes were dark and melancholy,
but her mood did not affect her appearance. He had never
seen her look better. "That woman really hounded me,"
she said. "If I didn't know how impossible it is, I'd be inclined to think she was jealous. I finally gave in, because it
was the wiser thing to do, all things considered."

It was an astonishingly mature evaluation, and it startled
Ruxton.

Tosti was speaking again, "I have told this husband of
mine," she said, "that there will be no sex relationship. So
you come to see me as soon as it seems safe, will you?" -

Ruxton nodded, not daring to speak. This was a new Tosti,
a woman to respect, and he'd have to try to figure out why
he had ever down-rated her. Of course, they had always,
when together, been aware of the importance of silence, and
there had been only a small quota of that conversation
upon which a woman, sooner or later, insisted. Her past history, as she had told it to him, seemed unreal in the face of
the calm assurance she was now displaying.

He recovered from his surprise, and said quickly, "I'll try
to make it tomorrow."

She inclined her head. "I've missed you," she said in a
low voice.

And that was all they had time to say. For the dancing
girl, who had snatched Ho Sin Go, whirled him back, and
he teetered breathlessly up to them, giggling from excitement. Ruxton reached over, patted the young man's arm, then
turned away and headed for the stairs. As soon as he was
out of sight, he went up the steps three at a time. He entered his room, cheerful, excited, and consciously reluctant
to realize that where women were concerned, he was as

big a phony as ever. He thought wryly, "All that stuff about the classical theater and what a great art form it is, is true. And that business of being afraid of what Mai will do—it's all real on some level." But it was the threatened loss of Tosti that had brought him emotionally low. And now, because he had her back, he was normal again. He remembered his rage at lunch time, the awful, murderous rage; and he thought soberly, "It's all still there. Being aware of the pattern hasn't helped me to change the feeling."

He felt himself to be in grave danger. But the high, cheerful state continued. Tonight, Phenix. Tomorrow, Tosti. Could he keep them both? Would there be trouble? Somehow, all that seemed unimportant, well within his capabilities. He would handle the difficulties when he came to them.

24

Phenix said, "I don't know why you excite me. But you do, tremendously. I suspected that such feelings were possible, because I tried to have them several times for my husband. But I simply couldn't sustain the feeling."

Ruxton made a suitable answer.

They were lying in the darkness on a blanket that she had thrown over the pile of mattresses. The woman whispered, "I'm sure it must be love. I feel so different."

Ruxton answered that with a tender remark. She snuggled up to him, and said, "Do you think you could learn to love me?"

Ruxton told her what she wanted to hear.

She said softly, "When you first spoke to me—remember that first day?"

"I remember."

"Remember how reserved I was?"

"Yes."

"But I was actually thrilled inside. This may seem strange, but my husband is such a forbidding personality that—till that moment—no other man had ever dared to show awareness of me as a woman."

Ruxton expressed appropriate surprise.

She went on, eagerly, "Naturally, it was too new a concept for me. But I wanted to show you some response. So I wrote that little note."

Ruxton expressed gratitude.

"It was a good thing I did," she said. "Because when I

talked to my husband I discovered he had formed a strong dislike of you. If I hadn't written that note, you wouldn't have called on me during the trial—isn't that true?"

Ruxton said truthfully that it was true. He guessed that she was trying to bind him to her.

She went on, "That first night, after the trial, he wanted us to make love. But I wouldn't do it. I felt as if that night I belonged only to you."

Ruxton stirred uneasily.

Phenix said, "Do you remember how startled I was when my husband called me in to your trial?"

Ruxton remembered. But he was thinking, too, "She's using up our entire store of intimacies and contacts this very first time." It bothered him, and he could only hope that she would not tire of those tiny details, and could repeat them again and again.

They separated about nine-thirty. She took her blanket, and went upstairs. When the inside basement door had closed, and not until then, Ruxton made his way outside. He had reasoned that if by any chance he were caught coming out of the house, a quick search of the basement would not find her there. It seemed fitting that the man should take the greater risk in so dangerous an affair.

He reached the gate safely. Once outside on the street, he walked swiftly to the hotel, and so to his room, and bed. He awakened shortly after dawn, and for the first time, then, in many hours, remembered Tosti. Instantly, he felt jealousy.

Ruxton lay there and seriously considered what he would do if Ho had gone out of his mild character, and enforced a relationship on his desirable wife. He had a series of murder fantasies, in each one of which he either stabbed, strangled, or beat Tosti's husband to death. He recognized after a moment that it was a vast development in him that he could be so sharply aware of his urge to violence. Time was when such impulses had been completely hidden.

On his way to the book room later that morning, Ruxton met Madame Mai. The meeting was no accident, since he took a walk in the opposite direction when he first went outdoors, and then—when he saw her come out of the Mai gate—he turned hastily back. As he approached her, he saw that a change had come over the woman. A certain severity of countenance had been softened. It was a subtle transformation. He noticed, too, that she had made herself up with extreme care. That warmed him, for it was unquestionably in his honor. It told him how far she had moved toward him emotionally.

As she came opposite him, she stopped. Ruxton paused also. She said in a surprisingly shy voice, "Good morning, Mr. Ruxton."

Ruxton said, "Good morning, Madame Mai."

"I hope all went well with you last night," she said, and her color was high.

"It went delightfully well," said Ruxton.

"For me, too," she said in a low voice. Abruptly, she became more of her old assured self, for she added quickly, "Listen, tonight is the Yang-ko Theater, and I shall have to go. Will you come also?"

Ruxton asked, "What is playing?"

The Girl with the White Hair."

Ruxton laughed. "That one." He added tolerantly, "Well, I don't mind seeing that again." He had another thought. "You mean, they're going to play that for the prisoners in the big prison?"

"Yes."

"They must be from a different class than I was given to understand."

"They're mostly from the mandarin and official class," she said.

"That's what I thought. Do you actually hope to get these people to appreciate *The Girl with the White Hair?*"

She said soberly, "Mr. Ruxton, a sentence of death humbles even the greatest of men to the point where each is, perhaps for the first time, willing to listen to other points of view. Of course, there are some who cannot be reached. Their fate is inevitable."

Ruxton had a flashing picture of the inevitability of his own fate, and another picture of his dead body being tumbled into a hole in the ground. He shuddered, and said quickly, "When is the next classical play?"

"Tomorrow night."

"May I see you then?"

"Same time, same place," she said breathlessly. "Goodbye, Mr. Ruxton."

She walked on.

Arrived at the book room, Ruxton browsed among the translations of the works of Mao Tse-tung, the Chinese Red leader, but he read paragraphs and single sentences only.

At half past ten—which was early for him—he sauntered

outside. He paused briefly on the edge of the garden, as if admiring the clear, bright day. The air had warmed, and it felt decidedly refreshing to his hot blood. Although the way was open—not a soul in sight—he felt uncertain. He realized that he was contemplating the prospect of Phenix walking in upon Tosti and himself. It gave him an unpleasant feeling.

But this was not the moment to hesitate. He had promised Tosti.

He proceeded to the side entrance, entered and, standing in the hallway, closed the door behind him with a loud click.

A pause. Quick footsteps. Then Tosti hurried in from the room beyond.

She seemed changed, more distraught. She drew him into her room, closed the door, and began to talk. She said something about the outrage of having to spend a night in the same room with her husband. As a Japanese woman of good family—

It was not, then, that he ever actually tuned her out. But he recognized turmoil talk when he heard it. He felt sorry for her, for all this had happened because he had ignored good sense. But it was too late, and quite useless, to feel guilty. So, as he undressed, he heard the intense emotion rather than the words. The meaning seemed to be in the feeling, not in what she said. Or so it seemed to Ruxton. The flow of words suspended during the physical act of sex, and then began again, and accompanied him to the door. As she let him out, she stopped, made a staunch effort, wiped a tear from her cheek, and said unhappily, "I talk too much. But I don't see him again for a week. So don't worry. I shall remain firm. You are my lover. No one else."

Ruxton squeezed her arm, and went out, touched. As he walked along the frozen street, he thought earnestly, "What is there about me that I who deserve nothing get all this loyalty from women?" There was a mirror in the main lobby. Ignoring the men who greeted him as he walked across the floor, he paused in front of it, and studied himself.

It was a stern face that gazed back at him but a healthy one. He was leaner than he had been, and paler. Which last was good. He had had a tendency to have his father's red face. He continued to study himself, the line of his jaw, the shape of his cheek, and the slope of his forehead. It was a well-balanced head and face; handsome, but more than that, strong and determined. Perhaps he was the universal father-figure to women. Perhaps women did not dare oppose him, just as they had been instantly obedient to father when they were children. And, somehow, they expected the same protection from him that father had given, in return for total surrender to his control.

And still he felt absorbed in his study of himself. In his time he had had—he estimated—over a hundred women. For a man, that was an achievement. Of course, any woman who let down her barriers could get a hundred—or a thousand—men. But he had observed that most men had a hard time getting women. For eighty per cent of men, each worthwhile woman had to be earned, so difficult did she make the conquest. Yet the Seal Ruxtons of this world did not encounter such difficulties. There must be a Gestalt here somewhere, a composite effect of all his separate qualities. He stood there, observing some of those qualities. He saw that his eyes were as gray and as bright as steel. They were surprisingly sane eyes—surprising because it was scarcely sane of him to be making love to the commandant's wife. Still, there it was. The Chinese Reds had captured a man whom women trusted, and who had during his adult lifetime taken full advantage of that trust to gain sexual satisfaction from them. The fact that the women desired him, apparently even more than he desired them, was what remained puzzling.

He turned away, shaking his head—and saw that several men were watching him with interest. Lemoine walked over, grinning.

"Well," he asked, "do you?"

"Do I what?" Ruxton said.

He felt no anger, though he realized he was about to be ribbed.

"Do you look more like a communist?" asked Lemoine.

Ruxton turned back to the mirror, thoughtfully. Without looking around, he said, "I'm going to take that question seriously, and the answer is no."

"How can you tell?"

Ruxton hesitated. The question had excited him. He felt an impulse to say his true thoughts. He said, "I don't see the streak of yellow as being big enough."

Lemoine stepped up beside him, so that Ruxton could see his sallow face in the mirror. The Frenchman said earnestly "That isn't the way these things happen. If *you* change your ideas, then you'll be the same brave person, but with the new thought. As for me, I have been a wishy-washy sort of coward all my life. No matter what ideas I supported, *that* didn't change."

Ruxton laughed. In these indiscreet, feverish daring moments of his, he felt completely free physically, emotionally, and mentally, and laughter in the face of danger came as easily as any other emotion. He said aloud, speculatively, "I remember communists I met in Hong Kong, and on my two trips into China. I'm sure their brains did not particularly need to be washed, since they all had rice bowl brains, and all they needed to know was, who is putting the rice into their bowl.

"What is surprising is that under the bowl is the sharp mind of a Chinese, than which there is none sharper. Yet this highly intelligent race has proved a terrible thing, that an entire people can be caught in a mold of static ideas for thousands of years. The Chinese have neither national nor individual goals that fit with the basic needs of a human being. Not once in their history—till the West forced them—was there a meaningful revolution. When these poor, miserable creatures rebelled, it was always because someone had appealed to an unbelievable streak of superstition that somehow went along beside the more gracious ideas of the wise men. The Boxers were fanatics who believed that bullets couldn't kill them. The Tai-ping rebellion was possible only because of an equally insane idea." Ruxton paused, drew a deep breath, and felt momentarily appalled that he had been swept along on his own mad emotion. He finished, almost lamely, "All I'm trying to say is that the color of communism is red and not yellow, and that therefore the Chinese will never make it."

Captain Gregory, who had been shifting uneasily in his chair by the window, stood up. "If you'll examine the chromatic scale," he said unhappily, "you'll see that the two colors are closer together than might appear." He added gruffly, "Ruxton, I'm surprised to hear you uttering ideas like that. Don't you think I proved that free expression doesn't pay. It will spoil my lunch if Mai hears about this."

As quickly as it had come, Ruxton's reckless mood passed. He went upstairs, chiding himself. Hard to believe that he could still be seized by self-destructive impulses and be inexorably forced by an intense inner need to babble out his incorrect concepts. But it had happened, and he could only hope that his suspicion about Lemoine was not true. But why had he been so indiscreet? As he lay down to wait for lunch, he realized that he was disturbed about something. As he knit his brow, a mental image of Tosti floated through his mind. He found himself remembering her unhappy face, and listening to her trembling voice. Because feeling guilt would do no good, he was trying to push all thought of her out of his mind when . . . he remembered what she had said.

Remembered it all, what he had actually seemed to hear, and what he had tried not to hear.

Ruxton sat up, to the hideous background music of a hundred protesting springs. He scarcely noticed the sound. He was thinking: "What did she say? *What did she say?*" Entirely apart from other significant statements she had repeatedly called herself a woman of good family—which didn't fit with what she had told him previously.

Slowly, he lay back, and considered the incredible drama that had so abruptly revealed itself. Tosti was not who she had said. Not a Communist convert. Not a poor little warehouse clerk caught in the defeat of the Japanese armies.

And that line of thought led him directly to the only possible explanation for such a deception as she was practicing here at the very center of a major Chinese experiment in future conquest. The truth about her must be on the level of either-or logic. Either Tosti was a former warehouse clerk, as she had said. Or she wasn't. And if she wasn't, she was a spy.

There was no third alternative of what a Japanese woman might be in a place where thousands of men were under sentence of death.

He saw clearly that only the most deep-reaching event could have stirred her to such an unintentional self-revelation. But she wouldn't be the first spy to be caught off guard. And so she had hastily agreed to marry Ho Sin Go.

It struck him that by now Tosti must be realizing that she had said too much. Would she come out into the open with him?

Or would she simply hope that perhaps he had been intent on his lovemaking, and so not divined the truth?

Whichever way she chose, she would have to trust him—with her life.

25

At a quarter to seven that night, Ruxton and nine other white prisoners, accompanied by interpreters, were led through the main gate of the big prison, across a courtyard, and into a huge auditorium.

The great room was packed with Chinese men. As he and the others followed the guide down the steps, Ruxton thought, "Attendance is not compulsory with us, but it must be for them, or there wouldn't be so many." An instant later a stray phrase in Chinese came to him from somewhere nearby: "When Koh told me the auditorium was heated, I decided perhaps I could love even the Yang-ko theater." Ruxton grinned. So that was it.

He and his group were led to choice seats near the front of the theater. As soon as he was seated, Ruxton looked around curiously at what he imagined were the former bigwigs. These were the Chiang Kai-shek supporters who had been captured by the Reds, and sentenced to death under the two year plan. It was a strange assortment of Chinese: little, wizened men sitting beside chunky individuals, bearded and beardless men, men with strong faces and steady eyes, and shifty-eyed, anxious-looking men. Only the fat Chinese of the Buddha-image tradition seemed to be missing from the assemblage. All through the large hall, hundreds of pairs of spectacles reflected the yellow lights that hung down from the ceiling.

Throughout his survey of the room, he had been looking for Madame Mai. Now he saw her. She was to his right, together with several women of her husband's staff. As he watched her, she turned her head and their eyes met.

It must have been exactly seven o'clock, for even as they were still gazing at each other, the lights went out, and on stage began a music drama that was simple and appealing— if one accepted the reality of it, as it was presented.

The Chinese Communists had taken an old Chinese art form, and modernized it. The music-drama from ancient times had concerned itself with highly artificial situations. A common plot might be the love of an emperor for a favorite concubine. In the drama, these two, singing falsetto, would state their conditions, their frustrations, their hopes; and, as the story ran its course, they would describe the fate that was befalling them. Other actors contributed their information in the same falsetto singing style.

As the centuries passed, no one thought of changing this form until the Communists, many of them educated in Europe and America, converted it to their own propaganda. *The Girl with the White Hair* was such a propaganda music-drama.

The story was about a peasant girl who was sold by her family into the service of the local landlord. The son of the landlord got her with child. When the boy's mother discovered what had happened, she feared that the neighbors would severely punish her guilty son, and urged him to do away with the girl. Terrified, the young, expectant mother, fled to the hills. There, in a cave, she bore her baby, but the experience had turned her hair white.

She maintained herself and her child by taking food left at the temple by the devout. Although she came down from her cave only by night, she was occasionally seen. And so, the legend of the white haired girl began. When the Communists finally "liberated" the village, they investigated and found the girl.

And so the whole story came out.

Ruxton, who had seen the play in Hong Kong with Anna Chen, recalled her tear-drenched face, and he also recalled his own thoughts as he had watched it with her. It had occurred to him that this simple girl was not, in fact, one of Nature's noblewomen. She had probably felt pride when someone of the landlord class chose her for his mistress. Nature had provided women with a weak defense against what looked like security, and the fact that the security could be false made no difference. He suspected that the white haired girl had been trapped by this same illusion.

His attention drifted back to the play. The old lady of the house was part of the ancient Chinese family tradition. Herself a victim of a lifetime of beatings, she went insane somewhere in the process, and was compelled by her psychosis to urge violence, particularly on the women who came under her jurisdiction. For two thousand years, millions of these insane creatures kept order in Chinese households on behalf of the men. However, the implication of the play, that the Communists were the first to put an end to the reign of this she-tiger, and of the system she represented, was a brazen lie. Laws to deal with her were on the Kuomintang books very early, but it was not easy to break the grip of the centuries. In some cities, thousands of young women, from the 1920's on, observing that the incorrigible male was reluctant even under law to give up his prerogatives, exercised that portion of the law which gave them the right *not* to marry . . . and they did not marry. These young women demonstrated how intelligent the Chinese were when given the opportunity. Until the Kuomintang passed liberalizing laws, women had no rights. Even marriage was arranged for them, and refusal was not possible. But though the burden of the ages was lifting long before the Communists seized power, the revolution did not instantly change people's minds about family relations. Ruxton recalled reading a Communist report in late 1954, more than five years after the "liberation," to the effect that in one province alone that year, more than ten thousand husbands had murdered wives who had tried to exercise their legal rights. One could imagine that millions of women, sensing the latent violence in their men, dared not take advantage of the new marriage law. It came down again to the basic question of the age: Which was better? The gradual release that democracy and education brought about, with its almost infinite variations of treatment for individuals? Or the enforced liberation, with its bloody toll of murdered women?

The end of the tearful melodrama came with the execution of the villainous landlord and his son, and the dawning of the bright, new Communist future for everyone. A few lights went on. And there was polite applause from the audience. The performers came back on stage, and were given somewhat warmer and more prolonged applause. It was a fine point. But there was no doubt, the acting had been splendid. The audience made a distinction between the play itself and the performance of it.

The actors departed, and a man came out of the wings. For thirty minutes he harangued his captive audience on the lessons to be learned from the play. The main items were: Hate the old feudal system. Notice that landlords despoiled young women as callously as they enslaved peasantry. Therefore hate and destroy landlords. Hate "Imperialist America" —which, in some way not clearly stated, was to blame for the old feudalism as well as for all China's present difficulties.

He ended with the ringing question: "Is it not wonderful that, under Chairman Mao, the People's Government is setting right all the ills and evils of old China, and is it not a pleasure to contemplate that China and her big brother, the

Soviet Union, will eventually settle accounts with that despoiler of civilization, Imperialistic America!"

The speaker, who must have been a familiar figure to the Chinese audience, was politely applauded. And then, as the rest of the lights went on, everyone stood up. There was a general movement toward the rear doors. Ruxton rose with the rest of his group, and was astonished to find Madame Mai at his elbow. It must have taken exact timing on her part, because many people were now milling around in the area between where she had been and where she was now. Ten seconds delay, and it would have been impossible for her to get to him.

Ruxton greeted her politely, and asked, "What comes next on the Yang-ko theater?"

Her color was high, but she answered calmly enough, "Tomorrow afternoon, the Yang-ko theater will present *A Question of Thought*."

Ruxton said, wonderingly, "You're really giving us the simple stuff, aren't you?"

"That is an incorrect concept, Mr. Ruxton." She spoke in a severe tone. "You should know, for your own future welfare, that everyone should be able to appreciate the theater of the masses."

To Ruxton, the notion that a communist propaganda play, based on fixed Marxist ideas and a fixed plan, was the theater of the people, was a distortion. The Party-line ignored most of the feelings of the masses, schemed to overcome their resistance, used death and other penalties where persuasion failed, and had therefore little true relation to the "people".

Nonetheless, as he waited with his group till the Chinese prisoners had completed their exodus, he temporized. "Thank you for telling me the correct concept," he said.

"What is wrong with *A Question of Thought?*" she asked, after a pause.

It was a query for which there was no answer, unless one could first agree how logical the discussion would be. It might be far better if she had asked, what was wrong with lying? Among the fantasies which it represented as truth, *A Question of Thought* had a group of professors in an Illinois university being the principal plotters in a scheme for America to gain control of the Chinese people. Ruxton sighed, realized that no discussion was possible, and said, "Nothing. It's an excellent drama. But not sophisticated enough for this audience."

She looked up at him with a worried expression. "Don't be so clever, Mr. Ruxton," she said earnestly. "Become simple again. That is the secret of being a Communist. Forget a lifetime of cunning, and place yourself at the mercy of your fellow human beings. They will recognize this quality in you, and respond with equal simplicity. Awaken."

Ruxton was suddenly curious. "Is that what is meant by awakening?"

"Yes." She nodded vigorously. "You awaken to your past crimes, reform your old society ways, and become re-educated. Don't you agree that would be wise?"

On the level of survival, Ruxton couldn't agree more, and he said so, sincerely. Under his breath, he added, "But how do you do it? How do you become a simple-minded communist?"

That amused him, abruptly. Because, of course, individuals like Mai and his wife were actually highly sophisticated people, and not simple at all.

They were moving now, and, except for a mumbled good night in answer to her "Good night, gentlemen!" when they came to the hotel, that was his final conversation of the evening with her.

26

Tosti met him at the door. "I was a very noisy and foolish girl yesterday," she said. "You must forgive me."

Ruxton followed her into her room, tense. The fact that she had brought the matter up so quickly indicated that she was going to try to find out what he knew. He was still undecided as to whether he should admit his suspicions or not.

She turned to face him. "Talk, talk was all I did," she chided herself. "I will never let my husband affect me that strongly again."

Ruxton believed her. He said, reassuringly, "I could see you were upset, and it hurt me. But I'm the one person in this whole world that you can be emotional with, and say what you please. Isn't that true?"

"But what happens after you get brainwashed?" she asked anxiously. "Suppose you become a communist?"

He was about to answer that soothingly, when he realized that her question was not an answer to what he had said. He countered, "Did you lose control of your mind when you were brainwashed?"

"No-o!" Her eyes were wide and innocent. "But they didn't waste much effort on a little warehouse clerk. I learned what the correct concepts are, and I learned to discharge my duty to the people through the proper working conception. You'll get the full treatment."

Ruxton said matter-of-factly, "I simply won't regard my relationship with you as any of their business. Do all these communists live up to the old rule of sex once a week?"

Tosti showed her teeth in a smile. "It isn't really a rule, now that they're in power," she said, "but *she* lives up to it against *his* will." She added thoughtfully, "But then, of course, she is a very unusual woman."

She discarded her coolie clothes, and came down into his arms. "I believe that you will take care of me," she said softly. "You will protect me."

"You can count on it," said Ruxton.

But he was uneasy, wondering if in the final issue he would have control of his mind.

For Tosti, even a hint that she was not who she seemed would mean investigation . . . and death.

She was silent during the lovemaking, and for the first time in their relationship he had the feeling that she was merely a recipient of his passion. When it was done with, she said unhappily, "I wish I hadn't talked so much yesterday. I disgraced myself. I was so full of personal emotion."

Ruxton pulled away and saw that she was on the verge of tears. That decided him. He had to make a more direct approach. He bent to her ear and whispered, "Do you think this room is wired?"

Her brown eyes widened. Finally: "I have checked everything every day. There's never a moment when I am not aware of the possibility. But there's nothing."

Ruxton accepted that, and took the big step. "You did talk too much yesterday. I didn't think about it at once. But afterwards it struck me that you are not what you seem."

She shrank away from him. Now it was she who temporized. "And if I am not who I seem, who am I?"

He did not hesitate. "It could mean only one thing. Do you have any direct contact with your people?"

She pulled away from him, and lay on her back with her eyes closed. At last, she whispered, "It would have meant my carrying a radio receiver and sender with me. Impossible.

I am therefore here for the full two years, and there is nothing I can do short of getting to Wanchan. There I could contact someone."

Having spoken, she opened her eyes, and looked at him. She said quietly, "That's what you wanted to know, isn't it?"

It was a direct admission. And what was disturbing now was that time was passing, and he should be on his way. He whispered quickly, "There's nothing *I* want to know. Except I want *you* to know that it's all right. I'm on your side."

Tosti said earnestly, "The hope is that one day the Mais will take me with them on a trip, and then I can contact someone. But they left me here that time they went to Wanchan so that he could see the classical theater. Remember?"

As he was leaving, Tosti touched his arm, and whispered, "I shall never let my husband affect me again."

Ruxton kissed her lightly, and they separated. He returned to the book room, relieved that the truth was out in the open. Whatever happened could now be dealt with on a basis of full communication. He found himself wondering what the Japanese expected to learn, and suddenly it seemed to him that what she was doing must be a relatively minor detail of a larger espionage system. They probably had agents in the great prison itself. Within that frame, their willingness to have her be where she was without contact for two years began to seem reasonable. He felt even more relieved. Not having to report was good for Tosti. For surely the nightmare of the intelligence agent was the risk that must always be present when he went to make his reports. Or, if he had a radio outfit, that his signal would be heard by police or military forces the moment he started his broadcast. Tosti was spared all of that danger.

He was able at that point to concentrate on the book he had picked up. It was about life in the United States, and it was such an account as would have astounded any American citizen. On every page, in words and illustrations, the United States was depicted as crime-ridden and poverty-stricken. Uncle Sam was shown either holding a hangman's noose, or with blood-stained hands, or in the guise of a carnivorous animal, or in the shape of a viper. He was always shown as evil and villainous. The words accompanying the picture were virulent beyond belief, with never a let-up on the theme that here was the new Nazi-Fascist country. The accusation of Nazism was propounded in a dozen tricky

143

ways. Uncle Sam was shown wearing a coat, with which he was trying—and failing—to conceal the Nazi swastika on his vest. Under the folds of the Statue of Liberty's cloak was an ill-concealed swastika. And so on, *ad nauseam*.

It was provocation at its most extreme. Reading it, Ruxton's initial reaction was a strong feeling of the need for the U.S. to awaken, and counter-attack. But when he had read further, it struck him that that was exactly what the Communists wanted: to drag the other group down to fighting at their level.

He was still thinking about it as he walked back to the hotel later. And so intent on his speculation that Madame Mai was almost opposite him before he became aware of her.

"Do you know what I've been doing this morning?" she greeted him cheerfully.

Ruxton withdrew from his introspection. "You look ravishing," he said.

"Thank you. It's entirely for your benefit. You know that, don't you?"

"I was hoping so." He paused; then, "What have you been doing this morning?"

"Your court record arrived in the morning mail, and I read it. I was surprised at some of the things in it."

Ruxton was taken off guard. He had assumed that all the information they had on him had been on hand from the beginning. He did a hasty look back over his trial, striving to recollect what might be in the record that Mai could use against him. He could think of only one thing: the prosecution had included in its otherwise baseless charge, a truth: that he was a wealthy man.

Standing there, considering that that knowledge had not hitherto been available to Mai in detail, he turned pale.

Phenix was speaking again, "For some reason, which I cannot explain to myself, I never thought of you as a married man. But there, by your own admission, was the statement that you were divorced."

Just what he had expected her to say was not clear to Ruxton. And possibly the shock that he had already experienced gave a special impact to her words. Somewhere in the enormous spaces of his head, there was a noise like distant thunder, and a sensation as of layer upon layer of all-enveloping blackness closing over his brain. He said something to Phenix, and walked on toward the hotel. It came as a puzzling thing to him that he was able to stay erect. For he was having fantasies of staggering, falling on his knees, pitching over on his face, struggling to stand up, and reeling forward again.

He was dimly aware of climbing stairs. On the third floor, he came face to face with the two sentries. They stopped as they saw him, and he had the distinct impression that they were amazed by something in his manner and appearance.

His awareness of them stayed with him only a moment. The next instant the floor arched up and struck him a terrific blow.

27

Ruxton had been at his office when he received the message.

Rainey was in the hospital with a broken leg. Her car had gone over an embankment and down into some brush and trees. Apparently, her leg had broken when she was thrown from the car. And she had lain there for nearly three hours before patrol car officers spotted the car tracks and glimpsed the car below.

Ruxton rushed to the hospital. A police inspector was waiting for him. "She's under morphine," he said, "and sleeping. She'll be all right. But let's you and I have a little talk." The man sounded grave.

He led the way into a small office, and turned. "Might as well just say it," he said grimly. "A tramp came by as your wife was lying there, and raped her while she was only partially conscious. She remembered it, and reported it to the hospital authorities."

The man paused, as if expecting questions. Ruxton stood numb.

"We've picked up a young bum," the policeman went on, "and as soon as your wife is able we'll have her try to identify him. He fits her description, and there is evidence of recent sexual activity. But still, we need the identification."

Ruxton, who had been listening almost blankly, mumbled at that point, "My God, what kind of a monster would assault a woman with a broken leg?"

The inspector went away, and Ruxton sat at his wife's bedside, fighting an irrational feeling. He blamed her for what had happened. He sat there beside the drugged body of the white-faced girl, and he framed words that he would speak to her when she awakened. She must understand one thing: she was no longer worthy of as much love as he had given her since their marriage, and she would have to make up for being possessed by another man. It seemed to him that the fact that he occasionally had had other women since their marriage was now completely justified.

Shortly after nightfall, Rainey opened her eyes, and said thoughtfully, "It must mean something, Seal."

"Huh!" said Seal, his own train of thought broken.

"I mean, a thing like that couldn't just happen."

Then he got it. He had often noticed a metaphysical tinge to her thinking. She was trying to fit a car accident, a broken leg, and the criminal assault of a male human animal into her superstitious philosophy.

Ruxton exploded: "For heaven's sake, Rainey—"

She went on, as if she hadn't heard, whispering, "When I realized what he was going to do, I begged for mercy. But he was like a man with a mission. And, Seal—through all that haze of pain, I responded to him. I never realized that agony and ecstasy were the same, but they are. It has to mean something."

Ruxton felt himself shrinking. His own resentment of the past many hours was overwhelmed by her crazy statements. Rainey went to church every Sunday. But he had always been convinced that her religion was not really Christian. A more primitive cosmology moved in the deeps of her mind.

Before he could say anything, two nurses entered the room. "We'll be fixing her up," one said. "Why don't you go out and eat?"

When he came back, Rainey was asleep.

Ruxton returned in the morning to find her awake and cheerful. She was astonished when he tried to resume the conversation of the night before, and denied even having spoken to him. Ruxton had heard of such things, so he hastily dropped the subject. In his relief, he scarcely noticed that all thought of his own blaming of her was gone from his mind.

But the conversations he had with her during subsequent visits seemed superficial. She was evasive—"I'd rather forget the whole experience—" Loving—"You poor darling, without your true love all this time—" And moody—"When a horrible thing like that happens, it makes you wonder about the meaning of life." That was as close as she got to her original thought.

The day she graduated to a wheel chair, the police brought a chunky and sullen young man for her to look at.

Rainey stared at him, and began to breathe hard. Then she shook her head, and said huskily, "No, he's not the one. I never saw him before in my life."

It was difficult for Ruxton to decide who was the more surprised, the police inspector, or the shock-haired young man with the blotched face.

Rainey went on contritely, "You mean, he's been in jail all this time?" She addressed the man, "Where do you live? We'll send you some money."

For once the suspicious Ruxton was dull-witted, as the man eagerly gave the name of a cheap hotel near the railroad tracks. It was months before he realized that he had been present while a man and a woman established the preliminaries of a rendezvous. One day, after he was motivated to follow her, he opened the unlocked hotel room door. And there she was with the chunky man in a bed with mended sheets, and a grimy looking blanket.

Incredibly, she tried to defend her lover. Ruxton beat him without mercy, till his face was a bloody mass, and his eyes were puffed and several of his teeth lay on the floor. By the time the police arrived, he had fought Rainey off and had her half-dressed. It was agreed that she would go home. Ruxton and his victim were taken to the police station. No charges were filed. The chunky young man reluctantly said he would leave town, which he evidently did. For that was the last Ruxton saw of him.

Rainey went to a psychiatrist, a saintly looking old man to whom she made a total transference. For weeks, she talked of no one else. But presently she ceased discussing him, and about that time also ceased to respond wholeheartedly to Ruxton's love making. She explained unhappily, "It's a phase I'm passing through. He says it's normal when you're getting along in therapy as well as I am."

Ruxton accepted that till one day he received a phone call from a business friend, who said, "Seal, telling you this may cost me your account. But I saw Rainey pick up a man in a bar yesterday afternoon. He was such a sleazy looking character that I was amazed and followed them to a motel. She drove her Cadillac, and she gave him the money to go in and register."

Ruxton said steadily, "Thank you, Bob. It won't cost you your account with us, I assure you."

Ruxton hired a detective. After two nervous weeks, he had a sordid story of a completely degraded girl who picked up male riffraff in back street bars. Armed with this informa-

147

tion, he had his attorney serve her with divorce papers. Since the detective had secured the names and home addresses of the men—some of whom were married—the attorney forced her to sign a stipulation admitting relations with eleven men. The stipulation also denied her any property rights, in return for a lump sum of $5,000. On that basis, the divorce was subsequently granted.

Ruxton heard vague reports of her after that. She was "shacking up" with this or that man, living in rented rooms, frequenting bars.

Then one day, his secretary came fluttering in. "Your wife is here," she said.

Ruxton said harshly, "I have no wife."

But he let her come in, a too-thin, colorless young woman in a gray dress that didn't quite fit her. Ruxton stared at her cynically. "Well," he said sarcastically, "what *did* it all mean, Rainey? Have you found out yet?"

She said wanly, "I wondered what it would be like to have as many men as you've had women. I don't think it was good for me."

Ruxton said, with a sneer, "So that's what you've been telling yourself. But I suppose even a little whore needs a story to kid herself along with."

She looked at him, her gaze far away. Then she sighed. "Seal—I'm broke. You have so much. Couldn't you put me on a small pension?"

There was a long pause, for he hadn't expected anything like that. The thought that motivated Ruxton finally was the honest admission that, in spite of pretending not to be disturbed, the truth was that it shook him every time he heard another tale about her and some man. He said now, deliberately, "I pay out money only if I get something in return."

"Oh, really, Seal, you don't want a little whore."

He said steadily, "I want to get you out of the motels, and the iron bedsteads of small hotels, and out of the back seats of broken down old cars, and I'll pay a price for that. So, here's the pitch. Take it or leave it. I set you up in a one-bedroom apartment, with a living allowance and you become my exclusive mistress. The day you break over the traces, your allowance ends."

At that, she cried softly. "Oh, I'm so glad," she whispered finally. "I'm so very glad. I'm sure you can trust me, Seal. I'm so tired of being free to every man who asks me. I think I should be paid for like any respectable prostitute.

But I've never had the nerve to charge." She began to laugh, wildly, choked, then sobered and came over to him. She reached out and touched his arm. "Don't start using me right away, Seal. I'm tired. Honest, I'm awfully tired. Maybe it's a tiredness of the mind. But let's get the apartment, and then give me a few days. Maybe I should even go to a doctor."

The doctor checked her out as being in good health but "run down."

"Whatever that means," said Ruxton's father, when Seal told him. He had come to his son's office to have a talk with him. He went on, gravely, "You and I are pretty much cut from the same cloth, Seal. At least, I tried to make it so. If it's true, then I have an unpleasant surprise for you."

"How do you mean?" Seal was startled.

"Let me tell you a story," said his father. "I've already described to you how your mother and I began our married life. Some time after you were born, I got fed up completely, and I left her. Then, when you got ill, she called me —and I came rushing, terrified that my going might have hurt you. Your mother took me back, but I guess she didn't forgive me. One day she left me. I fell sick. I've never been so sick in my life. That's when my heart trouble began, and my high blood pressure. The doctor told me afterwards that he gave me up at one point. Notice what happened. I leave her. No after effects. She leaves me. And I start to die. Similarly, you were able to leave Rainey. But now you've got her back—suppose she leaves you?"

Seal laughed. "Oh, for heaven's sake, Dad. I never heard such voodoo fantasy. Coincidence!"

His father stared at him, lips pursed, thoughtful. "Okay, boy," he said finally, "live through it. Your mother relented when I was in the hospital. But she was and is what is known as a good woman. And so she was moved to pity and toleration. Can you count on Rainey hurrying back to you?"

Seal was amused. "Look, Dad," he said, "I survived all those months when she was sneaking off to motels. If that couldn't make me sick, nothing can. I've got full control of this situation, believe me. One wrong move from her, and I'll kick her out without a qualm."

His father shook his head. "I hope you're right. But the way I see it is, we're the kind of men who can't have a woman leave us. Maybe, Freud had an explanation for it. I don't know what it is. I only know what happened to me."

Just five months later, in January, 1942 Ruxton entered Rainey's apartment, and found a note, which read:

Dear Seal:

Thank you for taking me back, but it's not going to work, so I'm leaving. I'm so far rehabilitated, if that's what it can be called, that I'm beginning to get mad at my position. Just imagine. I used to have the privileges of a wife, and now I have the duties of a paid mistress. I guess it's too hard for the same woman to play both roles. I still don't know why I got so debased so suddenly, and you who did the same thing before and during our marriage, are riding high. What is there about a woman, that she can be destroyed if too many men get her? I'm going to join one of the women's auxiliaries to the armed forces. At this moment, I can't imagine ever letting another man near me. And I'm only twenty-three. Think of that. Good by. Good luck. Don't try to find me.

Love,

Rainey.

She evidently meant it. Because it was the last time he ever heard from her. And he never saw her again.

He had no immediate reaction. But he knew she was right about the rehabilitation. Something had changed for the better. Perhaps it *was* a mounting indignation at the nature of their relationship. The other men owed her nothing, and she asked nothing of them. But possibly a former husband was different. One had rights with him, somehow.

He gave up thinking about it, and called one of his old girl friends. And then another. And a third. He began to feel quite cheerful. It almost seemed to him as if he hadn't given Rainey more than a passing thought—except for a few dreams in which she appeared. But even that faded. His dreams became more primitive, seemed to refer back more and more to his childhood. They were a little disturbing, but like morning fog yielding to the sun, they faded with full wakefulness.

Three weeks went by. About noon of the twenty-second day, he began to run a fever. Late in the afternoon his father dropped by his office, took one look, and called a doctor.

Just how many illnesses he had, probably no one ever knew. But he definitely had the flu, and he had double pneumonia, and a high fever with delirium. For a time, he even

150

seemed to have the measles. It was all pretty ridiculous and deadly. It was as if some tuning device inside him resonated with most of the early illnesses he had had, and his body reproduced them all, with scientific accuracy. Some of the diseases had no name. His eyes and ears became inflamed with painful cysts. His body was racked with one pain or ache after another from legs to head.

It required nearly five weeks for medical science to bring him back to the point where, pale and trembling, but with his temperature back to normal, he found himself on the road to recovery.

"It's as I told you," his father said. "There's something very special about the relation of Ruxton men to women."

Ruxton tended to dismiss his father's analysis as being incomplete. But then, he didn't understand it either.

28

Lying there in the bed of his room in the Chinese hotel-prison, Ruxton felt his fever begin to abate. It was so rapid that in a few minutes he opened his eyes.

He saw that it was night. But the yellow light was turned on. By its dull citron radiance he could make out that the room had changed. A table with an old-fashioned water jug on it, stood beside his bed. In one corner was a cot, and on it, sound asleep, was Father de Melanier.

The presence of the priest puzzled him at first. But Ruxton was fully conscious now, and he remembered fragments of scenes in this room with Father de Melanier. He had an impression now of many days and of many nights. And he realized that the other man had been his nurse. It gave him a warm feeling to realize that.

He recalled his prolonged memory of his life with Rainey. And he had a thought: "This is the same illness I had when she left me." He shook his head, wonderingly, remembering what his father had said about the Ruxtons and women. "But it isn't the Ruxtons," he thought heavily, striving for precision of understanding. His father and he were certainly similar types, but they in turn were undoubtedly sub-species of that larger group of intensely right persons whom he had labeled the terrorist type.

At that point he had a very definite feeling that, in having this recurrence of illness, he had almost died a second time. "Maybe—" hopeful thought—"it's now out of my system."

He felt no different. No change in personality. A strong feeling of disappointment came.

He recalled how his illness had started: Phenix mentioning his marriage, at a time when he was evidently under enough stress to unlock the door to a hidden room in his mind . . .

He must have slept on that thought. His next awareness was of it still being dark outside. But the priest was bending over him with a cup of water, and had him raised to a sitting position, so he could drink. Ruxton brought his hand up and took hold of the cup. He intended to be very firm about it. But his fingers trembled, and the water would have spilled had Father de Melanier not gripped the cup strongly.

The priest said in French, "Well, my friend, my prayers are answered. Your fever is down."

Ruxton lay back, gasping. He felt weak, but quite sane and conscious. He said huskily, "How long have I been ill?"

"This is the thirty-fourth day which is about to dawn. Once, we were all very afraid for your life. But Madame Mai procured some drugs, and so we have you with us still. You'll be all right now, I can see."

Ruxton thought, "Thirty-four days. Just about as long as I was sick that other time. And then, also, I almost died." It all seemed very futile.

The direction of his thinking changed: So Phenix had saved him once more . . . His attention drifted. The next moment—or so it seemed—it was daylight.

Father de Melanier rose up from his cot, came over, and said, "Soup, perhaps?"

It was while Ruxton was sipping his soup that Mai Lin Yin came in. He said, with a scowl, "I have never been sick a day in my life. How do you explain such foolishness as this, Mr. Ruxton?"

A wild thought leaped into Ruxton's mind. He wanted to say, "Do you suggest that illness is due to inadequate Marxist-Leninist indoctrination?" He restrained himself.

Mai went on, "I was told that your illness has taken a marked turn for the better. Is this a sign that you have resolved your inner conflicts?"

Ruxton doubted it, but he said nothing.

Mai glanced at Father de Melanier, then at the cot on which the priest had slept, and finally at Ruxton again. "What's he doing in here?" he asked brusquely.

Ruxton answered warmly, without considering that all human values were reversed in Red China, "He's been acting as my nurse, Major, a typical example of the kind of goodness which one finds so often among priests and ministers of Christian churches."

Mai's face twisted. He hissed, "Mr. Ruxton, have you ever studied the early Christian attempts to convert China?"

Ruxton shook his head weakly, appalled at his indiscretion.

"For your information," Mai spat, "the Christian missionaries came to China aboard the opium ships. Bible in hand, openly acting as agents for opium dealers, they invaded China, seeking converts from among the poor, bewildered, betrayed peasants and workers whose meager earnings were raided to enrich a pack of smugglers."

Ruxton sighed his frustration. He was pretty certain that Mai was somehow mis-stating the story, but it didn't matter. He said huskily, "Would you like some advice, Major Mai?"

"One of these days," Mai snarled, "we will repay these priestly hypocrites and other spies—" He stopped. He seemed to emerge from some distorted inner world of his own. "Advice?" he repeated. It was clearly the last question he had expected.

Ruxton said, "About twenty per cent of all males in this world are dangerous. That includes colored men and Chinese as well as whites. When you deal with any individual of that twenty per cent, be sure that your women are locked up, all available weapons are to hand, and that you're not vulnerable. China was very foolish a hundred years ago, Major. She was vulnerable."

The words must have seemed absolutely true to Mai. For there was a long pause, and then he said harshly, but with a measure of reasonableness in his tone and manner: "What is your advice?"

"Forget the past!" said Ruxton. "All those people are dead, the villains as well as the victims. Your job is to help make sure that you're not vulnerable today. It's a different world. Different people."

Mai gazed down at him, thoughtful now. "Sometimes, you are a wise man, Mr. Ruxton. But these Christians cannot even agree among themselves. Actually, they made very little headway. About three million converts after one hundred and thirty years is a pitiful record. And most of those were rice bowl Christians, who shed their Christianity the moment the rice stopped. But of the more intelligent groups—if there was a charge against a person, and he was also a

153

Christian, the chances of his being shot were greatly increased."

The conversation had tired Ruxton. He must have fallen asleep while Mai was still talking.

When he wakened next time, it was still daylight. Madame Mai was in the act of entering the room. There was no sign of Father de Melanier, and the cot on which the priest had been sleeping was gone. Phenix closed the door, came to the bedside, and looked down at him.

Ruxton turned partly on his side, and gazed at her intently. "What was the last thing I said to you that day just before I got sick?"

Her eyes widened. "You mean—you were already ill at that instant?"

"Out-of-my-mind sick," Ruxton said soberly.

She was nodding, half to herself. "That explains it, of course," she said. "And I was so mystified. Like any foolish woman I kept thinking to myself, it must mean you don't want me, or you wouldn't have turned and just walked away." She stopped. Then: "You said, 'I'll be right over.' Does that mean anything to you?"

Ruxton described to her his relationship with Rainey, and finished, "When the police inspector called that day, and told me my wife had been in an accident, and was at the Good Angel Hospital, I said, 'I'll be right over.' By the time I said that to you, I was evidently as completely regressed as if I had been hypnotized."

Phenix said softly, "You must have loved her very much."

Ruxton stared at her silently, displeased with her remark. He wanted an adult relationship with this woman, and he thought of Rainey and himself as two "kids." He glanced around the room, anxious to change the subject. "Where is Father de Melanier?"

"That's why I came up to see how you are," she said. "My husband ordered the priest out of your room, and commanded the sentinels outside not to permit him in here again." She broke off, "I'll have Lemoine bring your dinner." She bent over him, kissed him. "Get well quick!" she whispered. "I need you."

She went to the door, paused, and turned. "The priest is now going to have to show signs of turning over," she said. "Just reading is no longer enough for him."

Ruxton thought of the fact that there were probably as many Catholics in the world as there were Chinese, and that obviously the Reds had no clear idea of the kind of force that gave support to a devout Catholic.

Aloud, he said, "I don't see how he will ever be able to do it."

She shrugged. "Oh, he'll turn over. Don't forget, eastern Europe was strongly Christian, but today the Communists have control." She finished hurriedly, "But I must leave now. Good bye."

She went out.

Ruxton lay there, thinking, "I wonder if the Catholics in Poland have solved the problem of being Catholic and Communist at the same time."

He tried to picture Father de Melanier as a Communist. It was as impossible as trying to visualize himself as one.

He became very tired, and he slept.

PART THREE

29

Ruxton came down for breakfast on the third day after his illness abated.

Most of the men nodded to him when he entered the room, but he made no demonstration. After the meal—which was eaten almost in silence—Lemoine slipped out of his chair, came over to Ruxton, and whispered, "Maybe you have notice—the spirit is down. While you were sick, with no warning, Major Mai came in with soldiers and have that fat little German take out and shot. He say he has look us over, and every society have people in it who are no good for it. He say even though small in number we represent—what is it?—a cross section of society."

At that point, Ruxton interrupted with a gasp, "Holsenamer—shot!" He looked around the table hastily. There was no sign of the stocky German business man.

Lemoine shrugged unhappily. "It isn't as if one can say much good for the fellow, and maybe there was something we don't know about him, but then who can judge when a man is good for society?"

"Just took him out and shot him?" Ruxton persisted. He drew a long breath. "But that's ridiculous. That makes a mockery of this whole procedure. The three-month period —the two year suspension of sentence means nothing."

"We were very fierce afterwards," Lemoine agreed. "We say the same thing. It all happens so quick. Mai swear no one else will be picked for shooting for sudden reasons this three month period."

Ruxton sat back in his chair, stunned. Holsenamer's had certainly not been a heart-warming personality. But that didn't matter. The whole democratic theory that if one man was unjustly treated then all men were threatened applied here. Either the group made its stand on that principle, or surrendered whatever legal rights it possessed.

He sat there, shaking his head, cringing a little inside. For he knew what the answer was. Unknown to the others, a terrorist type who felt himself completely right was in charge of this project. The reasoning of such a man moved so easily from the most brilliant logic to the most perverted rationalization that, within instants, in his brain there could occur a breakthrough of turbulent emotion. Even in an established democracy, with its time-honored procedures, terrorist types confused justice. But at least the victim could not be punished arbitrarily. He had legal recourse to other courts.

Nothing like that existed here. Mai was an oriental potentate. His slightest murder whim could take a man's life and he need not account to anyone. Worse, if questioned too strenuously, his "rightness" challenged, he might fly into a rage and murder the questioner.

Lemoine whispered, "We have had many meetings, and we are all tire. Last night till three A.M. Even my bones feel fatigue. And of course everyone is now disturb over the good Father. The squeeze is on him."

"Father de Melanier?" Ruxton asked, unnecessarily.

Lemoine nodded. And Ruxton glanced to where the priest sat. The man's thin, intellectual face was pale. His eyes behind his glasses were watery, and—as Ruxton watched —he reached up and wiped them with a quick, almost surreptitious movement. Then he looked around with a guilty air. His gaze caught Ruxton's. He climbed heavily to his feet and came over.

Shaky though he was, Ruxton stood up, and shook the man's hand. "Thank you," he said. "You have my gratitude."

As he spoke, a wave of grief engulfed him. To his total shame, tears came into his own eyes. He shook the priest's hand again, silently, this time.

In his effort then, to gain control of himself, Ruxton said, "Sir, what is the truth of the accusation that Christianity came to China in the opium ships?"

Indignation transformed Father de Melanier's countenance. "So Mai told you *that* lie," he said. "The truth of the matter, Mr. Ruxton, is that one man, the Reverend Doctor Charles Gutzlaff, allowed himself to be persuaded to act as interpreter for the British firm of Jardine and Mathison, who were the great opium smugglers."

Ruxton couldn't help but notice that the priest slightly accented the word "reverend" but that was the only way in which he indicated that the culprit had been a Protestant, not a Catholic.

Father de Melanier continued, "In later years, all Christian Church groups, without exception, fought the opium trade and were in the vanguard of the forces that eventually ended that particularly disgraceful episode in Chinese-West relationships. However, I will say this—" he added, "the

British were sorely provoked by innumerable Chinese insults. It is doubtful if any people acted more insolently to foreigners than did the Chinese government in the 1830's. British emissaries were snubbed, or ordered to enter the Dragon's presence on their knees, bearing tribute.

"And so one day, the Mistress of the Seas, the great World Power that was the British Empire, sent an armed military group into China, and the Imperial might of China collapsed like a house of straw. Does anyone today suggest that old China could possibly have remained as it was? The Manchu Dynasty has disappeared, and I'm sure no one regrets its passing, least of all the Chinese."

Ruxton was nodding. "I see," he said. He felt contemptuous of Mai. It was the same old emotional stupidity, the attempt to use one incident as a reason for action. The brief interchange had exhausted him, and so he excused himself and made his way up to his room. Once in bed, he would have been glad not to think about anything. But the fact was, he kept wondering, "How is Father de Melanier going to survive?"

Ruxton awakened several times during the night. The first time he remembered the German, and thought, "I've already turned my attention away from Holsenamer." The next time he wondered, "Can a man's life be that unimportant that we don't even want to think about it?"

By the third time, his attention had shifted back to the priest. He lay listening to the footsteps of the guards in the hall outside his door, and he thought, "Really, there's no way out for him. The Chinese are trying to get a response that none of the European Communists are today asking of Catholics."

He felt enormously concerned.

30

Father de Melanier said in French, "The fact is, Mr. Ruxton, I have given no real thought to the problem of what may confront me at the end of the second three months, which —as you have pointed out—is now only six weeks away."

Four more days had gone by. The night before, Ruxton had still felt a touch of weakness, but this morning he had awakened completely well. Breakfast was over. The priest and he stood by the window near the door of the lobby.

For Ruxton, it was the marking time period. The realization had come to him this morning, in full force. They must all wait while winter thawed into spring, and spring hardened suitably for escape purposes.

The goal had its reassuring aspects. It meant all problems were modified. While you waited, you did what was necessary. Ate, slept, kept warm, had sex relations as often as possible, read Communist literature, participated in struggle meetings, bared your Capitalist soul, and agreed with Mai and his henchmen to their reasonable satisfaction.

Thinking such thoughts and feeling such feelings, Ruxton listened to the priest with the mixed emotions of tolerance and impatience.

The older man continued, "My long-run goal is to convert these godless men to belief in God and in the goodness of Jesus. Since my devotion is to spreading the gospel of Christ, I regard all earthly purposes as secondary but am quite willing to support economic measures that are truly designed to help the people."

"Father de Melanier," said Ruxton, "I don't know how this will all work out when the two years are over. But we don't have to concern ourselves with more than one step at a time. What can you do during the next few weeks that will satisfy Mai yet not compromise your position?"

"Nothing, sir."

Ruxton persisted. "Don't be another Captain Gregory. Think about it." His voice lowered, urgently, "Whatever you do must start now. I doubt if any last minute changes will be acceptable to our commandant in his present state of mind about Christians."

Father de Melanier shook his head. "Mr. Ruxton," he said sadly, "I am sure the ultimate goal of these Red Chinese is the elimination of all religion. The Taoists have been disbanded, their leaders shot. The Communists accused many of the Buddhist groups of being agents for the Nationalists, and in self-defense these have finally joined together and agreed to work with the government. The agreement includes a promise to expose any person who may be seeking to use religion as a cover for undermining the People's Government."

Ruxton said, interested, "You mean, the various living Buddhas and the great lamas of Tibet and Mongolia have banded together?"

"Yes."

Ruxton was silent. Though he was not familiar with the details of history, he knew that these people had not even

162

spoken to each other for hundreds and, in some instances, for a thousand years or more. Yet here, now, irresistibly impelled by a common threat to their survival, they had joined together. "Is it possible," he thought, "that I could change by regarding the Communists as a scourge of God, bringing a pause in the madness of divisive thinking, and so progress becomes possible again?" He pictured himself for a moment as an instrument of such a scourge, and, not too surprisingly, it fitted him to a degree.

Aloud, he said, "But you believe this is only a temporary alleviation which the Communists are allowing these religious groups?"

"Yes. Notice in spite of all protests the destruction of the smaller sects. It is a total destruction, without mercy. We Catholics protested the arrest and murder of the Taoist leaders, to no avail. Their ancient Nature worship is of course extremely pagan, and has in recent ages degenerated to a kind of animism, very primitive, even savage. However, it is a long time since civilized peoples have exterminated savages. The Chinese Communists have taken even this backward step. Less violent but equally thorough has been their treatment of the foreign missions. From the beginning, lip service was given to the idea that we would all be protected. But in fact, members of our congregation were forcibly restrained from attending church. Church property was suavely requisitioned—it was theft. We priests were progressively harassed until it was obvious that God's work could no longer be done. And still the words of the Government promised no interference. Such are the lies with which we had to deal. Meanwhile, the Buddhists, who have numerous followers, are temporarily being handled more carefully. Yet read the school textbooks. In them, most of the seven wise ones are ridiculed and degraded in every possible way. For example, Confucius is neatly lowered in public esteem by calling him a great thinker of the feudal period. What is the feudal period? It is the criminal time. So Confucius is the great thinker of the criminal time. The end will come for all of us, including the Buddhists, unless we agree to make no compromise. If even one person gives in, then the Communist hierarchy will be reinforced in its collective conviction that it is only a matter of maintaining a merciless pressure until all give in."

Ruxton could find no fault with the man's logic except that, if carried through, it meant that Father de Melanier would be shot to death. The realization brought a momentary return of his old cynicism. Human beings were the most irritatingly irrational of all creatures, and the most stubborn.

The annoyance ran its course. Ruxton said quietly, "Sir, I have been thinking about your problem, and it seems to me the solution for this next six weeks lies in one area."

Father de Melanier shook his head, and said sadly, "You mustn't try to tempt me, Mr. Ruxton. There can be no compromise."

"Very well," said Ruxton coldly, and turned away. A moment later, the outside door banged shut behind him.

The bitter cold January air evoked a gasp from him. The wind bit through his padded clothes with its icy teeth—and took some of the sting out of his irritation with the priest. He remembered that it was his idea that this was the waiting time. Those who didn't know that were bound to take this whole period more seriously.

With that thought, he stopped walking forward. As he stood there leaning into the wind, he realized for the first time that he had been heading in the wrong direction. He turned—and the wind caught him and pushed him. As he almost sailed back the way he had come, he saw that Madame Mai was already halfway to the hotel. She had her eyes covered by her mitts. But she must have heard the squeal of his footsteps on the hard ground. She peered up at him. And stopped.

"Mr. Ruxton," she gasped, "it's nearly fifty below. Protect yourself, or your skin will freeze!"

Ruxton said, "May I see you tonight?"

The woman stood stamping her feet for warmth. She asked anxiously, "Do you think thirty minutes will be long enough?"

"Of course," said Ruxton.

She went on quickly, "My husband goes to the main prison for about an hour this evening. So be there at seven." She started past him, then turned. "Such a short time together is all right with you?"

"Of course it's all right—under the circumstances."

"Thank you," she said. And hurried by him.

He walked on, not really cold anymore.

He reached the book room, found himself a book, and presently settled himself to reading.

After Ruxton left, Father de Melanier realized that he had exasperated that powerful man. He shook his head wearily, chiding himself. He thought, "I am so tired that I rejected his plan without even asking him what it was."

He was wondering vaguely why he was always so fatigued these days, when Mai Lin Yin hailed him from the stairway. "Priest—come with me to the big prison. I need you for something."

Simple, direct man that he was, Father de Melanier was strongly affected by the word "need." As he eagerly followed Mai outside, he thought, "To be needed, ah, to be needed at last." He envisaged the possibility that a group of Chinese Catholic prisoners were asking for spiritual solace. The picture was a little blurred in his mind. But he had a strong belief in the power of good, and in spite of the all-embracing cruelty of the Communists, he believed that they merely needed to be persuaded to a new way of thought, and all would be well again. Being straightforward, he would even have admitted that the treatment he, personally, had received from the Reds up to now was not cruel or inhuman. He anticipated no change as he fell in beside Mai and walked briskly alongside that grim-faced being.

The commandant was silent, and so Father de Melanier chatted about how the Church merely sought a *modus operandi* with governments, and sought only to ministrate to the soul of the individual within the State.

The two men entered the prison gate, and walked on into the courtyard. "Over here!" said Mai curtly. He led the way to where a rough-hewn board walk had been constructed beside a long, deep trench. The yellow substance at the bottom of the trench was frozen, but despite this it gave off a strong odor of urine. The priest realized that this was the outdoor urinal for the twenty-five hundred prisoners in the big prison building. And, since he had certain memories of what had happened to Christian Chinese in his own church, a sudden qualm seized him. He surmised unhappily that he was going to be asked to witness the further degradation of some Chinese Catholics.

As he turned to protest, Mai commanded, "Let me see those glasses of yours." He removed his hand from his padded jacket and held it out, palm up.

It was an unexpected request, and seemed to be entirely *non sequitur*. Father de Melanier was puzzled. He took off his mitts, and carefully handed over his glasses. "They're a little old-fashioned," he said apologetically, "but still—"

As Mai accepted the glasses with one hand, he quickly

165

placed the palm of the other hand on the priest's chest, and pushed. Father de Melanier stepped back involuntarily. As he teetered against the railing, striving to recover his balance, Mai shoved again. Groping wildly, the older man fell backward over the railing into the trench.

Had the fall continued uncontrolled, it might well have killed him. But—as he fell—Mai's hand reached down, caught his shoulder, straightened him out, and so he landed on the hard ice at the bottom of the trench partly on his heels and partly on his seat. The distance of the fall was a good eight feet. So that when he struck every bone of his body was jarred, and he sank down, dizzy, and gasping for breath.

As he lay there, he heard the beginning of a rumble of voices, and the sound of many feet on hard ground. Above him, Mai said, "Priest, I give you credit that you believe all that foolishness you've been chattering about. Your problem and mine is to find a way to knock it all out of your head." He said something else, sharply. But the mounting roar of voices drowned out his words. The next moment innumerable footsteps trampled on the board walk.

Painfully, Father de Melanier fumbled to his feet. He was too dazed to understand clearly what had happened or what was intended. But he now made his first tentative effort to reach up to the lip of the trench. He was vaguely appalled to realize that he could barely touch it with the tips of his fingers. He was in the act of groping for something to hold on to when a stream of urine struck him in the face.

He gasped, ducked, found a breathing space, and cried out in bewildered protest. "Major Mai, help me—"

And there he stopped, realizing at last the extent of the degradation that was being visited on him. He shook his head, wonderingly, and then he knelt in the growing yellow pool which was already turning to slush, already freezing— knelt, bowed his head, and began to pray.

He asked that the Almighty Father be merciful to the sinners. And that he be given the strength to endure whatever befell him.

He had no idea how long he prayed, but he realized presently, numbly, that the men were leaving.

As he knelt there, something struck him a tiny blow. A noose settled over his shoulders, and tightened around his frozen arms. He was drawn up and pulled over the railing. Two soldiers grabbed him, and started him walking. He wobbled, tottered, staggered, and slipped. But they held him

166

and they made him walk. And, presently, returning life came agonizingly to his body.

Father de Melanier moaned and twisted. But his two guides walked him into the prison. There he was taken into a heated room, his clothes were removed, and he was plunged into a tub of steaming water. A new, padded cotton suit was tossed to the floor beside him, and he was left alone to clean himself as best he could.

When he finally put on the new clothes he was surprised to discover his fragile glasses in the jacket pocket . . . undamaged. He felt relief. Shamefacedly, he realized why. It was not the end. He was not being wholly rejected. This was part of a program, and not the finale of it. He thought sadly, "How we cling to life, we possessors of the flesh."

As he finished dressing, still shaky but at least clean—Mai came in. He said, "You will be subjected to this beneficial shower every morning until you turn over."

Father de Melanier trembled before the threat. "I thought Project 'Future Victory' was not to use compulsion."

Mai pursed his lips judiciously. "Men of religion require special treatment," he said. "They are more given to old-style thinking."

"What will my fellow prisoners think of this indignity?" The priest spoke in a small, unsteady voice.

"You are not to tell them," said Mai. "If you do you will also receive the late afternoon deluge."

A tear squeezed out of Father de Melanier's right eye. He wiped it away, but he said heavily, "What do you expect to accomplish by a continuation of this—this outrage?"

"We have found," said Mai, "that urine and God do not mix. They are mutually exclusive." He was suddenly impatient. "Enough of this. As you can see, the choice as to how long the showers continue is entirely yours. However, if you were to tell me that you have decided to change, then I would suspend even tomorrow's bath until I could evaluate how much you mean it."

"Impossible!" said Father de Melanier, hoarsely.

Mai shrugged. "You make the choice." Curtly, he said, "Come with me."

He led the way out of the prison.

When they entered the hotel, the commandant headed for the stairway without a backward glance. Father de Melanier sat down near the door, and listened absently to a discussion which—with the usual delays for translations—was taking place between several of his fellow prisoners. It was being argued, with considerable agreement, that the Chinese Reds, having had twenty-five years to perfect their skill and harden their hearts, were much more determined Communists than their Russian counterparts. As a result, the take-over in 1949 was smoothly and confidently handled.

The discussion was absorbing to the participants, and no one even glanced at the priest. "They don't know," he thought. "They don't even suspect what I've just been through."

For the first time in his forty-plus years, he had a strong sense of life being unreal.

31

At a quarter to eleven, Ruxton glanced at his watch, smiled, and shook his head. He had decided not to see Tosti today. He couldn't trust Phenix on this first day of his being up and around. She might check on him.

And so he continued to read into a work that he had opened this morning for the first time: *Das Kapital* by Karl Marx.

It soon became apparent that Marx had based his rage reaction against Capitalism on a new evaluation of the historical data about the ancient labor groups. The discovery of such data in the nineteenth century had alarmed the ruling groups, and exhilarated all those rebels who saw in the facts thus revealed final evidence that the primal state of man was communistic.

It seemed to Ruxton that the hysterical intellectuals of the eighteen hundreds, and their monarchic opponents, were not capable of discerning truth in history. Throughout all time, people everywhere were confronted by ever more numerous masses of human beings, always hungry and fearful for their families. When crops failed, hordes of these beings descended on neighbors whose crops had not failed, attempting by violence to seize the food they so desperately needed.

It turned out that ways could be devised to control these poor, miserable beings, and that in fact they readily handed themselves over for some minimum of security, whether it was real or false. With this discovery began the betrayal and abuse of the poverty-stricken masses. Slavery, pay so low that survival was not possible—each owner-employer, operating entirely on self-interest and without governmental guidance, proved beyond all question that uncontrolled individual incentive could not, statistically speaking, be trusted to be humane in an economically meaningful way.

As a result, centuries ago, the tortured, starving menial turned to other ways of sustaining himself. The struggle that followed was probably closer to the true dynamics of human history than any of the accounts of the ruling families and their succession. Ruxton did not downrate the importance of the methods worked out whereby stable government could be passed on from one generation to the next; he suspected that success or failure of the communist states would hinge eventually on their ability to devise a technique for an orderly handing over of power by one group to another.

But, as he read Marx' famous book, he concluded that essentially the development of government was one, long effort to mobilize for the production of enough food to keep the hungry mob under control. When stopped by organized armies, and the cupidity of the unguided self-interest of his employer, the ancient lowly was a laborer by day and a member of a band of pirates, thieves or murderers by night. To Marx, these gangs of bandits, sometimes numbering tens of thousands, were the first labor unions, and Marx' claim to genius was that he correctly reasoned that such men, driven to the very edge of madness by the equal madness of the ruling classes, was a massive source of power.

It seemed to Ruxton that the Communists, in using this power, had in effect simply undertaken the same task as all governments everywhere: the task of providing food and shelter, and of setting up rules and regulations—along with the forces to administer them—which would actually control so many, many people.

Here in the middle twentieth century, the worker was still restless, still being abused, still justifiably dissatisfied—but the battle to keep him fed was slowly being won, particularly in the western world. It needed to be won everywhere.

During lunch, Ruxton glanced absently at Father de Melanier. Then looked again more sharply. The priest's face had a haunted expression. Ruxton hesitated, remembering his morning anger, but finally he stood up and went over.

"What's happened?" he asked.

The older man shook his head, mutely. "And, Mr. Ruxton, I want to apologize for my disregard of your good thoughts this morning. I was most impolite."

Ruxton gazed down at that tragic countenance with narrowed eyes. "Are you telling me that nothing has changed since this morning?"

Father de Melanier hesitated. A direct lie came hard for him. "Nothing, sir!" he gulped, finally.

Ruxton straightened. The strong feeling that something was wrong yielded before the other's denial. He returned to his chair and sat down.

As he finished his final cup of tea some minutes later, Ho Sin Go came over to him from the head table, and leaning down close to him, said in a low voice, "Mr. Ruxton, I badly need your advice."

Ruxton stiffened. He had a flash feeling that this was going to be about Tosti. The realization brought a peculiar, grim feeling, as he said, "What is it?"

Tosti's plumpish husband went on unhappily, "My relations with my wife cause me the utmost mental anguish. I feel that you are a person who understands such matters, and therefore I should like you to tell me what to do."

Ruxton was determined not to permit anything that was said, nor any emotion that was expressed, to stop him from doing exactly what he desired. He said, "Am I to understand that the petition that was circulated before the wedding was true? Tosti did not wish to marry you?"

"She is such a beautiful woman," said Ho in an agonized tone. "Don't ask me to give her up. As you know, she spends one night a week with me. I have begged her on my knees to accept me. She refuses. And at last I am becoming angry. Mr. Ruxton, you are an experienced man. Do women yield to anger?"

Ruxton gazed at the man, and bit his lip. He said slowly, seeking an easy solution, "Mr. Ho, your question startles me. Of all the people around here, you seemed the most gentlemanly to me."

"I confess," said Ho sadly, "I used to think of myself that way, also. No longer."

It sounded as if a crisis was indeed building up for Tosti. Ruxton said in a dissembling tone, "Mr. Ho, I doubt if my experience would be useful to you. In all my life I have never tried to win a woman after she indicated she did not want me. Sometimes a woman plays a game with the man she loves, whereby she seeks to be forced. But this is not your situation. You have a wife who did not wish to be married in the first place. My advice: Divorce her. Find yourself some delightful Chinese girl who does want you. End this tragic situation."

Ho shook his head. His moon face was so colorless it looked pasty. "I thought you might say that, Mr. Ruxton. But I can't do it. She is so devastatingly attractive to me."

Ruxton hesitated. In giving herself to him, Tosti had earned whatever protection he could offer. He thought, "In the final issue, I'll have to—" But the fact was, it would be better if a final issue could be avoided. He said in a low voice, "Have you told anyone else of this?"

Ho shook his head unhappily. "I have thought of going to Madame Mai, but I feel shamed by my predicament."

"I see." Ruxton nodded, relieved. "And when do you see Tosti next?" He realized that he was obtaining what information he could preliminary to action.

"Two days from now—Saturday."

Ruxton sighed with relief. Forty-eight hours. It gave him time to consider what he might do. Aloud, he said, "I'll think this over, Ho, and speak to you again before then."

"Thank you, Mr. Ruxton." Ho spoke gratefully.

Ruxton nodded, pushed back his chair and stood up. A few moments later he was outside and heading for the book room.

That night at seven, he entered the basement room without incident.

As he edged down the steps, Phenix' voice floated up from the blackness. "I'm waiting for you at the bottom of the stairway," she whispered.

Presently, he felt her fingers touch his arm, move caressingly down and snatch at his hand. Thus held, he allowed himself to be guided across the floor to the mattresses.

Despite the cold outside, it was cosily warm near the furnace. They spoke no words, and there was no sound except once, when she moaned softly.

Finally, Phenix stirred. She whispered into his ear, "I have good news. My husband goes to Peking in a few days with the prison commandant. They will discuss with the government the fate of various personages in the big prison. Of course, he wants me to go with him. But I have said that I do not wish to travel in the winter. So we shall have a week or ten days to ourselves." She broke off, breathless, "Please hurry now, and get dressed. We can talk of all this later."

When they separated, Ruxton waited till she was safely upstairs, then made his way outside.

As he entered the hotel, he saw that all the white men and interpreters, along with half a dozen soldiers, were

171

gathered in the lobby. As Ruxton paused, Lemoine got up from a chair and hurried over to him.

"Thank God you've come," he said. "We all wonder where could you be on a night like this."

Ruxton said, shivering, "I went for a walk."

"In this weather?" said Lemoine. "You mus' be made of asbestos." He broke off. "Major Mai call from the big prison. He want us all over there—I think to meet some Chinese big shots who are to be executed."

32

The little group of soldiers and prisoners, with the interpreters bringing up the rear, were led along dank, stone and concrete corridors, dimly lighted. At intervals were barred doors that were not doors at all but simply crossed metal bars that fitted into the openings, and each equipped with a massive lock. The interiors of those rooms were more difficult to observe. But by adding together what he saw in several glimpses, Ruxton was able to reconstruct their interiors. There were a dozen prisoners in each room. They slept bunched together on pads that lay on the floor. A table and some stools completed the furnishings, and a single bulb of no more than 15 watts hung down from a short cord in the center of the ceiling.

They came to a room where there were benches and a desk. Behind the desk sat Mai Lin Yin. He motioned them to the benches. Ruxton was glad to sit down. He felt shaken by what he had seen. He had sometimes imagined the conditions in the big prison, but had never quite conceived anything as bad as this.

There was a commotion at the door. Ruxton watched as a big-boned Chinese was pushed through the door by two soldiers. He had quick, dark eyes, and he gave everyone in the room a swift, searching look. Then he stepped over in front of the desk, and stood at attention.

Major Mai glanced down at some papers in front of him. "Aha!" he said in Chinese, "trained at the Whampoa Academy, attained the rank of general, to be shot on my return from Peking for failure to become a communist." He addressed the man directly, "What have you to say for yourself?"

"I am quite willing to become a Communist," said the

172

former officer. "However, I refuse to catch flies, or engage in day labor of my own free will."

Mai stared at the man, lips compressed, yet somehow respectful. Finally, he turned to the interpreters. "Translate the following: This is Brigadier General Mu Daio-tu, who retains his feudalistic ideas to the end. For such men there is no place in the new China."

He waited until the interpretations were made, and then again addressed the officer. "I believe there is a charge against you of having had the largest number of concubines accompanying you of any officer in the Chinese armies. Do you realize now what a crime this was?"

A faint smile creased the gloomy countenance of Mu Daio-tu. He said, "I was second, not first. After all, it was a widely known fact that General Lin Paio had the greatest number of concubines, and still has."

Mai Lin Yin changed color. It was visibly apparent that he hadn't known. Lin Paio was number 9 in the Communist hierarchy. Americans had faced him in Korea, and had found him a tough and skilful opponent. Mai after a pregnant pause said to the soldiers in a strident voice, "Take this man back to his cell."

Mu Daio-tu started out dutifully, but he paused when he was still inside the room, and turned. His eyes took in the white men. He said in Russian, "I don't know if any of you can understand me, but I am the officer who led the division that fought the Japanese at Hu-yang. Out of sixteen thousand eight hundred men, we lost fifteen thousand three hundred killed, eleven hundred wounded and about two hundred taken prisoner. I have often thought I should have died then with the bravest division that fought in recent Chinese history, and I assure you that I shall go to my death serenely, and in the hope that I shall again speak to, and see, those many dear friends of mine who fell at Hu-yang."

That he was able to finish the little speech was directly attributable to an error. His two escorts had stepped through the door, evidently expecting that he was following. As the officer made his speech, they stood in the corridor outside, apparently at a loss as to what to do. It was Mai who recovered, and bellowed, "Take him away, you idiots."

They rushed back in at the command, grabbed Mu Daio-tu, and thrust him through the door opening, and out of sight along the hallway. Mai turned to the interpreters. "What was the language?" he asked in a dangerous tone.

"Russian," said one of the men.

Mai seemed relieved. He stood up, and walked over until he was directly in front of Kuznetoff. To him, he said in Chinese, "If you translate that to anyone I'll take some kind of action against you."

Kuznetoff said, "It was the man's swan song. Would you deny him last words?"

Mai said in a more reasonable tone, "People under emotional stress merely create confusion and sympathy."

Kuznetoff said, "All right, I shall say nothing."

"Good," said Mai. "It will stand in your favor."

Kuznetoff shrugged contemptuously, but he said nothing. Mai turned away, and Ruxton waited, tensely. He thought, "Now I'll learn who else speaks Russian, because he'll have to silence them also." It was so important that, involuntarily, he held his breath . . . as Mai walked back to his desk and sat down. Slowly, Ruxton let the air out of his lungs. Mai's action had pinpointed Kuznetoff as the man who, with Gregory, had come to kill him.

He pushed the thought aside. There was something he must do. General Mu Daio-tu had made a statement of surpassing importance to all the white prisoners, and although he had said it in Chinese, it must be brought out into the open, and discussed.

Ruxton raised his voice, "Major Mai."

Mai turned, and stared at him questioningly.

Ruxton said, "It seems wrong to me that we are brought here, and then we are not allowed to hear the actual conversations between the Kuomintang person and yourself. In General Mu, we have a military man whose name I vaguely remember hearing—in what connection I do not recall. Can you explain to us why he failed to become a Communist?"

Mai said to the interpreters, "Translate Mr. Ruxton's words while I consider whether or not I shall answer him."

When the translations were completed, Mai said, "Unfortunately, he retained his feudalistic ideas."

"I presume," said Ruxton, "that he made some effort to become communistic, else he would not have survived the full two years."

"That is correct," said Mai. "This officer from the beginning expressed himself as being willing to become a Communist."

That was the key sentence.

"Then," said Ruxton, "all-out willingness is not enough?"

Mai must have realized the importance that Ruxton attached to the question. His eyes narrowed, and he smiled grimly. "No, Mr. Ruxton," he said in a ringing voice, "willingness is not enough, because we must assume that most men will promise almost anything in order to save their life." He had turned to face the benches, and now he was shaking his head. "Mr. Ruxton, the kind of communist we want you to be is such that, if we were to set you down in the heart of an American city, you would nevertheless remain a convinced Communist."

Ruxton persisted, "In what way did General Mu Daio-tu manifest feudalistic ideas?"

"One thing," said Mai. "He refused to catch flies." His tone grew indignant. "For thousands of years China has been disease-ridden. Flies are among the worst carriers of disease germs, and so, as you may have read, on several occasions Chairman Mao has ordered the entire nation to spend a specific period of time catching and killing flies. When six hundred million people devote a day in spring to killing flies, that is a mighty event indeed for the health of the nation."

Ruxton presumed that it was. Still other nations had solved the problem with chemicals and cleanliness of habit. He asked, "What else did the general do that was feudalistic?"

"He refused to volunteer for laboring work." Mai spoke heatedly. "Evidently, he considers himself superior to the workers and peasants. He did not awaken."

Ruxton hesitated. It seemed futile, and might even be foolhardy, to pursue the matter further. But the battle of Hu-yang must have been one of the great battles of all time. He said, "Is there no place for former Kuomintang generals in the Chinese People's Liberation Army?"

Mai was impatient. "That is not for me to determine, Mr. Ruxton." He held up his hand, although Ruxton was not planning to speak. "No more questions, now. I have asked for the thug, Chang Ku-tai, to be brought before us, and I hear footsteps approaching."

33

Mai asked roughly, "Did you fail to transform yourself into a Communist?"

The individual being interrogated was about sixty years of age. He was thin to the point of gauntness. His face nevertheless had the unlined youthfulness of many older Chinese men. His eyes ignored the white men on the benches, but they were dull and without hope. Surprisingly his voice had resonance and fire in it. He said, "I am thankful to be able to say that I shall die a sane man."

Mai said to the interpreters caustically, "He miserably confesses that he remains a Kuomintang beast and a running dog of the American Imperialists."

Ruxton sat stiff before the lying translation. A long moment went by before he was able to think, "It doesn't matter. I never saw this brave man before. I shall never see him again, and he doesn't even know that I understood what he actually said." It was certainly not the occasion for him to reveal that he knew Chinese.

By the time the translations were made, he had changed his mind about one thing. It did matter. He said to Mai, "May I speak to this man after you finish questioning him?"

Mai turned to stare at him, meditatively. He said at last, "Mr. Ruxton, you are a very persistent man. What is it that you have in mind?"

Ruxton said, "This is Chang Ku-tai, one of the—" He paused; he had been about to say, "one of the great men of the Kuomintang." He said instead, "One of the men closely associated with Chiang Kai-shek—correct?"

Mai nodded, lips pursed, eyes narrowed suspiciously. He said, "Perhaps the feeling I have against this is that you are asking too many questions."

Ruxton said, "I'm curious about Chiang Kai-shek. I'd like to ask this associate about him—that's all." He looked directly at Mai. "Do you have no curiosity yourself?"

Mai nodded at Ho Sin Go. "Translate for Mr. Ruxton." To the other interpreters, he said, "No additional translations, please."

Ruxton stood up, walked forward, and leaned against Mai's desk. "Mr. Chang Ku-tai," he began, "I have requested permission to interrogate you, and the permission has been granted."

When the translation was made, the older man nodded but said nothing. Ruxton continued, "All of the white men here are in the same position as you are in. An experiment is being conducted to convert us into Communists. At the end of five months, many of us in our desire to save our lives are willing to become Communists, but we don't know how. Your failure, therefore, is very disconcerting to us. How do you account for it?"

Chang Ku-tai answered promptly, "I know the truth of the Communist swindle. I cannot, and could not, blot that

176

truth from my mind." Ho Sin Go accurately translated the Chinese words into English.

Ruxton said, "What is the truth?"

Chang's bleak countenance broke into the semblance of a smile. He said, "I could do you a disservice by telling you, but if you wish—"

"I wish," said Ruxton.

"The Chinese people," Chang Ku-tai began, "have a history of good sense, and have demonstrated a desire to live by a philosophy of truth. And so, in this immense land, where there were no roads until a few years ago, a peaceful and industrious nation lived by a philosophy that revered the family. Three different times in China's history, three good-hearted emperors completely sub-divided the available acreage equally among the people. In each instance, it then required about two hundred years for the more shrewd and able to take over the property of the weak and the foolish.

"This supremely stable society was subjected in the middle of the nineteenth century to the impact of the commerce and military power of the white men of Europe and America. The people resented the foreigners and, in 1911, under Dr. Sun Yat-sen, the revolutionary Kuomintang overthrew the imperial house of the Manchus, and China became a republic.

"Before his death in 1925, Dr. Sun wrote the Three Principles of the People. It was on these principles that all subsequent governments, both Nationalist and Communist, professed to base their moral and political actions. The principles were Nationalism, Democracy, and Socialism. Each of these principles had a different meaning in China than elsewhere, in that Nationalism meant *against* foreigners, Democracy *for* only those Chinese who were loyal to Dr. Sun, and Socialism referred specifically to land reform. Utilizing this last point, the Chinese Communists subsequently duped thousands of people in America by passing themselves off as land reformers.

"After the death of Dr. Sun Yat-sen, leadership was soon vested in Chiang Kai-shek. At first Chiang shared Dr. Sun's admiration for the Soviets, and so the Russian General Galen and his aides became the military advisers of the Chinese government. The time came when Russian-directed mass demonstrations grew so violent that Chiang ousted the Russians and restored order.

"Chiang was then advised by the German General von Seekt, who was later one of the principal architects of the

177

German army. But with World War II came American military missions. These found a vast Chinese army under Nationalist direction. Still largely missing in China were armaments and the industrial base for armaments.

"The invasion and occupation of Manchuria by Japan in 1931 and 1937 had been a further degradation, which Chiang finally resisted. During this time, and later, the Reds were able to convince the world that they were doing most of the fighting—which was a lie—and so the enormous sacrifices of the Nationalists—more than three million dead—were nullified. As an example of the total duplicity of the Communists in their so-called struggle against the Japanese, Red losses during the entire Sino-Japanese war totalled less than one hundred thousand men."

He paused, then said, "I am still puzzled by the success of Communist propaganda in the West. I am thinking of Edgar Snow's book *Red Star Over China*—It was undoubtedly an honest reportorial scoop, but it was virtually a book-length false account, in which even the partially true statements made by leading Communists needed to be interpreted. For example, Mao Tse-tung stated truthfully that his younger sister and his first wife, Yang K'ai-hui, were executed for their Communist activities. Such simple truths need the additional comment that they participated in terrorist actions which caused many deaths.

"As an example of a significant false statement, there comes to my mind Mao Tse-tung's passing reference to a Chinese scholar, Siao-yu, that he was a curator of the Peking museum, and that he absconded with the property of the museum. It seems a pointless story, a casual thought which briefly associated in his mind, was spoken, whereupon the great man passed on to more important matters. But when we examine this tiny reference, it develops that Siao-yu was the founder of the Hsin Min Study Group, of which Mao was a member, and that for a time these two youths, at first in a friendly way and then in earnest, fought for control of the group. When it became apparent that Mao was successfully turning it into a Communist organization, Siao-yu withdrew from it. The two former friends now grew apart.

"Subsequently, under Chiang Kai-shek, Siao became curator of the Chinese library at the League of Nations, and he is still in charge of this extremely valuable collection, though I believe it was to be moved from Geneva to a place of greater safety.

"There is much more to the story of these two men, but you can see what must have been in Mao's mind as he spoke—apparently in passing—a gross calumny about his former friend, Siao-yu.

"All his other statements to Mr. Snow were equally slanted.

"Politically," continued Chang Ku-tai, "this was the period of Tutelage. Chiang had definitely decided in favor of democracy, but remembering Dr. Sun Yat-sen's experience, he set up a preliminary training period whereby the whole nation would, in a sense, go to school and learn democracy. But, of course, this great purpose was confused and seriously interfered with by the Japanese attack, and by the constant civil war which was the result of the conspiracy between the Chinese Communists and Soviet Russia.

"When it was finally decided to end Tutelage and set up a constitutional government—actually before the people were ready—the Reds showed their true colors by refusing to have anything to do with what they had been urging so long in their propaganda.

"Since, during this time, they had been supplied with massive armaments and training by the Russians—in direct and flagrant violation of post-war treaties, they now took off the mask, and stood revealed for what they were—the destroyers of democratic China . . ."

The former Kuomintang great man reached that point in his account, waited for the final sentence to be translated, and then shrugged. "Nothing more to say," he said curtly.

Ruxton said slowly, "What was the weakness in Chiang Kai-shek's character, in your opinion, that brought such a great disaster upon the Nationalist forces?"

The dark eyes of the elderly Chinese man were unwinking as they stared into his own. There was a long pause, and then the man turned to the interpreter and said, "Tell this American that in my opinion the Generalissimo Chiang Kai-shek had a faith in the intelligence and good sense of Americans which proved to be an error, and that his crime to China was that he trusted America, a country inhabited by the most stupid and self-centered people in the world."

"But surely," said Ruxton, after the translation was made, "the man must have some personal defects. Everyone else has."

Chang considered this, then shook his head. "I think we should end our conversation," he said.

From behind Ruxton, Mai Lin Yin said harshly, in Chinese, "I think we have indeed heard enough." As Ruxton turned to glance at Mai, the man stepped past him and pressed his face close to Chang Ku-tai. He said, "Why don't you tell him of your dealings with the Japanese invaders? Why don't you inform him of your visits to Japan? Why don't you tell him how, after your return from Japan, you became a leading advocate of the traitorous idea that war should *not* be undertaken against the Japanese invaders?"

The older man's thin, almost hollow face, was impassive. He turned to Ho Sin Go. "Tell this American that the real reason I am being kept in this prison is because of the Communist war-time propaganda claims that the Kuomintang did not join in the war against Japan, that only the Communists fought the invaders. Several former associates of Chiang Kai-shek have already been shot solely for the purpose of proving this falsehood. These Communists cannot let their own lies, which were useful at the time in deluding the Chinese people and the world, just sit there in the past. They keep looking around for ways to bolster the stories they told then. But what are the facts? Chiang Kai-shek, knowing the overwhelming strength of the Japanese forces as opposed to those of China, made every effort to avoid a Japanese invasion. But in 1937 the Japanese attacked China with their large and modern armies. This war could have been fought realistically—that is, as a limited engagement. Unfortunately one of the forces loosed by the Japanese was the force of emotion among the people, and this was cunningly taken advantage of by the Communists. Logic was over-ruled by war hysteria. Tears still come to my eyes when I think of all those millions of foolish people demanding total war. Subsequently, we experienced the frightful result."

Ruxton, listening to the translation, sighed within himself. For he had a sudden feeling that these Chinese were all very emotional. Including Chang Ku-tai. Including Mai Lin Yin, and Madame Mai.

Ruxton sighed again, and said quietly to Ho Sin Go, "Tell Chang Ku-tai thanks for his communication."

34

The third man was visibly in a state of shock. When one of the soldiers pushed him toward the desk, he staggered, as might a man on stilts, and swayed there in front of Mai, a glazed-eyed caricature of a man.

He was, Ruxton saw, not much over forty. His blanched face gave him the appearance of being ill, and there was a flabbiness about him that suggested he had once been plump. That brought a picture of a Chinese business man of a type Ruxton had often seen in Hong Kong—bright, westernized young men, whose attitudes and activities were far from the old Chinese tradition. The picture faded, and there was the reality to which this individual Chinese had come.

The voice of Mai said, sarcastically, "Well, gentlemen, here is your capitalist hero. He learned his lessons in finance from the Wall Street giants. But they're not giants when brought to justice for their crimes against the people. His terror derives from the fact that he is definitely one who will be shot. He only learned this a few hours ago."

When the translations had been made, Father de Melanier said, "Does he have faith, or is he godless?"

The sarcasm was even stronger as Mai said, "His god is money, and it has all been taken away from him. So, yes, he is godless."

Mai, who had been looking at the papers on his desk, re-shuffled them, glanced up, and said, "Actually, this is an unusual case. Fo Hin-di did everything in his power to become a Communist. He passed all the intermediate tests, and apparently willingly did field labor. But—" he nodded, half to himself—"what it finally came to is that they couldn't accept him. As you know, the People's Government tolerates a certain type of capitalist as a necessary evil. Manager-owners of factories, distributing organizations and retail establishments have been given a limited status in democratic China. It is a temporary matter, and the government will eventually buy into each business so extensively that the former owner will be an employed manager only. However, the money manipulators such as the Fo family are regarded as despicable."

Ruxton was becoming curious, and so he was relieved when—after Mai's words had been translated—de la Santa asked what turned out to be a leading question: "What is this man's exact crime?"

Mai said, "Like a gigantic octopus, the Fo family financial enterprises strangled the life blood of China."

"Yes, but what did this man do?" de la Santa asked.

Mai said, "Because of such financial bloodsuckers as this, China was caught in an inflationary spiral. We warned the corrupt villains then, but they took no heed. The people remember, and so the order came through yesterday not to spare Fo Hin-di regardless of his late attempt to atone."

The Catholic priest raised his hand, and said, "Tell him that if he would like to have the services of a priest, I shall be available to pray with him, with your permission."

"Absolutely forbidden," Mai snapped, then: "Are there any more questions?" His gaze shifted to Ruxton.

Ruxton shook his head. He could have given a much more searching interrogation than anything that the other men seemed capable of. But the fact was, he knew very little of the financial crisis of Nationalist China. Honest, conservative banking was one of the stabilizing institutions in all western nations. But like most capitalistic groups, banking and finance had needed regulation by the State. None —it had turned out—could be left entirely free of control. Prior to such control, and wherever governments eased regulations, capitalists had a tendency to get out of hand. At such times one might well reason that Karl Marx had been at least partly right. It was possible that the inexperienced Chinese Nationalists had failed to provide adequate regulations for its young, grasping financial community. But it was obvious that the financiers were only one of the bankrupting influences in pre-Communist China. Bigger than anything else was probably the costly civil war. In the face of that colossal drain on the public treasury, the negative activities of one or more financiers were probably of minor importance. Somehow, the government would have obtained even the use of the Fo money.

Ruxton glanced around at the faces of his fellow prisoners. They were relatively impassive. Clearly, Fo Hin-di had no sympathizers even among men who might in the not-too-distant future find themselves facing the same firing squad as he. It seemed vaguely unfair. But he said nothing.

Four more men were brought before them. Ruxton had lost interest, so he merely glanced at each, took in their identity from the words that were spoken, and made no comment of any kind. An absentee landlord—lucky to be still alive, for his was the breed most hated by the Communists; a former provincial governor, red buttons still in his cap; the publisher of a pro-government newspaper, long since taken over, its name changed, its news edited according to correct principles of Red journalism; a top customs official, accused of being a running dog of foreigners. The fate of these soon-to-be-murdered men, and millions like them, who placed their faith in the West, had actually been sealed when the United States decided it had no vital interest in the outcome of the civil war in China.

Ruxton's introspection ended, as Mai dismissed the last of the Chinese prisoners, and said to the white men, "I hope that you are learning lessons from the failure of these men."

The statement struck Ruxton as fantastic. But as the group of white prisoners made its way back to the hotel, and so to bed, it seemed to him that he had learned one thing from the visit. The Chinese prisoners, of whose presence he had been so dimly aware, were real people. Very superior human beings were imprisoned behind those stone walls.

35

Next day. A few minutes after nine o'clock.

Over in the latrine in the prison courtyard, Father de Melanier, stripped naked this time, was enduring his second urine inundation.

Ruxton had watched him go off with Mai, noticing his pale face, but without suspicion. He was thinking about the problem Ho Sin Go posed for Tosti. He headed for the library, and then, at his usual time, put away his book and went outside.

Tosti must have heard the click of the door opening, and must have known instantly who it was. She came running. Breathless, she flung herself into his arms. "So glad," she whispered as she clung to him, "so very glad."

She pulled away, and drew him into her room. "You have been ill?" she asked anxiously.

Ruxton said soberly, "No one has ever been any sicker than I was, and lived."

She watched him undress, and then slipped out of her clothes and into his arms. Afterwards, she sighed, and said, "I am having a hard time with my husband. I think he will try to beat me one of these days. What shall I do?"

Ruxton did not mention that Ho Sin Go had already spoken to him. He simply asked, as if he did not know, "When do you see him next?" She told him, and he nodded, and said, "I'll talk to him about it today." He finished dressing, embraced her briefly, whispered, "Don't worry!" and returned to the library.

He did not resume reading. Instead he sat with eyes narrowed, nerving himself to bring into full awareness a thought

183

that had been a tiny embryo in the back of his mind ever since Ho had asked his advice. The thought was, "It's time I did something." He realized with excitement that he meant not just about Tosti's plump young husband.

For nearly five months he had been effect and not cause. Except for the two women. Possession of them was no mean achievement, and was a positive action.

But the threat from Ho Sin Go and the visit to the big prison the previous night had brought him face to face with the fact that nearly one-quarter of his two year reprieve had slipped by. And it seemed to him, after reading as much of Marx as he already had, that he was further away than ever from conversion to communism.

He thought, "While Mai is working out a method whereby the Reds can conquer and take over a Western Nation, why shouldn't I work out a method whereby they can't?"

He was enormously amused for a moment, as he realized that only a terrorist type could have such a thought. His kind alone had the necessary rage at some level of the nervous system that could stimulate the sustained violence which might be required. Others could act under direction in a national emergency, or as units in an armed force. But he could plan action, and carry it out without someone else to spur him. He thought—the first real acceptance of himself since he had begun to understand his inner workings—, "I guess a few of us who feel 'right' within ourselves may even have a limited value in this primitive era of man."

It struck him that he felt a certain sympathy for Tosti's husband. Still, there was nothing he could do for a man whose intent was to force a woman who didn't want him. Ho's impulse to violence indicated that he also had terrorist tendencies.

The completeness of his understanding, and the release of tension that it brought, astonished and delighted Ruxton. He thought, "I've come away up, somehow, now that I've decided to act." He was clearly not made for fear. Rage, and its by-product, action *against,* was his forte.

As he continued to pretend to read, Ruxton realized that if he could persuade Father de Melanier to make certain suggestions to Ho Sin Go, then Tosti would be able to make contact with her fellow agents in Wanchan. First, therefore, speak to the priest, and then—

Excitement grew steadily in him, as he contemplated what else he had to do.

36

As Ruxton walked into the lobby a few moments later, he saw that Phenix was at the desk talking to the soldier-clerk. She turned, as he started to pass her, and said, "Mr. Ruxton, I have been asking this man if any of the prisoners have recently made any requests or complaints. Do you know of anything?"

She was gazing straight into his eyes as she spoke, and she evidently wished to convey something to him. He waited.

"Your room is warm enough?"

That was not literally true. But in freezing, starving China a room with a warm radiator in it during icy nights was the last word in comfort. In the daytime the room was only a little above freezing, but the lobby and the library were comfortably heated.

"Warm enough," he said in a slow, questioning tone. His eyes asked for more direct information.

"What about the mattress?" she asked.

And then he got it. This was a request for another rendezvous. Evidently, Mai would be occupied again. It remained only to discover the time.

Ruxton said, "The situation is the same."

She nodded, and said, "Good."

With that she headed for the outside door. Ruxton watched her go. He was thinking how impressive was the power of sex. He had always admitted its influence on himself, but Phenix had held off her own desire all these years. Now, with a rush, it was upon her.

He put that out of his mind, took a deep breath and braced himself for his next task on this day which he intended to be a turning point in his prison life. Today, he became cause.

He headed up to the second floor, a little shaky, but very determined. A soldier barred his way, as he started along the corridor. However, Mai looked up, saw the situation, and said in Chinese, "Let him pass."

A few moments later, Ruxton was explaining to the frowning officer that he had had an insight into his own rigidity of thinking. And that he believed that if he told his insight to the two Chinese prisoners, Statesman Chang and General Mu, they also might break through their own stubborn resistance to communist indoctrination.

Mai sat back in his chair, looked at Ruxton with bleak eyes, and said, "Has it made you into a good Communist?"

Ruxton replied, "Whether I said yes or no to that, we would have no proof, because nothing would show. The quickest way to determine its value is to try it on someone who is under maximum threat right now."

Mai smiled a faint, grim smile. But his eyes were like steel as he said, "Every time someone is to be executed for his crimes, I find you standing in my way, Mr. Ruxton. No one else seems to be as concerned."

Ruxton felt impatient, and made a gesture of dismissal with one hand. "I am concerned about them, yes. But that's a general feeling against any kind of killing." He broke off. "Let's not get off to discussing me, Major. I'm not important in this."

Mai smiled again, tightly. "Permit me to differ. To me, this group of twenty white men is by far the more important of the two groups of prisoners." He continued in a severe tone, "We are not interested in sparing everyone, Mr. Ruxton. When the living are venal, they sometimes learn their lessons correctly only by observing that punishment—after a certain point of venality is reached—is inevitable. Do you not agree?"

Ruxton hesitated. That the conversation was continuing at all was encouraging. The request for agreement was a device that had been used almost constantly in certain situations, and was evidently a technique of persuasion, and not of final judgment. He said slowly, "The way I feel, sir, death is too heavy a punishment for civil offences. People try to fit into the culture in which they find themselves, and all cultures gain their stability from the fact that once a majority has got set into its ways it cannot change easily. The hope of Communism is that, when it has had its chance, when everyone has given it years of time to prove itself, it will have been so successful that it has the support of the men and women of that era. However, if the people who matter in any group continue to resist it, then Communism will be overthrown at some future time. Since it hasn't yet proved that it can do any of these things, what is the point in killing a lot of people, particularly for what was not a crime when it was committed?"

Mai's dark eyes studied him, his face impassive now. He said finally, in a mild tone, "You have a long way to go, Mr. Ruxton."

Ruxton shook his head stubbornly. "My feeling is, I've

186

come a long way," he protested. "I'm willing for Communism to be tried out, to have its chance to prove itself. For the life of me, I cannot see anything wrong with that idea."

"You will, Mr. Ruxton," said Mai. "What you are expressing is one of those wishy-washy bourgeoisie concepts. This is an attempt to be scientifically objective and not involved in the struggle of the people. When you finally get the strength of will that comes with being a Communist, you will look back and be astonished at how weak you have been."

The conversation had deviated far from his original purpose, and it must be because Mai wanted it that way. Ruxton was disappointed. He said, "I'm sorry to have taken up your time, Major, with an unacceptable request."

Mai said, "Sit down. I shall take you over to the prison in a few minutes." He picked up the phone. ·

As Mai talked to someone in the prison, making arrangements for the visit, Ruxton thought wearily, "What was all that for? So much fuss, resistance, foolish talk—and then he gives in." He felt exhausted.

But his spirits began to recover on the way to the prison. And he quickly forgot the struggle with Mai as he contemplated the greater struggle ahead. His task was nothing less than to persuade two men like Mai, like Hitler, like Stalin— *two right men,* whose rightness had already brought them to the edge of the grave—that they must change all their basic ideas immediately.

37

The two Chinese prisoners entered the interrogation room uncertainly. Seeing them, Ruxton was surprised to realize that General Mu Daio-tu was not really a big man. The previous night he would have estimated his height at five feet eleven. Now, he revised the figure downward by several inches.

Mai barked at the men, "Sit!"

Listlessly, the men obeyed, and there was a pause while Ruxton gathered his thoughts. He frowned at the ceiling and noticed that a skylight brightened the room considerably over the night before. The light of day was, he observed, not kind to the prisoners. They looked very drab in their tattered clothing. Tufts of cotton poked out from the padded sections. Their faces were gaunt. Even General Mu looked older by many years.

Mai gave an accurate translation of Ruxton's analysis of the "right" person. The lack of distortion in his interpretation of Ruxton's ideas suggested a genuine interest in the method. When Mai was finished, Chang Ku-tai said, "But how does all this affect the truth of a matter?" And General Mu Daio-tu asked, "Are you suggesting that I fought the battle of Hu-yang in my own head, and that it didn't happen as I said?"

Since Ruxton presumably knew nothing of the battle, he asked about it, and when the details had been given him, he said, "No, I believe the facts. But only a 'right' man could have insisted on 16,000 troops fighting to the death."

"The order to do so came from the Generalissimo Chiang Kai-shek, and I carried it out." Mu was calm. "Under the Chinese principle of *nien-tao-fa*, the military law of collective reponsibility, I would have been shot had I disobeyed. And the man next in line would have been shot had he disobeyed me."

"That proves my point," said Ruxton triumphantly. "I cannot believe you would have saved your own life at the expense of 16,000 men had you believed you were wrong. Therefore, you felt 'right.' And therefore, my question is, how 'right' does a man have to feel to be able to sacrifice an entire division in a single battle?"

It was a tricky argument, Ruxton realized. General Mu might feel threatened at the implication that he would save his own life at the expense of his men. Actually, that had nothing to do with the argument. Abruptly, Ruxton realized that the trickiness of the argument had penetrated to the officer. The man's eyes narrowed, and—just like that —he was angry. "The battle was fought in the Chinese tradition of bravery!" he yelled.

Ruxton was not prepared to argue a military point, or the merits of a battle. These, of course, did have a terrible reality of their own. What he wanted to bring to the attention of the two men was that eighty percent of human males did not have the kind of character to maintain such a death stand. They were not mentally and emotionally constructed to direct a battle. It took a special type of personality to do what Mu and Chang had done. Such a personality might well be the optimum type to command an army corps or head a diplomatic mission. But now, here in this prison, each man must break free of the rigidities of the past, surrender the certainties that had once been so successful, and adjust to the new requirements.

He was explaining this carefully in English, when Mai Lin Yin cut him off. "Ah-ha," said Mai to Mu Daio-tu, "so you are angry at last, General. So this American has found your secret guilt. In the most cowardly fashion you allowed an entire division to be destroyed to save your own hide."

"That's not true," said General Mu. But he looked shaken.

"All these months," said Mai with excitement, "you have been calm in your successful evasion of guilt. Exposed at last, you bellow like a wounded tiger."

Mu was beginning to recover. He said, "The next time a general officer of the Chinese People's Army is ordered to fight a severe engagement, it would be interesting to hear your opinion if he failed to assault the enemy as directed."

Ruxton stood helpless before the useless argument. It was in Chinese, and therefore he was not even entitled to understand it, let alone participate. He said to Mai, urgently, "Are you translating what I said? What is he saying?"

Mai turned to face him. He looked pleased. "Mr. Ruxton, your method is an excellent one, for it has done something all our tactics have up to now failed to do. It has brought out strong emotion in General Mu." He went on with satisfaction, "What I particularly like about the method is that it is a direct attack on the false values to which these men cling. I have to admit that up to now it has never occurred to anyone to challenge Mu Daio-tu's military career as such."

Ruxton gazed at the man gloomily. Mai was missing the entire argument. "Right" people could support true or false values with equal fervor. He was minded to say to Mai, "What about the possibility of the false values of communism to which you have attached your rightness?" He didn't say it. He said instead, "Will you ask Chang Ku-tai, does he comprehend what I have been trying to explain?"

Mai translated the request. Chang replied, "It is your contention that human beings derive a feeling of being 'right' from events with which they are intimately connected."

Ruxton said, "No. My contention is the opposite of that. Certain people—not everyone—have an innate feeling of rightness, and then they *think* the events prove them right. Yet they believe they are gaining their rightness from the event, when in fact the feeling of being right existed first."

Chang looked troubled. "Events are a truth in themselves, and accurate analysis is not subjective."

Ruxton said, "People who feel 'right' the way I have described are often able to be analytically accurate, and sometimes not. It is my observation that they are never aware of the areas in which they are not able. For example, my guess would be that General Mu fought an analytically skilful battle at Hu-yang. But I believe from, uh, observation that his need for so many concubines is not normal."

"I agree with you," said Chang. "I never had more than three women at a time in my life. What can a man do with a dozen?"

"In America," said philanderer Ruxton mildly, "we believe that a man should have only one woman."

"Impractical," said Chang impatiently.

General Mu interrupted, "Perhaps you gentlemen do not understand true virility. Under normal circumstances, I needed sexual release only three or four times a day. But during the stress of battle a dozen times was not too frequent for me."

It was an area in which Ruxton felt analytically incapable of sound judgment, so he said, "An American psychiatrist might say that the general is suffering from sex anxiety. Please notice that he does not seem able to analyze his need as abnormal."

He glanced at the officer, and saw that the man's eyes were bright, and that he seemed to be in a state of trembling excitement. Sex stimulation? Perhaps he now would be motivated to play the Communist game so he could start copulating again.

He considered that for a moment, recalled a half year period of impotence that he had experienced, hitherto inexplicable, and decided that in the final issue sex would take second place to rightness.

He watched as General Mu walked over to the wall near the door. The man's bony frame was stooped. His face twitched.

Seconds, and then minutes, went by.

Presently, the mental battle became unbelievable. Ruxton thought, "If death is forever, and life worth living, he has everything to gain simply by admitting error."

A tiny sweat broke out on General Mu's forehead. The room was icy cold. But he stood there and perspired. And still no words passed his gray lips.

Ruxton said gently, "General, were you wrong at Hu-yang?"

The man's attention seemed far away, and for a long moment it seemed as if he did not hear Mai's translation. Then, he nodded. "Yes, I was wrong."

Mai translated that tensely. Ruxton waited.

The officer continued thoughtfully, "The concept of collective responsibility has value where forces are relatively well matched. Under such circumstances a small degree of extra bravery and determination can sway the balance. The Japanese welcomed our death stand. It gave them an opportunity to destroy with their mechanized forces one of the German-trained divisions they were anxious about. While the cost was heavy to them, they could afford their losses and we could not afford ours. Similar stands at Nanking and Shanghai cost the Chinese forces ten percent of the entire group of trained officers in the country, and sixty percent of the manpower of the forces involved in the fighting. All the troops that were killed were potential officer material for the vast Chinese armies that were needed to save China. Nationalist Chinese forces never completely recovered from Nanking, Shanghai and Hu-yang. When later, in the first Burma campaign—"

He stopped, hesitated, and said, "That's not important. What matters is that when the orders arrived to make the stand, I called General Pai to protest, and he agreed with me, and as is well known, he later became a master of strategic withdrawals. But he said that the Generalissimo would not hear of anything but a death stand. I accordingly fought the battle with grief in my heart. I was not wrong in doing this, since even generals must obey their superior officers, but I was wrong in later justifying the battle and in taking pride in it."

He had spoken without looking directly at anyone. Now, he turned and faced Mai, "If it is not too late, I am willing to do field labor, and catch flies, and whatever else is required."

When Mai had translated that, Ruxton said, "What about Chang?"

The former Nationalist emissary shook his head, and said, "My analysis of events is documented and on record. It has proved to be a true prediction. What can I say except that I *was* right?"

Since the rightness or wrongness of a particular action was not at issue, Ruxton merely said, "Now, come, sir. Find some way in which you were wrong in all this."

The small, dark eyes were bright. Chang cupped his chin in his hands and stared at the floor.

Time passed.

Finally, Ruxton turned to Mai. "Ask him if he doesn't think that at least he was wrong in the sense that anyone on the losing side is wrong?"

Chang glanced up as Mai translated the question and stared for a long moment at Ruxton. Then he nodded. And said, "The fact is that much of my position has been wrong. For a hundred years, China's only valid goal has been to become a strong military power. How this was accomplished, whether through Russia or America, should not have been an issue among Chinese people. I allowed myself to become an advocate of American aid as distinct from Russian. I was wrong also in allowing myself to be sidetracked into social issues, when the fact is that the type of economic structure adopted by China at this present stage in her development is of minor importance, so long as the method used included the mobilization of the country's manpower for industrial and military purposes."

He smiled. He seemed more at ease. He said, "I'm sure we can all agree that China has come a long way since that day in 1894 when the Imperial Chinese government informed the American diplomat, the Honorable Charles Denby, that China had not a single soldier with which to oppose Japanese seizure of Korea." He smiled again, more bleakly this time. "You may be interested in the reply given by Mr. Denby. He said the Japanese invasion was not a threat to the vital interests of the United States, and that China should seek diplomatic help from Russia, the vital interests of which—it was held by the American government —were affected."

Ruxton began, "Sir, what I want you to become aware of is not the wrongness of an analysis, but that quality in you that—"

He was interrupted.

Mai barked at Chang, "What about your mission to Japan? What about your advocacy of a no-war policy when Japan seized the five provinces in 1937?"

The old man said, unhappily, "As you know, my advice was not accepted. On July 21st, 1937, military leaders from all over China met in the auditorium of the Central Military Academy and pledged their loyalty to the nation, determined to offer a united front against the invader, resistance to be based on a policy of *k'ang-chang tao-ti,* a fight to the last. Was I wrong to feel grief-stricken at that decision? In view of the fact that these areas are now back in China's possession, I must confess, yes, I was wrong. My error lay in my narrow identification of China as being Kuomintang. From the point of view of their interests, I was right, since—except for those who have been accepted by the Communists—not one of the persons who attended that July meeting is now in power. But as things stand, China is governed by Chinese. The inequitable foreign rights have been forcibly abrogated. China has a front-line force of 1500 planes, and has become a military power to be reckoned with. All of these things are right. I cannot be sure that they would have happened had my advice been followed. Therefore, I was very probably wrong to advocate the views that I did advocate."

After he had translated Chang's words for Ruxton, Mai said, "I plan to recommend that these two prisoners be given an additional three months to correct their views."

Ruxton was silent. All three men had missed his point.

On the way back to the hotel, Mai confided, "Actually, having Chang Ku-tai make such a confession will be welcome news in Peking. His name is known all over Asia, and his admission of error is valuable propaganda material."

Ruxton thought, ruefully, "To think I put in all that time and energy just to add two more communists to the large group that already exists."

But he knew after a moment that he had accomplished more than that. Men who were neurotically "right" in the way that he was could not be persuaded to give up their rightness, but they would give ground on a point of logic into which they had projected rightness provided it was called to their attention, and provided they were, at the time, also standing on the trapdoor of a gallows. The gallows by itself was not enough, and the information by itself was not enough. As witness Mai, a "right" man, who had not for an instant considered what was said as applying to him.

It was all pretty grim. But it was something to know.

38

It was half an hour later.

The day had been particularly dusty, and Ruxton headed for the washroom in the hotel, and gave himself a refreshing rinse. On the way downstairs, as he approached the second floor, he heard a woman—not Phenix—speaking in Chinese.

She said, "How long will you be alone?"

"Two hours." The answer came from Mai Lin Yin, but he spoke in such a low tone that Ruxton stopped short on the second step from the bottom, just out of sight.

"Then we have time?" It was the woman, and her voice also sounded conspiratorial.

"Yes."

"Then please come to me at once. I long for your arms around me."

"And I yours," almost whispered Mai Lin Yin.

Ruxton hesitated no longer, but came down the remaining steps, and so into Mai's range of vision. The commandant was standing, watching the thin, plain wife of Fa 'tze walk off along the hall.

He gave Ruxton a startled look, then an expression of relief flitted across his face. He acknowledged Ruxton's greeting with a curt nod.

Meanwhile, Madame Fa 'tze had paused further along the corridor, one hand on a door knob. At that point, the armed sentries walked past her, coming toward Mai. Her gaze followed them for a moment. Abruptly, she turned and disappeared into the room across the hall.

That was as much as Ruxton saw. He made his way to the lobby, bemused. He was thinking, "Of course. I should have guessed. Having more than one woman is part of the neurosis."

It wasn't—he analyzed—that infidelity was confined to the "right" personality. Since some seventy per cent of American women were reputed to be partially or totally frigid, millions of normal men were compelled to seek other sexual resources.

. . . He wondered if Phenix knew.

Ruxton decided, after a moment's consideration, that she did. That was why she was sleeping with a white man, the one forbidden sex behavior in Red China.

How he might make use of what he had seen and heard, Ruxton had no idea.

That night he and Phenix made love in the hurried manner of thirty-minute lovers. All too soon she was gone, her footsteps a whisper retreating up the stairway. Ruxton dressed hastily in the darkness, found Tosti's flashlight by the door, and allowed himself two minutes to catalogue items stored in the basement. What particularly interested him was an aluminum extension ladder which, he estimated, was long enough to reach the top of the big prison wall.

Ruxton walked back to the hotel sobered by the realization that his next cause action, the freeing of Fo Hin-di, was actually possible. Every step was solved, except the important one of communicating with Fo and gaining his cooperation.

Arrived in the hotel lobby, Ruxton was about to sit down when he saw that the soldier at the desk was motioning to him. The man pointed at the dining room, and gestured imperatively. Ruxton, surmising that he was to go in, walked over, and glanced through the portieres. He saw that a meeting was in progress, since the white prisoners were there, along with most of the Chinese interpreters.

For an instant he hesitated, then he shrugged, and thought, "Let's see what price I have to pay for having the commandant's wife as my mistress." He clamped his teeth together, pressed lips against each other, entered and sat down.

After a moment, the chief interpreter stood up, his thin, intellectual face tense, his eye glasses bobbling. He waved one hand at the Chinese who was speaking, and addressed Ruxton sharply through Ho Sin Go, "Where have you been, Mr. Ruxton?"

Ruxton stiffened at the tone, but he waited patiently for the translation, and then he said, "I thought these meetings voluntary. But here I am—so what's the problem?" That was his story and he intended to stand by it to the last available moment of love-making.

Fa 'tze said, "We sent the priest over to the library to find you, but you weren't there."

Ruxton realized that they might have looked other places, so he could name no specific location where he might have been. He said curtly, "Obviously, I didn't run away, if that's what bothers you. So let's resume the meeting."

Fa 'tze hesitated. He was a mild-mannered, intelligent man for whom the severity required by the regime came hard. After a moment, his face relaxed. "Yes, you are here, and as we can all see, somewhat antagonistic. However, you are correct. Attendance at these meetings is voluntary." He turned to the others. "Let us continue," he ordered.

What followed then seemed to be simply another drab meeting. Ruxton had no premonition that this would be different.

39

It was, Ruxton discovered, a meeting against stock exchanges and grain exchanges and in fact against any kind of price setting on the open market. And it wasn't so much, then, that the arguments were entirely irrational as that some of them were out of date.

The Chinese Reds were pretending that United States grain and stock exchanges still operated as they had prior to the depression. The American farmer, in reality relatively comfortable under the protection of price controls, was depicted as a victim of depression and of Wall Street manipulation.

Shortly after midnight, Mai came in and listened to the halting arguments with a scowl. After a while he went up to the front and took over the meeting with a curt "I'll handle this" to Fa 'tze.

To the group, he said, "You have now undoubtedly heard the Communist case against Wall Street. I fully expect that you are capable of asking intelligent questions about any point of doubt you may have. I want to hear some questions."

From Ruxton's left, Lemoine said in an irritated tone, "I don't see the value of this. I have a better subject for discussion."

Ruxton glanced at the young Frenchman, and noticed that he was very pale. He watched with interest as Lemoine continued, "I have been a Communist three times of my own free will. I thought I would have no trouble at all becoming one for a fourth time. But I seem to have great difficulty. Have you any advice for me?"

Mai said, in a hard tone, "The first three times you were not a Communist, Mr. Lemoine."

"I felt that I was," Lemoine answered. He seemed not to notice the commandant's intense emotion as he went on warmly, "I attended meetings. I marched in parades. I helped over-turn a street bus."

Mai answered grimly, "These were undoubtedly commendable actions, but in your case they were obviously the behavior of someone playing at being a Communist."

Lemoine said peevishly, "All right—so I played. Now I sit here night after night in these groups, becoming more and more tired each evening, but no closer to being a Communist. Where are these brainwashing methods that we have heard about? I need them used on me."

Mai seemed to be involved in a mental struggle. When he finally spoke, it was evident that he had partially taken control of himself. "I should remind you that your task in Project 'Future Victory' is to brainwash yourself. These group meetings are designed to help you."

"They haven't helped me a bit," Lemoine said stubbornly.

"In fact, they've just made me increasingly irritated. If this is brainwashing, it will never work."

Mai studied him with narrowed eyes, then said in a voice thick with rage, "Just one minute, Mr. Lemoine, while I get the equipment, and we'll do a little old style brainwashing. Just one minute."

With that, his face dark as thunder, he strode out from behind the table, across the room and through the portieres.

Gregory turned and said to Ruxton, "In Korea, many of their brainwashing stunts were directed at more than one person. But a number of them could be used on one individual."

Mai came back into the room, an automatic revolver in his hand. As soon as he was back at the table, he said, "Mr. Lemoine, stand up."

Lemoine, a startled expression on his face, climbed to his feet.

Mai raised the automatic. "See this?" he asked. "It contains eight shells. Seven are blank, one is loaded. Come up here!"

Lemoine, gray and visibly shaken, walked to the table. Mai held the gun out to him. "Take it!" he said in an inexorable tone.

Lemoine slowly reached out with trembling hand and took the weapon. He stood holding it awkwardly.

"Raise it!" commanded Mai. "Place the muzzle against your head."

Like an automaton, Lemoine brought up the gun, and pointed it at his head.

"Pull the trigger!" Mai snapped.

Lemoine lowered the gun. He stared for a moment at Mai, and he was breathing hard. "Are you crazy?" he gasped. "Why, the first bullet may be the one that's loaded."

Mai smiled a tight smile. "Yes, Mr. Lemoine. You asked for old-style brainwashing." He held out his hand. "Give me the pistol."

Lemoine reached across the table and placed the weapon in his hand. Mai stood fingering it, the same fixed smile on his face. He removed his attention from Lemoine, and his eyes took in the other prisoners. He said in a ringing voice, "Gentlemen, we're going to have a demonstration whereby someone this evening will lose his life. Since you have Mr. Lemoine to thank for this, you may by a two-thirds majority vote, select him as the victim."

De la Santa stood up, and his words were translated. "Mr. Mai," he said, "we could all see you losing your temper with

197

Lemoine. I think you should recognize that strong emotions have been stirred in you. Why not withdraw and let this meeting continue as it was before you came in."

Mai said savagely, "We will proceed with the vote."

As a murmur ran through the room, Ruxton closed his eyes and waited for fear to strike him, but there was none. Far in the back of his head, a hot point of anger burned a little hotter, that was all. By that time the interpreters were barking out names, asking each man "yes" or "no" as to whether or not Lemoine should be the one executed.

The vote was 20–0 against execution.

Mai stood at the head table, the smile fading from his face. His gaze flicked from person to person, and came to rest finally on Ruxton. He said, with annoyance, "Mr. Ruxton, how do you explain a 20 to 0 vote, which, had it been reversed, would have freed every other person from jeopardy?"

Ruxton stiffened to a conscious coming-to-grips with the reality that this man and what he did was part of his daily life. He said slowly, "Whenever a crisis comes upon us here my impulse is to put off a decision in the hope that it will not really happen. Perhaps at some level of the mind I expect that the anger you display on such occasions will evaporate."

Mai stood with the pistol, scowling, then he explained patiently, "There is no anger in me, except the anger of an indignant father whose moral sensibilities have been outraged by the behavior of his children." He finished, "Would you change your vote, now that I have explained my motives to you?"

It struck Ruxton with a pang that he had actually been brought to the center of the stage, and that therefore the threat had shifted from Lemoine to him.

The realization put extra care into his next words. He said, "No—because I still hope that the father, however angry, will have mercy on his children, and that this evening will not bring severe punishment to any person."

Mai said harshly, "The ideal father does what is necessary, and since this is an analogy only—I, as the father who represents the welfare of the people, declare that you gentlemen, by your unfortunate 20 to 0 choice, have voted yourselves into the game. Accordingly, we shall now draw lots, that most democratic of all methods of selection." He turned to the interpreters, "A sheet of paper and a box, please." When these articles were brought, Mai sat down and, while total silence reigned, wrote on the sheet of paper, tore it into

198

pieces and dropped the pieces into the box. "Shuffle those," he said to Fa 'tze.

When this was done, Mai reached in without looking down, picked a slip of paper, and then read the name on it: the Dane, Niels Madsen. The second name was Gregory; the third, Jarnoz; the fourth, the Portuguese, Diogo; the fifth was Ruxton; the sixth, the priest—

Mai scowled at that, then threw it on the floor. "That doesn't count," he said. He drew another slip for six, and read the name, "Kuznetoff." The seventh was Tittoni. At that point, Mai said, "I arbitrarily name the eighth and last person to be Lemoine."

He waved an arm excitedly, and pointed at the right wall. "Those persons named will please line up over there."

There was no doubt but that he was serious. Ruxton, a little numb now, got up with the others who had been named, and walked over to the wall. He had a sense of being in a fantasy. But it was real enough to be standing there, presently, one elbow touching Jarnoz and the other the Dane.

As Mai walked over to the group, the sly smile was back on his face. He held the automatic pistol, and, as he came up, he motioned with it in a peremptory fashion. "Mr. Ruxton, you get over to the end of the line!"

His hand movement suggested that the end of the line was to his right. Ruxton walked over and took up the indicated position.

Mai pointed the pistol at Lemoine, and waved it in the same commanding fashion. "You," he snapped, "fourth position!"

Lemoine, gray and grief-stricken, obviously in deep shock, obeyed.

At that point, there was a sound from beyond the portieres. They parted, and half a dozen soldiers with fixed bayonets came running into the room, and took position facing the prisoners.

Their arrival brought an electrifying sense of immediate action. Ruxton felt himself shrink, felt a sudden tension. But the hot center of fury behind his eyes won that battle of sensations. He continued to stand there, calm but keyed-up.

Yet he was uneasy. Being moved to the end of the line gave him a shaky feeling of having been selected for something.

But for what was not clear.

40

Standing there, Ruxton thought, "And the fact is, I personally cannot do anything." It was a feeling he had had before, that Mai could only take so much communication from him. He had used up his quota of the man's good will on General Mu and Mr. Chang, and on what he had already said.

Someone else would have to change this situation.

Pistol in hand, Mai now walked over to the Portuguese, who stood first to his left. The commandant was at ease, smiling. He said in a genial tone, "I recall, Mr. Diogo, that you advocated that your compatriot, that reactionary agitator, Gongoe, show courage—"

Ruxton thought, "Is that how he labeled that frightened boy in his mind? Reactionary—"

Mai continued, "How do you feel, Mr. Diogo, with an 8 to 1 chance that the first bullet is not blank?"

"I feel extremely angry," was the reply, "but I have nothing to say."

"Surely, you have some last words," Mai tantalized.

Diogo pursed his lips, and then said, "I cannot see the value of this reckless method. What am I to believe except that you consider individuals of so little worth that you subject them to a meaningless test?"

"Am I to understand," Mai asked in a dangerous tone, "that after all these months of reading Communist literature, you still retain the bourgeois inability to subordinate yourself to the good of the people?"

"I don't think," was the steady reply, "that at this moment I am anything but a human being confronting the threat of death, and trying not to be afraid. In my present state of mind, I cannot appreciate your motives."

Without another word, Mai raised the automatic, paused momentarily while he aimed directly between the eyes— and pulled the trigger.

There was an empty click.

Ruxton, who had flinched and closed his eyes, opened them and realized that he was in a state of incredulity. Then he thought, "They say that this was the feeling of the Jews about to be murdered in Germany in World War II, of the Kulaks about to be murdered—millions of them—in Russia in the long ago of the 1930's, and of the Chinese landowners confronted by the Three Anti and the Five Anti movements just a few years ago. They couldn't believe they were being murdered in the twentieth century."

He saw that Mai was staring at Diogo. "Well, my friend, you won the gamble—which is only right, since it would be a shame if an 8 to 1 chance did not pay off. You may sit."

Without a word, Diogo walked to a chair and sat down. He leaned on the table, forehead cupped in his hands, and stared down.

Mai stepped over to Gregory. "Well, Captain," he said, "yours is the seven to one risk. Do you have any comment?"

The officer ignored him, glanced at Ruxton, and said quickly, "Ruxton, what do you think of all this?"

There was a quiet dignity to the question that lifted it above the personal. Ruxton felt impelled to answer. "How do you mean, Captain?"

"Mai is killing us one by one without waiting for the two-year period to end, and without even adhering to the three-month rule he laid down—so what do you think is the *real* purpose of Project 'Future Victory'? Obviously, it has nothing to do with turning us into Communists. Major Mai couldn't care less."

Mai snapped, "Captain Gregory, I asked you a question. Address yourself to me."

The American officer turned to him. "You want a comment?"

"Yes."

"Very well. I don't believe that was a fair drawing. When I look at the men whose names came up, they appear to me, with one possible exception—that Dane—" he nodded at Madsen—"to be individuals whom you want to beat down. Show me the slips in that box. Either you just wrote nonsense on those papers, or else we're the only ones who are named on them."

Mai glared at him, then said in a quick aside to Ho Sin Go, "Do not translate that."

To Gregory, he said in a smooth-as-silk tone, "I cannot permit your words to confuse these others. You evidently have no comment to make."

"I even believe," went on Gregory, "that you have the pistol set, so that you know who will get the bullet. Somebody here you want to get rid of. I wonder who—and why?"

A look of extreme irritation erased Mai's smile. He said sharply, "You are certainly a man who can arouse me to annoyance. Take care! But obviously you feel you are not the selected person. Is that true?"

"I've been a good boy," said Gregory. "I go to the library every day. I make no disparaging remarks. No, I don't think I'm the one. My turn will come later."

"Cling to that hope!" said Mai, and raised the gun.

The sensitive mouth of the officer compressed. The lean face grew taut. He looked straight ahead, as the automatic pointed at his temple.

There was a hollow click.

Ruxton, who had kept his eyes open, saw that little beads of sweat stood out on Gregory's forehead. The officer slowly unclenched his fists, and without waiting for permission from Mai, walked over to a chair and sat down.

Mai gazed after him, as if he intended to say something. Evidently he thought better of it, for he glanced past number three in the line-up, and confronted Lemoine at number four position.

"Well, my friend," he said accusingly, "what do you think of the effect you created?"

Lemoine stared at him dully. "All these meetings," he mumbled. "I am going crazy."

Mai studied him with eyes narrowed in calculation. Then he nodded half to himself, and said, "You undoubtedly have strong feelings over having created such a deadly threat to your fellow prisoners. Accordingly, I offer you a second opportunity at this stage to end this situation. Take this pistol, select one person from among this group, and fire it at him. I want you to select the person who, in your opinion, is the least likely to be useful to the world Communist movement. To eliminate a useless person would be worthwhile, don't you agree?"

Lemoine said almost blankly, "You mean I—shoot one of these people?"

"It's a five to one chance that the shell will be blank," Mai urged. His dark eyes glittered eagerly.

Watching him, Ruxton suddenly realized the truth. All this was for Lemoine. Mai had spotted the young Frenchman's mental disturbance, and was trying to push him over the brink.

Since it was a trick designed to break a man's mind, obviously the next bullet was not the one. His reasoning carried him instantly past his early decision not to interfere in this situation.

He said aloud, in French, in a tense voice, "Lemoine—

choose me! Take the chance. Otherwise, we all have to go through it, anyway."

Mai gave him an astonished look, then turned to the French interpreter. "What did he say?"

The translator told him.

The Commandant walked slowly over to Ruxton, and stared up at him, lips thin, eyes hard. Ruxton returned the look steadily, and asked, "It's logical, isn't it, Major?"

Mai said angrily, "This is bourgeois nobility, Mr. Ruxton. I will not tolerate such an emotional gesture from you."

The man was so ice-cold in his manner, so deadly in the rigid way he held himself, that Ruxton backed down. He said, "How can I withdraw my offer?"

Mai said to Lemoine through the interpreter, "You may not choose Mr. Ruxton. His offer bars him. And, furthermore, your failure to reply at once now endangers a third person. Silence!" He made a violent gesture at Lemoine. "You may have another chance in a few minutes."

41

Smiling, showing his teeth, Mai Lin Yin faced Kuznetoff, who was third in that line-up. The commandant was clearly enjoying himself as he said in an expansive tone, "Well, my White Russian comrade, do you have anything to say?"

"Many things," was the steady reply, in Chinese. "Do I have time?"

"All the time in the world," was the answer. "You may bare your innermost thoughts."

At that point, Ruxton had another thought. Gregory was right. There had been no true drawing by lot. Mai was putting the "intelligentsia" among his prisoners under pressure, and he wanted reactions. Therefore, his statement that Kuznetoff had "all the time in the world" was almost literally true.

Kuznetoff said, "I am puzzled about this project."

"In what way?"

"Several points."

"Name them."

"While China starves," said Kuznetoff, "we are fed excellent food. It certainly lulls us."

He went on, "The indoctrination is painstakingly detailed, as if you meant it, so your aides unquestionably believe their task is to convert us. Such apparent sincerity lulls us.

"Even middling high Communist officials don't have heated quarters in winter. The fact that we do makes the project seem important, and that lulls us."

He continued, "When somebody is being yelled down and executed, we see that his fate is the result of some kind of strong emotion on the part of the commandant—yourself—and so we think we must do nothing to rouse you, and so long as you are not aroused, all seems to be well, and that lulls us.

"Yet one by one," Kuznetoff concluded, "we are being killed. What can we decide except that conversion to communism is not the true purpose of this project?"

Mai said sarcastically, "These are bourgeois arguments, Mr. Kuznetoff. You are concerned with individualistic fantasies. This is unwise. Your energy should be directed to a sincere effort to discover what false conceptions prevent you from becoming one of the people."

Kuznetoff said, "Everybody is an individual. You are an individual. That cannot be a bourgeois idea."

"I have subordinated myself to the people," said Mai, "and you continue to think of your own selfish interests and cannot bring yourself to cut your family tails."

Kuznetoff said, "You seem very much an individual to me, motivated by highly personal emotions."

"Many have misunderstood this," said Mai, "and since it is one of the distinguishing marks of a Communist, I shall answer you carefully." He barked a command at Fa 'tze, who opened a drawer in the table where he sat, searched in it, took out a booklet, and brought it over. From where he stood, Ruxton could see that it was printed in Chinese.

Mai read from it in a staccato voice: ". . . Within recent years, the tendency towards individualism, disorganization and indiscipline has been found among the cadres—" Mai glanced up and explained, "The cadres are the Communist group leaders." Looking down again at the page, he read on: "Some cadres thought that since the revolution was successful, they should be rewarded according to their contributions. They no longer performed their duties with scrupulous care but sought recognition, position, and pay. They weighed every assignment in the light of personal gain or loss and were reluctant to work in poorer or troublesome districts—"

Mai paused and glanced up at Kuznetoff. "The moment we hear such a thought, we know that we are dealing with a bourgeois masquerading as a Communist. Such people are quickly marked to be sent to those districts which they detest. There they are urged to meditate on a correct working attitude and learn obedience to the collective interest."

Kuznetoff said, "I sense an injustice here, since no doubt the innocent wife must accompany her husband to the place to which he has been demoted."

"There is no demotion," Mai explained patiently. "Demotion is a bourgeois concept. If you will bear in mind that it is better to endure the worst conditions under Communism than the best conditions under Imperialism, you will have a clearer picture of the truth."

Kuznetoff said slowly, "The best conditions under Imperialism include the wearing of fine clothes, living in fine houses under impeccable conditions, and for a man having a well-groomed and beautiful woman to make love to. And the worst conditions under Communism might be a remote, desolate area among primitive people without adequate shelter or food . . . This is better than what I have just said?"

Ruxton saw that Mai had relaxed, and was watching the younger man tolerantly. He said, "These are some of the bourgeois ideas of which you must rid yourself. The men and women whom you describe are criminals. You must learn that there is no real pleasure in exploiting the masses, and that this appearance of comfort and bounty, which seems to have impressed you, makes people empty not full. When we liquidate such persons, we are shooting hollow human shells and not real human beings at all."

Kuznetoff became very pale, and stood clenching his hands. Ruxton thought, "He's remembering that his family were among the 'hollow human shells' liquidated by a similar monstrous concept in Russia." It was the old labeling of one's enemies as sub-human. Hitler did it with the Jews and Slavs. Apparently, it was necessary mentally to animalize people before you could comfortably destroy them.

Since everybody did it, the method must be exactly and precisely human.

Mai was continuing in a severe tone, "As for the position of the wife in the circumstances you have described—how can she have good will, let alone feelings of love, for someone whose old-style thinking makes him a potential reactionary? She should be the first to denounce her husband for holding incorrect views." Mai's voice was resonant as he went on, "No, no, Mr. Kuznetoff, women have assumed the dependent role long enough. They must now learn to be realistic. And so, you can see that if you find a wife with her husband at some remote area, she is there because she shares her husband's backward views. So do not feel sorry for her. She is exactly where she ought to be."

It struck Ruxton that one could not escape the inexorable logic of these fanatics. Reasons served no useful purpose. For the masses, to live in hell was being held up as being the same as living in heaven. Meanwhile, Mai himself had a dozen spare mattresses in his basement and lived amid the glittering furniture of a murdered mandarin, and slept with more than one woman. In Peking, Mao Tse-tung dwelt in one of the old Imperial palaces, and exercised despotic power of life and death over hundreds of millions of people.

Kuznetoff was staring with fixed gaze into space. "I have no further comments, Major Mai," he said icily.

Mai had been leafing through the booklet. For the moment he was intent, and seemed unaware of the emotion he had aroused. "One more quotation," he said. He found the page, glanced up and said, "Liu Shao-ch'i in speaking of the five loves of a Communist—these being, of course, love of country, love of the people, love of science, love of labor, and love of public property, made the following statement—"

He looked very moved as he spoke, and Ruxton stared at him. This was a new Mai. Was the man really that impressed by one of the top Communists, which of course was certainly what Liu Shao-ch'i was?

Mai read: " 'To sacrifice one's personal interests and even one's life without the slightest hesitation, and even with a feeling of happiness, for the sake of the Party and the Class, for national liberation and for the emancipation of mankind, is the highest manifestation of Communist ethics. This is a Party member's highest manifestation of the principle. This is the manifestation of the purity of proletarian ideology in a party member.' "

Kuznetoff stared straight ahead, and made no reply.

Mai blinked at him, and then seemed to realize for the first time the hostility he had aroused in the other. His body stiffened. He said, "Keep Liu Shao-ch'i's self-sacrificing thought humbly in mind as you play your part in this worthwhile brainwashing drama."

With that he raised the pistol, and pointed it at Kuznetoff. The blue eyes of the White Russian gleamed with hatred. His face twisted into a contemptuous smile. His body, which normally looked tightly wound-up, was, perversely, relaxed and casual.

He was still in this state when Mai pulled the trigger.

There was a metallic click.

Kuznetoff drew a deep breath and said acidly, "I don't believe the gun is loaded."

But perspiration mottled his face where a moment before his skin had been smooth and dry and colorless.

The Chinese officer said with curling lip, "I won't bother to have that translated. In a few moments there will be an explosive sound, and someone will fall dead, and you will have been proved wrong."

The younger man's hatred suddenly thinned his mouth to a slit. He said harshly, "I don't understand why I am in this project at all. During World War II most White Russians fought with Hitler, and though I was not there in body I was certainly there in spirit."

The statement was so obviously dangerous; it seemed totally to brand him as a Fascist, that Ruxton held his breath. He let it out again as Mai said without rancor, "These are matters we leave to our big brother, the Soviet Union. You represent as much Fascist venom as any man anywhere, and we were curious. By observing you, we may learn lessons of great value, and perhaps at some later time we can even advise our big brother on how to deal with similar descendants of the despoilers of old Russia."

"Bah!" said Kuznetoff. "All that anti-fascist stuff is just surface talk. It is a well-known fact that some of the top German Nazis have been seen on the streets of Russian cities. There is even a story that Hitler is alive today somewhere in Russia."

Mai said, "You are again expressing bourgeois concepts. One of the psychological phenomena, which is understood by our theory, is what occurs when someone reacts against Communism. Such people can be forced to react more than is good for them—forced so easily by skilful propaganda that we Marxists have an exact word to describe them. We call them reactionaries—that is, people who react. All Communist propaganda is directed toward producing a paranoid *react*ion of response. This, in turn, produces a compulsive paranoid revolutionary feeling in the liberal groups. These two groups then inter-react until they are quite insanely furious at each other. But it is the first reaction of the more conservative types that requires the massive propaganda and agitation. What follows is essentially automatic."

Kuznetoff was silent, scowling.

Mai smiled at him blandly. "You mentioned Hitler. Hitler understood revolution and counter-revolution as thoroughly as we Communists. Yet our world-wide organization of relentless propaganda, utilizing Marxist ideology—which holds that capitalist countries would inevitably war with and destroy each other—completely nullified Hitler's pitiful international propaganda."

Kuznetoff said, "His murder of the Jewish people lost him world support."

"Nonsense," said Mai. "Hitler lost the propaganda battle long before his extermination program." He ended curtly, "I urge you to correct your bourgeois attitudes. Be prepared to share comradeship with anyone, even a former Nazi who is working toward the same goal. Now, step aside!"

Kuznetoff hesitated. He looked resistant. Then he seemed to think better of it, for without a word he walked back to his chair and sat down.

But he had put on an impressive show of the virtually unqualified courage of hate.

42

Mai stepped up to Lemoine.

"One more chance for you," he said. "Select anyone in this room for the next shot, and that will end this trouble which you have caused."

The young Frenchman was gray with fatigue as he answered huskily, "I'm not choosing anyone, Major. I'm sorry I started all this but I'm not going to make it worse by saving my own life at the expense of someone else."

"In that case, Mr. Lemoine," Mai said deliberately, "I think I'll let you wait again." He nodded at Jarnoz. "Step to fourth position. I have decided to give you an extra chance. You get the five to one opportunity."

When this had been translated, the two men exchanged positions, without a word.

Mai stepped back, and stared at the big man. "We Chinese have often wondered about you Turks," he said. "A stubborn people, the Turks, and, like the Chinese, victims of western aggression and insult."

Jarnoz said steadily, "Like the Chinese, we were very backward, but we have no enmity toward the people who forced us to modernize. The dynamic forces of mankind's growing pains worked inexorably to snap us out of our old ways, and we are grateful."

Mai said in a dangerous tone, "Are you comparing the

ancient Chinese culture with the primitive religious system of the old Turks?"

Jarnoz looked thoughtful. "No," he said. "Come to think of it, I'd better not. When Gongoe made a slighting remark about China, you had him killed. When the Swede criticised China, you had him killed, and when Holsenamer made that coarse remark about your country, you had *him* killed. Therefore this is an emotional point with you, and I should not have made any comparison. The truth is that the Chinese should solve their own problems, and we Turks, ours. Comparisons are odious and unjustified."

Ruxton listened to Jarnoz' words, staggered. He was implying race prejudice, total and all-embracing—depicting Mai as simply another Xenophobic Chinese, who at some organismic level operated entirely on the basis of tribe and blood and skin color.

He recalled flashingly what he himself had said that first day when Mai had invited him into his automobile. And there it was: he also had been critical of the Chinese. Within hours Mai had had him on trial for his life.

As his thought reached that point, he saw that Mai was gesturing at the interpreters not to make a general translation of Jarnoz' words.

The man stood for an entire minute of silence gazing at the bigger man. Finally, he stepped forward and without warning slapped Jarnoz' face.

The Turk winced but made no move. He said, "You see. My analysis strikes deep."

Mai said in a husky tone, "Your attempt to ascribe narrow motives to my actions is an insult to all Communists, and for that I slapped your face. We Communists are the true internationalists."

Jarnoz said frankly, "I had to say what I did, Major, because I believe it is true. I also believe you don't realize that you have these basic feelings below all your Communist training." The dark grimness of Mai's face seemed to give him pause, but he went on, "May I continue my analysis?"

Mai nodded. To the interpreters, he snapped, "No general translations." But the words were translated into Chinese for Mai. And so Ruxton followed the argument, as before.

"Consider," said Jarnoz. "An enormous propaganda is directed toward having the Chinese people be friendly toward the Russians. But the truth is that the Chinese people hate all Russians with whom they come in actual contact. So that the one authorized association with foreigners means nothing."

"Go on!" Mai was watching Jarnoz, eyes unblinking.

"Historically," said Jarnoz, "the Tai-ping Rebellion of the 1860's was anti-Catholic and anti-foreign. It got out of hand and millions of people were killed. Finally, the empress-dowager's forces surrounded Nanking, caught and beheaded the religious maniac and his relatives who were in command of it."

He went on, "The Boxer Rebellion at the turn of the century was anti-Catholic and anti-foreign. It was connived in by the old empress-dowager, who wrote many cunning memorials designed to encourage and inflame the anti-foreign passions of the people."

Mai's face was dark, but he did not interrupt as Jarnoz went on, "The Three Principles of the People, propounded by so enlightened a man as Sun Yat-sen, are essentially against foreigners. In fact, not until Chiang Kai-shek did we have in China a distinctly pro-foreign atmosphere, and so for the first time we saw in China itself Chinese friendly to foreigners."

"White Chinese!" said Mai with a sneer.

Jarnoz said, "Yes, I know what the Communists call them. But these White Chinese are all dead or in exile. Major, the pattern of anti-foreignism seems pretty clear."

"Are you completely finished?" Mai was stiffly polite.

"One more point, small but not to be dismissed. There are heavy penalties in the Red Chinese society for a Chinese girl who has sexual relations with a white man. I think you should consider what I have said, sincerely—don't you agree?"

Mai stood tapping with his finger on the butt of the pistol he held. His lips were pressed together and on his face mixed emotion showed. Presently, he swallowed hard, and said testily, "You seem to have quite a knowledge of things Chinese. Are you familiar with our history?"

"Yes." Jarnoz' tone was even. "I am professor of the Oriental cultures in my own country. I came to China to make a first hand study of China today—and here I am."

Mai said grimly, "Then you know that the opium wars were the most immoral wars in the history of the world— for their purpose was to force upon China a trade in drugs which she was making every effort to stamp out—"

Jarnoz said, diplomatically, "It was still the feudal period in China, and in other parts of the world, the merchants were not yet controlled. These two weaknesses combined to bring China misery."

"And you also know, then, that the Chinese people," Mai rushed on, as if he had not heard, "were subjected to the degradation of having most of their principal ports taken over. Through these ports foreign manufactures poured into an unprotected China. Machine-made goods competed with the work of craftsmen whose skill had been built up over the centuries, and wiped them out. For every ten thousand craftsmen of old days, there are now ten. These ancient arts were swamped by a deluge of worthless articles—"

"It was a great tragedy," Jarnoz agreed. "But the destruction itself was not by design. No human brain has ever been able to foresee the impact of new methods. In a world where high fences are still necessary, China's fence was taken down. But now you hate most the only country— America—that tried to prevent anyone from taking full control. The open-door policy—"

"It was the greatest of all disasters!" Mai suddenly yelled. "It had the worst effect of all. The British, wherever they have been in full control, eventually took some responsibility for the development and protection of the country they illegally occupied. In China no one was responsible. A pack of wolves was let loose upon a countryside which was forbidden to defend itself. Don't speak to me of the benefits of the open-door policy by a country that put up immigration barriers against the Chinese as early as 1880."

Jarnoz said, "America was almost last among the great powers to pass such immigration laws. For years the United States Congress maintained an attitude that a Chinese immigrant was the same as an immigrant from a European country. But gradually it was realized that the migrants from China had fantastically low standards of living. Even in the days of the frontier West in America—where standards were not high—the Chinese immigrants lived in quarters that were like pig pens. These men were products, no doubt, of the feudal period in China but such conditions had to be dealt with in a practical fashion by those who had to live with them."

Mai snarled, "Stop talking nonsense in defense of prejudice. People learn to live better as quickly as they can. The Chinese laborers who built the great American railroads were paid starvation wages."

Jarnoz said, "They saved their money and returned to China rich men, in terms of Chinese standards. But in both

211

China and America they lived like animals." He nodded judicially. "Culturally, it was a transition period from extreme poverty. I recognize that."

"Perhaps, you do not recall," bellowed Mai, "but there were signs at the entrances to parks and walks in the treaty ports. Do you know what those signs said?"

Jarnoz nodded soberly. "Yes, I know."

Mai was oblivious to the acknowledgment. "Those signs," he shouted, "had printed on them DOGS AND CHINESE NOT ALLOWED. Who was prejudiced? The Chinese? Or those who put up the signs?" His voice dropped to a low, tense tone. "Yes, the Chinese learned to hate these arrogant foreigners. But there's a difference between hate and prejudice. Prejudice contains no hate. Prejudice despises. We Chinese hated those who despised us. But we judged them not on race or color, but on their deeds—

"Wait!" He held up his hand imperiously. "Wherever the foreigner brought his so-called civilization, there corruption flourished. Shanghai, in its foreign time called the wickedest city in the world. Canton, Foochow—I could name all the treaty ports, and give a picture of the moral decay of each, as the Chinese realized that they were second class citizens in their own country."

Jarnoz said, "All that you say is true—up to a point. The white man is only slowly becoming civilized. Yet historically, China is not innocent. For 250 years, all trade with the West was done through the Canton hongs. All other traffic with foreigners was forbidden. Foreigners were insulted and despised. This was long before they did anything to merit it. You may well imagine their angry joy when they began to realize that the Chinese armed forces could not defend China. After all, the British force that landed in 1841 consisted of only 2300 men, and a year later less than 10,000 men defeated the Chinese forces at Chapu and Chinkiang, even though those forces with traditional Chinese valor, fought to the last man. The people, of course, did not realize that the hatred required of them was motivated by Manchu cunning and so they were easily persuaded to hate the foreigners. What followed was not pleasant, but out of this travail has now emerged a new China. The People's Democratic Dictatorship should be the first to realize that only after the old was destroyed could the new begin."

When Jarnoz had finished, Mai stood with mouth slightly open, his eyes glinting. He seemed to be having a battle with

212

himself. Abruptly, he exploded. "Perverted liar!" he yelled. "White men stink with prejudice, smell with the foul odor of false superiority, are rotten with race hatred—and you accuse the truly superior Chinese people of having feelings that are only possessed by foreigners."

Involuntarily, Ruxton took a step forward. He felt a desperate worry for Jarnoz as that mad shouting began. Yet after a moment he stepped back, his fear diminishing. Because the man was screaming arguments, not commands for execution.

Jarnoz said evenly, "I made these statements at your request. Perhaps, we had better get on with the torture."

There was a long pause. Mai Lin Yin stood leaning slightly forward, and he was breathing hard. Slowly, he straightened. A moment later he seemed to have recovered his self-control. He raised the pistol.

Jarnoz shrank a little, and said, "I have one more thing to say. The Chinese have the longest recorded history in the world—true?"

"True." Mai was wary.

"And as far back as their history goes," said Jarnoz, "they have been notorious for torture methods, of which this is only a mild version—true?"

Mai held out his hand warningly to the interpreters. Rage reflected in his posture, and there was no question but that Jarnoz should not have continued the argument.

Once more Mai's arm came up as if he were intending to aim the gun. Then he made a sudden move.

Down on Jarnoz' head came the barrel of the gun.

The big man stood trembling as if he were cold. Then with a moan he fell to the floor. He lay there, twitching.

"But he's not dead," Ruxton told himself shakily. Jarnoz had survived the longest criticism of China undoubtedly ever offered by one person to Mai Lin Yin. So his analysis must have penetrated and struck home.

Mai was yelling at the interpreter, "Take advantage, you fool!"

The interpreter, a little man, ran over, stood astride the fallen giant, and shouted at him in Turkish. As he jabbered, he nudged Jarnoz with his feet. He was so insistent that presently Jarnoz stirred, sat up, and mumbled something in return.

He recovered rapidly at this point. Mai, who was standing by, said to the interpreter, "Tell him to go to his room and go to bed."

When this had been communicated, Jarnoz stumbled to his feet, and shakily walked out of the room.

Mai turned back to the line-up of men, now reduced to four. His manner was grim and threatening. Nevertheless Ruxton said to him, "Major, why did you have someone talk to a half-conscious man?"

The other's forbidding countenance creased into a smile. "None of your business, Mr. Ruxton."

Ruxton regretted his question. The intention was quite obvious. The talking to a semi-conscious man must be a brainwashing technique, an attempt to wreck Jarnoz' mind.

He felt furious, but presently he realized that the anger was futile, and that the nightmare game was continuing.

43

Mai said harshly to Lemoine, "Move over to sixth position. You can wait one more."

Tears came to the young Frenchman's eyes as the words were translated. "Major," he half-sobbed, "all I asked was a faster way to become a communist. These men had nothing to do with my request. Spare them this torture."

Mai taunted, "This is brainwashing, old style, as per your request."

"I was tired," Lemoine sobbed. "So many meetings. I didn't know what I was saying."

Mai ignored him, and addressed Tittoni, the more intellectual of the two Italians: "Well, my friend, so at last I confront the mystery man, who has never explained his presence in China. In this hour of testing, do you care to reveal your secret?"

Tittoni was pale. "All I ever said," he muttered in a low voice, "was that my coming to China was a mistake. I have no secrets. To tell would make me look foolish. Therefore, I prefer silence. Raise your gun. Fire your bullet. My reasons for coming to China were as stupid as the actions of any person driven by religious impulses."

Mai said, surprised, "You are not religious? I thought all Italians were either Catholic or Communist."

"Not true. I am a rationalist, willing to believe in religion if something sensible ever offers, but all present day organized religions are to me merely nonsense from a superstitious past."

As these words were interpreted, Ruxton saw Father de

Melanier stand up in agitation. The priest said in French, "Were you born a Catholic, Signor Tittoni?"

Mai looked around, irritated, and asked for the comment to be translated. When that was done, he said sharply, "Tell the priest to mind his own business."

Nonetheless, a moment later, he had the question repeated to Tittoni. The long, lean Italian nodded.

Father de Melanier muttered aloud, "A renegade. I thought so."

Mai ordered the comment translated into Italian. "I reject that," Tittoni said indignantly. "However, I have more respect for him in his ignorance than he has for the struggle it cost me to free myself from superstition, so I shall not engage in an argument."

Mai pursed his lips. He seemed to be in a dilemma. Then he said, "I find myself having thoughts and feelings of leniency. These religious views which you have expressed are essentially my own." He motioned peremptorily at the Italian, and at the Dane who was next in line. "You two may sit. I order you out of this line-up."

The two men hesitated, looked uneasily at Ruxton and Lemoine, and then with shame-faced relief walked back to their chairs.

Mai stepped close to Ruxton. He said, "At this point, my friend, I should be inclined to end this game—except for one thing. Your urgent request that Lemoine fire at you still fills me with great eagerness to pull the trigger once more. And since you asked for it, I believe that you should be the victim of this final shot."

Ruxton looked down into that stubborn, angry face, and felt the color drain from his cheeks. He was thinking that all this delay in firing the fourth bullet meant that it was the one that was loaded.

His initial intuition that he should not interfere in this situation had been correct.

His one impulsive deviation would now cost him his life.

44

As the first intense fear began to fade out of him, Ruxton made a kind of truce with imminent death. He was able to say earnestly, "Major Mai, once the main drama began, I only said two things. Apparently, you took great offense at one of them."

Mai's manner was one of unrelenting stubbornness as he said deliberately, "I shall make you and Lemoine a proposition, Mr. Ruxton. Only one of you will receive a shot. Which one? Since you have attracted my attention, I permit you to decide whether the shot shall be fired at you or at Lemoine. Because of my leniency with these others, the chances are still four to one in favor of the person at whom the bullet is fired."

Ruxton didn't believe that. He said, "I might as well be frank. I believe the next bullet is the one that's loaded."

Triumph glinted in the other's brown eyes. He asked softly, "Would you like the following gamble? I shall fire the next shot at the floor. If it is not the one, then you will make a choice as to which of you will be shot at next. Agreed?"

All in a flash Ruxton's certainty that the next bullet was loaded, gave way to confusion.

Mai, watching him, said, "You realize that the chance then goes down to three to one?"

Ruxton was realizing. It was the dilemma of this deadly game of Russian roulette. He also realized with a belated awareness of how severe an experience it had been, that three men had already confronted the insane threat of the game. Each man in turn must have experienced the anguish that he was now enduring. He shook his head, and said unhappily, "Major, the victim cannot make such a decision."

Mai said quickly, "You are wrong. All through China people have been confronted by the need to decide who is fit to survive in the new age. This is the great problem of our time, Mr. Ruxton. The individual wants someone else to determine his value to society, but he must do it himself."

Ruxton felt no desire to engage in dialectical argument, and he said so. "You cannot expect a sensible decision from a man facing death."

Mai said, chidingly, "Mr. Ruxton, obviously the pressure you are under at this moment is approximately the right amount for you. Anything less, and you will continue to manifest those bourgeois characteristics which have already enabled you to waste—essentially waste—the first five months of your suspended sentence. You will admit, you show no sign of turning into a Communist."

It was true, but Ruxton remained silent.

Mai continued, "There are predominantly two types of irresponsible people: the simple, ignorant person, and the rigid, prejudiced person. In their millions, these two types maintain a stubborn adherence to old-style thinking. You cannot beat such thinking out of them, and of course you cannot reason it out because, amazingly, as you address these persons, you discover that it is their prejudice and their old-style thinking which responds to what you are saying. How do you alter the responses of the individual who is like this? We use force and emotional impacts. We teach him, using killing as a method of driving home the lesson. Whom do we kill?—people who represent ideas from which we want him to dissociate himself. To drive this lesson deeply into his simple, or his devious, mind—depending on the type —we Communists generally do not do the killing ourselves. *He* does.

"Even this sinks in slowly, for of course he didn't really want to do it. So we must have him tell us why he did it. You see—" Mai smiled slyly—"if we left him to his own justifications, we would discover that he had disowned personal responsibility for the act. When he has participated in enough killings, and told us the correct reasons each time, presently he will think first of the correct reason, and then, and only then, does there come a faint echo of the old-style thinking.

"Now, you may ask, what about the man who has been executed. Surely, he is an object of pity. No, in his millions, he was the backbone of a feudal system that has held China in chains for centuries. His death is necessary to teach the lessons we want the people to learn. But it is also necessary because if he were not dead he would be scheming for a return of the feudal system under which he flourished. We do not need this man, Mr. Ruxton, and we will not allow him to live wherever we find him."

Even as Mai spoke, Ruxton negated the reasoning that underlay it. All totalitarian revolutions were a waste of time, and a complete tragedy. Communism, like other total control systems, had taken the exact form it had because it was a means whereby compulsive terrorists expressed their irrational need to kill and dominate.

Nothing else was involved. Nothing at all. Nothing, nothing, nothing.

He came to this point in a rapid sequence of thoughts, and said, "Who will you kill in America, which is not a feudal state?"

Mai said, "That will be determined by the success of this project. But I can answer your question in a general way. America is, as you say, not a feudal state. It is an Imperialist state. First, we shall kill all the Imperialists, the Wall Street

217

exploiters, and all the people who are on lists which have already been prepared by the American Communist Party. A few hundred, or a thousand, rightist writers will have to be shot, and perhaps those labor leaders who have betrayed the revolution. From there on, we judge according to the recommendations that I shall make at the end of this experiment."

"I see," said Ruxton. He was shaken. He had never thought of it quite so concretely before.

"You see, Mr. Ruxton," said Mai tolerantly, "there are enough differences between Americans and Chinese to justify careful research. The Chinese is more of an individual than your American—"

Ruxton interjected, in astonishment, "I would have thought it was the other way around."

"No, no!" Mai spoke vehemently. "Consider. Americans buy only advertised goods, think only thoughts which they learned at school or at home, or—if they are rebels—the reverse of those thoughts. This makes them the most stereotyped people in the world, for they have been subjected to more of this for a longer period of time than any other nationals."

After a moment's startled contemplation of that, Ruxton decided against it. Uneducated people, like the Chinese, were, alas, not princes of Nature but were instead prey to the maddest superstitions. The American people had many faults, but not so many as foreigners believed.

Mai was speaking again. "In a struggle meeting," he said, "those who truly accept responsibility for the good of all mankind, do not hesitate to vote the death penalty for an individual whose existence is inimical to the welfare of the people. Bearing this in mind, will you now render a verdict between your value and Lemoine's value to the future of humankind?"

Ruxton shook his head, grimly. "Major, I see this little game of Russian roulette as suitably deadly, but I also see that the purpose of it is to get one of this group to turn against the others. You want to break through a kind of basic unity that we have, the existence of which surprises me. In Korea, you broke up the most personal friendships. Have you now decided to do the same here?"

Mai hesitated, then in a tone of genuine curiosity, he asked, "What are your reactions to the Korean brainwashing?"

"It's generally admitted that you were successful. So I

218

should like you to answer me one question. When the Americans returned from Korea, it was established by subsequent interrogation that over three thousand had been more or less seriously affected. Only a few hundred were not affected."

The brown eyes gazed at him enigmatically. "What is the question?"

"Periodically," said Ruxton, "during these past few years, American and European persons, held in Chinese prisons, have been allowed to proceed to Hong Kong. A percentage of them act like people on whom brainwashing has been successful."

"You wish me to comment on this?" Mai asked.

"In a moment—" said Ruxton. "First, one more point. Here in China, hundreds of millions of people have been forced to participate in these study groups, and prior to the liberation—" the word came surprisingly easily—"the Communist armies maintained discipline and a unified purpose by constant use of the study group system among all soldiers and officers—for example, the 'let us see' program just before the big Communist push that ended in victory—"

"What is the question?" Mai asked, his voice suddenly impatient.

Ruxton said frankly, "With all that proven success behind you, why are you really experimenting on twenty white men. Why bother? Why don't you just turn us over to a subordinate and have him put us through the old mill? You've proved that is all it takes."

The eyes of the Chinese commandant continued to stare at him for some moments. Then Mai pursed his lips. Finally, he said in a bleak voice, "Mr. Ruxton, brainwashing does not work. Not as it has been practiced up to now. That is why you and I and the others are here. Among us all, we will find the answer. We shall find the method that does work."

He finished harshly, "*This* method shall now continue."

The admission seemed to lift the entire project out of whatever organized meaning it had, and into a new realm of chaos and potential violence.

45

It was at least half a minute later.

The statement that made virtually meaningless the torture

and murder of millions, was behind them, and Mai was elaborating, moving his hands expressively as he talked.

"Of the three thousand prisoners in Korea, only a score—as you may recall—actually stayed behind. These results might be compared to the outcome of the early riots which we communists created. In those days, we were satisfied if we stirred things up. The aftermath of such foolishness was that the government forces executed all the communists they could capture. Today, whether in brainwashing or rioting we do not wish to be involved in actions that lead nowhere. Hence, old-style brainwashing techniques, which merely frightened, are of no value. The man must give himself to us all the way, and only methods that will get him to do this are of interest. If the brainwashing of three thousand American prisoners in Korea had been successful, they would have cut their tails of loyalty and family relationship and remained in China."

He made a dismissing gesture, and finished, "As for those persons who were permitted to go to Hong Kong after being brainwashed—the ones you mentioned probably divide into two groups: the cowards, who must make a big thing out of brainwashing in order to hide their cowardice, and those who gained a unique identity from the experience, which they would have to give up if they admitted it hadn't worked. So they pretend. China, Mr. Ruxton, is today a vast world of pretenders."

That was so exactly Ruxton's belief that, for a moment, he had nothing to say, for fear of saying it wrong.

Finally, he said earnestly, "If what you say is true, if such tactics as this—" he indicated the gun—"do not work, what can you or I or anyone gain by a continuation of this game?"

Mai stared at him in stony silence. Finally, he put the gun into his pocket and said, "You're a clever man, Mr. Ruxton. You led me such a devious verbal route that—like an unskilful chess player—I was unwary and now find myself checkmated. However, this merely wins you another gamble. Answer two questions, and I may indeed end this game. First, do you find anything bad about America?"

"One thing," Ruxton replied after a thoughtful pause.

"Details, please!"

Ruxton did not hesitate. Truth was truth no matter where it was told. He said frankly, "There are too many men like myself in the United States."

"Like yourself!"

Ruxton explained. "A percentage of American men are not faithful to their wives—"

He had a side thought, "Let him think that one over, considering Madame Fa 'tze—"

He continued aloud, "As a result many families break up, and as an additional result there is an immense amount of emotional upset in the homes. This affects the children, and they grow into emotionally shallow people. The United States is just beginning to pay the price of these broken families."

"You say you were this type of man yourself?"

"For many years. The truth of all this only recently dawned on me."

Mai pursed his lips. "What I really wanted from you," he said, "was a political answer and you have given me a social one."

"Political—is that your second question?"

Mai scowled. "Do not be so clever, but—" Pause—"Yes, I'll accept that as one reply. Now, my second question: do you see anything good in Communism?"

Ruxton said, "Oh!" And was silent.

After a long moment, there was still no way to avoid an answer, and so he said, "In reading Marx and Lenin, I was struck by the fact that these men were satisfied to win the State. They both felt that those who controlled the power of government would then, by experiment and right purpose, be able to achieve communism."

"What point are you making?" Mai sounded fretful.

"In the Communist Manifesto," Ruxton continued, "Marx of course stated many ideals which he thought should be achieved. It is these ideals that continue to win the support of idealists all over the world. Since half or more of the ten points have been the subject of social legislation in enlightened countries, it is obvious that Marx described a number of basic human needs. I find these ideals admirable," he finished glibly.

He added, under his breath, "But I don't agree that some of them can be achieved under communism. Also, it is significant that child labor—one of the main points of the Manifesto—has been abolished everywhere but in Communist countries."

Mai was nodding judicially. "You have much to learn, Mr. Ruxton," he said, "but your answer shows serious thought, and wins you the reprieve you have sought."

With that, Mai started for the door.

Beside Ruxton, Lemoine said in a low voice, "Is it over?"

He seemed confused, as though he had not been able to follow the sequence of events.

Ruxton shook his head. He did not look at Lemoine, as he said in French, softly, "No—that man is charged up to commit murder, and he hasn't murdered anyone yet."

Fascinated, he watched the retreating figure of the commandant.

46

Halfway to the door, Mai stopped. Turning, he walked rapidly over to Kuznetoff.

"So you don't think the gun is loaded?" he said.

Kuznetoff glared up at him, shrinking, his face suddenly waxen. But he did not reply.

Again, Mai made a quick turnabout. He strode over to Pescara, the Italian sailor, whose crime was seduction of a Chinese teenager. Out came the pistol from Mai's pocket. Before the startled seaman could more than stiffen, the barrel was pointing at his head, only inches away.

The explosion shattered the silence of the room. The blood came rushing, pouring down over his face. Pescara pitched forward to the floor.

Mai screeched at the soldiers, "Carry out the body of this foreign dog, and bury it!"

With that he walked quickly from the room.

Somewhere to Ruxton's left, Fa 'tze was yelling, "Everybody remain motionless!"

The interpreters, in turn, yelled the command in several languages.

Silence fell, and the men watched without a word as three soldiers lifted Pescara and carried him out.

Fa 'tze held up his hand. "Wait!"

There was a waft of cold air as the outer door of the lobby opened and shut.

In a severe tone of voice, as if he were a parent speaking to naughty children, Fa 'tze declared the discussion ended for the evening. He concluded, "You may now retire, and we can only hope that you have learned correct thoughts here this evening."

As Ruxton started for the door with the others, it seemed to him that he had all the correct thoughts but one:

The first correct thought was that the Chinese Communist leadership was made up exclusively of 'right' men.

The second correct thought was that they were racists above everything, and emotionally judged all things in relation to non-Chinese, exactly as Hitler, for example, had judged any Jewish situation.

The third correct thought—and this was worst of all—was they *didn't know* that race prejudice was the basis of their actions. They thought of themselves as internationalists. This created an incredible confusion, for their actions were never related to their statements.

And the last correct thought, but not the least, was that Project "Future Victory" was not basically intended to convert the little group of white men into Communists.

That left one large question: What was the project for?

47

He was about to leave the room when, from the corner of one eye, he saw Lemoine stagger to a chair and slump into it.

Ruxton was exhausted. Yet, impelled by pity, he walked over and with one hand reached down, took Lemoine by the collar and raised him to his feet. "Come along," he said heartily, "it's bedtime."

He had swung the younger man around as he spoke. Now, he saw that Lemoine was perspiring, and very pale. As Ruxton released him, he headed for the door, unseeing, muttering, "This Wall Street madness—we have heard it six times. The farmer. The worker. The small capitalist. The intellectual. These are the victims of Wall Street. We go over and over the same falsehoods."

The man was not well. His mind had regressed to before the murder and was again revolving around the complaint that had triggered Mai's violence.

Ruxton said gently, "This is no place for anti-Communist talk. You need sleep."

"You're just like all the others," Lemoine complained in a pettish voice.

Ruxton, who did not feel like "the others," said acridly, "How did you get so out of favor? I thought you were the Mai fair-haired boy."

"So did I," said Lemoine. "I tell them things. I even spy a little on the others, like a good little stool pigeon—not you," he said hastily, "but on some of those s.o.b.'s. Yes, I thought I was with them, but—" he shook his head indignantly— "what good is that if you can't even speak a few plain words of home truth?"

He seemed unaware that he had revealed a secret. He muttered, "Maybe in the final end, I am the only brave man in the group."

Ruxton said impatiently, "Look, friend, why don't you go to bed and get some rest?"

"I can't rest anymore," said Lemoine. And started to cry.

It was a soft crying, like a man at a funeral. Ruxton was embarrassed. He had in his time struck crying women, but crying men he had simply avoided. Now, he reached forward, took Lemoine by the arm, and started him toward the stairway.

Lemoine stumbled along for half a dozen steps, then he stopped. He pushed Ruxton away. "Leave me alone!" he mumbled. "I'll be all right." He walked erratically across the lobby and sat down. He was obviously not all right. But Ruxton didn't wait. He had his own tiredness to contend with, and his tiny quota of good will was exhausted. He headed upstairs.

Ruxton was wearily opening the door of his bedroom when footsteps sounded behind him. As he swung about, Father de Melanier slipped by him into the room.

The priest turned, caught Ruxton's arm and pulled him inside, then hastily but quietly closed the door. He said in a trembling voice, "I realize you are very tired, Mr. Ruxton. But I need most desperately to talk to you."

Ruxton said, "You seem more wide awake than I am, sir."

"I slept this afternoon," the priest admitted.

"Then give me fifteen minutes' sleep," Ruxton said. "During the war I found that I had my wits again after a quarter of an hour."

He didn't wait for a reply, but lay down on the bed.

It seemed only an instant later when he was being shaken awake. "Excuse me," said Father de Melanier, "but I allowed you twenty minutes."

Ruxton struggled awake, and presently sat up. It was hard. "I guess I'm not up to my war-time energy," he mumbled, "but I'll make it."

He stood up, squeezed his eyelids again and again, rubbed his body, and paced the room. "What is it?" he asked.

"First," said the priest, "I have spoken to Ho Sin Go. He will take Tosti to Wanchan the day after tomorrow. He sees the possibility that if she starts to spend his earnings on clothes, she will begin to accept him."

Ruxton nodded curtly. It was good news, but he could have waited until morning to learn it. He said, "Thank you. But this isn't what you came to tell me."

"No!" The priest was silent, miserable, for he didn't quite know how to begin. He trusted Ruxton, but he had so much to tell.

All these months he had deplored the situation, held himself to a dignified resistance, and prepared his soul for the brief agony of death by shooting. Since his urine experiences, that decision was meaningless. Tonight's murder had created a frantic feeling. He was aroused to the need for immediate action.

Ruxton sensed the man's dilemma without knowing the details, and said, "Tell me first what's most important."

Father de Melanier, in a hopeless voice described his degradation in the big prison open latrine. He was almost in tears, as he finished, "Perhaps worst of all is the icy cold that comes so quickly. I'm sure it's only a matter of a few days before I catch pneumonia and die. So you are speaking to a doomed man, Mr. Ruxton."

Ruxton mentally conjured the physical agony—and shivered. "My God!" he said aloud. Yet after a moment he realized that he was not surprised.

Another one of the prisoners was in process of being killed.

Soon five out of the original twenty-three would be dead, nearly a quarter of the "population."

His silence as he thought this gave Father de Melanier his opportunity. The priest had decided to pass on to at least one other person all the information he had about Communist methods, and Ruxton was to him the logical recipient of what he knew.

He began by stating that the Marxists were scientists of revolutionary tactics and strategy in the same way that Napoleon and other military geniuses were scientists in warfare. "Mr. Ruxton," he said earnestly, "what I have witnessed in China in the past two decades has been both fascinating and frustrating. The entire western world was taken in by the propaganda of a revolutionary group, and failed to understand the dilemma of the Nationalist regime. The Kuomintang, sir, was confronted on the one hand by scheming, crafty traitors to the democratic idea and to their own country, and on the other by the stupidity of their friends, who expected them to achieve perfect democracy in a country that was under mortal attack, and whose people had no background in democratic living. The confusion was of course unbelievable."

He must have said more, but Ruxton dozed. When he came to, the priest was concluding a point gloomily, "—Such has been the travail of China . . . And," he continued, "the United States is next, of the big nations. The signs are everywhere. The constant labeling of America as Fascist—you've seen the incessant vitriolic propaganda—"

He paused, and Ruxton nodded. He had seen it, indeed, complete with swastikas, and the shrieking naming of every American act as Imperialist.

When next Ruxton came to, the older man was saying soberly, "—Consider the adjoining prison, with its 2500 prisoners. There are less than a dozen such prisons in China. Even if there were half a hundred, it would have little meaning in a country of six hundred million. Since 1949, between 18 and 25 million human beings have been executed in China. That is the equivalent of the entire adult population of France. Compare this to the total of 25,000 prisoners under sentence of death in these few reform prisons. Less than one in ten thousand has been given the highly publicized opportunity to live by turning Communist within two years. If you add to this the seventy-odd million who cannot get normal jobs—it's a policy—or who do forced labor in labor camps, you can see the total meaninglessness of it."

Ruxton was startled. Without thinking about it, he had assumed that a rough measure of justice was being meted out within the harsh frame of Communist theory.

But it wasn't justice.

What a deadly discovery the Communists had made about human beings. Control communication, then out of every 15 or 20 thousand potential victims, kill all but one without trial. Give immense publicity to an apparently fair treatment of that one. Maybe later kill him, also.

Nothing more was needed. Everywhere people believed, accepted, agreed sufficiently, that all twenty thousand had been given fair treatment.

Fo Hin-di, the financier, had done everything required by the reform theory, yet the order to execute him had come through anyway.

"Oh, Mr. Ruxton," said the priest sadly, "the total murderous logic of these people has no parallel in history since Genghis Khan."

Ruxton scarcely heard. Recollection of Fo Hin-di had brought a thought. He straightened so dramatically that the priest stared at him. "What is it, Mr. Ruxton?" he asked in alarm.

Ruxton said in a tense voice, "Do you expect to be put in that urinal again tomorrow?"

Father de Melanier nodded sadly. "There's no sign of this torture ending."

Ruxton said urgently, "Do you remember what the prisoner, Fo—the bank family man—looks like?" he asked.

Father de Melanier blinked at him. He seemed to be having a hard time grasping what must have seemed a totally alien thought. Finally, he nodded. "Yes—a man about my age—I remember."

"The one who is to be shot?" Ruxton persisted.

"Poor fellow," the priest nodded. "Yes, I remember."

"I'd like you," said Ruxton steadily, "to walk along the bottom of the latrine until you see him, and then give him a message from me."

The older man stared at him blankly. "Are you mad?" he blurted. "I don't look up at these people. I turn my back on them."

"Identify him," said Ruxton relentlessly, "and then speak to him, and give him the following message: tell him not to return to his cell after the nine o'clock visit to the urinal on Sunday. Tell him to hide near the center of the north wall. I shall rescue him there shortly after nine—day after tomorrow. That's Sunday night."

Father de Melanier was silent, his face a study in confusion. He stood up and paced the floor. "Mr. Ruxton," he said finally, weakly, "you overwhelm me."

Ruxton said nothing. The priest wrung his hands. "The big problem," he said in a voice that trembled, "will be to identify him among 2500 prisoners—particularly under such unfavorable circumstances."

Ruxton stood up and shook Father de Melanier's hand. "Thank you, father. I think we ought to go to bed."

The priest seemed to have forgotten his own purposes. "Center of the north wall," he murmured. "Nine P.M. Sunday. Very well, Mr. Ruxton. Though I don't know what you're up to."

He walked out into the hall. Ruxton closed the door after

227

him, and went to bed. He must have fallen asleep instantly.

He dreamed that he was dying, and awoke struggling with someone who was in the bed with him. Appalled, desperate, Ruxton fought in the dark with his unknown adversary.

48

Exactly how he had gotten on top of the man, he could not be sure. But he could feel the other's throat between his hands, and he squeezed with the strength of fury. Beneath him, the man twisted weakly. His fingers clawed at Ruxton's wrists. The resistance was so ineffectual that Ruxton realized he was no longer in danger. He let go of the man's neck then, and groped for the light. Failing to find it easily, he was about to make a more determined search, when a stunning awareness struck him: this bed didn't squeak.

He thought, "My God, I'm not in my own room!" Following hard on that was an even stronger realization: "He's not trying to kill me. I'm trying to kill him!"

With a single movement, Ruxton was off the bed. A crack of light at floor level located the door. He ran to it, fumbled for the knob, and then hesitated. Whom had he tried to kill? His confusion was too great. He turned the knob, jerked the door open, and hurried along the bright hallway.

As he was opening the door to his own room, his error dawned on him. Out of which room had he come? He turned, and gazed helplessly along the corridor with its nine doors on one side, and eight on the other. One of the farthest six—he was sure. But which?

Reluctant now, he entered his bedroom, pushed the bed against the door—just in case his victim counterattacked—and then flopped down. What had happened was disturbingly clear.

For the first time in over seven years, he had again attempted a sub-consciously motivated murder—with one difference: He had gained awareness of his action in the middle of the attack, and had immediately become fully rational, and all violence had subsided.

The difference was so reassuring that he was able to go to sleep.

When he awakened it was daylight—and he was in a rage. He climbed out of bed, and looked out of the window. The glass part glittered in the frosty air; the rice paper was curled and crinkled. "Still freezing cold," he thought. But he thought it absently. He wondered if he were angry at Mai for what had happened the night before. But he decided that the murder was merely one factor in a complex of extreme exhaustion and tension. It was this entire complex that had stirred the old psychosis. As he slept, it had broken through, seized control, and made him go through the motions of the old, stereotyped attempt-at-killing pattern—as before, short of actual murder.

The analysis calmed him, and he went downstairs.

As he ate breakfast, the shock of the night before lifted from his body. Presently, he was able to look at the other prisoners. He wondered again: "Whom did I try to kill?" His seeking gaze moved over the room, met Gregory's narrowed eyes; paused momentarily to receive a hard, answering look from Diogo, the Portuguese; moved on to Jarnoz, whose head was bandaged and who did not look up as he ate; passed on to meet the icy blue glaze of Rudolph Spie; skipped over Tittoni, whose secret reason for being in China was still secret; moved on . . . When he came to Kuznetoff, Ruxton glanced away quickly, before the man could catch his eye. Because, who else? It was Kuznetoff who had come that night with Gregory, to murder him. Logical, that in the cunning depths of his brain, where rage monitored thought and action, Kuznetoff would be the man marked for death.

Breakfast over, Ruxton walked to the library, and sat down with a book. He was thinking, "All right, so maybe I know who I nearly choked to death. Now what?" Ruxton pictured himself telling that hate-filled young man exactly what had happened. Simply to confront that thought made it obvious that he could never admit the truth.

But he felt uneasy, since he could assume that Kuznetoff would be trying to determine who had attacked him. That was something he'd have to watch out for . . . Keep the bed against the door at night, be alert whenever the man was near . . . simple precautions.

Later, as he lay beside Tosti, so great was the tension within him that he was only vaguely aware of the woman. But as he completed dressing, he came alert enough to tell her what he wanted her to say to the Japanese spy contact in Wanchan.

Tosti listened calmly. "I'm sure they'll do it," she said. "It will be a test of their organizational skill, and they need to find out about that."

"You can give me the details when you get back," Ruxton whispered. "Don't take any chances, though."

"It'll be a phone call entirely in code," she said, "so don't worry." She was outwardly at ease, but she held him a moment at the door, and kissed him lingeringly.

At lunch, Ruxton kept glancing casually, but with underlying tension, at Father de Melanier. Finally that guilty man looked up, shook his head slightly, and then became absorbed again in his food.

Ruxton settled back, shocked. It was staggering after a moment, to realize how much he had counted on instant success. He was uneasily considering the consequences of failure to contact Fo, when he became aware that the priest was coming over to him.

Father de Melanier bent down, and said softly, in French, "I did my best."

Ruxton nodded, and he had a feeling of acceptance of the man's statement, but all he said was, "Try again tomorrow, sir, and thank you."

As he headed for the library shortly after 6:30, Ruxton was disconcerted to see by the sparkling glow of the ice-laden string of lights above the street, Phenix coming toward him.

She stopped, and said quickly, "I had forgotten that tonight is the night when my husband normally possesses me, and I am sure that he plans that it shall be so. I'm sorry. I don't know what my situation will be tomorrow night."

She walked on toward the hotel, and Ruxton continued on to the Book Room. He was thinking, "I'll read until five to seven, then join the group discussion. No reason why I should be late tonight."

It would be a good idea to have his attention elsewhere at the time when Phenix and her husband were making love.

His watch showed exactly seven as he walked into the hotel. He paused to get a drink of water at a faucet next to the stairs, and then he entered the dining room through the portieres. The moment he was inside he realized that something was wrong. One of the interpreters was shouting at De la Santa in Spanish. And the Spaniard was shouting back.

As Ruxton sank into a chair, Jarnoz slipped over beside him, and whispered in his halting English, "Trouble. Lemoine missing since last night."

49

Ruxton leaned back with a sick thrill. Another murder? Had Lemoine somehow irked Mai again? Before he could think further, the interpreter with whom De la Santa had been arguing began to translate the argument into Chinese. As he got the drift, Ruxton listened with fascination.

"We have a report," the interpreter translated De la Santa's words, "that Lemoine's mind has broken under the strain of the fatigue of these meetings, and that the break occurred last night. The report further states that the purpose of these long meetings is to bring us all to the same fatigue, with the intention of destroying our brains also."

"Who told you this?" the interpreter asked.

"Who said it is not important," was the Spaniard's angry reply.

The translation reached that point when there was a sound from the door, a man clearing his throat. Ruxton and the others turned. Mai Lin Yin stood there. He was evidently aware that something was wrong, for he said quickly, "What is all this?" When he had been told, a peculiar, sardonic look came into his face.

The interpreter concluded, "I took the view that the most important fact is, who introduced this negative thought into this group of men."

Mai was scowling. "Quite right," he said. He walked forward, and faced the prisoners. "Well—" he demanded, "who was it? Come, come," he rapped sharply. "We'll get the information sooner or later. Who said this?"

Father de Melanier stood up. He was pale, but his body was straight and his voice was firm as he said, "I am familiar with these monstrous Pavlovian ideas. And I felt it my duty to inform my fellow prisoners."

Mai's eyes narrowed to slits, as he almost spat the next question. "To whom did you tell it?"

De la Santa said quickly, "He told a group of us in the lobby just before the meeting."

"Who? Name each person present," came the relentless command.

The Spaniard hesitated. He took a deep breath. "Am I in danger of being shot?"

"No side issues," Mai retorted. He twisted toward Father de

Melanier. "You have one chance to rehabilitate yourself. Name the men you talked to."

Father de Melanier shook his head firmly.

De la Santa said something to his interpreter. To Ruxton's relief, the words when translated, were: "There is no point in making an issue of *that*." He addressed the white men: "Those who were present, stand up!"

Mai ordered, "Translate that."

Presently nine men rose to their feet.

Mai glanced at Ruxton. "You remain seated? You were not present?"

Ruxton shook his head. "I was not present," he said.

Mai stood frowning, staring off into space. He nodded finally, and his face was dark as he said, "I shall deal with this priest most effectively one of these days. Now——" He confronted the group. "For your information, fatigue does not damage or destroy the brain. This is a fallacy, which evidently derives from some mystical picture of what the brain is and how it reacts to weariness. Normally, a human being develops a vast pattern of nerve inhibitions, and these may be said to constitute his stereotyped reactions to life. Fatigue excites a more general inhibition, in three steps to change. It would be unwise of me, if you desire change, to tell you in detail what those three steps are. But there is no brain damage. Also, I should remind you that your attendance at these group discussions is voluntary."

"What happens if we don't attend?" asked someone from behind Ruxton.

Mai smiled, and spread his hands. "We may take it into account. We may not. All we desire is the change itself. How it is achieved by each individual is up to him. We simply offer the group discussions as a more rapid method. Truth, as you know," he smiled again, "may be all that you need."

Twice during the subsequent discussions, Ruxton dozed, and awakened with a start to realize that the translations and interrogations continued in their forever fashion. The subject matter was, what backward thinking had made each individual react unfavorably to the revelation of the brain changing effect of fatigue? Additional questions were asked on the same idea: "Why had the individual not refused to listen to a negative report as soon as he realized that it was negative?" And, "Why did not each person on realizing the negative nature of the communication chide the person giving the negative communication?"

Father de Melanier was asked to explain: "What is the

nature of your emotional attachment to the defunct Nationalist regime that made you act the role of Nationalist agitator?"

The priest vigorously denied that any such motives were
involved in his action.

The evening ended at three fifteen A.M. As Ruxton headed
wearily for his room, he realized that the naps he had taken
during the group meeting were attempts to avoid extreme
fatigue.

"What a paradox," he thought. "A few weeks ago I was
practically begging to have my brains addled. Now I can
wait."

He slept peacefully.

At breakfast, Lemoine's place was empty.

50

His compatriot's absence seemed to disturb Father de Melanier more than it did anyone else. The priest ate very little, and
presently he pushed his chair away from the table, came over
to Ruxton, and said in a low voice, "He is not in his room
again. His bed was not slept in—again."

It was Ruxton's first specific awareness that Lemoine had
not been in his room two nights before.

Father de Melanier hesitated, then: "After I left you the
other night," he whispered, "I saw Lemoine coming up the
steps. He seemed dazed. He paid no attention when I spoke
to him. I became alarmed. But when I started to help him,
the guards brushed me aside and took him downstairs. That's
the last I saw of him."

Ruxton said quickly, "You mean, the two sentries on our
floor grabbed him?"

The priest nodded. "One of them said, 'Look—fatigue!'
And they brushed me aside and took him off."

So it had been that dramatic.

Ruxton was curious now. "What did he look like to you?
Lemoine, I mean."

"He was crying," the priest said commiseratingly. "It was
terrible to see the poor man in that condition."

Ruxton nodded—a nod of dismissal of Lemoine. He said
decisively, "I'm sure the pressure on him was not as great
as it is on you." He lowered his voice. "Don't forget who
you're looking for." He broke off. "Better go now. We can talk
later."

He watched the priest walk away to his purgatory.

When Ruxton emerged from the hotel a while later, he was pleasantly surprised by the breeze that met him. It was far from being a summer's day. But the ice was gone from the air. The sun's rays definitely seemed to warm him as he strode to the library.

He spent a restless morning in the Book Room, finally settling down to a reluctant reading of Marx' The Communist Manifesto.

Ruxton ate lunch scarcely aware of his fellow prisoners. Another, though related, train of thought occupied him. It was actually a great loss to the Western civilization that so many Chinese intellectuals had accepted communism in preference to capitalistic democracy. He was now convinced that part of the answer was—native Chinese people were antiforeign. Those individual Chinese who had started the long climb up to tolerance had either escaped abroad, or were born abroad, or were dead.

Ruxton sighed, and he was still thinking about it when— accidentally—his eyes were engaged by Father de Melanier.

The priest gave an almost imperceptible nod of his head, then turned away.

Ruxton sat, stiff and numb. After a moment he realized that he was in a state of shock, so powerful was the impact of the silent message the priest had given him. He continued to eat, but he was scarcely aware of taste. His mind darted feverishly around and about and over the fact that the monstrous prison was penetrated and defeated, and that, if all went well, the financier Fo Hin-di would be rescued at nine P.M. Sunday night . . . tomorrow!

Gradually, his excitement yielded to curiosity for details. Lunch over, he accompanied Father de Melanier out to the lobby. They stood by the window, unfrosted now but blurry with streaks of water. Ruxton asked in a low voice, "Did anyone notice?"

Father de Melanier shook his head, and said, "Fo said no one in the vicinity was from his cell, so even if someone reports our conversation it would be difficult to identify him."

Ruxton grew aware of a change in himself. In his deepest inner being, a taut feeling was gone. And only now that it was no longer there did he realize that it had ever existed.

The release extended to other perceptions and to his emotions. He had been gazing at the tormented face of the priest, unconcerned by the anguish that was written there, not really aware of it, shutting it off. Suddenly, he let it come in upon him. He thought, compassionately, "What a remarkable feat he has just accomplished, and all I cared about was that he accomplish it, and never mind the difficulty of doing it." He pictured the other, naked, standing on ice, being subjected to incredible shame.

Guilt touched him, and pity came. "Why don't you lie down, sir?" he asked gently. "I think your sleep will be more comfortable, since the day is considerably warmer."

"You noticed it, too?" said Father de Melanier. There was an eager note in his voice, that caused Ruxton to look at him quickly. The man's eyes were bright, almost feverish, his color high. The priest continued, "Just as I despaired for my life, warm weather descends upon the land."

Ruxton guessed uneasily that he was being given a Catholic view of God interfering in the affairs of men. Such things were outside his own reality.

He shrugged, and thought, "But why not? Such thinking will make it easier for the good father to contend with the grim fact of extreme physical exposure. People need an attitude to torture."

He slept that night with a deep sense of being in command of the situation.

51

Morning.

He was with Tosti in her room, and she was whispering, "They will do it. Expect them tonight. They will pass Fo along their network."

Afterwards, as he was leaving her, her fingers on his arm gently restrained him. "Perhaps you should not come for a few days. There will be turmoil," she said softly.

Ruxton patted her hand. "I'll wait," he said, "then come when it seems right."

She nodded. "I'm sure it is best."

A few minutes later, as he looked over the books on the shelves of the library, it struck him that the feeling inside had expanded again. Even with the books, his outlook was different. He had previously examined only English language works. Now, he glanced at some of the foreign language volumes. First, a collection of Mao Tse-tung's wartime speeches, a limited edition, printed in Chinese. As he leafed through it, he came upon one paragraph that was easily the most cynical of all the statements given out by that sanguinary individual. The speech, made during World War II to top Communist leaders, made idiots and madmen of those Americans who had urged support of Mao "the agrarian reformer." When the war against Japan was at its height, when China was bleeding, with more than half her territory in the hands of the invader, at the time of the big Communist propaganda about how the Reds were the only ones who were fighting the Japanese, Mao said, "Our determined policy is 70% self-development (consolidation of our own position, politically and economically), 20% compromise (with the Nationalist Government), and 10% fight the Japanese." There it was in black and white, printed by the Communists themselves. Thus was the big lie of the war in China exposed.

Ruxton realized that the real truth went deeper. Whether a statement was a falsehood or not was not actually the issue any more. By the time you found the correct data, nobody wanted to hear it anyway. What was needed was far more perceptive understanding. The Chinese Reds were "above" the war in the same way that Lenin had been above World War One. Mao Tse-tung, the Chinese Red leader, had based his program on the weakening of the Nationalist government forces by the Japanese, while his own Yenan-based troops strengthened their position, infiltrated Chiang's government and expanded the land area under their control. It had all worked perfectly, first with Lenin, in that the German government, facing defeat, had been motivated to support his efforts at subverting the Russian people—and now with Mao, in that he had successfully destroyed the future democratic China.

Ruxton was casually glancing through a French book when the door opened, and Phenix came in. She caught his eye, and he inclined his head, whereupon she walked over. Ruxton noticed that the other prisoners had looked up from their reading and were watching her.

Phenix said briskly, "What books are you reading these days, Mr. Ruxton?" Ruxton handed her the book he was holding. She glanced through it, but when she handed it back there was a note in it, which read: "Not tonight. My husband will be in the house packing for a trip."

Ruxton stared at the message, shaken. Mai in the house while he himself was in the basement getting materials for the rescue.

"You read French?" Phenix asked.

She repeated her question twice before he could recover. Then he nodded. "And speak it," he said.

With an abrupt movement, Phenix walked away from him. He stood watching, then, as she went over to the other prisoners, and glanced at the books they were reading. When she finally departed, Ruxton wondered if her little game had fooled the men. He sincerely hoped it would be difficult for these fellow prisoners of his to conceive that a liaison existed between a prisoner and the commandant's wife.

Later, on his way to the hotel, he tore up the note Phenix had given him, and surreptitiously dropped a few of the pieces. There was a breeze of sorts, and the tiny fragments drifted . . . and were gone.

In the afternoon he went for a short walk in the opposite direction to where the rescue would take place, past the soldiers' barracks, as far as the end of the street. By the time he returned he had discarded one by one what was left of Phenix' note. It seemed to him that the wind from the east was strengthening. Clouds appeared in the sky, and raced westward. The possibility of overcast heartened Ruxton even more.

As he ate dinner that night, he thought, "So far, only two setbacks. I'll be absent from the group meeting two and a half hours at least, and Mai will be upstairs in his house while I'm fumbling around with that damn ladder. If I should make a sound, and he hears it—"

He refused to consider the dangers any longer. Thinking of such things could only lead to anxiety.

The moment dinner was over, he left the hotel and headed for the library. He sighed with relief as he saw that the sky was gray and, equally important, the wind had died down. The night promised cloudiness.

52

As he approached the Mai residence, he grew aware that two men were shouting at each other in Chinese in the darkness ahead. It took several minutes for him to distinguish who it was. Then he realized that the chunky guard at the gate was exchanging yells with the sentinel on the big wall.

Ruxton stopped. He could not go to the Mai basement door while the soldier on the wall was looking down into the yard. As he stood undecided, listening, he realized that they were talking at an abysmal level of intelligence.

The guard wanted to know when the Kuomintang s.o.b.'s in the main prison would be shot, since they were obviously sick in the head. The sentinel said that the prisoners would first be given a chance to mend their ways and then they would be shot. The guard thereupon good-naturedly called him a Nationalist spy, against which charge he was stoutly defending himself when Ruxton decided not to wait any longer.

As Ruxton went through the gate, the sentinel wanted to know who Ruxton was, and why don't you shoot these Imperialist bastards. He would have none of the argument that the American was mending his ways. You couldn't change these Wall Street dupes just by having them read books.

Ruxton sat with a book in his hands, and was greatly relieved when the shouting outside finally ended. He waited until three minutes after seven, then put away the book and went to the door. A minute later he was inside the basement, and his rescue mission was under way.

Using his flashlight, he edged down the steps to the concrete floor, and so over to the ladder that was leaning against a wall. One end was behind a metal barrel, and several boxes were piled up against the other end. When he peered behind these barriers, he saw that a variety of small objects were also entangled with the ladder; two metal buckets filled with nails, a piece of chain, several leather straps, hatchets, hammers, a saw . . .

Ruxton removed one item at a time, for he had to avoid knocking anything over. At the end of twenty-two minutes by his watch, he had the ladder outside. He left it there, and re-entered the basement. This time he procured a rake with metal prongs.

What he did then, while he was still in the Mai yard, was to be the pattern, with variations, for the rest of his journey. He crept to the fence, and used the rake to erase all signs of his creeping. Once over the fence, with only open ground ahead of him, he walked slowly, body bent low, rake in one hand, ladder in the other. The ground was cold and hard, but so dry that even now, in the very middle of winter, little dust clouds rose up behind him.

For a hundred yards he was meticulously careful. He walked, crouching, and after each step turned and used the back of the rake—and his fingers in several instances—to obliterate the footprint.

It was intensely dark, and so after the first prolonged careful effort, he straightened his body and began a machine-like action. He took a long step, used the rake, and then another long step, and the rake again—step, rake—step, rake—step, rake—

When he estimated that he had gone half a mile, he turned north at a sharp angle and started to lope along with the steady pace of a long distance runner. He made only a half-hearted attempt now to hide his footprints, simply dragged the rake behind him. It bounced and banged along, and he could imagine that it missed its mark almost as often as it hit. But he felt that it would take sharp searching indeed to find the marks he was making.

He ran a whole half mile past the north end of the big prison, and then turned again, and ran westward, until he was able to make out the vague mass of the prison beside the street lights directly south of where he was. He turned toward it, and slowed to a walk, again becoming careful, and using the rake to cover each step that he took. As he came near the prison, he bent lower, and watched for his contacts.

Suddenly, a soft whistle sounded. It came from his left, and a little ahead of him. Ruxton walked on slowly, veering to the left. And he felt a thrill in spite of himself as a man's figure rose up beside him. The man, smaller, thinner than Ruxton, came close to him and whispered, in perfect English, "There are four of us, sir. We have a stolen jeep parked on the old Japanese air strip, a few miles north of here, and we are dressed in the uniforms of Chinese Communist soldiers, and in fact are Chinese, not Japanese. We should tell you that Tosti is a Japanese agent working, with her government's permission, for the Nationalist government." He broke off, "That's our story. Now, three of us will go up the ladder with you and—"

He outlined his plan, and finished, "Does that sound all right, sir?"

Ruxton said that it did. The thin man thereupon made a tiny clicking sound with his tongue, and three more shadowy figures joined them. It was then, as they edged forward in a group, staying close to the ground, the Ruxton had a peculiar feeling. In that instant, Tosti became entirely real to him as a spy. The phenomenon of this realization was impossible for him to define in any precise terms. All these weeks he had known that she was what she was. He had often recalled the discussion when she had revealed herself. But that was talk.

This was real.

For the first time he realized that his keyed-up feeling was joy. He *liked* this dangerous job. And yet he knew that he could be killed at any instant. But that didn't really matter. Life was important, yes, even delightful. But it would end eventually. It must be an illusion of some basic race impulse that the time of the ending mattered. Perhaps there was a specific mechanism in the brain that got excited when a threat to survival occurred. Whatever it was, it was now at peace, not reacting in its idiot, automatic way, *not* a factor in his forward drive.

They had come to the base of the prison wall. Hugging the wall, utilizing the scant concealing foliage of some shrubbery, they carefully unfolded the extension ladder, and placed it against the wall. At a steep angle, it reached to within an inch or so of the top—a fact which Ruxton observed as he eased himself onto the parapet.

The two men who had preceded him up the ladder were already vague shadows crawling on their stomachs toward the sentry's tower. The leader of the group of four now climbed up, and he and Ruxton raised the ladder rapidly, assuming that the guard was being taken care of. But they were cautious and silent nonetheless, making every effort to control their swaying, flexible instrument. Ruxton sighed with relief as the ladder touched the soil of the prison compound, touched it so gently that he heard nothing. He was about to lower himself over the edge when his companion caught his arm, and whispered into his ear, "Wait! I think he's coming."

In the dense darkness beneath them, a figure seemed to detach itself from the shadow of a building. So black was the night that a man's body was virtually indistinguishable from the ground, and Ruxton was beginning to think they had been mistaken when the ladder trembled. A moment later, as he held it steady, he felt the strain and give of the metal as someone climbed toward them.

It was fifteen feet to go, and Ruxton imagined a weakness in the man's knees and stomach was slowing him. For it seemed a long time before a hand groped over the top of the wall. Ruxton leaned forward, took firm hold of a smooth wrist with one hand, and pulled. With the other hand, he reached down and held the ladder steady. As the climber's head came up, Ruxton's companion whispered in Chinese, "Who are you?"

"Fo."

The word was a soft, gasping sound. Nothing else was

said. The former financier was pulled all the way to the top of the wall and shoved slightly to one side. Then the ladder was drawn up, and lowered again to the outside. Ruxton went down first, followed by Fo. Then came the two men who had gone after the guard, and finally the leader of the rescue group. In the darkness they folded the ladder, and presently they were on the move, carefully covering their tracks. Soon, they were walking. And then they came to the parting of their ways.

Ruxton said, "We were lucky that the guard didn't hear us."

"He'll never hear anybody again," was the reply.

Ruxton was shocked. "Your men killed him!"

The other man laughed softly. "It's always good to leave a dead man behind, because it's important to impress on people that the Reds are not all powerful, and because war on the espionage level is so unreal that we need impacts periodically to make it all come alive. This is why we welcomed your request. All across China groups will now be activated to do their part in passing Fo along. Perhaps several more people will be killed. This is all to the good. The disaster of China's capture by the Reds will be complete only when all activity against them ceases, and friend and enemy alike collaborate in suppressing opposition." The man finished, "Besides, to be a soldier at all, this guard will have participated in more than one struggle meeting that ended in an execution."

Ruxton did not question the man's explanation. But he made a mental note to aid no more prisoners.

The leader of the rescue group was speaking again. "You go back to your prison. We will find our jeep. Nice to have met you." He whistled softly. The little group of small men hurried off into the blackness, and Ruxton was alone in the great night on that remote Chinese plain in mid-winter. Except then, for the sounds he made in retracing his footsteps, it was an icy-cold world of complete silence.

53

The illuminated dial of his watch showed two minutes to ten as Ruxton opened the Mai gate, and stepped through it to the street beyond. He closed the gate with the studied movements of a man who is exhausted but still in control of his body. He did not glance at the sentry, as he turned and slowly walked toward the hotel. His feeling was that if he moved faster or slower, he would either fall back or pitch forward. A band of pain clamped across his chest, there was a salty taste in his mouth from over-exertion, and he trembled inwardly from head to foot. He sensed that he needed more oxygen than he was allowing his lungs to have. In spite of the need, he held his breath to normal until he was nearly halfway to his destination.

There he stopped. There he stood, gasping for air, taking in great, cold breaths. Minutes went by. He would have liked to sit down on the hard ground, but that he dared not do. At last, he began to feel better. He started forward again, still with that inner tremble, but he had paid the main price for the colossal physical effort that had brought him to the gate of the Mai residence within the time limit.

As he came into the dining room he paused and once more considered his story. He was more than two and a half hours late, and if he were asked to account for his absence, he intended to say that he was evaluating the effects of over-fatigue, trying to decide whether or not he would seek such effects.

It was a good story, he decided—and drew the portieres aside. He sat down in a chair near the back of the room, and looked at the men seated around the head table.

Fa 'tze glanced up at him, and said something to Ho Sin Go, then resumed reading a book that lay on the table before him. Ho stood up and came over. He looked in a good humor as he explained to Ruxton that some of the prisoners had expressed emotional interest in the condition of Lemoine. It had therefore been decided that they would visit the young Frenchman. They were now awaiting the arrival of Mai Lin Yin, who would guide the visiting party.

After Ho had walked away, Ruxton leaned back in his chair and realized that it was actually possible that his absence would not be reported. For half an hour, he and the other prisoners sat silently waiting, before Mai Lin Yin, dapper in his uniform, arrogant of manner, a faint, insolent smile on his face, entered the room.

He barked an order for everyone in the room to accompany him. The interpreters, who were already on their feet, came forward, uttering their translations.

Out into the night went the entire group of prisoners and interpreters. Mai headed along the street toward the most distant barracks, and led them inside. As Ruxton entered, he saw long rows of bunks, and at the far end, two tables set up for table tennis. The whites were evidently expected, for the soldiers were fully dressed. At a sharp order from a non-commissioned officer they stood at attention.

Major Mai proceeded to a rear room, which was a sort of ante-room. Several doors led from it. At Mai's command, the non-com opened one of these doors. Ruxton was among the first dozen white prisoners who crowded with the commandant into the room.

The scene before them was primitive in the extreme. Lemoine lay on a bare, rough-hewn wooden bunk. Though it was winter, and the room was unheated, he had no covering. An offensive odor of urine and feces permeated the chill atmosphere. Somewhere, during his degradation, Lemoine must have become conscious that he was in danger of soiling himself, for he had made a half-hearted attempt to remove his trousers. Ruxton felt a strong revulsion and was glad to move aside as Father de Melanier pushed past him and spoke indignantly to Mai.

"This is an outrage," he said. "A criminal action against a citizen of France."

Mai stroked his cheek, and looked at the priest with an obviously sincere hatred. But all he said was, "The outward appearance of the first step to change is unfortunate; but he can be washed."

The priest said, heatedly, "He has become worse than an animal. He doesn't care, has no feeling about his surroundings. Everything equals everything else. You see, I am familiar with these vile Pavlovian experiments."

Mai gazed at him with narrowed eyes, speculatively. Finally, he turned to the nearest Chinese, "Translate what we have said." As the jabber began, Mai took a small sheaf of papers out of his pocket, glanced at it, waited until there was silence again, and then continued, "What has happened here is a form of inhibition. The particular result is that it requires the most violent stimulus to produce a response. The condition of course could be permanent but we do not plan to let it remain that way. Your compatriot Lemoine will be moved on by the fatigue route to the next phase."

The priest chided, "What you are doing will produce permanent brain damage, for what is inhibition of nerve activity at such a level but destruction of the normal functioning of the brain?"

Mai said evenly, "Every act of restraint imposed by society inhibits the activity of nerve cells. The great Pavlov discovered methods of doing this which could be utilized to transform sick personalities to well ones in the most dramatic fashion. By this means the sickness in the capitalistic soul is cured in three steps to change."

"It is an outrage and a lie—" Father de Melanier was grim. "The excessive fatiguing of individuals has always been denounced by civilized people everywhere."

Mai was contemptuous. "The physiological reality of the fatigue condition is extremely simple," he said. "The fatigued nerve refuses to transmit an impulse. When enough nerve cells are fatigued, and there is an enormous scarcity of nerve impulses, that is, millions of nerve cells are refusing to transmit messages, perception from the exterior world is cut off, the individual's muscles may not function, he feels an area of blackness in the brain itself, and he may actually fall because he is not in control of himself. This is a relatively elementary process. It is feared by capitalistic slaves because they have been kept in ignorance of any kind of mental phenomena.

"You may ask, who has been giving this beneficial therapy to your compatriot, Lemoine? There they are!" He indicated two lumpish looking, moon-faced privates, and finished proudly, "In a few days these two worthy but, we must admit it, not highly educated individuals will have achieved for Lemoine a personality transformation of major proportions. This is a common ability of all first class privates in the People's Army. Respect them, my friends! These are the men who shall change the world."

He beckoned the two. Holding their guns, they pressed past von Spie and the two Scandinavians, and came to attention in front of Mai. He congratulated them, and they beamed. Ruxton stared at them with a dawning comprehension of the hideous power they had been given. A psychiatric method had been discovered, so basic that any person who was even slightly familiar with its principles could enforce it on another human being. Needed only was the will to exercise such a power over other persons, and here in this ignorant people a group of schemers had found, not criminal willingness, but something fundamentally more useful. Here were millions of minds so plastic that such control methods could be taught as part of a new way of life.

The priest was speaking again: "Entirely aside from the atrocious degradation suffered by Lemoine, what we are witnessing is the de-humanization of a harmless, friendly person. The body may live on. The mind is destroyed—obviously destroyed because it is no longer recognizable."

The smile faded from Mai's face. He looked impatient as
244

he waited for the interpretations, and then he said sharply, "Very well, priest! I have permitted you to say these things because the men now may judge for themselves, as Lemoine moves through the three steps. It is a hard way, admittedly, but the criminal capitalist personality is set hard against easy transformation. The decision to undertake the fatigue route is up to each person. I recommend it. Now, are there any questions?"

Ruxton asked soberly, "I gather that the first step to change is a nerve condition where the person responds only to yelling, or to a big shock, and is unresponsive to any normal request or disturbance."

"That is correct," Mai answered.

"What," Ruxton asked, "are the manifestations of the second and third steps?"

Mai hesitated, and Father de Melanier said in French directly to Ruxton, "The second step is a nerve condition where the individual makes an exaggerated response to small stimuli and no response at all to shouting or any big—"

A yell from Mai interrupted him. The priest faltered and looked questioningly at the commandant, who said savagely, in Chinese, "If you are giving Mr. Ruxton information, stop it at once." Mai turned to the interpreter and asked for a translation of the priest's words. When this had been given, he said, "Do not translate. Say this: It is better that the individual not know the additional steps."

As these words were being translated, Mai turned to Ruxton, and said, "Your question was perfectly legitimate, and you have received, of course, a partial answer from this—" He paused, then silently motioned at Father de Melanier, but his body was trembling with a strong emotion, either rage or hatred. He bit his lip, and then added more slowly, "Make no further attempt to obtain this information, or the priest will suffer."

Ruxton argued with the injunction in a mild tone. "It seems to me we could make our decision easier if we knew all the facts."

Mai laughed mirthlessly. "You don't think, my dear Ruxton, that any of these—uh—colleagues of yours, will actually decide to undergo the fatigue cure."

Ruxton protested. "But why did you bring us out here? We all thought—"

Mai was calm again. "This is a propaganda visit," he said.

"Propaganda!" Ruxton echoed. He motioned at the disgusting spectacle of Lemoine. *"This?"*

Mai was derisive. "Mr. Ruxton," he said, "we Communists understand the cowardice of the peoples of the West. All over the world these capitalistic slaves and their captors are quailing as it begins to come to them that a way has been found at last to free the slaves and bring the enslavers to justice. Your people, Mr. Ruxton, do not have the kind of courage it takes to defeat what these two men and millions like them can do!" He indicated the two privates, who evidently recognized that they were being talked about, for their round faces broke into grins.

Ruxton said nothing. He was realizing with a sinking sensation in the pit of his stomach that he believed what Mai was saying.

There was an interruption. Footsteps sounded on the concrete outside the room. A man yelled, in Chinese, "Major Mai—urgent message from the big prison!"

As Ruxton turned, he saw Mai straighten, and peer over the heads of the prisoners. Then he saw the messenger, a soldier, waving a letter. Mai spoke to the interpreters. They began to yell and push at the prisoners. The room was quickly cleared, and Mai took the letter, opened it and read it. His eyes widened, then he scowled and folded the letter with jerky movements of his hands. That was all Ruxton saw. He ceased looking back, and pushed with the others through the barracks and out into the street.

But he guessed that Mai had been advised of the escape of Fo Hin-di.

There was a lump in his throat as he walked back to the hotel, that had nothing to do with Fo. It was pity for Lemoine. He thought, "My God, that poor guy has still several days of that to go through."

Father de Melanier fell in beside him, and said, "Mr. Ruxton, we have just witnessed a significant change in the Red Chinese brainwashing program. Although I had previously read of these obnoxious Pavlovian techniques, I had not seen them introduced into the *Hsio Hsi*—" He paused, and explained, "That is the Chinese name for these group and self-criticism meetings. I have seen people exhausted by the long meetings, but no savage advantage was taken of their weariness. If a man, for example, a landlord, was marked for death, they didn't try to tire him. The method used was to turn everybody against him, and the meeting ended with

246

the entire group shouting for his death, no one, you understand, daring to do otherwise."

Ruxton nodded, but said nothing. He was impressed by the reasoning, but he had no experience with which to make a comparison.

When, a little later, the prisoners were dismissed, he went to his room and to bed. At first his sleep was fitful. He kept seeing the haggard face of the young Frenchman lying on that primitive bunk amid the fetid odors and substance of his own droppings.

Twice he awakened to the sound of trucks and the shouting of men. The search for the escaped prisoner must be on. The thought made him feel better, and he slept soundly.

Breakfast next morning was a peaceful meal. The prisoners were generally silent. The group of interpreters seemed cheerful. Ruxton studied them surreptitiously, not quite daring to believe it, but they acted as if they had not been told of Fo's escape.

Ruxton went to the library as usual after breakfast. It wouldn't do to change his habits now. At a quarter to eleven, he returned to the hotel. Father de Melanier was sitting in a big chair in the lobby, and he looked surprisingly at ease, almost jaunty.

Ruxton strode over to him. "Good God, sir," he blurted, "what are you doing here so early?"

The priest's pale blue eyes blinked at him cheerfully from behind the pince-nez. He said, "The ways of God are mysterious, Mr. Ruxton. Major Mai left early this morning for Peking. The story is that he will be gone ten days. Since the major was personally attending to my morning bath, and he is gone, I find myself with a vacation on my hands, and nowhere to go."

It was a moment for rejoicing. Ruxton grabbed the priest's hand and pumped it heartily. He sincerely hoped that God was indeed involved in this matter, and that He would continue to act on the priest's behalf.

He felt slightly surprised that Mai had departed on schedule, despite Fo's escape. He must be intending to see important personages, who expected him, and who could not be kept waiting. Whatever the reason, the monster was gone, and Father de Melanier had another chance for life.

Ruxton said, "I have just the place for you to go, sir. Will you get your coat and come with me?"

"Are you serious?" Father de Melanier seemed uncertain.

Ruxton was serious. It was time to stop his own nonsense and carry out his plan for the priest without delay.

54

The day continued cold, as they walked along on the hard ground toward the village on the other side of the prison. Ruxton noticed that his companion was affected by the freezing temperature. The priest held his ears, clapped his hands frequently, and stamped his feet.

He caught Ruxton's gaze, and said apologetically, "After those days in the urinal, I seem to get frozen easily."

"Let's walk a little faster," said Ruxton. "We have still a distance to go."

"But what are we going for?" the priest protested.

Ruxton explained his purpose. "One of the dozen or so Communist points is reform through labor. If you align yourself with any of their basic principles, you cannot be said to be resisting. Reform through hard work is my recommendation for you until spring."

Father de Melanier slowed down, then stopped and shook his head. "Mr. Ruxton," he said gently, "clearly God intended me to face this trial, and I plan to place myself entirely in His hands."

"Still," Ruxton urged, "you should meet these people. Then you can decide."

The priest hesitated. Finally, he agreed. "It will be a pleasure to talk to your friends, but I make no promise."

"Fair enough."

They walked in silence then along the full length of the north wall of the big prison, and so to the home of the cadre.

The woman who opened the door to their knock was young and rather pretty in a youthful, Chinese way. Ruxton had never seen her before. He motioned to Father de Melanier, who had fallen back courteously, to come forward and interpret for him. Before the priest could do so, the woman ran back into the house. Ruxton heard her say something about strangers—it was one of those exotic insulting Chinese references. She used the Chinese word that meant goat.

A few minutes later Johnny Liu, accompanied by a thin-faced young man with a lean body and hard eyes came to the door.

"Changes?" Ruxton asked, though it was obvious.

248

"The old cadre is to be tried," said Johnny Liu. "Too easy."

The thin-faced Chinese said sharply in Chinese: "What is he saying?"

"He asked me who you were and I told him you were the new cadre—the new leader; the old cadre is on trial."

"What does he want?"

Johnny Liu turned to Ruxton and asked the question in English.

Ruxton told him. Johnny said to the cadre, "These two are tired of not doing anything. Would like to work."

"Oh!" The cadre stood considering that, a slightly less severe frown on his face. Finally, "We have no work right now—later."

At that point Father de Melanier broke in. "What about preparing the seeds?" he asked in Chinese.

A startled expression crossed the cadre's face. "What is this?" he yelled. "Interpreters—yet one of them speaks Chinese."

It had all happened so naturally that when Johnny asked for an explanation Ruxton merely indicated the sequence of events. But he was thinking with pained contempt, "All these Reds are stupid people." Already he knew that here was another terrorist type whose intelligence was blurred by an overwhelming suspicion and rage.

Johnny Liu said, "The new cadre's name is Wan Yo-hil." He turned to Wan, and said, "This is the prisoner who helped us last fall."

Wan's rage seemed to go away.

The priest said, "I will come in the morning to begin."

Ruxton said to Johnny, "Tell him I can come only in the afternoons. I have morning studies to do, but my friend has already completed his study and can come all day."

Johnny translated that for the cadre, and added the comment that it would be an excellent thing for the peasants to learn what was good seed grain by the standards of these "foreign scientists."

Wan merely nodded.

The entire interchange had taken place with Ruxton and Father de Melanier standing outside. Now, without further words, Wan closed the door on them.

Ruxton said ruefully, "We'd better get back to the hotel before we freeze." He was beginning to feel the chill himself.

Father de Melanier was thoughtful on the way back. He said at last, "We mustn't interfere in the trial of the former cadre. I tried interference with accused persons in the district where

249

I lived and it made the situation worse. These are very simple people. They put two and two together on the level of 'Why is the foreign goat helping the demoted cadre?' Their answer: 'It must be because the cadre and the goat are secretly working together.' They can't seem to imagine that objective feeling of justice is the answer."

Ruxton noticed that Father de Melanier seemed to have forgotten his initial refusal to engage in reform through labor.

As they entered the hotel, Phenix came forward and spoke to the priest in Chinese. "My husband asked me to tell you," she said, "that you must make up your mind to abandon Christianity by the time he returns." She held up a warning hand as the man seemed about to speak. "Don't answer," she admonished sharply. "You have ten days to think about this. And now, please depart, since I also have a message for Mr. Ruxton."

The priest hesitated, then bowed and walked off. Phenix said to Ruxton, in a low voice, "Why don't you come early tonight, at about six-fifteen. That way, you can get to the group meeting on time for a change."

Ruxton said gratefully, "I'll be there, and thank you."

That night, despite her promise, Phenix held him on the mattresses until ten after seven. When they separated, she seemed unaware of what she had done. She whispered, "Since I am in command while my husband is away, I have ordered that there be *Hsio-Hsi*—group discussions—only every other night. Tomorrow night we shall have a longer time together. Come at seven . . ."

55

When Ruxton reported the following afternoon to help pick over seeds, he found Father de Melanier in a low, barn-like structure, with more than a dozen peasants. The priest had a grief-stricken look on his face, and every little while a tear would trickle down his cheek. But he shook his head warningly when Ruxton expressed concern. They worked at a long bench under a skylight, silently, until the afternoon waned. Then the two white men walked back toward the hotel prison.

As soon as they were out of the village, Father de Melanier said, "I must stop shedding tears over the inequities and brutality of Communist China. They shot the old cadre this morning."

"Lo Hin Yo!" Ruxton exclaimed. He remembered the sturdy-built leader who had been anxious to ensure that he was properly educated about Wall Street. He said uneasily, "What in God's name for?"

"The big shift is taking place," sighed the priest, "from Mutual Aid to Collective Farm."

"Oh!"

"Until now," said the priest, "the peasants have been given to understand that each owned his own land but that they must help each other under the guidance of a cadre. Now, the land is taken from them and lumped into a collective farm."

"But why kill Lo?"

"He represents the Mutual Aid period. He was probably chosen for his congenial nature. From what I hear, everybody liked him. By killing him, the new cadre frightens the villagers into accepting the seizure of the land."

"But he was working for the Party."

The priest was gloomy. "Mutual Aid is the old idea, and it has to be stamped out." He added, "They don't kill all these old cadres, mind you, perhaps only those they feel cannot make the next step."

"I see," said Ruxton thoughtfully. There was inexorable logic here. It was not the first time that Communists had executed their principal allies and supporters, and it reflected once more Lenin's hard philosophy of the one step backward and two steps forward. Lies, deceits, violence. No holds barred. No mercy shown. Because when you were right, you were justified. With that postulate, all morality became nothing. Goodness, warm-heartedness, normal human behavior ceased to be taken into account. The individual had no rights and no protection. Lo Hin Yo, a staunch supporter of the regime in his own mild way, had been murdered so that a few dozen peasant farmers would be frightened into acquiescing in the theft of their property. Undoubtedly, some of those farmers were guilty men in that they had accepted land taken from murdered landlords. For them, awareness of their stupid cupidity must now be dawning. But this action in this remote village was only a single, tiny, visible movement in one of the most violent revolutions in the history of the world.

It was night. Again, they were together on the mattresses in the heated darkness of the basement room. Once more, he held a woman whom he could not see but who responded with intense excitement to his lovemaking.

Afterwards, Ruxton whispered, "I don't understand why

you people are bothering with this project. As I see it, if Communist forces ever capture America, they'll liquidate twenty per cent of the population, which will terrorize the rest into submission, at which time through a correct working conception and group guidance they'll get the idea of what's expected of them and will conform."

"The West is different," she answered. "They realize it in Peking. Those who have been overseas have talked to Mao Tse-tung, who himself never left the country. My husband has been finding out what that difference is."

Ruxton said, "Everybody can be scared. Statistically, no one is immune to a campaign of terror."

She rejected his argument with a movement of her body. "There's a difference. We're smart enough to know it, but we didn't know what it was." She went on quickly, "For example, in Korea 3,000 of 3,400 American prisoners collaborated. Yet at war's end all but a handful wanted to go home. Why? This was a question we had to answer."

"Now you know?" asked Ruxton.

"Yes. The American soldiers wanted to get back to the corner drug stores and soda fountains, to juke boxes and to GI benefits, to imported motor cars, to easy high-pay jobs and homes with electric lights and television. The last thing they want to do is the hard labor that will be needed during the next half century to change the world to Communism." She ended, "All this had to be explained."

Ruxton nodded to himself in the darkness. It did indeed. Since she was describing the truth, the question was, how would the Communists use the information?

He asked the woman. She said, "I'm sorry. I can't tell you that. But really it's obvious. People who have luxury needs are more easily kept under control than those who can get along emotionally and morally on bare necessities."

Ruxton said, astonished, "I should have thought the opposite is true."

"Oh, no. Not with military occupation."

Ruxton pictured that, but he was still not convinced.

Phenix said, "That's all I'll say. The details are my husband's secret."

Ruxton returned to the hotel, troubled by the fact that these clever Chinese had accurately analyzed the American character. Somehow, he never would have expected Mai to pin it down so unerringly.

During their time together the next night, Phenix whispered, "My whole life has changed. Every day has new meaning in a way I never dreamed possible."

It was one of her frantic nights, and Ruxton realized that her relationship with him was actually too exciting for her. Not for the first time the thought came that their sex idyll couldn't last because she was becoming unstable.

Again, she held him past the starting point of *Hsio Hsi,* and it was nearly a quarter after seven when he walked into the hotel.

As Ruxton parted the portieres and glanced into the meeting room, a shock went through him, and all thought of Phenix was instantly blotted from his mind.

Lemoine sat in a chair a few feet from the door.

56

Ruxton stepped into the room, gripped by the excitement of the unknown. Nonetheless, as he walked to a chair, he was already gaining control of himself. He sat down, and outwardly then, his attention was on what Ho Sin Go was telling him: that the subject for the evening was the distribution of goods, and of how the distributor must receive only ordinary working man's pay, like anyone else.

Since that was part of basic Communist theory, Ruxton had considered it before, so he did not have to hear the arguments. He rejected the whole thing out of hand, for the instant the right to allocate goods was given to any person, he could charge for it. He could accept in exchange other goods, the special blessings bestowed by pretty girls, or other favors too numerous to think of.

It didn't take much of a gift to influence most people in a land where everything was scarce. Ruxton recalled hearing how, in Korean prisoner-of-war camps, some Americans gave up their meagre food rations for a cigarette butt. Entirely aside from what this implied about the true power of the cigarette habit, it provided a telling example of how little need be given by the distributor for his own private ends where all resources were controlled.

A loud voice interrupted his train of thought. Lemoine was on his feet. Angrily, he asked, "Why weren't these truths presented earlier in the group meetings?"

He was politely heard through, then requested to sit down, which he did. But shortly after that he was on his feet again. He looked around the room belligerently, and said to the interpreters, "I know several persons present who are very definitely not becoming Communists, and who, I am sure, will not turn over until a much more positive statement is required of them."

The man seemed unable to keep quiet. Several times during the evening he exploded into speech. Ruxton observed him closely and saw that his face was an angry red, and that he clenched his jaws. His eyes were slightly narrowed, as if with suspicion.

When the meeting ended at two-thirty, which was early, Ruxton walked over to the young Frenchman and deliberately held out his hand. Lemoine glanced down at it, then without a word turned his back on Ruxton and walked over to the French interpreter. The two men spoke together in low tones. All the anger was gone from Lemoine's manner. He seemed eager to please. Every word and gesture accepted that the Chinese was his friend. Finally, Lemoine walked to the door, and without speaking to any of the white men, headed upstairs.

The next morning was clear and cold and dusty. The steel blue sky was typical of northeast China in mid-winter.

It was the day he resumed his visits to Tosti.

They discussed Fo. Tosti said, "Of course, he has escaped. If he hadn't I should have heard something from one of those two." She often referred to the Mais as "those two." She went on, "Besides, I'm sure there were no problems. In such a big country, with so many people, one disguised Chinese with correctly forged papers cannot be picked up."

His affair with Phenix continued its uneasy course that night. She was passive this time, but she held him very tightly. "I've been disgracefully aggressive," she murmured. "A woman shouldn't act like that."

She was again dangerously possessive. And she kept him until seven-thirty. It occurred to Ruxton after he had left that he actually felt more threatened now when Mai was away than when that grim, suspicious man was at home.

Another night.

Phenix was tremendously emotional, so much so that it affected Ruxton, and he found himself involved in a fierce whispered discussion about the good heartedness of the Chinese and the evil intentions of the whites.

Phenix argued so long and so late that he barely got to the gate before ten P.M.

The following night, he was more than twenty minutes late for the group discussion.

It seemed a foolish way to arouse suspicion. But women had held him before. What such a woman did was require a man to measure up to a standard of manhood that had nothing to do with the affair between them. In order to meet that standard the man had to brace himself inwardly to reject his wife's legitimate inquiries as to where he had been until five A.M. Over the years, in reading newspaper accounts of divorce suits where the wife reported her husband consistently out most of the night, Ruxton had realized that his were not the only females who played that game. Yet he had never found a way to get around it, and so he did not seriously resist the same compulsion in Phenix.

On the eighth night, Phenix over-shot the mark finally and irrevocably. As she hurriedly pushed him to the door, she whispered, "Oh, I'm so sorry. The guard will be coming to look for you. It's twenty after ten."

Ruxton made no comment. He had known for twenty-five minutes that he was in trouble.

"Go on upstairs," he whispered. "They may knock on your door."

"You'll be all right?" Her tone was agonized. But it was a little late for that. The destruction was done.

"I'll do what's necessary," he said.

"But—"

"Please go," he urged. "If they come to your door, you should be there."

It was evident that she agreed, for her hand caressed his arm, a fluttering motion, and then she was gone. He heard her pad across the floor, and the faint, faint sound of her soft steps on the stairs. A door opened and shut. Silence.

Alone, Ruxton thought, "It's simple. Either the guard did notice that I failed to leave, or he didn't notice. If he didn't notice, no problem. If he did—trouble."

Trouble was a mild word. Danger, suspicion, exposure!

57

Ruxton slitted open the door that led outside. He had a quick glimpse of brush. Because he felt fearless, he was about to push the door wide and step out boldly—when he heard footsteps.

The Chinese gate guard came into view.

Ruxton pulled the door shut, and listened to the retreating sound as the man walked around to the back of the house.

Once again, he opened the door. There was no one in sight. He slipped through it, and closed it carefully behind him.

He took three swift steps and then lowered himself partly behind and under a bushy evergreen. The hard parched ground was icy cold against his body. But he had a limited view of the yard, and he himself was concealed in shadow.

He waited, expecting reaction.

The stillness of the night was broken. A door opened. Tosti's voice came. A man spoke in Chinese, asking for Madame Mai. Ruxton suppressed a strong impulse to remain and hear the conversation. Bu the knowledge that the guard was occupied spurred him to his next step.

He had been tugging with stiff fingers at his shoe laces. Now they came loose and he pulled off his shoes. A moment later he was on his feet, and padding softly over the hard ground. He darted from one bare-branched tree to another, seeking his concealment close to the ground.

He came to where he could see the gate. As he had feared, the Book Room guard stood in front of it.

Ruxton waited in the shadows, watching the second guard, estimating his chances. They seemed small. The gate was open. The guard stood half in and half out of the yard, partly facing away. But obviously able to see movement out of the corner of one eye.

Ruxton was silently cursing the situation when Madame Mai and the first guard came suddenly into his line of vision near the gate. She had led the man around the far side of the house.

She spoke to the two soldiers. "Go to your quarters. If this prisoner is missing, he will be found. But I'll take charge now, and see if he has returned to the hotel."

One of the guards said, "We searched the yard, but there was no sign of him. Perhaps we should look again."

It was a perfectly valid suggestion, but obviously one that Phenix could not permit. "Do as I say!" she commanded sharply.

They walked off, one grumbling that it would be her own fault if anything went wrong.

Ruxton waited. His impulse was to take advantage of the lull. But his problem was complicated by the possibility that Tosti might come outside.

He didn't want her to find out either.

He grew aware that Phenix was looking around anxiously. He shrugged, and emerged from hiding.

The woman came over and said in a low voice. "We have been very foolish. The gate guard says that you have been leaving at 10 o'clock, and the book room guard says no, you leave shortly after seven." She broke off, urgently, "You'd better go back to the hotel. We'll decide in the morning what to do."

Ruxton returned to his room, went unhappily to bed and to a restless sleep.

He awoke with the thought: "I'll have to watch out for Madame Mai. She's likely to take some further action without telling, and women don't always make sensible decisions in situations like this."

. . . Nor did men.

He dressed with a heavy heart. Logically, he was a dead man. Although the absence of Mai Lin Yin would cause a slight delay in his extermination.

58

As Ruxton approached the gate of the Mai residence, he saw that a new sentry was on duty. The guard inside the library was also a new man.

Ruxton pondered the changes as he looked for a book. It seemed to him Phenix had made an error. Yet he had no clear idea of what she should have done.

Shortly before lunch he returned to the hotel, and went hopefully up to the second floor. She was there with two Chinese who did not speak English, and so she said openly, "As you have seen, I have acted. I sent them away in the middle of the night." She was calm. "You never let a subordinate get into a position where he can argue with you. They understand punishment, and have been told that they were let off lightly. Also, I sent them to their home units, and had their immediate superior tell them that the disciplinary action is not shown on their records. So they won't talk about it."

Ruxton nodded his grudging admiration of the solution. By getting the men away before dawn, she had minimized the possibility of the story spreading. Still, it wasn't over. And it wouldn't be until Mai had had time to react.

"Do I see you tonight?" he asked.

"Of course." Her tone was sharp. She seemed to realize it,

257

for she softened, and said, "Tonight, but not tomorrow night. My husband returns tomorrow evening."

Ruxton left her, encouraged but not convinced.

That day passed. That night for the first time Phenix let him go at ten to seven. "We should have been more careful in the past," she said with a sigh, as they separated.

The next day and evening ran their course. Shortly before midnight there was a sound of motor cars. Ruxton got up and looked out of the window. The headlights of four automobiles were coming along the road from the east.

In bed again, Ruxton presumed that Mai was back.

He was still awake thirty minutes later when someone knocked on his door. As he tumbled out of bed and slipped into his trousers, Ruxton thought, "Already?" But it was Gregory's voice that came through the panel: "Ruxton, open up, will you?"

Ruxton opened the door. Several of the white prisoners stood there, partially dressed.

Gregory said, "Come to von Spie's room. You can see into the prison from his window. Things are happening over there."

Ruxton said, "Things?"

It developed that von Spie, watching Mai's arrival, had seen him and the prison commandant order out the entire prison garrison. Swiftly the soldiers marched through the gate into the prison compound. Shortly afterwards, gunfire had started. It was still going on.

Executions!

Ruxton gazed out of one of the two windows in von Spie's room at the scene beyond the prison wall. By the bright lights streaming from the prison they watched as three or four men at a time were grouped against the wall. There would be a rattle of gunfire. And the men would crumple to the ground.

For over an hour the white prisoners looked down as some seventy groups of men were led out and shot.

At last it was over. The lights went out.

Silence.

Presently, the prison gate opened, the soldiers came out and marched away.

Ruxton went back to his room, and to bed. There was an empty sensation at the pit of his stomach. He thought, "It's time. Whatever I do, it's got to be done quick."

He had for a long time now had the feeling that his

knowledge of the "right" man would stand him in good stead in his dealings with Mai.

But how?

59

Jarnoz, Tittoni and Niels Madsen were in the washroom when Ruxton entered the next morning. The Turk still wore his bandage, and he seemed very sober. He said, "Mr. Ruxton, I need advice, help."

Ruxton, who needed advice and help as much as anyone, felt too low in spirit to resist. He did glance questioningly at the other two men. Jarnoz said quickly, "They not understand English. We talk, hey?"

Ruxton asked wearily, "What's the trouble?"

"Since the other night—" Jarnoz touched the bandage on his head—"my spirit not good. Bad thoughts, bad ideas, sick head. Strong desire to believe all this communist madness. Too tired up here—" he pointed at his bandage again—"to resist."

So the hypnotism had taken effect. Ruxton did not doubt the cause. "Take advantage!" Mai had commanded the interpreter, and the man had yelled in Turkish at the confused and injured Jarnoz as he lay on the floor. But how did one undo that? He shook his head gloomily. "I don't know how to help you," he admitted. "Let me think about it."

Jarnoz caught his arm. "Please—we talk."

Ruxton hesitated. The truth was, of course, that he might as well be listening to Jarnoz. This was the day when Mai would discover that the regular sentries were missing from his home. And the fact was that he had nothing to do until Mai reacted to their absence. He said without enthusiasm, "All right. Talk."

It turned out to be not a conversation but another lecture. A desperate and despairing Jarnoz felt the need to impart to someone the essence of *his* observations on the Communist menace. Most of what he had to say was old stuff to Ruxton now. But it was evident that for each man it was a new and disturbing revelation, and Jarnoz was no exception. Yet he did have several fresh thoughts. In his halting English Jarnoz pointed out that Communism had learned its first lesson from the short-lived French Communes of 1848. The methods discovered there, and analyzed correctly by Marx, given a cruel and remorseless leadership, were actually capable of producing a powerful state. That was what fooled many people. They couldn't seem to realize that, like the czarist regime, the Marxists had achieved another of the interminable line of successful police systems with which history abounded.

Jarnoz pointed out that Hitler also created a new state, complete with communist-style party. If a method for creating a state by violent means was the criterion, then several other systems deserved loud applause: The Turkish janissaries of the not too distant past were certainly not a bourgeois group. Genghis Khan's system of exterminating all city and town dwellers, and of basing his state on nomad herders, maintained his dynasty for more than a hundred years, and Tamerlane's empire, founded on entire divisions of berserks, lasted longer.

Dictatorship of nomads and berserks, dictatorship of the janissaries, dictatorship of the proletariat—the end result was that the great Khan, and Tamar the Lame, and the Turkish Caliphs and Stalin and members of the Communist Party lived better, much better than the average man. How else could one judge a system other than by observing who rode the fine horses, who travelled first class, who ate and dressed well?

Jarnoz completed his diatribe, laughed apologetically, and said, "Now, we go to breakfast—hey?" He started for the door.

Ruxton held him with a gesture. The man's talk had helped him. He thought, "Who would have dreamed in their day that nomads could seize Asia? Who would have thought that men could be trained to go berserk and so be used to conquer half the world? That children taken from conquered people, as the old Turks had done, could be turned into the fierce janissaries who held an empire together? And certainly, before Marx the idea of arming the poorest people in order to defeat all the military forces of a state was not conceivable."

Surely, in his knowledge of the "right" man, he had an idea of equal power to anything that had ever existed.

There were gaps in his knowledge, of course, but the main outline was there.

He felt the strength of that conviction as he said to Jarnoz, "Fight this weakness!" He pointed at Jarnoz' head. "I'm sure that the blow you received gave you a feeling of a system too powerful to overcome. Historically, when these new systems are on the rise it sometimes seems as if nothing can .

ever stop them. Millions of minds are overwhelmed by this thought alone. Nations fall, almost as if by mass hypnosis, and yet, when history has rolled over the event, we can look back on it dispassionately and see that the great tide went only so far, and then rolled back. Sometimes the speed of the recession astonished all onlookers. I think it will be the same with Communism."

Jarnoz' heavy face was somber. His bright, intelligent eyes blinked at Ruxton.

"Good thought," he said at last. "Thank you."

60

The earth rotated on its axis. The morning lengthened. Ruxton went back and forth between the Book Room and the hotel, hoping to have a chance to talk with Phenix.

There was no sign of her.

During the afternoon, he helped the priest pick over seeds. As, in the gathering darkness, the two of them walked to the hotel, he tried to feel confident that he needed only a few minutes' conversation with her to set in motion what he believed would be the inevitable self-destruction of any terrorist type.

Neither Mai nor his wife showed up at the hotel that night.

The group meeting was about correct working principles, and Ruxton and Father de Melanier were commended for their labor "for the people."

Ruxton was too tense to appreciate the praise. He went to bed with the conviction that the next day would bring a decision.

Morning.

Ruxton loitered outside the hotel until he was freezing cold, but Phenix did not emerge from the Mai gate.

He walked to the library, thinking, "I've got to make up my mind. Do I face all this with a heavy heart—"

His body felt heavy, his spirit sagged—

"—or do I brace myself and take it in stride?"

He straightened, and did that peculiar internal pushing away of negation that he had learned in the air force. What it did was black out—something. It wasn't exactly that he was no longer afraid. What happened had some of the aspects of automatism. A part of his brain was blocked off. But he could think, and function. He felt very hot, and a constant anger seethed in him. Accompanying the rage was a restless feeling.

And recklessness!

The slightest sound outside sent him racing out of the library to intercept Phenix. But it was never she.

Inside again, he no longer cared if he were observed reading foreign literature. In fact, he spent his time reading bound scientific journals in Russian. The journals contained Pavlov's own account of his fatigue experiments. There was the objective story of the research which had led to the three phases of fatigue. What concerned Ruxton was, what would fatigue do to a "right" man?

Pavlov's report clarified for him that the final, fatigue effect was an inversion. In dogs, the visible symptoms were exactly as Father de Melanier had described them: the turning against the beloved master, and affection for someone formerly hated. In human beings the transformation was more complex, but the change in personality had the same reversal aspects.

The only reference to what might happen if fatigue were continued too long was that in some instances, the dogs died.

Ruxton put the Pavlov book away, shuddering, but with his mind made up. He could wait no longer for a chance encounter. He walked outside, and around to the back of the house. Tosti answered his knock. Her eyes widened as she saw who it was. Ruxton said softly, in Japanese, "I must speak to Madame Mai. Will you tell her privately—"

She was shaking her head. "They fight all night," she whispered. "They went out early, shortly after seven. I couldn't hear what was said."

"Where did they go?"

She shook her head again. "I heard him say she had exceeded her authority, but what about I don't know."

Ruxton nodded. "I'll see you tomorrow," he said.

But he didn't believe that.

He went back to the library, and he was settling down with another book, when the door burst open. Two soldiers leaped across the threshold and came to attention at either side of the door.

There was a long, pregnant pause. Then Ho Sin Go appeared in the doorway and stepped diffidently inside.

Ruxton gave a lightning side glance to the three other whites in the room, de la Santa, Tittoni, and Niels Madsen. They seemed shocked. No one moved.

Ho Sin Go marched straight over to Ruxton. His plump,

blotched face looked waxen. "Mr. Ruxton," he said, "you will accompany these soldiers—at once!"

Ruxton could feel a thick sensation in his throat. Resistance, rage—but he walked slowly across the room. He paused beside de la Santa. "I don't know what this is," he said in French, "but it looks bad. I wish you and these other two gentlemen the best of luck."

De la Santa murmured an earthy curse. Then he looked up, and there was a tear in the corner of one eye. "In many way," he said, "you have been a difficult man for me to like. But a man indeed you are. Good luck, sir."

He stood up and offered Ruxton his hand.

As Ruxton passed Tittoni, the Italian reached up and patted his arm. Niels Madsen saluted him.

Outside, Ruxton was directed by Ho Sin Go to walk away from the hotel.

They came presently to the same barracks building in which Lemoine had been held. Ho Sin Go motioned Ruxton to enter, but did not follow him inside. Once in, Ruxton looked back and saw that the two soldiers were taking up sentry positions at the entrance. That was all he saw. He faced about, walked in through an outer door, and so into the barracks proper.

There were no soldiers inside. But Mai Lin Yin sat in the chair beside the warrant officer's desk near the door, and Phenix sat on one of the bunks.

61

There was a warning in the way the woman sat. She was hunched up, her legs drawn under her, as if her body had contracted, as if she had tightened all her muscles and become smaller. She did not look at him, and after her first fleeting glance and his formal nod, which she significantly failed to return, Ruxton ignored her.

But he had accepted the possibility that their liaison was discovered. And so he gazed at Mai with an outward calm and, more important—an inward willingness to be immensely flexible in his reaction. Now that the crisis was here, he could deny or admit, and face the consequences with equal grim determination. He had confronted angry husbands before. That, at least, was a situation he understood.

He looked at Mai a trifle too guilelessly. But then, it was not a normal situation. Mai sat behind his desk and he had a faraway look. Finally, he grimaced and said harshly, "Mr. Ruxton, my wife has confessed that for many months she has been your mistress. What have you to say for yourself?"

So that was the approach. Ruxton said, amazed, "Your wife has *what?*"

Mai bit his lip. He had evidently thought to solve the husband's dilemma on the opening accusation by making one of the oldest gambits in the history of infidelity. And now the accusation was made, he had lost the advantage of surprise, and he was no further ahead. He said bitterly, "Your pretended astonishment gains you nothing, Mr Ruxton. We are not here for histrionics. I am trying to determine what punishment shall be meted out to my errant wife. As for you—I have no doubt about what I shall do with you."

Ruxton continued to gaze at the man, but he could not help wondering at those duplicities of life which had made it possible for him to rescue Fo without incurring penalty. Yet now, by the well-defined route of a woman's emotions, he was trapped. For he suspected that guilt or innocence made no basic difference in this situation. But the game of words was not played out; the penalty might still be alterable by masterly denial.

He said slowly, "Major Mai, I cannot pretend to know what has transpired between you and your charming wife that would lead you to accuse her. As for me, what you say is fantastic. This is a military prison. Everywhere you look there is a soldier on duty—"

"Except in my wife's bedroom!" Mai snapped.

So he didn't know about the mattresses. Ruxton drew a deep, slow breath, parted his lips to speak again, and then closed them. He had made his main points. He was convinced now that Phenix had confessed nothing. Therefore he had nothing to fear except the madness of a man who correctly divined a truth, and might strike suspected offenders dead even though he had no evidence against them.

The silence lengthened, and finally there was a movement from Phenix. She was uncramping, expanding her body. She had taken on the look of a woman who knew herself to be secure, as she said in a voice that was perhaps too high pitched, "Mr. Ruxton, as you have no doubt surmised, I have a jealous husband, who does not shrink from degrading his wife. I beg you not to make this accusation common talk among your fellow prisoners."

Mai said acridly, "Mr. Ruxton has been discreet all these

264

months. I'm sure he will continue to be so." He went on savagely, "Don't believe for one instant, my dear, that these denials have changed my mind. I have an instinct for intrigue, and once my suspicion is aroused, simple logic leads me unerringly to the truth."

The stubborn look was on his face, and there was no doubt but that he meant it. And of course, his analysis was right.

It was no time to hold back. Whatever cards he held, he now had to play. He hesitated a bare instant longer, and then he said, in Chinese, "Major Mai, don't you think you have killed enough of your prisoners in the first six months?"

Silence.

Mai sat back in his chair and gazed at him. Ruxton watched him tensely for a reaction that would reveal that he understood that Ruxton was giving him a message. The unspoken message was: "Now that you know I understand Chinese, you will realize that I know about Madame Fa 'tze."

The silence ended. Mai laughed curtly, and said in Chinese, "Mr. Ruxton, my wife understands and tolerates the emotional turbulence of her husband—isn't that right, lover?" He glanced at Phenix.

The woman was staring at Ruxton. "You've understood Chinese all this time?" she asked. She sounded disconcerted. She glanced at her husband uneasily. "What has he overheard, do you think?" she asked quickly, and she spoke in the crude north country Chinese.

"He overheard me and Fa 'tze Jui-fang arrange a rendezvous. I told you that he came by, remember?"

Ruxton had no intention of letting them know that he also understood their northern dialect. He had made known his knowledge of Mandarin Chinese for a reason. That reason was now proved meaningless, because Mai was one of that majority of "right" men who had his affairs openly.

Mai faced Ruxton. "How many languages do you speak, Mr. Ruxton?"

"Four," lied Ruxton. "French, Chinese, English and Latin."

It was a respectable total for an American, and therefore sounded plausible.

"I see." Mai stared off into space. His expression gradually hardened. "Your attempt to blackmail me gets you nowhere, Mr. Ruxton, but it does establish your guilt."

"I don't follow your reasoning," Ruxton said.

"We won't argue the details," said Mai, "unless you have some other point of blackmail you would like to discuss."

Ruxton's thought went to the escape of Fo Hin-di. But

that was against him, not for him. Then his mind flashed to what he knew about Tosti. Impossible. An instant later, his attention settled on his next move.

"Are you going to execute me?" he asked.

The brown eyes stared at him grimly. "And if I am?"

Ruxton had no illusions. This was the crisis. There was no one to save him; he had only his own devious mind. And any schemes he had would have to be solidly based.

"I have some money in Hong Kong," he said. "My life savings. I'll place 25,000 U.S. dollars to your personal account in Hong Kong if I survive the full two years and am not executed."

"You are offering me a bribe?"

There was no turning back. "They call it ransom," said Ruxton steadily, "and I am offering 25,000 dollars ransom for my life."

Mai stood up suddenly, and walked over to Ruxton. His hand came up and he slapped Ruxton's face. "It's not enough," he snapped. "You'll have to do better than that."

Phenix said wearily, "Mr. Ruxton, agreeing to be bribed is a tactic for a Communist. Landlords, officials, officers, Kuomintang dignitaries—all have offered ransom. It has always been accepted, and afterward they were executed just the same. Please do not add further disgrace to this degrading situation in which my husband has placed me by being taken in by one of his little games."

Mai walked back to his desk and sat down. "Well, Mr. Ruxton," he asked, "any more schemes?"

Ruxton shook his head. "That completes my blackmail possibilities," he said evenly. But his heart sank.

"Naturally," Mai went on in a relentless tone, "I do not confuse my personal life with my public life, and so what I shall do, Mr. Ruxton, is simply speed up your conversion. We shall follow the route of maximum sustained fatigue through the three steps to change."

He clapped his hands, and yelled in Chinese, "Attention!"

The two soldiers came through the door on the double.

Mai commanded, "Take this foreign—" he used a colloquial term, literally meaning building, but which, given a special streetside meaning, implied an obscenity, "into the fatigue room."

The soldiers motioned Ruxton toward the rear door. Thereupon he became the first in a procession which consisted of himself, followed by the two soldiers in single file, with Mai bringing up the rear.

They passed through the room where Lemoine had sat mindless on a bunk, and entered a long, large rear room which was unoccupied and unfurnished except for a treadmill and some chairs.

Mai motioned Ruxton over to the treadmill.

62

Ruxton walked to the machine. It was a typical treadmill and differed from the kind used for work in that there was a rear wall, and this wall had tiny sharp nails about half an inch in length protruding from it.

Mai pointed at them. "You won't need these claws at first," he said, "so I'll just draw them in." He manipulated a lever, and the nails receded. Mai continued. "You may not be aware of it," he said, "but the original treadmill was a big drum shape invented by China as a practical way to pump water. When the British took it over, they promptly used it as an instrument of punishment. It was installed in some British prisons to provide artificial hard labor. It is not generally realized that the immediate ancestors of the present English treated the lower classes more cruelly, probably, than any other people."

Ruxton had cringed as he saw the nails. Now he tore his attention away from them. He said, "The human race, Major, is just coming up out of the age of cruelty. In all the world, the English were among the first to have humane laws. The Chinese are apparently going to be the last."

Mai stared at him a moment, eyes narrowed. Then: "Get on!" he said curtly.

Ruxton was recovering. He asked, "What is this supposed to do?"

Mai said, "You step onto it a Capitalist and you step off a Communist."

Ruxton felt blank, but he asked in a steady voice, "How long do you think it will take?"

Mai seemed to consider that. His face, which looked heavier, more fleshy than when Ruxton had first met him, grew pensive. Whatever emotion had been in him seemed to have subsided. Apparently, the punishment fitted the crime, and so he was at ease in contemplation of it. "Fifty hours," he said finally.

Ruxton said, "Impossible. I haven't had enough exercise to be able to do anything as sustained as that."

"You have an incorrect view of human functioning," explained Mai. "Fatigue is merely a phenomenon of the cells and their connections. But now, onto the treadle, if you please!" He spoke sharply.

Ruxton hesitated, stirred to anger by the tone of voice. He glanced at the two privates. They gestured menacingly with their bayonets. Since there was no escape, he tentatively placed one foot on the treadmill.

The tread made a soft, sliding sound, as it moved several inches. It was evidently kept well oiled.

Ruxton glanced back, met Mai's cold gaze, and faced the treadmill again. This time he put his full weight on the treadle, felt it start moving, dragged his other foot on the floor to slow it, then raised that foot also. And he was on.

He spent the first few minutes sensing the responses of the treadmill to his weight, and movement. He hoped that control was possible, that he might find a way of manipulating its sliding motion—slowing it, even stopping it.

He could not stop it. But it had a drag of its own that kept it from madly accelerating. Its slowest speed was slightly faster than a man normally walks, and this was the pace he brought it to.

He became aware that Mai was watching him with sour amusement. However, the man said nothing. Simply turned away finally, and walked out of the room. The two soldiers sat down in chairs on either side of the treadmill, and watched him stolidly.

Ruxton walked his brisk walk and, already feeling tense, made a further analysis of his situation. At this rate he would be completely exhausted in less than an hour—unless he could work out a system of oxygen intake that would support his accelerated motion.

He began breathing slow and deep. It was an unaccustomed rhythm for him. It required about as much of his attention as he could spare from the complicated task of keeping the speed of the treadmill down to its minimum.

In less than ten minutes, he began to feel confused, like a man who is required to do too many things at once. He knew then that the pace was beyond his strength, and that the crisis was only minutes away.

But an hour must have passed before he fell the first time. What happened was, he suffered a momentary blackout, like an over-tired driver who falls asleep for a few seconds, and wakes up with a start to realize that he is off the road.

Ruxton hit the rear wall of the treadmill with a crash that

made him dizzy. The tread stopped as he half-leaned, half lay against the slanting wall of metal, gasping for breath. Quickly, he was quite alert again. He saw that one of the soldiers was standing up. Before the man could menace him, Ruxton stepped gingerly onto the middle of the tread and began his futile walk again.

The soldier sank back into his chair.

As he walked that too-rapid walk, Ruxton watched the soldiers and his whole body trembled with hate. Marx had reasoned that such people would respond with a stereotyped brutality to the responsibility forced on them. All across the world they were proving that the analysis was absolutely correct.

His ferocious hatred subsided gradually as the pace took its toll of his energy. He began to feel surges of grief, and then he seemed to be without emotion but immensely tired.

Crash!

He grew shakily aware that the Chinese soldier was standing over him, angrily gesticulating. Before that threat, Ruxton climbed to his feet. He felt weak, and his legs were trembling as once more he started on that merciless march up the treadmill.

This time he fell without any sensation.

His first awareness was that he was lying on the floor, and rough hands were jerking him back onto the machine. Something hard jabbed his side.

He blacked out.

Yet the next time that consciousness returned, he was walking quite firmly on the treadmill, as if he had recovered his strength.

Again the blackness closed over him, and when he had his next fleeting awareness he was still walking the treadmill. And he was thinking of a friend of his in the air force who, while acting as co-pilot, grew aware that the door beside him had sprung open. He felt an awful suction. That was the last thing he knew. When he came to, he was on a rubber raft. He had evidently opened his parachute, fallen 11,000 feet, landed in the ocean, freed himself, swam to a raft which his companions dropped to him—and he had done all of these things without being conscious of a single action.

Ruxton thought, "There is another part of the brain that can take over in an emergency—"

Whatever it was took over again, even as he had the thought about it.

From somewhere to somewhere came a voice, saying, "Tosti is a Japanese spy. She's a spy—spy—" Ruxton listened to the sounds, at once alarmed and puzzled. He was alarmed that another person had discovered Tosti's secret, and puzzled as to whom the information was being given. He grew so anxious that he was able to focus his eyes blurrily on his surroundings.

He was still in the barracks, still on the treadmill, still moving forward, but on his knees now, automatically straining to get away from the needles. His back felt numb. There was a feeling that the needles had been used many times now. Two soldiers, new to him, sat in the chairs. One seemed to be sleeping.

Although Ruxton had no particular conscious thought about it, as he turned his head aimlessly, his gaze flitted across the barred window, and he saw that it was night.

He crawled on, becoming more aware with each passing moment, so much so that the steady mumbling of his own voice suddenly roared in on him. And he was saying: "Tosti is a Jap spy—she's a spy—a spy—"

Ruxton bit his tongue. It was not a small reaction. He bit so hard that blood gushed in his mouth, and his tongue hurt with an excruciating pain. The silencing act was so violent he stopped his movements on the treadmill and instantly the needles drove cruelly into his back. He jumped with the agony, and frantically scrambled forward, as he had done so often, earlier. He thought, "You scum, you're betraying that girl—"

He forgot about it.

He seemed to be falling into some incredible distance. And as he fell, he dreamed.

A thousand dreams there were, that opened wide as many doors, and there, suddenly, was not a dream at all, but a complete memory.

Instantly, he felt feverishly ill. But it was a small child's sickness. He was lying in bed, dying, because he wanted his daddy, who had gone away . . .

Ruxton came up out of some great depth of torture, and he thought in amazement, "My God—that was the time my father left my mother. Why, he even told me about it, and that he came back because of me . . ."

His mind wandered. He heard himself raving; then—blackness. And then, as plain as if she were in the room, his mother's head, face and shoulders loomed above him. She looked like a giant, completely out of proportion, and very young—a girlish mother. "Like that picture of her when she was in her twenties," he thought. The large, pretty face was streaming with tears, and every word she spoke had a sob in it. The deluge of sympathy and sorrow was like a palpable force. She cried, "Oh, Seal, Seal, please get well. I love you. I'll take care of you. You'll be all right. You're all that matters. You'll always be my baby, and I'll take care of you forever."

He felt the meaning of those words then, and the power of that emotion, through the mist of his fever. The words came into his unprotected body, penetrated to every cell. The sympathy engulfed him with its warm, sticky wetness, and then like an all-pervading gas, saturated his being. The meaning and the emotion became as much a part of him as his arms, his legs, his head.

He started to sob, "Why, why isn't she taking care of me?" But it was a young boy, then a teen-ager, then a youth, asking the question at some gut-level of life. The feeling never came near the surface of his thinking mind. It quavered at some deep of the self in the form of an awful grief. A promise betrayed. The terrible, unforgivable perfidy of women.

He had finally realized: "Those goddamned female bastards are all wanting to be taken care of themselves."

On the day of that realization, he knew somehow that no woman would ever really take care of him. Not mother. Not all the mother substitutes that he had slept with, seduced, taken away from other men, struck, punished, mauled, betrayed—Not one of them would ever fulfill the promise made to each and every cell of his body.

As that truth began to penetrate, his father's training of him, his father's—and certain other men's—ideas about women and life grew real to him. He became a man in his father's image, thinking the same casually superior thoughts, feeling automatically that women belonged in a low category. He rejected their feelings, catered to a woman only to the extent necessary to get sex from her, and never felt any genuine respect for her as a person. Women were like children, to be tolerated by a grown man, and never granted equality.

It was the basic incorrigibility of the 'right' man.

A man's voice said, in French, "All right, Ruxton. Get off!" The words echoed in his mind like a senseless rhyme.

"Get off!"

"Get off!"

271

"Get off!"

And echoed. And re-echoed. Hands grabbed him, and shoved him violently, breaking the repetitious pattern.

"I said, GET OFF!"

The floor came up. He had a momentary glimpse of it coming toward him. Involuntarily, he put out his hands to stop it.

The next moment, or so it seemed, somebody was shaking him.

Ruxton had no means, then or later of determining how long he lay there on the floor. But when he opened his eyes he felt quite sane. His body ached a little, but otherwise he was normal.

His head had been facing toward one bare wall. Now, as he was about to sit up, he turned it automatically.

And stiffened.

Kuznetoff sat in a chair beside him. As Ruxton moved, the man placed the point of a short, thin knife against his throat.

"Stay right there, Ruxton!" he said in an even purposeful voice. "I have a question to ask you, and your answer will determine your fate. Were you the man who came to my room and tried to choke me to death?"

63

Kuznetoff went on tensely, "Don't expect any interruption. I've killed your guards. If you try to get up, or call for help, I'll shove this needle knife right into your throat, and no one will ever know what happened."

Ruxton lay there, stunned. He believed that Kuznetoff would do exactly that. He said at last, "I don't understand what you are talking about. And for God's sake, what would bring you here at a time like this?"

He spoke automatically, because he had no plan. Yet when the words were uttered, he realized that denial was his best reaction.

Kuznetoff said deliberately, "I'm trying to decide whether to kill you, or merely make you squeal for mercy. As for why I came here under these conditions, when I discovered that you might lose your memory in this fatigue treatment, I knew I had to find out about your attack on me before that happened. If it wasn't you, then who was it. My life may be in danger."

Ruxton lay back, breathing hard. He was amazed, again, that his brain was as clear as it was, and that he did not seem particularly tired. But, then, Lemoine, except for the new rage in him, had not appeared exhausted from *his* ordeal.

Before Ruxton could think further, Kuznetoff's voice came, low and sharp, "Don't brace yourself. Don't try to roll away. I can push this knife faster than you can move."

Ruxton hadn't realized that he was tensing again. With an effort of will he forced himself to relax, and he said, shakily, "I can't see what killing me will gain you—and I still don't know what all this is about."

"You deny that you came to my room one night and tried to choke me to death?"

"Look, brother," said Ruxton harshly, "if I had ever started to choke you with the intention of killing you, you wouldn't be here."

Kuznetoff was silent for a moment. He said at last, slowly and implacably, "That makes some sense, but the more I thought about it, the more I became convinced that the voice was yours. So I'm not concerned with what scared you off. You've got one minute to go . . . Unless you tell me exactly why you attacked me. If you tell me, I may let you live—provided you beg for your life. One minute, Mr. Ruxton."

Ruxton had no intention of begging, but it struck him now, finally, that with such a man he would have to admit the truth. And so, hastily, he cast about for a way of telling what happened that would be understandable to Kuznetoff.

"Hitler!" he thought abruptly. "Of course, Hitler."

He said aloud, "You remember all that stuff we used to hear about Hitler and his rug-chewing rages?"

"Hitler!" Kuznetoff echoed. "What has he got to do with—"

Ruxton went on, "Those persons who watched him when he was eating the rug were convinced that he was completely out of his head. However, unlike what happened to me, I feel that he had a low-grade awareness of what he was doing. Which made it worse, of course. He could rationalize his behavior. I couldn't."

"Are you saying?—" the White Russian began. He stopped. He seemed to be out of his depth, and groping. He said then, irrelevantly, almost defensively, "Hitler was a genius."

"I thought you might think so," said Ruxton. "That night, with me it was not like that at all. When I woke up, there I was in the act of choking you."

"You admit it!" The man's face was livid. His voice held a

triumphant grate. "All right, Ruxton, your confession earns you the privilege of begging for your life, as I promised."

The threat was hard to take. Yet Ruxton's mind remained steady. He thought, as much in amazement as dismay, "Hatred really has no give in it." But it seemed to him that the man's admiration for Hitler was still his point of entry into that rigid brain.

"One minute to start begging, Ruxton."

Ruxton said in a steady tone, "I've been thinking a lot about this recently, and remembering what Mai said about Hitler understanding revolution." He went on, "Hitler surprised the Communists by understanding their tactics, and by manipulating the reactionary energy the Reds had stirred up to gain control of the streets, and to then capture the state. In the final issue in Germany, it turned out that reactionary energy was actually more powerful than revolutionary energy, and I wouldn't be surprised if that were true everywhere. Now, if Hitler had used his method in a strictly scientific way, we would have realized that he was operating above the consequences of his actions, and been interested in what he was doing. But because of his psychotic hatred of the Jewish and Slavic peoples, he never could convince us that what he did was based purely on method, whereas Stalin, who seemed to adhere to his own theories, but who probably murdered just as many people, lived to be called Uncle Joe, and we still have an image of a pipe-smoking, fatherly figure. Fantastic, eh?" said Ruxton—and rolled over, away from the knife.

Thus ended his delaying tactic.

64

As Ruxton flung his body along the floor, and leaped to his feet, he felt, rather than saw, the White Russian make a belated thrust at his back. For Kuznetoff, it was a fateful effort. He lunged up out of his chair, lost his balance, and staggered within reach of Ruxton's arms. Ruxton caught him in a grip of iron, slapped one arm around the slender, wiry body, and with his free hand grasped the man's right wrist. He squeezed mercilessly until the knife fell to the floor. Instantly, he slammed his foot down on it, and with a lurch of his own body to give power to the thrust, sent him spinning back into the chair.

Kuznetoff brought himself to a precarious stability, and

from this position stared up at Ruxton with glazed eyes.

The look of confusion on the man's face stopped the attack Ruxton had been about to make. He drew back, and it was then he noticed that he felt dizzy. It was a wild sensation, as if something big inside him had gone out of control. The threat had been too great. He grew aware of a warmth around his neck and upper body. Rage! The same fury that had been in him when he found himself choking Kuznetoff that night, the same overpowering anger that he had awakened with the following morning. Only now it didn't seem to be "over there." He could feel himself sinking into it, identifying with the anger. Briefly, then, it was as if he had three distinct awarenesses. He was himself, somehow detached, viewing the rage, and at the same time there was his own developing entanglement with a passion that grew more blinding every moment.

Ruxton saw that Kuznetoff was staring at him, his blue eyes wide. The man said in a low, urgent tone, "For God's sake, what's the matter?"

Ruxton couldn't speak. The choked feeling in his throat prevented him from talking. And the haze in his brain made his vision blur. Yet, he noticed the fact vaguely, he was still holding back. Could it be that the tiny portion of good sense that he had gained through understanding himself was restraining an anger that almost seared him, so white hot was the sensation of it in his head and body? A faraway thought came, that this was what the men who faced Hitler had been up against. This was the mental, physical and emotional madness of Stalin when he was angry, and in Mao Tse-tung. Many had reported the fury of these men at key moments. It was the same rage that had been in Mai Lin Yin at the time of the execution of Gongoe and the others.

Kuznetoff said, uneasily, "Mr. Ruxton, my attack on you has evidently put you into such anger that this conversation should—"

"What you're looking at," said Ruxton thickly, "is a reasonable copy of Genghis Khan and Mao Tse-tung, and Mai Lin Yin, and Hitler and all the little Hitlers, and Stalin, and that whole breed. This is how they reasoned when someone crossed them. So let's see how it comes out, hey, Anton?" He went on recklessly, "Speaking of my attack on you, how about your attack on me—with Gregory?"

He was thinking: "I'm crazy. I shouldn't be staying here. I should be deciding what to do next."

But his voice went on, "Remember that, Mr. Kuznetoff?"

The startled look on Kuznetoff's thin face was replaced by an expression of relief. "That makes us even," he said quickly. "I'm willing to call quits."

"How do you know," Ruxton demanded irrationally, "that I won't sleep-walk into your room again?"

Kuznetoff admitted that he didn't know. Ruxton stared at him blurrily. It almost didn't feel like anger, but rather some body turbulence which he was confusing with that emotion. He thought: "I'm standing up here like a drunken sailor. But if this isn't rage, what is it?" But that thought was over there in the distance. He heard himself say, "Why don't you sleep with your bed against the door, like I do?"

"I will," said Kuznetoff. He added hastily, "That solves that."

At that point Ruxton saw the two Chinese soldiers sprawled on the other side of the treadmill. The sight slowed the violence inside him.

He blurted out, "Good God, you really did kill them!"

Kuznetoff made a dismissing gesture. "I'm sure they deserve it," he said. "One of them was sleeping," he explained, "and the other dozed for a few moments. That's when I came in through that backroom window—" he pointed vaguely—"and cut their throats." Again he gestured. "But we can solve that problem later. It's a few minutes before four in the morning. Gives us time."

Time for what, he didn't say. They were more than a thousand miles inside China, and it was winter, and they were not going anywhere. Inside Ruxton the rage subsided, even more, like a wave striking a rock and shattering into spray, still in motion, but its power diminishing second by second.

He thought of Tosti. "I've got to get her to Wanchan," he told himself, "before they put me on that damned machine again."

It was a complete purpose. So subjective and all-enveloping, that it took no account or consideration of others. He had the idea. Instantly, he leaped at Kuznetoff. The man jerked away in alarm. But Ruxton merely grabbed his arm, and pulled him.

"Show me how you came in!" he whispered fiercely. "Then you get back to your room before we're discovered here."

65

Outside was a great stillness. In the darkness the two men removed their shoes.

Ruxton swallowed his shock as the chill of the ground instantly penetrated through the thick socks to the skin. Yet after a moment the cold was somehow bearable, and they were moving with relative safety behind the row of houses, away from the lighted street.

When they came to the rear of the Mai house, Ruxton whispered, "You get back into the hotel as best you can. I'm stopping here."

"What are you going to do?" Kuznetoff sounded alarmed. "If you murder Mai, we'll all be killed."

"Don't worry," Ruxton said. "I'm not the killer type." He added, under his breath, "At least, not yet."

Kuznetoff caught his arm, then grabbed his hand and shook it. "Good luck," he said, "whatever you do. I regret the violent feelings I had for you."

"Thank you for rescuing me," said Ruxton.

"I came to kill, not to rescue," was the sardonic reply.

They separated.

Ruxton watched him out of sight. And he was about to climb over the fence, when a man whispered from the shadows.

"Ruxton! It's me, Gregory."

Ruxton had started to react at the first sound. In a single convulsive movement he jerked Kuznetoff's knife out of his pocket. Slowly, he shoved it back, and scanned the intense darkness beside the fence.

"There are four of us here," Gregory whispered. "Let's talk."

Ruxton had the men located now. They were crouching, spread out, further along the fence. As he knelt beside Gregory, who was nearest, the other three crept up and formed a little group around him. Besides Gregory, there were de la Santa, Jarnoz, and Tittoni.

Gregory said, "We were determined to rescue you, and then saw that it was already done by someone else."

As he heard those words, Ruxton felt a warmth creep over him. Silently, he shook each man's hand. It struck him that if this little group of nineteen prisoners were actually a nation in miniature, then Mai had better take note. He was evoking resistance of a high order. These four men had come out prepared to fight, if necessary.

But he didn't need them.

Beside him, Jarnoz said, "Question—what now?"

Ruxton whispered, "I want you to go back to the hotel. Let me make my own attempt. Don't get involved in an escape in the dead of winter."

After Ruxton had repeated his words in French to de la Santa, that individual exclaimed, "But how can you hope to escape without help?"

It was no time for argument. Decisive minutes were passing. Ruxton said savagely, "Get back to your rooms, damn you! You're endangering me!"

In the darkness, de la Santa chuckled, "Same old angry American. Good luck."

Bending, he whispered to Tittoni, and the two men crawled off toward the hotel. Gregory said, "Sure you don't want any help?"

Ruxton said, "I either make it, or I don't. Goodbye. If anyone can do it, I can."

And still Gregory hesitated. "I don't see how you can get to Wanchan," he said uneasily. "It's thirty miles."

Ruxton said, "I don't think I should tell you my plan, Captain. It's too late to change it. But for God's sake, be on your way, and let me get on mine."

Jarnoz was tugging at Gregory's arm. "Come. He right. Mass escape impossible. Let him try to make it."

Gregory allowed himself to be drawn away. As he left he whispered, "Ruxton, you have my sincere good wishes."

Ruxton believed him. "Thank you, Captain," he said gratefully.

But he was glad when they were gone, and glad that they had not insisted on hearing his plan. He might have told them, in his urgent need to get rid of them. And it would not be wise to tell anyone about Tosti. For if she were ever exposed, and trapped, there would be no escape for her. The rest of them might continue to hope that Project "Future Victory" would end up with some of its experimental subjects still alive. But a Japanese spy would be doomed on discovery.

His plan for rescuing Tosti was not simple. He intended first to arouse Tosti; then, when she was dressing, he would go to Ho Sin Go's quarters, explain the situation to that unhappy young husband, and either solicit his support, or

278

force it. It was a night for decisive actions, and Ruxton dared not shirk a single logical possibility.

Gingerly, he climbed over the Mai fence. As he lowered himself on the far side, a figure rose up a few feet away, and a whispered voice said, "It is I, Mr. Ruxton. Ho Sin Go. You have come, perhaps, to see my wife."

Ruxton grabbed at him, but Ho retreated. "I have a gun," he said. "Hold still."

Utterly appalled, Ruxton hesitated. And realized that he could not accept any threat from Tosti's plump young husband. He crouched, and braced himself for an attack to the death.

Ho said, "Do not fear me, Mr. Ruxton. I came earlier to the torture chamber, and I heard what you said about Tosti. Instantly, my eyes were opened. I want to know what I can do to help."

Slowly, Ruxton let the tightly-held air from his lungs. He whispered, "You expected me to escape?"

"I came out to help you escape," said Ho. "Then I saw that someone else had already achieved my goal."

Under his breath, Ruxton said, "Good lord!" And then he was silent. There no longer seemed any question but that Mai, in torturing him, apparently without cause so far as the other men were concerned, had released emotional forces of the strongest kind. For they had all risked death, each for his own purpose.

He caught his tense thought, and hurriedly explained the problem of getting to Wanchan to Ho Sin Go. The distance required vehicle transportation.

Ho said, "Mr. Ruxton, when I heard you say those terrible words about my wife, I went out in a stunned state. But soon I recovered, and knew what had to be done. I have here a forged requisition for Major Mai's own car. Will that be satisfactory?"

In the darkness, Ruxton squeezed the man's arm in a gesture of affinity. "Go and get the car!" he whispered. "Drive out about a mile along the road, and wait. I'll bring her there."

"Very good, sir."

"And get your own things," said Ruxton. "You'll have to go with her. You can't remain here after this."

"I have every intention," was the fierce reply, "of accompanying my wife wherever she goes."

Ruxton decided to digest that idea later.

66

Quickly, he helped Ho over the fence.

Turning, he crept across the yard, making his way to the side door. And so, softly, into Tosti's room. A vague light came through the bamboo blind, and presently he was able to make out her form on the pallet. He reached down and placed one hand over her mouth, and encircled her body with the other.

He felt her grow tense. And then—

It was like trying to hold a wild animal, so violently did she struggle. But after a little, his whispered words penetrated, and her fight ceased.

In the darkness, as her breath gradually became normal again, he told her what had happened, but not why it had happened. About the fatigue treatment, but not about Phenix. About his mental disorder, and the betrayal. About meeting Ho Sin Go outside, and what Ho was doing at this very minute.

"You mean," she whispered, "that husband of mine—"

"Yes," said Ruxton.

She was silent, then: "Tell me again, what did you two plan?"

"To take you to Wanchan, turn you over to—well you know, your associates, in the hope that they can get you out of China."

"And what about you?"

"You told me they wouldn't take me—" he let the sentence hang.

"That's true." In the darkness, she seemed to be thinking hard. "What about Ho?"

"He says he's going with you. He's burned his bridges."

Another pause. Then, "What am I going to do with him, Seal?"

"Take him along," said Ruxton, "then divorce him."

"I'm not sure he can be trusted alone with me," she said. "He's getting to be a man, and one of these days he's going to have me, if I don't watch out."

Ruxton was silent. He had the same conviction, and he had no idea what to do about it at this penultimate moment.

"Get ready!" he commanded. "We'll talk on the way."

"Wait."

He was aware of her bending down, and in the darkness

he heard her fumbling **in** one corner, near the floor. Then he heard her speak in a low voice, in Japanese. Another voice sounded metallically, like someone on a phone, but very muffled.

Amazed, Ruxton realized that she was engaged in two-way radio communication.

The conversation lasted several minutes. Then she rose to her feet, and whispered. "I brought the radio back from that visit to Wanchan," she said simply. "You understand—for extreme emergency only. I couldn't even tell you."

Ruxton understood all right.

"A jet will come for Ho and me," she whispered. "I'm sorry, Seal, they won't take you. I begged, but they won't."

Ruxton was astonished at the idea of such a magical device as a plane flying all that distance into a hostile China. But her words gave him an empty feeling.

"For Christ sake, why not?"

"They want Project 'Future Victory' to go on. They will not interfere. It's a merciless decision."

"But why take Ho?"

"He may have information."

It was all too logical. Grimly, Ruxton inquired if the plane would land on the abandoned airstrip to the north. Tosti said it would, and added that it would arrive shortly before dawn.

"We'd better leave as soon as I'm dressed," she whispered.

Ruxton, considering what his own plans should be, took along the blankets from her bed. As soon as they were well away from the prison area, they talked of many things. What would happen to her?

"My term with the Nationalist Intelligence Service can end in six months," she said. "My family wants me to marry. There was a young man selected."

Ruxton surmised aloud that the marriage to Ho would have to be taken into account.

"Yes, the Japanese courts are very strict."

There was such an odd tone in her voice that Ruxton said finally, "Why don't you stay married to him. Have many children. Live happily."

"Are you serious? He's Chinese."

He had forgotten that Tosti was a strongly prejudiced racist. He sighed, and thought, "There's no place in this world for just us people."

He could see the car parked in the near distance ahead, and he said, "I'm going to have to leave that problem for you to solve. Just explain to the courts how the marriage happened, and they'll release you."

"I feel sorry for the poor man," said Tosti, perversely.

Ruxton remained silent. He suspected that in Japan Tosti would be far more bound by custom than her behavior in China might indicate. If that custom favored a continuance of the marriage to Ho Sin Go, then the young man was in luck.

A few minutes later, they joined Ho, and explained about the plane. Ho said, "I know where the road leads off to the air strip."

67

They spent the next hour feeling out the dimensions of the strip. Since the plane would have to land into the wind which blew gently from the east, they finally stationed themselves at the western-most end, and sat in the car wrapped in the blankets.

The darkness was barely beginning to soften when the familiar jet hissing came. As the plane roared by in the deep greyness above, they turned on the car lights.

The jet made a wide turn, and came down toward them. For a hundred yards the airstrip was lit up, and what was revealed must have made the pilot cringe. The years had split the concrete, dust had settled over the handiwork of man, and Nature had wrought a thousand destructions. Ruxton, who had landed on poor strips in his time—landed hard, landed with a lump in his throat, but landed—knew that a pilot with sharp night vision and a perfect courage, could do it. He was not mistaken.

As the machine roared over the car, the pilot turned on its landing lights, and a moment later it struck the ancient field, bounced, struck again and then, on its next strike, held; and presently it made a turn and came hissing back to where they waited.

Ruxton recognized the plane as a long-distance two-jet trainer, capable of carrying a pilot and two persons. And, being Japanese, two relatively small persons. It was not constructed for six-foot Americans.

He had hoped until this instant that he might force his way aboard. Now, finally, with a silent curse, and an emptiness in his stomach, he accepted his fate. Wordlessly, he lifted Tosti through the narrow door, and then helped Ho up beside her. The woman leaned out anxiously. "But what shall become of you?" she asked in Japanese. "Seal, you must take the car, drive to Wanchan. Don't go back to the prison." She sounded distressed.

Ruxton said, simply, "Good bye. Good luck."

There was no time for further speech. The pilot waved him off, urgently. The door closed. Ruxton, knowing what was coming, began to run. The jets hissed with their sound of power, and the plane moved, gathered speed, and made its take-off.

He heard its fading roar for several minutes, though he did not see it again.

68

The light of dawn increased rapidly now. Soon, he was able to make out mounds of stones piled off to one side or another of the strip. To pilots they were familiar sights, common to all hastily cleared fields, or back country air strips.

Ruxton left the car lights burning, and, taking the blankets, hurriedly but carefully made his way to the most distant rock pile. He worked fast, rearranging the rocks until he had a narrow cave, big enough to hold him and the blankets, and with one rock that he could lower to cover partially the entrance to his hideout.

He was in process of easing himself into the imperfect shelter, when the first jeeps appeared on the horizon. Hastily, Ruxton lowered the rock into position, crouched down in the blankets—and waited tensely.

From his place under the rocks, he could not see what was happening, and the sounds were a confusion. The jeeps arrived, and their motors were either left running, or else the machines were actually driven slowly around the strip itself. Such details of movement could not be clearly interpreted by the sounds alone. Once, he heard a shout. After more than an hour, the jeeps went away and there was silence.

Ruxton waited. When he could endure his cramped position no longer, he lifted off the rock, and crawled out. A survey of the horizon showed no sign of life. Mai's car had been driven away. He stretched and exercised. Feeling better, he crept back into his hideaway, and promptly fell asleep.

He awakened with a start to the realization that the jeeps

were back. He thought tensely, "Mai must be with them, this time." It was a surmise only, and if it were correct, it made no difference. Mai, too, must have accepted the evidence of his eyes. For presently those jeeps also went away.

About mid-afternoon Ruxton crawled out of his cramped quarters for a second stretch. Then numbly, he crept back into the shelter and drew the rock down.

He must have slept again, for the night came with surprising swiftness, and at last he was able to come out of his hiding place without fear of being seen.

He still had time to pass. Obviously, it wouldn't do, with what he had in mind, to get back before midnight. But he looked for, and found, the glint of snow. Soon the awful need for liquid was satisfied, and once more he settled down with his blankets to wait.

About eleven o'clock, he set out, and what he did then was typical of a peculiar high energy that he had always shown in crisis. To cover the final quarter mile to the Mai house, he literally and patiently walked it on the blankets. He spread one, walked across it, spread the other, and so on, all the way to the fence, and then—inside the yard—all the way to the basement door.

He spent the night cutting up and rearranging the mattresses. First, he removed all except the bottom two. Then he built a latticework from the numerous props and pieces tucked away in the cellar. Next he cut and ripped solid sections from the centers of five of the mattresses. He fed this slowly into the furnace during the next several hours, taking care not to stuff in too much at one time.

What was left of the ripped mattresses he fitted around his latticework. After which he piled the remaining, undamaged mattresses back in place. When his task was completed, the pile of mattresses looked as it had before—but now there was a cosy little home for him thirty inches high by about three feet wide and nearly five feet long.

To get inside, he merely forced his way between two of the mattresses. Once in, he used chunks of wood to prop open two ends of a mattress where—he had already determined— there was least likelihood of the aperture being seen. This gave him a cross sweep of air.

For emergencies, he planned to close even these openings. He had a piece of thin metal piping through which he intended to breathe whenever someone actually came into the basement.

Satisfied, he removed his shoes and some of his clothing.

He would have liked to sleep, but his mind was too active for that. It had become obvious that his only hope was his knowledge of the true nature of the "right" man. Lying there, he clarified for himself every aspect of the behavior of that twisted personality.

Mentally, he wrote an essay, summing up his observations, objective and subjective.

69

The type of person I am describing (*wrote Ruxton with his mind pen*) sees everything that ever happened to him in a distorted fashion, which in essence shows him to have been a hundred per cent right and everyone else to have been wrong.

The following description of his behavior, while by no means complete, is exact as far as it goes:

He is a man. His problem revolves entirely around his ally-substitute: his wife. Prior to, or shortly after they are married, something happens after which he postulates that she is no longer worthy of his complete love. There is no appeal from his judgment of her, once it has been rendered.

Although married, he must be free to do as he pleases, with no questions asked. He may talk as if the woman is also free to do as she pleases. My observation is, he doesn't mean this. He will spy on her if his slightest suspicion is aroused.

If she crosses him, or brings up to him some aspect of his misbehavior in a critical way, he either withdraws into a resentful silence which may last for a week or even longer, or he expresses unqualified rage. A percentage of him hits or chokes with a violence that does not shrink from causing damage and disfigurement.

If she leaves him, he must die.

This can be actual death, or the symbolic death of alcoholism, drug addiction, or insanity, or an illness so severe that when he finally recovers he is no longer the same person.

If she leaves him, or starts divorce proceedings, he presently goes into a frantic emotional state: tears, wild appeals, desperate anxiety—"Don't leave me. I love you more than life." This desperation is always confused by him, and for a time confused by the wife, with love. Many wives, after many bitter disillusionments, refuse to accept this madness as love. But a surprisingly large number cling to the idea that it is love of an especially intense type.

If the wife leaves him with any kind of finality, he may attempt suicide, or he may die in one of the ways already described, for this man must control his ally-substitute, or he must die, except—

He can leave her, and live.

If he does the leaving, he still tries to control her by withholding child support, or alimony, to the limit of the law, or often he seeks a lover-mistress relationship with her, his argument being that this is the least she can do for him in return for financial support.

I estimate (*Ruxton wrote mentally*) that eighty per cent of family break-ups everywhere are caused by this man, in his myriad numbers.

With this outline in mind, many otherwise inexplicable events in any neighborhood, and a particular type of news headline or news story, take on new meaning.

Soon after the wife leaves this man, he either buys a gun and keeps it handy, or if he already has a gun he now purchases ammunition for it. Often, he will carry it with him for a time. A noble fantasy seethes in his brain. Somehow, the woman whom he has been unfaithful to a hundred times is mystically visualized as his lover for all eternity. In his feverish dream-world, he plans to make sure of this by murdering her, and then committing suicide. He may kill her; only rarely does he kill himself.

And so we have the type of headline that gives the public its first awareness of the drama. I can recall several:

HUSBAND INVADES CHRISTMAS PARTY—SHOOTS WIFE—Griefstricken When She Would Not Reconcile, He Claims.

ENTERTAINER STABS ESTRANGED WIFE TO DEATH—Unfaithful, He Says. Amazed Friends Say He Was Unfaithful, Not She.

WIFE RUN OVER IN STREET—Accident, Says Divorced Husband-Driver, Held on Suspicion of Murder.

WIFE BEATEN BY FORMER HUSBAND—Unfit Mother, He Says. Neighbors Refute Charge, Call Him Trouble-Maker.

HUSBAND FOILED IN ATTEMPT TO PUSH WIFE AND MOTHER-
IN-LAW OVER CLIFF—Wife Reconciles, Convinced Husband Loves Her.

I can also recall (*Ruxton thought*) typical news stories like
these:

> When they were married, her husband would stay
> away from home for a week at a time—now that they
> are divorced he won't. This was the testimony yesterday
> of Mrs. Edie Street, seamstress. She told the judge she
> divorced Street, 35, in January on grounds of cruelty.
> Since then he keeps showing up intoxicated at her
> place of work. He caused her to lose one job by creating
> a disturbance, and is threatening to force her out of
> her present job by embarrassing her, she said. The
> judge granted a restraining order to forbid Street from
> annoying her.

*   *   *

> For the first time in his fistic career, Mickey Balisco
> insisted yesterday that he took a beating—and from his
> divorced wife at that. He even showed scars to prove it.
> But police, who investigated a complaint of his wife,
> Gina, 30, that Mickey beat her up and tried to run over
> her with his car outside her home, booked him on sus-
> picion of assault. Mrs. Balisco's story was that the 31-
> year-old pugilist, accompanied by his latest girl friend,
> came to her home late Sunday to see his two children,
> who live with the mother, demanding entrance for both
> himself and the young woman who was with him. . .

*   *   *

> Hard-living artist Roger Grant, a World War II guer-
> rilla fighter, and estranged husband of singer, Susan
> Hill, was in court for the fourth time in as many
> months, on a charge of knocking his wife down in front
> of their child. . . .

Of course (*Ruxton continued*) these are examples of terrorist types at the level of the average man. My estimate is
that for every actual murder, there are several thousand
assaults, and for every man who assaults there is an even

larger total of males who, though they have the potentiality for violence, do not become overt.

There is a way to recognize this latter type: He is wholly or partially being supported by a woman—usually the wife or the mother. And it is conceded by almost everyone that it is a shame that such an essentially capable man is going to waste.

Obviously, terms like evil and good, moral or immoral, do not readily apply to what this man is doing. Deep in the neurosis of the right personality is a compulsion to die. This is where the frantic element comes from, and this is why—if they can invert the feeling and project it outside of their bodies—they can kill. Unknowing man is confronted in such compulsions by an internal chemistry that is beyond his control. Perhaps the knowledge necessary to control it is still a hundred million murders away.

Are there two sides to this story? Is the average wife somehow guilty also?

Not at all (*Ruxton concluded*). Whatever individuality she brings to the marriage is soon overwhelmed by the formidable reality of her "right" husband. For example, although I tend now to doubt my father's account of how his marriage began with my mother, if what he said *was* true, then we can see how her pitiful attempt to keep love pure by restricting sex, was swept aside—not by persuasion, or through the help of a counsellor—but by total and casual infidelity.

And I can see now that I build up a twisted version of what happened to my wife, Rainey. I believe the truth is, she went into a dazed state shortly after we were married when she became aware that I was continuing to have other women. I wouldn't be surprised if she drove over that cliff when she was regressed in grief and hopelessness.

I, not she, should have gone to the psychiatrist.

At least two types of woman can defeat the "right" personality. One does so by becoming ill at key moments, and somehow this reduces him, disturbs him, defeats him. If she is ill often enough, and severely enough, one day he becomes hopeless and dies. The other type of woman is even more subjective than he—more demanding, requiring that he live up to her standards, impatient of any weakness of character that he manifests. She makes him feel wrong so often that he is not able to stand the pressure, and leaves.

My best analysis of the making of the "right" man is that he is the product of a male parent who does not know how to be a father. He either deserts the family, or neglects his children, or else exercises discipline and training for which a boy is not ready at the age that it is administered. Whichever circumstance is involved, the boy feels impelled to turn to his mother for protection. This need is reinforced by the entirely desirable care she gives him during illnesses. However, in that percentage of children who become ill unto death, the reinforcement is abnormally strong. She becomes his ally for all time.

Later, when he becomes closely associated with other women he confuses them at some depth of his being with his mother, and expects them to be his allies also. He would like to be able to tell these mother-substitutes about his other loves. He would like to bring the other women home with him. He can really never understand why the wife objects to such behavior. Her antagonistic reaction makes him feel critical of how mature she is.

These are the common denominators, and they are so important that the multitudinous variations that one might expect in so many thousands of different persons are accordingly of minor significance.

From earliest times, courts of law have been lenient with the right man's "crime of passion." Far more protective action for the woman is in order.

The outward appearance of conformity to society, which one often finds in the right personality, is merely part of his effort to feel right. He actually considers himself above the mores, and has a world view that places him well outside the need to conform, except insofar as it seems practical to him. However, if he is an apparent conformist, he may support strong measures to control others.

It should be noted that all persons feel better when they are right. This normal impulse ought not to be confused with the neurotic or the psychotic drive of the person whose need to be right has caused so much misery and destruction.

(*Ruxton completed his mental summation, and fell asleep.*)

70

Someone was in the basement.

Gently, Ruxton pulled out the props holding open his air holes. In the place of one of them, he shoved the metal pipe, eased himself into a comfortable position where he could suck air through it—and waited. He had no idea of what time it was.

A woman's voice said softly, "Seal, are you here?"

Phenix! Hurriedly, he pulled back the metal pipe, laid it aside and, raising the end of one mattress, poked his head out.

"Here!" he answered. "Under the mattresses."

She came swiftly around the pile. She exclaimed a little as she saw his stubble-bearded countenance; but then she rubbed her cheek against his, lovingly. And then she said, "I saw you after that White Russian helped you to escape. My husband is a very sound sleeper, and so I sneaked out. I was going to rescue you—"

Ruxton thought, "You, too!"

"There was so much confusion yesterday, I dared not come down here. But I knew you hadn't gone off with that woman and her husband—"

Ruxton had eased himself to the floor by the time she reached that point. He knew that Tosti was "that woman." But he said, as a matter of course, "What woman?"

When that had been explained, he said abruptly, "Phenix, I want you to leave your husband. Tell him you plan a divorce, and that you are leaving for good. Pretend to return to your family, but actually go to Hong Kong, and wait there. I'll write a letter which will authorize you to receive funds from my bank while you're there."

It was a long message, but he was able to say every word of it before she reacted. She said in astonishment, "Leave my husband—whatever for?"

"I realize," said Ruxton, "that for a Chinese woman, acceptance of the rights of a husband go deep. But you've broken one barrier, in taking me for a lover. I'll tell you why you should break through the biggest barrier of all."

As quickly as he could, he told her of the "right" man, and of how Mai would temporarily abandon his mistresses in a desperate need to have his wife back. He pointed out, "Once you discover how he responds to your departure, you can control him completely if you wish."

She was quick. Her first words went instantly to the heart of the idea. "You're implying that Marx, Lenin, Stalin, Mao Tse-tung, my husband, and all their kind merely projected their "right" personality into the ideals of Communism. That the ideals have no reality in themselves." She sounded shocked.

Ruxton explained patiently, "The truth or falsehood of the ideas is not a factor. There *are* true ideas in the world, but they are not involved in a 'right' man's responses when he is manifesting his rightness."

She murmured, half to herself, "It's true that my husband is a very disturbed person."

Ruxton suppressed an impulse to make additional abstract explanations. It would be a mistake, he realized, to shift from the personal to the general. The truth was, that it was all personal. There were no objective actions. Every human being acted in a situation and attached himself to systems and philosophies according to the way he was as a person. It only looked like mass movements because there were so many people in each category.

He said, "Let me make clear what will happen to your husband when his mother-substitute—you—leaves him."

As he told her how Mai would react, her eyes grew wide. "I don't believe it," she whispered. "That hard-hearted man hasn't that much feeling in him."

"It isn't feeling, as you mean it," Ruxton explained patiently. "It's madness. But if you ever hope to find a way to live with this man, as you evidently feel you will have to, then you ought to discover if he will have a response to your leaving him, in the way that I predict he will."

There was a look on her face that was half-doubt, half belief. "He's told me many times that I can go whenever I want to." She said it slowly.

"That's typical," said Ruxton. "And the fact is he'll have a temporary feeling of relief when you first leave. Your departure will give him the sense of freedom that his neurosis tells him he wants."

She bit her lip, nodded as at some secret thought, and then, as if his answer would decide her, said, "Tell me again, what will actually happen in your opinion?"

"Your husband," said Ruxton, "will either take to drink—"

"Impossible," she said. "He detests alcohol."

"—Or," said Ruxton, "he will start using drugs."

"He despises drug addiction more than anything in the world."

"—Or," continued Ruxton, "he will temporarily become insane."

"I can't imagine it," said Phenix.

"—Or," said Ruxton inexorably, "he will start to die. That," he lied, "will take a while, of course."

The woman was silent for a long moment. Finally, the look of decision came into her face. She said, "The whole thing sounds completely fantastic, but the truth is I've seen people —men—do things like that and so I'll do as you ask. What do you want me to do?"

Ruxton said, "As soon as you can, get me paper and pen, and I'll write a letter to my business manager in Hong Kong. It will instruct her to supply you with an income that will enable you to live in an apartment in Hong Kong for as long as you wish."

"But what's going to become of *you?*" Phenix asked plaintively.

Ruxton said quickly, "We can talk about that before you leave for Hong Kong. You understand—you must tell your husband you wish to divorce him, and you must pretend to be leaving to go to your family—"

"Yes, yes, I know."

"Right now," Ruxton urged, "you better go. You've been here long enough."

She evidently agreed, for she left precipitantly.

71

At the end of three weeks, the food that Phenix had prepared for him was completely gone. Although he had kept it in a space where the outside cold penetrated, and thawed only what he needed at any time, the remnant, for several days, had been extremely unpalatable.

Accordingly, Ruxton emerged from his hiding place one morning just before prison breakfast time. He made his way outside, stood blinking at the brightness of the day, and then climbed over the rear fence, and walked around to the hotel.

He was a dirty, bearded monster, but he got all the way to his seat at the breakfast table without being stopped. Several of the other prisoners saw him, and gaped. But it was a piercing cry from a Chinese at the head table that produced a chattering pandemonium.

Ruxton sat down, drew a serving dish toward him, and began to eat of its hot contents. From the corner of one eye, he saw Fa 'tze wave his colleagues to silence, and stand up.

"Mr. Ruxton!" he said through the French interpreter.

Ruxton turned. "Yes?" he said, in Chinese.

There was a long pause. Then, in Chinese: "Where have you been?"

"I've been hiding from torture," said Ruxton, who had planned this dialogue for weeks.

"Very grave charges have been made against you," said

Fa 'tze. "The murder of two soldiers. You have been sentenced to death."

Ruxton shook his head. "I know nothing of that. I must have fallen off the treadmill, and I presume they were already dead when this happened, or they would have put me back on. I evidently lay there until I recovered consciousness, at which time I crawled out of a back window, and hid."

"You've been in hiding for 22 days!" Fa 'tze exclaimed incredulously.

"Is it that long?" Ruxton said. "I didn't know. I lost touch with time."

Fa 'tze demanded in a severe tone, "Where have you been hiding?"

"That information," said Ruxton firmly, "I think I shall give only to Major Mai."

Fa 'tze hesitated, then turned to his colleagues, and there was a murmured consultation among them. Presently, Fa 'tze said, "You will resume your former activities until further notice. Major Mai is incapaci—he has a severe cold."

Ruxton's grim guess was that Major Mai's cold was going to get worse. And, at this remote outpost, the medical science available would not be able to save him.

Father de Melanier, de la Santa, Gregory, Jarnoz, and Tittoni came upstairs with him. They stood by in the bathroom while Ruxton lathered up with cold water, and stropped one of the razors. His face was extremely painful, and his near-month's growth of beard wouldn't shave.

Jarnoz laid his hand on Ruxton's arm. "Wait! We get hot water."

He grabbed Tittoni's arm, and pulled him. Though the two men did not speak the same language, the Italian seemed to get the idea. They went downstairs together, and in less than ten minutes came up carrying a kettleful of steaming water.

"Better hurry!" Jarnoz said. "May be trouble."

Ruxton hurried. And, though he was bleeding from several cuts when he finished, the job was done by the time Fa 'tze came to the door.

The tall Chinese looked subdued. "We have a complaint from the kitchen," he began. "Two prisoners forced their way in—" He glanced at the kettle and at Ruxton's face and evidently got the picture. "Oh!" he said. He was apologetic. "Under the circumstances, I should have seen to it that you received the hot water. I shall explain."

72

Ruxton asked, "Did anyone fail at the end of the six-month period, besides myself?"

The question was addressed to Gregory, who shook his head.

The four men and he were conversing as best they could. And Ruxton's first order of business was to fill in the twenty-two day gap in his knowledge.

In a few minutes he had the details. The disappearance of Ho and Tosti, the departure of Mrs. Mai, Mai's illness—which had begun about six days before. De la Santa said, "The rumor is that he's actually very ill. Meanwhile, the group meetings go on, and we continue our cooperation."

Father de Melanier said in French, with a wan smile, "Do you think we will end up with the twenty-three of us all murdered, yet with all of us having cooperated to the end?"

It seemed almost facetious; it was almost like a poor joke, and it didn't sound right coming from such a man. But Ruxton believed that, on some sub-level of Mai's mind, that *was* the purpose.

He conceded that intellectually the members of the Chinese People's Government probably attempted to operate on Marxist principles, but a primitive racism was one of the driving forces behind the violence of Mao Tse-tung and his associates. Not only did they kill to break up the old state machinery—which was Marxism—but they also killed to break up the inroads that foreigners had made. And that had nothing at all to do with Marxism. It was predictable that, unless their Xenophobia was brought to their attention, soon they must evict the Russians also.

These thoughts moved through Ruxton's mind. Then he looked at the priest, and said, "How have you been treated, sir?"

The older man made the sign of the cross. "God has been good," he said simply.

Ruxton thought: "God, and the machinations of Seal Ruxton." But he felt no cynicism.

The minutes had flown, and it struck Ruxton that he wouldn't have many more. He gazed at Tittoni, and asked, "My Italian associate, what did bring you to China?"

When de la Santa had translated that, there was a pause,

finally the man smiled shamefacedly, and said, "I was one of those intellectuals who felt sorry for the downtrodden. When the Reds won in China, I considered it a victory for the people, and I decided to come and see the results for myself. I was arrested by madmen. I am embarrassed for myself because I turned out to be just another idealistic fool."

Before they could speak further, there was a clatter of footsteps. Someone yelled a command. An instant later the door was thrown open.

The two sentinels stood there with fixed bayonets. From somewhere outside the room, Mai Lin Yin yelled, "Mr. Ruxton, drive out those foolish men who are in there with you!"

Ruxton motioned to the four men. "Outside!" he said grimly.

They went, for the most part silently, a pat on the arm, a quiet word. The priest murmured a prayer. At the door, Gregory turned and offered his hand. "You're a damned phony!" he said, but he sounded gruff. "You were in the air force, weren't you?"

"Yes."

"A pilot?"

"Yes."

"Then you were an officer?"

Ruxton, who had been a lieutenant colonel, realized what was coming, and hesitated. During the long, slow hours in the Mai basement, he had thought about his truculence while in military service. And he had revised downward his estimate of the number of s.o.b.s among the officer corps, and he had also taken a look at the type of G.I. who resisted orders. About one-fifth of soldiers were the troublemakers. The others, officers as well as men, were law-abiding and did their duty to their country. . . . Twenty per cent of the G.I.s and perhaps forty per cent of the officers—the figures were probably true of all armies—were the terrorist types.

Standing there, he accepted Captain Gregory as an honest man. "You have my best wishes, sir," he said, and held out his hand.

They shook. Gregory said, "And you, mine."

Turning, he left the room.

There was a pause, and then a pale, hollow-eyed Mai walked in through the open door. The caricature of what had been a well-groomed Chinese officer motioned the two guards to enter. When they had taken up position, one behind Ruxton, the other on the far side of the bed, Mai closed the door.

He said then in a low, tense voice, in English, "Mr. Ruxton, do you know where my wife is?"

"Yes," said Ruxton, "I know." He went on, and his voice was slightly uneven, "When she rescued me—"

"Rescued you! My wife?" Mai spoke sharply.

Ruxton continued as if he had not heard the interruption, "When she rescued me, she told me that your accusation against her degraded her, for she was a good woman who had been faithful to an unfaithful husband." He spoke the entire lie without any personal revulsion. Besides, it was true in a way; the woman had endured her husband's behavior for many years. Ruxton continued, "She felt that she owed me at least an opportunity to escape, and so she rescued me from my torture, explained her plans, and I presume presently carried them out, since you are asking these questions."

All the time Ruxton was speaking, Mai had stared at him with unblinking eyes. Now, he said in a dead level voice, "Mr. Ruxton, where is she?"

"That information," said Ruxton, and abruptly he was sweating, "has a price on it."

"What is the price?"

Standing there, not really knowing what to expect next, Ruxton told him.

73

The tableau of Mai facing him, rigidly held for several seconds after Ruxton had spoken.

Abruptly, the man uttered a screech, and leaped forward. Using his fists, he struck at Ruxton's face, at his chest, and at his arms. And he screamed, "I'll have the information whipped out of you! I'll burn out your eyes! I'll skin you alive! I'll bury you in an ant hill!"

Ruxton held up his arms to avoid the other's blows, but in spite of all his will, he shrank before those horrendous threats. There flashed through his mind stories he had heard of the terrible actions of the Red leader, Mao Tse-tung, in the districts where he had been in charge for the Communists in his younger days—stories of people buried alive, burned to death, crucified, and tortured in every conceivable fashion. The man had been a fiend, without mercy.

But then a new thought came to Ruxton. That was *after* Mao Tse-tung's first wife was executed. Since he couldn't bring her back to life, he had his emotional release from an endless series of murders.

Mai Lin Yin had another way out.

Presently the man ceased his wild hitting and shouting. He stood gasping for breath. Then he staggered to the bed, winced as it screeched under him, but he sprawled down on it, and for several minutes lay there breathing hard.

At last, without raising himself, he said, "I am greatly relieved by your statement that it was my wife who released you."

Ruxton merely stared at him.

Mai continued, "One of our hopes for Project 'Future Victory' has been that we might learn so to manipulate individuals from different western countries that they would always think of their own skins first. This has now been established as a truth."

Ruxton realized that he was being given a part of the goals of the project and discreetly kept silent.

"It would have been unfortunate," said Mai, "if, by yielding to personal feelings, I accidentally achieved for the prisoners a united resistance front."

Ruxton, having the memory that no less than seven persons had been motivated to free him, did not trust himself to say anything.

"So," said Mai, "we may safely assume that in a crisis, the threatened country will find itself deserted, its former friends cautiously sitting on their hands. There is an old English saying that, since they dare not hang together, they will therefore hang separately."

Slowly, he sat up.

"You must not think, Mr. Ruxton, that what I have said to you will go any further, since you are next on the list of those to be hanged, or rather, shot."

He motioned to one of the soldiers. "Open the door!" he commanded.

The men jumped to obey.

To Ruxton, Mai said, "Get outside!"

Ruxton went, the soldiers alertly urging him.

Mai followed them into the hallway. "As you have been told," he said in a quiet voice, "you were sentenced to death *in absentia*. The sentence will be carried out immediately."

As Ruxton walked down the stairs, his knees felt watery, but otherwise he had no fear and almost no thought. And still he believed that his analysis of what was happening in the brain of Mai, the "right" personality, was correct. But maybe, he thought wryly, it was a case of the-operation-was-a-success-but-the-patient-died. Evidently he didn't know how to use his knowledge in a specific situation.

This bitter reflection was with Ruxton as he was led along the street, and tied, spread-eagled, to the rings in the concrete wall.

Even as he was being tied, a squad of six soldiers came running along the street. They took up position opposite him, and unlimbered their rifles.

Without a word, Mai turned his back on Ruxton, walked over behind the firing squad, and faced about.

"Ready!" he cried in an inexorable voice.

Ruxton felt blank and unbelieving. It all seemed far away. He wondered if Lund and Holsenamer, and the other about-to-be-murdered prisoners, had felt this same sense of unreality.

"Aim!" Mai yelled at the firing squad.

Ruxton closed his eyes. There was a pause, that lengthened. He opened his eyes in time to see Mai waving the guns down. The commandant walked across the street to where Ruxton stood against the wall.

"Well, Mr. Ruxton," he said savagely, "are you prepared to talk? You have a final opportunity."

Ruxton stared at him, and he was thinking, "All these people are implacably following the principles of control Marx discovered. Now I've found a deeper motivation for what they do. It reaches past all their training into the mind itself. Why shouldn't I follow through on what I think I know?" The truth was, he had no alternative. There was nothing else that he could trust. Mai's handling of the project was marked by broken promises and vicious acts.

Ruxton shook his head. "You have my offer," he said.

Mai said, "You persist in this plan to ruin me?"

Ruxton shrugged, "You're ruining me."

Mai snarled. "You're a white man—of no value in the new age."

Ruxton asked coolly, "Do you include your Big White Brother, the Soviet Union, in that sweeping statement?"

Mai was silent; he was pale, and seemed distraught.

Ruxton continued, "You see, Jarnoz analyzed you correctly. Your attitude is simply and backwardly based on race prejudice. There is not a New Age bone in your body. So I think we can do without your contribution to the future of mankind."

It was immensely dangerous talk. But—again—there

seemed no alternative. Nonetheless, Ruxton decided that he had said enough.

What his knowledge of the "right" man could do for him was done.

PART FOUR

74

The Chinese, Ruxton decided, were the greatest spitters in the world. The fact had never been so strongly borne in on him as on that long railroad ride to Hong Kong.

In his brief journeyings through China, he had generally stayed in his seat, content to be unobtrusive. Now he was too concerned to be inactive.

He paced, rather, he skidded, along the aisles. The floor of each crowded car in the speeding train was slimy with sputum, and more was being added every minute, as all around him people kept clearing their throats and expectorating.

Restlessly Ruxton walked back and forth. As restlessly, he sat at intervals with the little party of white prisoners. He kept looking the men over, counting to make sure they were still present. They were always all there except Lemoine who, in the final issue, he had not dared to include. Several times he checked to make sure that each man had one of the automatics that Mai had reluctantly brought from the prison storeroom at Ruxton's insistence.

He kept an eye on Mai, too. But that was no problem. The man sat hunched in a seat, staring mindlessly at some blank distance within himself.

Once, when Ruxton sat down, Father de Melanier indicated the commandant, and shook his head in bewilderment. "What did you do to that man?" he asked. "What's holding him? He'll be killed for this, if they ever catch him."

Ruxton, who had earlier described the violent type of man to the priest, sighed at these unperceptive questions, and wondered if he could ever put over his concept. He doubted it, and so now he gave a more pedestrian explanation: "His wife hid me when I escaped. She told me she was leaving him, and where she was going. I'm taking him to her."

Father de Melanier said, wonderingly, "Love is a strange phenomenon."

"It's not love," said Ruxton.

The priest seemed not to hear, for he went on, "Makes

303

you realize that these people still have human qualities after all."

"What the 'right' personality has," said Ruxton, "makes people *in*human."

Something of that seemed to penetrate, for the other man continued, "One thing I don't understand about this type of man you have described—from what you say there are just as many of them in America as in Russia and China."

"My estimate is twenty per cent of the male population everywhere. Undoubtedly, there are equally as many women but they handle it differently, and I couldn't tell you what they do with it."

"If it's the same everywhere, how do you explain?—"

"The difference is in the economic and political system under which they live," Ruxton explained. "In the United States, the successful terrorist type hands over power to his elected successor, because the system of government by law leaves him no alternative. Believe me, he tries hard enough to get around the law, but he can't for long. However, in Russia and all communist countries, the system plays into his hands. His problem is to retain control against a variation of an old-style palace-type conspiracy, and this requires secret trials, or out and out murder. He cannot surrender control quietly, because he might be killed by vindictive friends and relatives of people he harmed."

The next time Ruxton sat down beside him, Father de Melanier said, "Do you know that the Chinese railroads never had the problem of a frontier country. The first train from Canton to Nanking was jammed with passengers overflowing the aisles and the rear compartments." He smiled. "Of course, the Taoists preached that the river, sky and forest gods were outraged by the trains, but after the suppression of the Boxer rebellion that kind of thinking lost ground."

"I wonder," said Ruxton. The Taoists had been in the vanguard of anti-foreignism in old China. Again, the new China seethed with anti-foreign feeling. It didn't seem very different.

Father de Melanier said, "I find it hard to believe that there is race hostility in the Chinese people. Perhaps there is a difference between race-prejudice and hatred of foreigners."

Ruxton considered that, saw that there could be a distinction, and said, "Perhaps; you may have a point."

On a third occasion, the priest sat down beside Ruxton

304

and asked simply, "Now that we are getting away, what do you think of communism? For example, how does it happen that not one person in our group turned into a communist of his own free will? After all, we know there are millions of people in non-communist countries who are pro-Red. In many instances, no one even had to argue very hard with them. They seemed to be natural communists."

"I don't see it that way at all, sir," Ruxton said. "The truth is, there are as yet no communists in the world."

"Oh, come now, Mr. Ruxton, you're splitting hairs."

"Not at all, Father," said Ruxton. "The communist intellectuals are the first to admit it. For them, communism is an ideal that will someday be realized. Meanwhile, violence, enforced labor, semi-slavery . . . in their books they don't deny it. As for their sympathizers in other countries, they think of themselves as idealists. It's a way of feeling right, I'm sure. Most of them know very little about communism itself, and none of them have had the experience of living under it. My guess is, they're all basically very angry people."

"But," the priest asked, bewildered, "what did they expect of us?"

"To become fired by the goal, to start to act as if the goal is realizable, to involve ourselves in the struggle to achieve it—" Ruxton added, "That's what they would have wanted, I mean, if the project had been honest."

"Very well," said Father de Melanier, "so my question becomes, why did not one of us involve himself?"

"I'm sure," said Ruxton, "most of us were willing to cut our tails and adopt a correct working attitude. To that extent, we were as willing to be Communists as the millions in eastern Europe and in China. I don't see how they could trust us with further involvement, except slowly, with small tasks. No matter what we did or said in the project to prove that we had turned over, they could only accept us in stages. Don't you agree?"

"But surely there is somebody in the Communist hierarchy who is more than an automaton blindly trying to save his life?"

"Yes," said Ruxton. He indicated Mai a few seats away, sunk low in his seat. "There he sits."

"But he has become a pitiable object," said the priest.

Ruxton said earnestly, "It is only an accident that the man sitting in that seat is not Mao Tse-tung or Nikita Khrushchev. All terrorists are equally vulnerable."

The older man's eyes were wide with wonder. "I'm sure I

don't really know what you're talking about, but I believe you, for most certainly there sits the formidable Mai Lin Yin."

Ruxton went on, "Marx discovered how a relatively small group of terrorists could take over a state. However, he offered no method whereby the state could ever get rid of the terrorists. And so, communism is now caught in the trap of its own takeover techniques. Like an endlessly repeating computing machine, the system invariably picks the most violent of the intelligentsia for the top positions, and these men then project their psychosis into the society. In order to feel justified, they mercilessly promote the cause of communism, and they can't turn back because the compulsion inside them prods them as mercilessly."

The priest asked, "What shall we do with this Great New Power in the Pacific?"

"What do you suggest?" Ruxton asked. "You know more about the Chinese than I do."

Father de Melanier brightened. "I trust the Chinese people to come out of this eventually in good shape. After all, the angry old terrorists—as you call them—will soon be dead. And if they are succeeded by angry *young* terrorists, at least they won't have anyone to blame for failures and misfortunes. It's up to them to make it work." He paused, and blinked behind his glasses. Then: "Suppose they succeed? Suppose communism does prove to be a superior economic system?"

"Impossible!" said Ruxton scornfully.

That was his only philosophical discussion on that tense journey.

Ruxton had several low-voiced conversations with Gregory, with Kuznetoff, with Jarnoz and de la Santa. These were the men he could talk to directly. The problem was, how were they going to get by the frontier station five train hours from the border?

He pointed out, "We cannot afford to have our guns taken away from us when we're still that far from safety."

De la Santa, who was silent when Ruxton first broached the dilemma, returned from a walk along the aisles, and said, "I think we should count on Mai's authority. The way the police respect our travel permits shows that the authorization stamp Mai used is very special. We've got to recognize that the man in charge of Project 'Future Victory' would be an important personage with considerable powers."

So Ruxton said to Mai, "Under no circumstances are we to be searched or interrogated at the frontier station."

The sick eyes looked up at him. "There will be no problem," Mai mumbled, "so long as I talk on the phone with my lover before we actually cross the border."

Uneasily, Ruxton reported the words to the others. "Right there," he said frankly, "is the blank in my plan. I don't know what will happen when he has talked to her."

He was tense, but not really surprised, when they were passed at the frontier station without comment or interference.

Five hours later, the train, having traversed the coastal mountains, pulled up at the border station, and there, only a short distance along the bank, was the bridge that separated Red China from Hong Kong.

Without hesitation, Mai commandeered the border inspector's private office for the phone call to his wife.

75

There was a thrilling moment when Anna Chen's voice came over the phone. Her tone was businesslike in the extreme. But when she heard Ruxton's voice, she burst into tears, and that was so familiar, Ruxton felt a lump rise in his own throat. When she had finally controlled herself, and when he had asked the question, there was a long pause; and then, in a subdued voice, Anna said, "We're all very guilty here, because undoubtedly someone talked too much to Madame Mai. Or perhaps she is a woman who can put together a few facts. I'm afraid she suddenly got a picture which you didn't want her to see."

The long and roundabout account gave Ruxton a terrible, sinking feeling, and no information. "What are you talking about?" he yelled. But he was afraid, not angry.

Anna started to cry again. "I think she found out about me and Antonina and Celeste and——"

"Oh!" said Ruxton.

"——And so she went back to China," said Anna, sobbing.

Ruxton swallowed hard. "When was this?" he asked finally.

"Four days ago."

Ruxton glanced through the open door at Mai in the inner office listening on the phone extension. He steadied himself. "Okey, Anna," he said, "I'll talk to you later."

He hung up, walked in to the inner office to face a slyly smiling Mai, and closed the door behind him.

"Well," said Major Mai Lin Yin, and he was as of old, "your little scheme to use my love for my wife didn't work."

"It isn't love," said Ruxton. He had his hand in his pocket, where he still had Kuznetoff's knife, and he did a strange thing with his muscles; he braced himself to commit murder. He thought, "I mustn't weaken. I mustn't fail." Aloud, he repeated, "It isn't love, Major."

The man was savoring the situation, and he was growing progressively gleeful. He paid no attention to Ruxton's remark. "As you can see," he said, "I will lose nothing by this episode. I don't have to explain my actions to my subordinates, and when I turn up with all the prisoners, no questions will be asked. You see that, don't you?"

Ruxton not only saw, but far worse he suddenly felt weakness sweep over him. He thought, in anguish, "Oh, God, am I going to betray us all by not being able to strike hard—or even strike at all?"

Aloud, Ruxton said, "You think your wife returned to the prison?"

He spoke automatically. He was having a second, stronger reaction, an awareness that he who understood the Mais—and Ruxtons—of this world so perfectly, could not kill except as a last resort.

Mai said, "I'm happy that you raised the point. I'll phone the prison. She's had time to get there."

Ruxton, watching him, saw that the man's hand shook, and his voice trembled, as he put the call through. When he looked up at Ruxton, he was perspiring. "I'm not well yet," he said.

Ruxton did not answer. As he waited for China's old-style phone system to make the connection, Ruxton stared through the window. He could see an open stretch of track and, beyond it, the bridge between the Hong Kong area and Red China. A party of Chinese were walking across the bridge into China.

It was all so near, yet now a single, living man barred the way. One man—and his own inner restraints. . . . He became aware that Phenix must be on the phone, for Mai burst into tears.

"Oh, my dear, my dear sweetheart," he sobbed, and his speech was the rough, North China dialect. "You must never leave me again—" The sobbing and the protestations of love went on for some time, but Mai presently recovered. In the end, he said in his normal voice, "I'll be back in a few days. Don't ask what happened. I can't explain it on the phone."

At the point, Ruxton said, "May I speak to her?" He held out his hand for the phone.

Mai said into the receiver, "One moment, lover." Then he looked up, his eyes narrowed, his face pale. Slowly, then, he extended the instrument.

The white man, Seal Ruxton, who took the phone from Mai's fingers, was not quite the same person who had walked shakily into the room a few minutes before. In those few minutes Ruxton had realized what his weakness was, and had made his peace with the exact nature of the violence that would shortly have to be done here, a stone's throw from safety. Win or lose, he was committed.

"Madam Mai," he said into the phone.

There was a pause. Finally, Phenix' voice came coolly, "Mr. Ruxton."

"Do you realize what you have done, after our agreement?"

She replied, "I am in my husband's house, where I belong."

Ruxton said grimly, "What you have done is typical of the wife of such a man. Trapped by some last minute foolish emotion of her own, she rushes back to receive again his false assurances of love."

"At least," came the reply, "I shall not be just another foolish concubine in your extensive harem."

He was not reaching her, and so the deal he wanted would have to be cold as ice, made of steely actions and not from the heart at all. He said, "Madame Mai, tell you husband that you will join him in Hong Kong, and nowhere else."

He heard her draw in her breath. Then she said, "Mr. Ruxton, there is a saying in America, 'My country, may it always be right, but my country, right or wrong'. That's the way I feel about China. Surely, you don't expect me to betray my own government?"

He was not touching her. He said urgently, "Look, your husband has learned how to exterminate the people of the West. He doesn't need us any more."

"That is not the goal of the project!" she flashed.

"Your husband is a master at this game of brainwashing, and therefore he produces exactly the feelings he desired. Each time we took a step toward becoming communistic, he did something to push us back. That must have been deliberate."

"You're drawing the wrong conclusions!"

"I believe," said Ruxton, "that the top communist brass studied the results of the Korean brainwashing of Americans, and decided it wasn't worth it. The decision to figure out how to exterminate all white people was probably made then. I tell you, Phenix, throughout history 'right' men have been able to make decisions like that, and have tried to carry them out."

"*White* men," she said acridly, "are not in a moral position to talk against extermination. In Africa one or more attempts were made, and in America the Indian *was* almost exterminated."

"You are absolutely mistaken," said Ruxton. "No such attempt was ever made. The Indians suffered from local conditions of the frontier, and the government was and has been their protector. As for Africa—" He broke off. "Then you support this policy?"

"No, I don't. There is no such policy."

Ruxton thought hopelessly, "Actually my little power system is the most vulnerable ever devised. I lose the woman, and I've lost everything. And she is so easy to lose . . . or is she?"

The final question contained a desperate possibility. Suddenly breathless, he said—and he virtually gasped every word, "Madam Mai, what you discovered in Hong Kong relates to the old-style me. That was the way I was before I began to analyze the man who has to be right. In coming back here, I didn't know what I was going to do, or be. Obviously, it would be different, but how is not clear to me even now. Because, of course, desire goes on. Sex goes on. We don't have to argue that point, I'm sure. But you should make allowances for change in a person who has begun to understand himself."

The phone was silent after he had spoken. Ruxton was beginning to fear that she had hung up or laid the receiver down, when a small voice said, "Seal, forgive me! You must not think I have lost feeling for you, but you cannot imagine how hurt and confused I was in that big city. It was terrible. I rushed home like a sick child. From what you have said, I realize there is truth in you, and that I was wrong to think otherwise. Yet you must know that I cannot do what you want. However, there is a solution. Seal, put my husband back on the phone!"

"What are you going to do?" Ruxton was uneasy.

"I shall tell him to release you but not the others."

310

Ruxton's first reaction was relief. Then the exact meaning of her words penetrated. He protested violently, "Phenix, it's got to be all or nothing."

"You know that's impossible. It would ruin him. Give him the phone!"

Suddenly he felt confused, his arguments swept aside by her Solomon-like decision. Shaken, Ruxton handed the receiver over to Mai. "She wants to talk to you," he mumbled.

He was vaguely aware of their conversation, and that Mai was objecting to his wife's suggestion. Yet the man was quickly convinced, for his final words were, "Very well, my dear, I think your solution is a correct one, under all the circumstances, and I bow to it."

Mai replaced the receiver on the phone, and he gazed up at Ruxton soberly. "My friend," he said, "we both have my lover to thank. As you know, I would inexorably have been compelled to do my duty. Yet I realize my position with so many armed and desperate men. I don't think any of you could get away, because there are several hundred soldiers at or near this border station. Nonetheless only you and I know the situation. Therefore, you may cross the bridge, but the others remain. Agreed?"

Ruxton stared into the man's narrowed brown eyes in utter fascination. He did not question that this was a legitimate offer. In asking for and obtaining from Phenix, understanding, he had gained the final advantage over the "right" man here in front of him. Of all the people in the world, he was best qualified to realize what a complete personal victory it was.

Lone wolf Seal Ruxton was free—if he wanted to be.

Mai said, matter-of-factly, "It is understood, of course, that you must not mention Project 'Future Victory' to anyone. Someone will suffer, if you do."

Ruxton heard, but made no acknowledgment. He was absorbed in a sudden awareness. It was a thought on a different level than anything he had ever had.

The thought was, "I've got to decide now! . . ." For him, rightness meant, Go! He was a man alone in the world, living his own life, with his women and his businesses, and his hard philosophy.

The alternative was to make a fight for it, and very likely get killed. How wrong could you be? Dead . . . He had a strong, strong feeling that he owed nothing to anyone.

Mai spoke again, "You agree that I have stated the situation correctly?"

"Yes," said Ruxton, "it's correct."

Mai urged, "And remember, you are the only one under sentence of death. Therefore no one but you need escape. But you must escape."

The logic was unquestionable. Ruxton had no feeling of making up his mind. Without a word, and without a thought, he took out his pistol.

Mai glanced fearlessly at it, and said, "A single shot will end all chance even of you escaping."

"I know," Ruxton said. "And I agree that my position is exactly what you say it is, and just as you acceded to the logic of my position—when I alone knew where your wife was—so now I accept your offer to cross to Hong Kong by myself."

With that, he tossed the gun onto the grass mat covering the floor.

"I won't be needing that," he said.

Mai looked startled at the action. Then an expression of pure delight fleetingly illuminated his sunken cheeks. The next instant, his face was blank of all emotion. He stood up. "You are very wise," he said, and moved around the desk toward the door. As he reached the gun, he turned, and stooped to pick it up.

There was still no conscious tension in Ruxton as he watched the man. But the thoughts he had had earlier were still with him . . .

The truth was that the West was not yet motivated to kill communists. The battle of mind and idea was not lost. The world was poised in a dreadful balance between mass destruction and peace. That balance should not be upset by single persons on their private decision. And so, Mai—though he had murdered thousands, and by all the ancient codes of man deserved death—would now benefit from the uneasy truce that was still in force. Ruxton knew how to damage without killing.

He struck a single, incapacitating blow with the knife.

Mai straightened slowly, and gazed up at Ruxton in surprise and puzzlement. He whispered, "Mr. Ruxton . . . what have you done to me . . . this past month . . . ?"

"If you stay real quiet," said Ruxton, "you'll be all right." He helped the man back to his chair.

312

76

Outside more than a dozen newly arrived young Chinese men were being efficiently relieved of their possessions by a crew of girl interrogators. Some of the youths looked crestfallen, but they had evidently accepted the propaganda inviting overseas Chinese to return "home." And now they were in, and it was too late. Ruxton had seen their kind on his other trip.

Striving for casualness, Ruxton spoke to Gregory, loud enough so that two nearby, uniformed officials could hear. "We're to go," he said.

And he started to walk toward the barrier. He was vaguely aware, as he partly turned his head, of the Chinese chief inspector coming out of a building, and looking after them. The man spoke to the two officials, and one gave an answer.

The inspector yelled a command at a platoon of six soldiers. As these men trotted after the little party of white men, the inspector turned and went back into the building.

Ruxton restrained his panic with the thought, "He can't know anything till he tries to talk to Mai."

But he said now to Gregory, "I wounded Mai, and I think he'll be found any second. We can't allow these soldiers to take us back. It's a fight to the death right here."

Quickly he walked forward until he was opposite Kuznetoff, and gave him the news in French. He saw that Gregory was speaking to Jarnoz. Presently every man was walking with hand in pocket, gripping a pistol butt.

The soldiers loped past them, and took up position at the barrier. One of them spoke to the officer in charge, and it was he who stepped forward and, in a distinctive British accent, addressed Ruxton, who was first in line.

"I have instructions to pick up your authorization permits. This should have been done at the station."

Ruxton reached in his pocket, and handed his over. Then he gripped his automatic again and waited while all the permits were given to the man.

As this task was completed, a train from Hong Kong started across the bridge. They stood aside as it moved slowly by.

Farther up the track, at the border station, some Chinese soldiers were gesticulating at the barrier guards.

The last car rolled by, and the white men stepped onto the

bridge. Ruxton looked back, and saw the inspector and some soldiers hurrying toward them.

"Run!" yelled Ruxton.

As they reached the Hong Kong side, a scattering of rifle fire made everyone dive for the nearest cover. For Ruxton, this consisted simply of lying flat on the ground. From his prostrate position, he could see that on the far side of the bridge, soldiers were milling and gesturing in the excitable Chinese manner.

As he began to edge away from the bridge, Ruxton stared mentally into his future, and it was a big picture indeed that he saw.

He thought, "I have the power of special knowledge, equal to Marx's armed proletariat, Hitler's understanding of reactionaries, and Tamarlane's berserks.

"And, more important, what I know can reach past the cannon and the jets, past the million-men armies, and the armored divisions, and past any technology, no matter how advanced."

The logic of it was remorselessly simple. Everywhere, those few "right" men who had not fallen by the wayside lived in that state of heightened, feverish activity which had substantially given them control of the world in this as well as all other periods of history. Always, each "right" man had ruthlessly utilized all available techniques of control to maintain his power.

The Marxists were only the latest of a long line of people who had chosen to use their knowledge to gain power, no matter what the cost in human lives.

His dilemma now was: Should he use *his* discovery to take the world away from other "right" men? Or not?

He had crept into the shelter of a British frontier station as he had this thought. He did not climb to his feet immediately but sat, grinning at an idea that suddenly popped into his mind.

"Mrs. Khrushchev," he said aloud, "why don't you leave your husband? Let's change the world in one step."

He began to laugh. It was an uproarious laughter that soon verged on the hysterical. He grew aware of the other men gathering anxiously around him. Ruxton ignored them. He was caught in a vortex of mad humor.

"Madame Mao Tse-tung, walk out on that fat, little, old man," he gasped, "and with the greatest disrespect, if you please."

He had a fantasy, then, of the Russian leader, and the

Chinese fuehrer untangling themselves from their concubines, and gazing in amazement after the fleeing wives. Then, for a time, returning to the daily round of mistresses. Ruxton was completely convinced that that was the main activity of the two men. Since no person understood the wellsprings of his actions and thoughts, it was obvious that politics was merely another stimulant to sex. So it seemed to Ruxton, as his mental picture of the aging lechers doubled him up for nearly a minute.

When he could breathe again, he looked at the other men, grinning broadly.

Jarnoz said to Gregory, uneasily, "Have he gone crazy?"

"No," Gregory said, "he's just throwing off six months of fear. I've seen it before." He added enviously, "I wish I could do that, but I only lock it away somewhere inside me."

Ruxton was still grinning. "I'll bet," he said, "that an entire economic system could be built around 'right' men, particularly around the millions who have failed. Of course, there will be problems. They'll probably start arguing about which one is really 'right.' "

This time he laughed till his sides ached, and his breath came in great gasps. It was so painful he would have liked to stop, but another thought had come, and he was grinning again.

He looked around at the sympathetic, smiling faces of the little group, and he raised his voice, and said cheerfully, "Right men of the world, unite! Together we can not only get each other's wives but all the other women in the world as well. Isn't that worth fighting for, men?"

More laughter.

"Besides, the women will love it. We're all such charming fellows—when you first meet us . . ."

There was more, but finally the hysteria began to wear itself out. A British border policeman came over. He said, "That sounds like the funniest joke that was ever told. Can I get in on it?"

Gregory said sourly, "He seems to be the only one who knows the punch line. We haven't heard it yet."

Ruxton was climbing to his feet. He was still smiling, but he was in control of himself now. "You will," he said, "one of these days." He stood, arching his back, stretching, feeling a strange confidence. He had conquered the confusion of the twentieth century. It was a dynamic age, and there would be many changes. But through it all, he would

315

be able to stand up to his full height and live each moment according to what it had to offer.

". . . One of these days," he repeated softly.

Later, straight and tall and thoughtful, he went into the great city.

REFERENCES

Author's Note: Aside from several novels about China which I have not listed, two items deserve mention—an article which appeared in the *Manchester Guardian* in 1954, by a British Labour Party member who visited a prison of the type I describe in my novel; and a taped talk by Lt. Col. William F. Mayer, psychiatrist attached to the Fourth Air Force, who discussed the actual degree of collaboration by Americans captured in Korea. The markings below represent my personal estimate of the books listed.

A. E. v.V.

★ Interesting   ★★ Useful   ★★★ Important

★ *Brainwashing in Red China,* by Edward Hunter, Vanguard Press, N.Y., 1951.

China, A Short History, by Owen and Eleanor Lattimore, W. W. Norton, N.Y., 1944.

The Chinese Conquer China, by Anna Louise Strong, Doubleday, Garden City, N.Y., 1949.

★★★ *China Under Communism,* by Richard L. Walker, Yale University Press, New Haven, 1955.

★ *China Under the Empress Dowager,* by J. O. P. Bland and E. Backhouse, Lippincott, Phila., 1910.

★★ *The Communist Persuasion,* by Eleutherius Winance, O.S.B. P. J. Kennedy, N.Y., 1958.

★★ *Foreign Mud,* by Maurice Callis, Knopf, N.Y., 1947.

The Long March, by Simone de Beauvoir, World, Cleveland, 1958.

★★★ *A Military History of China, 1924–49,* by F. F. Liu, Princeton University Press, Princeton, 1956.

Prisoners of Liberation, by Allyn and Adele Rickett, Cameron Associates, N.Y., 1957.

★ *Profile of Red China,* by Lynn and Amos Landman, Simon and Schuster, N.Y., 1951.

★ *Report on Mao's China,* by Frank Moraes, Macmillan, N.Y., 1953.

★ *Ten Years of Storm,* by Chow Ching-wen, Holt, Rinehart and Winston, N.Y., 1960.

★★★ *Third Force in China,* by Carsun Chang, Bookman Associates, N.Y., 1952.

Yankee Ships in China Seas, by Daniel Henderson, Hastings House, N.Y., 1946.

★★★ *Soviet Russia in China,* by Chiang Kai-shek, Farrar, Straus and Cudahy, N.Y., 1957.

★★ *Out of Red China,* by Liu Shaw-tong, Duell, Sloane & Pearce, N.Y., 1953.

★ *China: New Age and New Outlook,* by Ping-Chia Kuo, Knopf, N.Y., 1956.

★ *The Yellow Wind,* by William Stevenson, Cassell, London, 1959.

The China Story, by Freda Utley, Henry Regnery, Chicago, 1951.

★ *The New Face of China,* by Peter Schmid, Pitman, N.Y., 1961.

★★ *Mao Tse-tung and I Were Beggars,* by Siao-yu, Syracuse University Press, Syracuse, N.Y., 1959.

All the Emperor's Horses, by David Kidd, Macmillan, N.Y., 1960.

China Shall Rise Again, by May-ling Soong Chiang (Madame Chiang Kai-shek), Harper, N.Y.

Treaty Ports, by Hallett Edward Abend, Doubleday, Garden City, N.Y., 1944.

★★ *From One China to the Other,* by Henri Cartier-Bresson, Universe Books, N.Y., 1956.

Report on China, The Annals, Vol. 277, American Academy of Political and Social Science, Philadelphia, Pa., Sept., 1951.

Contemporary China and the Chinese, The Annals, American Academy of Political and Social Science, Philadelphia, Jan., 1959.

★★ *Blunder in Asia,* by Harrison Forman, Didier, N.Y., 1950.

China and Her People, by The Hon. Charles Denby, L.L.D., L. C. Page, Boston, 1906.

★ *Hunger In China* (Letters from the Communes), Introduction and Notes by Richard L. Walker, 46 pp., *The New Leader,* N.Y., May, 1960.

★ *Let a Hundred Flowers Bloom,* by Mao Tse-tung, with Notes and Introduction by G. F. Hudson, 58 pp., *The New Leader,* N.Y.

★ *The Hundred Flowers Campaign and the Chinese Intellectuals,* by Roderick MacFarquhar, Praeger, N.Y., 1960.

★★ *Chinese Proverbs From Olden Times,* ed. by Peter Beilenson, Peter Pauper, Mt. Vernon, N.Y., 1956.

Hurricane From China, by Denis Warner, Macmillan, N.Y., 1961.

★★★ *The State and Revolution,* by Vladimir Il'ich (Nicolai Lenin), International Publishers, N.Y., 1932.

★★ *Red Star Over China,* by Edgar Snow, Random House, N.Y., 1938, 1944.

What We Must Know About Communism, by Harry and Bonaro Overstreet, W. W. Norton, N.Y., 1958.

Brainwashing, by Edward Hunter, Farrar, Straus and Cudahy, N.Y., 1961.

Chinese Thought (from Confucius to Mao Tse-tung), by H. G. Creel, Mentor Edition, N.Y., 1960.

The Russian Revolution, by Alan Moorehead, Harper, N.Y., 1958.

★★★ *Darkness at Noon,* by Arthur Koestler, Macmillan, N.Y., 1941.

★ *Eastern Shame Girl, and Other Stories,* Avon, N.Y., 1947.

Coercion of the Worker in the Soviet Union, by David Rousset, Beacon, Boston, 1953.

Police State Methods in the Soviet Union, by David Rousset, Beacon, Boston, 1953.

The God That Failed (Andre Gide, Richard Wright, Ignazio Silone, Stephen Spender, Arthur Koestler, Louis Fischer), Harper, N.Y., 1950.

★★★ *The Seizure of Political Power,* by Feliks Gross, Philosophical Library, N.Y., 1958.

★★★ *The Ancient Lowly* (2 vol.), by C. Osborne Ward, Charles H. Kerr and Co., Chicago, 1888.

★★★ *The Nature of Human Conflicts,* by A. R. Luria, Liveright, 1932.

★★ *Chinese Theater,* by Kalvodova-Sis-Vanis, Spring Books, London.

★★★ *Democratic Ideals and Reality,* by Halford J. MacKinder, Henry Holt, N.Y., 1919, 1942.

The True Believer, by Eric Hoffer, Harper, N.Y., 1951.

★★★ *Speech and Brain Mechanisms,* by Wilder Penfield and Lamar Roberts, Princeton University Press, Princeton, 1959.

The Authoritarian Personality, by T. W. Adorno and others, Harper, N.Y., 1950.

Must We Fight Russia? by Ely Culbertson, Winston, Phila., 1946.

★★★ *Das Kapital,* by Karl Marx, Henry Regnery, Chicago, 1959.

★★★ *The Communist Manifesto,* by Karl Marx, Henry Regnery, Chicago, 1960.

The Sayings of Mencius (tr. by James R. Ware), New American Library, Mentor Edition, N.Y., 1960.

"Hseüeh-Hsi: The Real Threat from Red China," by George R. Price, *Think* Magazine, published by IBM, N.Y.

"The Killer Had Been Paroled," by Robert P. Crossley,

an article in *The Ladies' Home Journal,* Phila., Feb., 1962.

★★★ *Battle for the Mind,* by William Sargent, Doubleday, Garden City, N.Y., 1957.

★★ *No Secret is Safe,* by Mark Tennien, S.J., Farrar, Straus and Cudahy, N.Y., 1952.